An Acciden

The A

This is Steve's first venture into novel writing and is set in a place dear to his heart in the Derbyshire Dales.

The author began his professional life as a uniform police officer and then as a detective for the Derbyshire Constabulary in the Derbyshire Dales. In his later police service he specialised in both domestic and international fraud, as well as money laundering investigations.

After retiring from the police he qualified as a teacher lecturing in Public Service, Law, and Criminology before joining the private sector as a Management Training Consultant.

Steve is now 'retired' from both policing and teaching but retains a lifelong passion for writing. He lives in Derbyshire with his wife Beverley.

For Beverley

An Accidental Death

Steve Winnard

<u>Copyright</u>

Book cover design by Emma Bradford

ISBN 978-1-7398572-0-2

www.swpublishing.co.uk

<u>Acknowledgements</u>

As a first novel I have had many people giving me good advice and help with both the story structure and editing. I would therefore like to thank Karen Kennedy Sue Mutch and Margaret Miller for their help with editing and Gail Radka with the story structure.

As a special acknowledgement I would also like to thank Emma Bradford for the book cover design.

Chapter 1 – – A Dead Girl At White Lodge

Tuesday 14ᵗʰ January

Dave Baker, through half asleep eyes, peered at his mobile phone that had woken him with its 'Waves' ringtone. The time of 6.30 a.m. illuminated mistily through his gluey eyes together with the 'Work' caller ID.

"Not today" he sighed and answered the call.

"Detective Constable Baker?"

"Yes, what's happened?"

"We have had a call from a water bailiff, who was checking for poachers at a trout pond near White Lodge Car Park on the A6 at Ashford In The Water. It looks like he's come across the body of a woman on the track up to the pond."

"Is he sure she's dead?"

"Yes he's absolutely sure; he says that it looks like she's been there since early last night as she's covered in snow. One of the uniform officers covering the area is at the scene and his supervision is on the way."

"Alright I'll be there as soon as possible, tell everybody to stay away from the scene unless absolutely necessary."

He didn't ask who had found the body as there was only one water bailiff for that area and he knew the body finder would have been Stan Moore. Dave had worked occasionally with Stan when he was a uniform police officer. When Stan had retired, like many retired police officers in the Dales he had gone to work for one of the local landowners. Most went to be security or gamekeepers, but Stan had chosen to be a water bailiff. It was a job that he was as committed to as his previous police one, and a joke amongst his ex-colleagues that he protected the local fish as much as he had previously protected the local population. The fact that he was checking for poachers, in the dark at 6 a.m. in the morning on a freezing snowy day in early January, was not a surprise.

Dave Baker slid quietly out of bed and tip-toed half-awake to the bathroom, trying not to wake the other occupants of the house. He shaved quickly with the razor on the side of one of the dual hand basins that he had left there the previous day and then made his way into the large walk in shower.

He caught sight of his slim, muscular body in the full length mirror and the glimpse was enough to remind him that he needed to get back to the gym as soon as his work commitments allowed. He usually worked out in the gym every day, but since

Christmas because of work and his new girlfriend, he had not found the time. Dave tensed his stomach muscles. Yes definitely turning flabby he thought. He would go to the gym later if work and Helen commitments allowed.

There was a large bottle of a French labelled aftershave on the vanity unit. Dave took off the top, sniffed it and sprayed it onto his face…. and then under his arms in the absence of any deodorant. Eight minutes after the call, feeling clean and fresh, he went back to the bedroom and took out the shirt, that he had ironed the previous night, from the wardrobe.

The wardrobe was full of pristinely ironed shirts but none of the others were his. The shirts had belonged to a man a good three inches shorter than his six feet two inches and a good twenty pounds more in weight. He hung the shirt on the handle of the wardrobe and looked at the warm bed he had just got out of.

Helen's wavy blonde hair cascaded onto the white cotton pillow and her slow sleeping breath whispered from her small perfect mouth through pale rosy lips. She looked like a sleeping angel he thought.... his angel. Dave leaned across towards her and gently shook the t-shirted shoulder that poked out from the grey silk duvet cover. She opened her bright sleepy blue eyes that immediately sparkled awake on seeing his naked body above her.

"I've been called out and got to go into work."

"Have you got time for a coffee or something?"

"Yes if you make it, I've got to get dressed and get away as soon as possible."

Helen slid to the side of the bed and swung her feet to the floor. She stretched her arms above her head, her tousled blonde hair falling over her shoulders. Seeing his eyes on her she reached down grabbed the bottom of the t-shirt and pulled it over her head and dropped it to the floor.

"Are you sure we haven't got ten minutes...for the something......and time for a coffee" she asked putting her arms round his waist.

Dave looked at his watch; it would have taken him forty five minutes to get from his house in Chesterfield to White Lodge but only ten minutes from where he was. There would be questions asked if he turned up fifteen minutes after being called out, questions that he knew he wouldn't want to answer.

"Alright I've ten minutes but you will still have to make the cup of coffee."

Thirty minutes later DC Dave Baker was driving north on the A6 from Ashford In The Water towards the car park at White Lodge. As he always did on the way to any job, he was running through his mind the various protocols and policies that he would have to follow when he got to the scene. The crime scene protocols he had been taught on his Policing Degree at Derby University had been embedded with practical experience once he had joined the police. Dave had been in the police five years. For the first three years as a uniform officer, he had been based at Bakewell and then following his appointment as a detective, he was working in a small team of three detectives based at Matlock covering the two hundred square miles of the Derbyshire Dales and its small towns and villages.

Dave ran through the likely scenarios of what may have happened. He knew the rural location well. It was a popular car park just off the main A6 road between Bakewell and Buxton. The car park catered for walkers, weary motorists and as a source of income for many of the thieves who preyed on handbags left in unattended vehicles in remote rural parking areas. A track led off from the car park and wound its way uphill to an old limestone quarry that had been flooded and stocked with trout and other game fish.

He found himself hoping that it was a suicide. At the moment that would be the least-worst option because of his workload. It had been a bad three weeks over Christmas for sudden deaths. Two accidental deaths just before Christmas had meant that he and his colleagues had a desk full of paperwork, on top of the usual, burglaries, thefts, and assaults, and he did not want either his boss Detective Sergeant Hollins or the Coroner taking him to task for not completing his paperwork on time.

He considered what type of suicide given the circumstances he had been given. A body on the track ruled out suicide by a car gassing, but it could be pills with a nearby note explaining why life was so futile and promising everlasting love to those left behind grieving. It could be a walker who had slipped and broken their neck. That would be the best scenario he thought, and he tried to persuade himself that he would be attending a fatal accidental slip on the icy track. As he got closer to the car park however he could feel a rising sense of foreboding in his mind that the morning was not going to be a straightforward one and that he would neither be seeing his own home nor Helen that night.

It was 7.30 a.m. when Dave pulled onto the car park at White Lodge. Tuesday 14th January was a typical day for the time of the year weather-wise in the Dales. Cold and frosty. The frost baked car park had been covered in a layer of overnight snow. Virgin tyre tracks led to a couple of white luminescent chequered police vehicles parked up in front of him. Cold foggy breath exhaled from the two police officers at the side of the police vehicles as they chatted on the snow covered car park. Puddles of light brown frosted ground had appeared around them where they had disturbed the dusty snow and it had blown away.

Dave got out of the car. The cold hit him like a truck, and he shivered instinctively. He went to the back of his car, opened the boot, and took out his old uniform yellow fluorescent hooded jacket. It was the warmest coat he owned, and it was windproof as well. On cold mornings like this it was a lifesaver.

The three stripes on his black jacket and bald pate identified one of the police officers as Sergeant William 'Bill' Fry. Bill was the Station Sergeant at Bakewell but would supervise the uniform officers from Matlock and Ashbourne on the same shift pattern. Dave Baker knew Bill well. He had been his shift Sergeant five years ago when he had first joined the Derbyshire

Constabulary on the graduate entry scheme. Even then Bill would have been described as a 'veteran.'

Bill had been a police officer for thirty years. A spell as a detective in Derby and then the Regional Crime Squad had been followed twenty years ago by a promotion to Sergeant at Bakewell. The routine of uniform duties had allowed him to settle down with his wife Judy, three children had followed, who were now all teenagers at the local Lady Manners School.

Fifteen years ago, he had bought the police house where he was living on the council estate at Moorhall, and the permanence and longevity of his police role in the town had led to his acceptance as 'one of them' by the townsfolk of Bakewell. Bill's local knowledge was legendary amongst his work colleagues although the source of the knowledge remained unknown to most.

Dave was one of the few who knew that those unknown sources were usually to be found in the snug bar of The Manners pub. Knowledge he had gained from a brief period of time when he had lodged with Bill and his family on his appointment at Bakewell as a police officer.

Bill stamped the snow from his shiny black boots, reached into the upper left pocket of his tunic on which the blue and white striped Long Service and Good Conduct ribbon had been proudly sewn and removed a packet of Marlborough cigarettes.

The cigarettes were half-way out of his pocket as Dave joined them.

"Morning Excy" Bill greeted him.

Excy was the nickname that DS Hollins had given him when he had joined Matlock CID a couple of years ago. He had been told that it matched his determination to solve crimes with the way that an Exocet missile hit its target. Dave liked the nickname, which was just as well, as like a virus it had passed from those in the CID office to all those who knew him.

"I'll tell you if that's the case in a bit Bill," Dave joked back at him with a smile.

"Want one Bod?" Bill asked offering the half empty packet to his colleague.

"Don't mind if I do." Bod reached over and took a proffered cigarette.

"Excy?"

Dave raised the palm of his hand towards Bill

"No thanks, not had one for weeks I'm trying to give up."

"Me too for the last 30 years" Bill retorted drily as Bod took out his Zippo lighter and lit both cigarettes.

Dave was not surprised to see Bod at the scene even though he was based some fifteen miles away in Matlock. He would have been on nights and covering the sub division with another officer. The two hundred square miles of the Dales sub division ranged from Buxton in the north and then eastwards towards the outskirts of the Yorkshire city of Sheffield and then swept down around the west of Chesterfield and on towards Belper and Derby before circling round and gathering in Ashbourne, Hartington, and the other Derbyshire villages on the Staffordshire border, before heading back to the outskirts of Buxton.

The three main towns in the area, Ashbourne, Matlock, and Bakewell, all had police stations where one Sergeant and eight officers were based to cover the area '24/7'. None of the police stations had been open to the public since the government cuts to police budgets a few years ago and had been replaced by a centralised command and control centre which took all reports and calls for service for the area through the emergency 999 number or the national police number 101. With only one other officer, Bod was responsible for covering the whole of the night shift for the best part of a third of Derbyshire.

Bod stomped the snow off his muddy and scuffed boots that had probably last seen any polish in a Northampton shoe factory several years previously. His uniform trousers, draped like overlong curtains over those same boots, gave the impression that sometime in the recent past it had belonged to someone several stones heavier and at least six inches taller. Bod was thin. Wiry would be a better description. His long and pointed nose was his main facial feature, growing like a craggy outcrop from his heavily sun and wind tanned face.

Bod had picked up his nickname from his initials. Brendan O'Donnell. It had originated in his schooldays and stuck with him all his life. If you asked his close family what his Christian

An Accidental Death

name was it is unlikely that anyone would have known. Bod was the only name that he was known as, and the only one Dave had known him answer to. Dave had worked with Bod for the last couple of years and they had struck up a good relationship despite the difference of age, over the occasional beer after a shift.

The contrast between Bill Fry and Bod in appearance was amplified by Bod's mop of unkempt black swept back hair compared to the speckled bald head of Bill and it gave them the appearance of what the two extremities of a 55-year-old man could look like to a god with a sense of humour.

"What do we know so far then Bill?" Dave asked.

"In a nutshell, Comms got a call from Stan Moore about 6 a.m. this morning. He was checking on his fish, as he's had a bit of poaching over the last few weeks. Says he was driving up to the pond when he sees what appears to be a large snow covered rock on the track. Stan stops, gets out to move it, and sees it's the body of a woman. He's checked if she was breathing but she was obviously dead. As an ex police officer, he didn't want to disturb the scene any more than he had to, so he has run back down to the car park to get a signal and ring it in."

Bill paused to see if Dave needed any clarification of what he had said. Dave nodded and so Bill continued.

"Comms sends Curly who is night cover with Bod. Curly meets Stan in the car park, and they walk back to the body where he confirms that she is dead, and they leave the scene. As supervision cover I've come across from Matlock with Bod. So, to summarise we've got a dead woman, only Stan Moore and Curly have been to the scene and Stan's Land Rover is still there. Bod's seized Curly's clothes and he's now sat in the back of the Panda in his underwear and a fluorescent jacket!"

Bills serious face broke into a wide grin.

"For Fucks sake! I might need him for a cordon"

Dave complained expressing mock anger at the practical joke played on the young officer.

"You will be alright, No-one's going to be here for ages and the place is in the middle of nowhere. He's only been in the job six months, so he was fair game, I'll send him back to the nick to get his spare uniform and he will be back in twenty minutes."

"Alright, but we will need him Bill, so let's get him back here soon as."

"Where's Stan?"

"Top end of the car park up there."

Bill pointed to an army camouflaged figure about fifty yards away partly hidden by a line of silver birch trees.

"Gone to ring his missus, wants her to take some boots and clothes to the nick for when we seize his clothes off him. She's a bit fiery and I don't think he wanted us to hear her bollocking him for waking her up at this ungodly hour in the morning."

"Well, that's the scene covered, what is the best way in Bill?"

"Probably up the track, over the wall and through the copse of trees, then over the top wall and back down to the Land Rover. How you approach it is up to you when you get up there."

Dave walked towards the dry-stone wall adjacent to the two police vehicles and noticed Curly sat in the driver's seat of the police car with his bare legs and fluorescent bib clearly visible through the window. Dave gestured for him to wind down the window.

"Ayup Curly, you alright, first body you found?"

"Yes, I'm OK, it's quite exciting really."

" Did you notice anything about what might have happened to her?"

"Not really, she's no clothes, there was some blood. She was definitely dead, so I left and waited for supervision and CID to turn up."

"You did right" Dave assured him.

"Is it a murder do you think?"

"We won't know yet, but if we do the basics right at the start we won't come unstuck later on. Get yourself off back to the police station, get some new gear on and get back here soon as. You will be needed later, and you won't be much use in just your skiddies and a fluorescent bib."

"Will do Excy. Be about thirty minutes."

Curly wound his window up and drove out the car park and turned south down the A6 back towards the police station at Bakewell.

Dave shouted back to Bill.

"I've told Curly to nip back, get changed and get his arse back here soon as possible, if that's alright with you?"

"Yeah, no problem do you want me to come up with you?" Bill offered.

"Won't do any harm and two heads are better than one, I'm still hoping it will be some poor bugger that's wandered off, slipped, knocked themselves out, and frozen to death or topped themselves with a bottle of pills and lovely suicide note in their pocket."

"With no clothes on as well, you always were an optimist!" Bill joked catching him up.

"It's as likely to be a stowaway dropping off the landing gear of a passing plane as that. I've got a feeling this is going to be a wrong un. It's too remote and wrong time of year to be natural causes."

Dave walked through the open gate and then turned to the dry stone wall on his left. He felt the cold snow, and hard roughness of the wall on his hands. Dave immediately regretted not putting on some gloves and his walking boots as he then scraped his leather brogues on the rough gritstone of the wall as he climbed over it. A thought that was repeated as the smooth leather soles slipped on the frosty grass, and he was forced to grab the branch of a silver birch to stop himself landing on his back.

Bill chuckled at his plight "You should have put your boots on!"

"Thanks for that Sergeant Hindsight!" Dave replied laconically.

Dave righted himself, pushed through the trees and began the trek up to the Land Rover, whose green roof could be seen over the top of the next drystone wall about fifty yards away where the track turned back on itself. If they went straight up the hill and then got over the next wall the Land Rover belonging to Stan Moore would be facing them thirty yards down the track.

"You were on last night, what time did it start snowing?"

"There wasn't a lot as you can see, but there were a few showers. Started just after 1 a.m. I think. I had a cuppa back at Matlock nick with Bod about then. Was clear when I went in but there was a covering when I came out. Stopped about 4 a.m. I reckon."

"Might give us an idea of when she got here." suggested Dave.

"According to Stan she wasn't here yesterday morning when he came up to check on his fish about the same time, so that would be about 5.30 a.m. to 6.00 a.m. says he's been coming up every day as he has lost a lot of fish in recent weeks. He reported it just before Christmas and asked us to keep an eye out on nights. You know what he's like with his fish. He has been pretty wound up about it and threatened to 'shoot and kill the bastards!' if he got them before us."

"If she's got a sack of fish and been shot we've got a good suspect then" joked Dave.

Once they had climbed over the wall, Dave and Bill stopped and scanned the scene. There was no sign of footprints or tyre marks in the frost and snow in front of the Land Rover. There was, however, a small pale white snow sprinkled mound. They looked at each other and Dave nodded. Bill moved to the verge side behind him, and they walked silently towards the Land Rover, hugging the wall and hedge that lined the bridleway. When they were about twenty yards away from the Land Rover, Dave checked for footprints down its nearside, there were none. Stan Moore had obviously got out the offside driver's door and not returned back along its nearside.

Dave nodded again to Bill, and they continued forward squeezing against the hedgerow.

"Sorry about that!"

Dave laughed as a shower of snow came off the wall of bare hawthorn as he pushed through it, and it sprung back throwing snow over Bills now cold red face.

"Just call me Rudolph the snow-covered reindeer!"

"Well, you've got the nose for it!"

The jocularity came to a halt as they came to the front of the Land Rover.

Five yards away a snow covered mound lay curled in the roadway. Dave could see it was a young woman; her knees and legs were in a foetal position. The torso lay on its side hiding the left arm. The right arm was outstretched on the frozen track as though grabbing for some invisible rescue. Red nail varnish caught Dave's eye against the white snow and dark rocky track surface. She was naked, the snow merging with the pale pearl sheen of her white body. Her auburn hair clung wetly to her skull, flowing stream like into the snow covered rocky track. A recent heavy foot had stood on an auburn tress leaving it embedded in a muddy imprint.

"Fuck!" Dave exclaimed quietly.

"Yep" whispered Bill.

Dave carefully approached the body along the side of the bridleway, taking care to tread on virgin ground, until he had a better view of the corpse on the ground. The long red hair had fallen away from her face revealing her open green lifeless eyes. Early twenties Dave guessed, attractive as well. She was small, around five feet tall he reckoned.

A rivulet of blood had trickled from a large cut above her right breast. It had run across her sternum and over her left breast before falling into what was now a small frozen dark pool that spread under her partly hidden left arm. Another incision about two inches in length showed clearly above her left breast. Blood had trickled from this cut downwards before joining the small frozen pool on the rocky floor.

Dave had seen enough. He took out his iPhone from his pocket and started to take pictures of the scene from his crouched position. He dropped his blue Bic pen by the side of the footprints in the frost around the body. This would give some idea of shoe size if CSI turned up after the snow had thawed.

He photographed the two different shoe prints which he assumed were those of Curly and Stan Moore. There were no others visible, which indicated to Dave that the body had been there before the snow had fallen. He put his phone back in his pocket and waved to Bill to back away.

Both men carefully backed away, taking care to follow the pathway they had created to the scene. They went back over the wall and down the hill towards the stamping Bod and anxiously looking Stan Moore, still waiting in the car park.

"Well looks like we're here for a while!" Dave quipped to Bod as he walked up to him in the car park.

"Is it a Murder?" Bod asked, as Bill and Dave stamped the snow off their respective shoes and boots.

"No, it's a suicide. She's stabbed herself multiple times, then run half a mile up a farm track completely naked on the coldest night of the year. Once in the middle of nowhere she has collapsed and died to just fuck up the local police's first brew of the morning."

A broad smile passed across Bods face at Bill's sarcasm.

"Well, I'm not missing my brew Sarge, so I suppose best thing I can do is nip back to the nick and get some teas and coffees up here, while I can, what you reckon?"

Bill looked at Dave for a decision as the detective at the scene.

"Get back within half an hour Bod. Don't put sugar in the coffee and sort out a regular supply there's going to be lots of people here in an hour or so and they're going to be here all day."

Bod nodded, gestured for Stan Moore to get in the back of the police car and got in the driver's seat to wait for Bill.

Dave turned to Bill

"Right Bill, there's going to be more brass than a pub's snug here in about an hour so let's at least look as we know what we are doing. Get Stan Moore down to the nick, get a statement off him and his clothes. We don't know when she died, so let's have all cars stop checked on this road, ask them if they've seen anything over the last few days and get details of the drivers and passengers. We will need someone up above the body on the track to stop anyone and particularly the press, stumbling down to the scene and buggering it up, that is a priority. Three questions then - Who have we got on and available? How long before we can get that all up and running? Is it possible to get it done before the brass get here?"

Bill looked at him as though he had just asked him to jump into the river Wye that ran along the valley below the car park.

"Not a snowballs chance in hell Excy. I'll do what I can but that box of policemen back at the nick was emptied about ten years ago. I'll take Stan Moore and sort him out, Curly should be on his way back and will be here in about fifteen minutes so you can send him up to cordon the scene. I've got four officers coming on at 8 a.m. two at Matlock and two at Ashbourne. They can make their way here soon as they book on, which is about now so I'll get on the radio to Comms and get them travelling. They should be here in no more than half an hour and can do the stop checks. Bod and me were off half an hour ago but can stop on. That leaves Bod spare when he gets back with the drinks, and you can sort him out with whatever you want him to do. I reckon the brass will be here between nine and ten, so I will do a ring round at nine and get whoever is spare from an office up in Buxton down here as well. That's the best I can do Excy. What about Holly and Cath?"

"On at 9 a.m. but I will see if Comms can get them out earlier. See what you can do getting anybody else here. While you're doing that I'll hold the fort here and update Comms as we will need to get the circus on their way here. Nothing on the radio yet as we don't want the place crawling with press before we get going. Put some road closed signs out on the car park as well, otherwise there will be the public causing chaos on here when everyone turns up."

"No problem, consider it done, there's one in the back of the car" Bill assured him.

Bill got in the passenger seat of the marked police vehicle and was driven away by Bod. Dave watched as the car stopped at the car park entrance. Bill got out, opened the boot, and put a sign up at the car park entrance, got back in the car and was driven away along the A6 towards Bakewell.

Chapter 2 - The Decision

Friday 20ᵗʰ December

Some three weeks earlier, at 7.15 a.m., on the last working Friday before the Christmas holidays, the electronic alarm belonging to Paul Trueman sounded its first gentle 'beep.' By the much louder third 'beep' Paul was awake and did his first morning stretch in his grey silk-sheeted king size bed.

Bright winter sunlight shone through the blinds of the bedroom in the large stone detached house half-way up Eaton Hill in Baslow. Paul looked at the sunshine induced ribbons of light and shadow across the bed, and smiled to himself, it was going to be a beautiful day, He swung his red silk pyjama coated legs out of the bed and onto the oak whitewashed floor, stretched for a second time, stood up, and went for a shower.

Twenty minutes later, after blow drying and sweeping back his grey collar length hair in the back lit mirror, he walked back into the bedroom and with a flourish of his arm, opened his walk-in wardrobe door. Paul hesitated, examining with his eyes the line of starchly ironed shirts, before deciding on a white cotton one to go with his grey Ralph Lauren suit.

An Accidental Death

He admired his reflection in the mirrored door. He was not tall at a little over five feet nine inches and his once slim figure had been expanded by middle age and fine dining, but he could still give an image of authority and wealth from the scum he would be dealing with in court that morning. He breathed in, pulling his paunch above his waist and practised a stern withering stare at himself in the mirror. That was the look he wanted his criminal victims to see as he sentenced them. He would look authoritative to his peers and the press, and his clothes would distinguish him as well above the social status of those he would be dealing with that morning. He put the shirt and trousers on, chose a pair of grey cotton socks and made his way downstairs to the kitchen.

Of all the rooms in the house, he loved the design of the kitchen best. The room had a black and brilliant white colour scheme whose ambience was enhanced, in his eyes, by the quality of the glossed unit doors and appliances. He looked around and admired his interior design capabilities. The gleaming black granite worktops complimented perfectly the black mirrored marbled floors and white walls; the colour scheme was broken only by a grey granite vase of pink lilies, (whose perfumed pollen stems he had expertly removed as they flowered) and a grey sixty inch Bang and Olufson TV on the wall.

Paul had designed the kitchen, as he had all the rooms in the house with the help of his partner. The house reflected their own personalities, everything was smooth, sleek, polished, and in its place. Out of sight until needed and then at hand, to then be cleaned and put away until the next time. Having looked around the kitchen and praised himself, he did what he did every morning, and poured himself a bowl of granola with soya milk and a blended banana and strawberry smoothie. Before eating his breakfast he rinsed all the utensils he had used, placed them in the dishwasher and wiped down the work-surfaces.

By 8.05 a.m. he had finished his granola and smoothie while listening to the news headlines on the TV. He neatly stacked his used pots in the dishwasher and checked his Breitling wristwatch. He had twenty minutes to spare; plenty of time he decided to complete his next task that morning.

Paul walked through to the living room. On the smoked glass coffee table was an ultrathin MacBook and two brown cardboard boxes. He unpacked the smaller of the two packages and forced out the USB memory stick from its plastic holder. He then unpacked the second box and removed an identical ultrathin MacBook and placed it next to the one already on the coffee table. Paul carried both MacBooks into the kitchen with the USB, and with great care he positioned them equidistant apart on the worktop.

Sitting comfortably on the white leather topped bar stool he opened up the first MacBook with his thumbprint. He was by no means an expert on IT matters, but believed that a biometric thumbprint was much more secure than some random password that could be guessed or forgotten. He put the USB stick into the port and copied the contents of the MacBook onto it. He then busied himself in the kitchen making a pot of ground Arabica coffee whilst the contents of the MacBook downloaded onto the memory stick.

When it had finished downloading he opened the second MacBook and set it up for biometric access using his thumbprint once again. Satisfied that it was secure, he transferred the memory stick to the second MacBook and sipped his coffee without milk or sugar, whilst it downloaded the files he had just copied. Paul saved the copied files and then erased everything from the memory stick, and removed it. He then broke it in half and deposited it in the bin with the packaging. Satisfied the copying had been successful he then picked up his phone and opened a contact.

"Hi it's me, ... can you talk....... great .... it's been hectic this morning, but I've managed to copy over the files to my new Mac.......... I hate having both of them at the same place so could do with giving you your MacBook back as soon as possible......... I can't drop it off on my way to work as I'm sitting today, but you could pick it up if you want....... well, if you're calling I'll make you a coffee before Court......... alright I'll see you in the back kitchen.....I've booked us in at Fischer's for dinner tonight if that's alright with you, we can walk from mine .... that's brilliant .... remind me that I will need to allow you to thumbprint access my new Mac when you come over later .... alright see you in an hour or so .... Bye."

Paul checked his wristwatch again. The twenty minutes he had allocated for the copying task were now up. He poured the remains of his coffee into the sink, ran the residue away with cold water and was putting the mug into the dishwasher when his mobile phone rang. Paul saw the caller was "John Squires" a fellow Conservative councillor for the Derbyshire Dales.

"Morning John!" he answered the call.

"Good Morning Paul, are you on the bench this morning?"

"Yes, starting about 10 a.m. and finishing hopefully about 3.30 p.m. Is there a problem?"

"No, just trying to schedule a meeting of the Conservative Group to discuss whether to allocate money for a couple of grit bins at the bottom of Eaton Hill. The good lady wife told me she almost slipped there a few days ago and I was hoping for your support as you live on the road. It's a bit of a rush I know but we can make a decision tomorrow at the highways subcommittee meeting if you can make it."

"Well, I'm free after golf tomorrow, if that's any good John?"

"That seems alright. about 2.30 p.m. then and I'll let you know if any of the Labour smelly socks look like buggering up the decision at the meeting in the clubhouse in the morning!"

"Sounds fine, John."

"That's the plan then Paul. Send a few felons down for me, today will you!"

"Not a problem, I'll mention your name and address as I do it… if you like!" he replied laughing.

"There's no need to go that far, I don't want the great unwashed buggers coming around and putting bricks through my windows! See you tomorrow on the tee." John laughed back and hung up.

Paul put the appointment in the diary app on his phone and checked his watch again; he was now running late. He went upstairs to his bedroom, taking the stairs two at a time and quickly chose a silk tie and a pair of rubber soled black brogues from the wardrobe: it was frosty outside.

As he put on his suit jacket he remembered that he had not put away his new MacBook. He scurried back down the stairs to the kitchen, picked it up and took it into the study where he sat in the black leather chair at his desk. He pushed the chair back from his black onyx topped desk, opened the singular central drawer to the desk and placed the MacBook inside it. Paul locked the drawer and crossed over to the bookcase where he removed his copy of 'The Song of Achilles.' Opening it in the middle, he placed the thin desk key in the small hole cut into the pages and replaced it on the bookshelf.

Paul then picked two more books from the lines of books in the bookcase - A Magistrates Court Guide and Magistrates Sentencing Guidelines that he would need later that day and put them in his large black calfskin Dior messenger bag that had been left at the side of the desk. The messenger bag and an identical brown one had been mutual presents that he and his partner had bought each other the previous year on a weekend break to Capri. Happy memories. He looked out of the study window onto the heavily frosted lawn. He hated the cold. If only the weather was as warm here as it had been there he thought to himself.

Walking back into the kitchen he looked around. Good. Everything had been put away in its place. Then he saw the second MacBook on the worktop. He chastised himself for his forgetfulness and opened the messenger bag, lifted the full-length calfskin flap that covered the secure hidden zipped pocket and placed the MacBook in it. Paul zipped up the pocket and refastened the calfskin covering onto its Velcro fastening and checked his watch again.

"Damn" he exclaimed aloud to himself.

He was now four minutes late from the schedule he had set himself that morning. His brogues were upstairs but there was a pair of grey Sebago moccasins neatly placed at the door, where he had removed them the previous day. He could save some time by putting those on rather than going back upstairs and retrieving his brogues ….and they would go just as well with the suit he had chosen. He slipped on the moccasins, placed the messenger bag over his shoulder and shut the kitchen door behind him. As he closed the door, he felt the reassuring weight of the door and the heavy lock drop into place.

Twenty yards along the path he looked back at the house and checked that the windows were all secured, and then checked his watch again. If there was not much traffic on the road to Bakewell he could make up the time.

Paul hurried along the slate path and then slowed as the smooth soles of his moccasins slipped on the overnight icy covering. He cursed himself for his poor choice of footwear and considered going back to the house to replace them with the brogues that had a better grip. He checked his watch again; he didn't have time, and so carried on carefully walking along the path to the garage that housed his five month old Porsche 911 Coupe.

Paul drove the six miles from Baslow to Bakewell at speed, pushing the car into all thirteen bends of the A619 and enjoying the feeling of power in the performance car. At Pineapple Bridge, just outside Bakewell, he came up behind a slow-moving Honda Jazz. The clock on the dashboard showed that he was now back on the time schedule he had set himself. Paul put the Porsche into third gear, dropped thirty yards behind the Jazz and cruised into Bakewell along the well gritted Baslow Road, tapping the steering wheel and listening to Sade. Life had been good to Paul Trueman, and he could see no reason why that state of affairs should not continue.

At the car park on Granby Road, he parked his car directly opposite the police station for security and paid for a day's parking at the nearby machine. After placing the ticket in the windscreen, he put the messenger bag over his shoulder, and as he locked the Porsche his eye was drawn to a hooded figure across the road, outside the entrance to the car park.

The young man was doing small circles on a hand painted black mountain bike. The cyclist turned towards him, and he recognised him immediately. It was Gary Traynor, otherwise known as Little Shit. Gary Traynor was on the list of offenders he was dealing with that morning and Paul was particularly looking forward to sentencing him for the thefts and burglaries that he had admitted to at his first hearing four weeks ago. At that time sentencing had been adjourned for reports and he was very hopeful the probation report would recommend a substantial prison sentence for the serial offender now he was eighteen.

He envisioned himself regaling his friends at the golf club of his involvement in ridding the Derbyshire Dales of its one-man crime wave. It was just a shame he couldn't send down his father Ron as well. "Like father, like son" he thought. He wondered which one of the duty solicitors would have the misfortune of representing him today. Probably that druggie Bernie Marples he thought to himself. Not that Gary Traynor needed one, as he was as well versed in his rights and the law as any solicitor.

Paul walked from the car park up the heavily salt gritted Water Street and crossed the one way system to The Old Post Office. The Magistrates Court sat one day a week in Bakewell Town Hall, the entrance to which was just ten yards across the road in front of him. He waited whilst a red saloon passed and then stepped forward. Paul's right foot landed on the black icy road, and he felt his smooth soled shoes slip on the deadly covering. His arms flew into the air as he fought to keep his balance and the Dior bag fell from his shoulder into the roadway. A uniform police officer appeared from nowhere and grabbed his arm, steadied him to prevent him from falling and then gathered up the bag from the road with his other hand.

In the police officer's grip Paul regained his balance and exhaled loudly in relief. He turned to his rescuer and saw the three stripes on his arm.

"Thank you Sergeant."

"No problem Councillor Trueman, strong arm of the law sometimes comes in handy to our elected representatives"

Sergeant Bill Fry, let go of Paul's arm and placed into his hand the dropped Dior messenger bag.

Paul gripped the messenger bag tightly with his left hand and quickly finished crossing the road onto the pavement on the other side. The pavement was ungritted and icy, so he took a right footed short leap onto a dry, ice-free patch of pavement outside the door to the Town Hall and then leapt left foot first onto the paved entranceway. As his foot landed on the smooth wet floor he felt his leg slide forward.

Paul Trueman, for the second time in a minute, struggled to regain his balance, but this time there was no police officer to prevent him falling backwards. As he fell he was aware that his messenger bag was falling out of his grip behind him. At that same moment he saw the blue and yellow stained glass skylight in the ceiling of the entranceway for the first time in his life and then felt the back of his skull hit something hard. He realised it had to be the floor.

Paul lay there looking up towards the stained glass skylight. He was alright. There was no pain, but he could feel rising nausea and there was an ache at the back of his head. He went to raise his head from the floor and as he did so he felt his hair grab stickily at the floor. His head was bleeding. Then he smelt the blood as its wetness pooled against his cheek. His mind started to panic, and he tried to raise himself again from the floor, but he couldn't make any of his limbs move. Above him the blue merged into the yellow so that it looked like a Caribbean beach. That's odd he thought to himself then his vision went into opaqueness and a blurred figure was turning him onto his side.

Paul blinked and vision swam back to his eyes, and he realised that the side of his head was now resting in the warm blood coagulating on the cold hard floor. He could feel blood running down his neck, but was still surprised that there was no pain. He blinked again. He was facing the road in the entranceway to the Town Hall. Paul could see his messenger bag in front of him, lying on the footpath where he had dropped it as he fell. At that moment, a bicycle wheel appeared at the side of it, and a hand reached down and grabbed the strap. Paul saw the unmistakable face of Gary Traynor come into view at the side of the arm, and then hand, arm, face, and bag disappeared from his sight, followed by the bicycle wheel.

Anger rose inside him, how dare someone like Gary Traynor steal something from him! The silent angry scream of "Leave that you fucking thieving little shit!" left his brain but did not reach his mouth as the blackness of unconsciousness enveloped him.

The first person to come to the aid of Paul Trueman after he fell was Bill Fry, the police sergeant who had stopped him from falling a few seconds earlier, followed by Mrs Teresa Bagnell the Magistrates Clerk who was entering the courthouse at the same time. Teresa, a woman who was always willing to help others in emotional distress, if only to have something to tell her friends about later, 'in confidence' of course, knelt at the side of Paul.

"Are you alright Paul? It's terrible that the council has allowed the entrance to become so slippery."

There was no reply.

Bill knelt at the side of Teresa and cleared Paul Trueman's tongue from his throat, then rolled him onto his side into a recovery position. Then without asking opened her handbag and searched through it before taking out a handkerchief that he passed to her. Teresa was about to ask him indignantly what he thought he was doing when she saw the gaping wound at the back of Paul Trueman's head.

Bill placed the handkerchief into her hand and then pressed both against the bloodied wound. The blood immediately soaked the handkerchief and ran over her small, manicured fingers. Teresa, repulsed by the warm stickiness, tried to remove her hand but the sergeant held it even tighter against the gaping flap of skin.

Teresa felt the blood matted hair and the hard bone of his exposed skull against her fingers. She closed her eyes, and the acrid taste of bile filled her mouth as she gagged and then swallowed it back. She did not want to be where she was. There was no way that she could tell her friends of the horror of this moment without reliving it, and that was something even now she knew she could not do.

Theresa took a deep breath; she felt the tears seeping through her tightly closed eyes and Paul's blood seeping through her tightly clenched fingers.

"You will be alright; you're going to be alright," she reassured herself and Paul's unconscious body with little confidence.

A warm spurt of liquid on her wrist caused her to open her eyes; the profusely bleeding wound was now rhythmically like a small fountain ejecting bright red blood onto her wrist and forearm; she moved the tightly scrunched bloodied handkerchief to cover the pumping stream of blood and closed her eyes again. She wanted to be sick and gagged again at the mingling smell of blood and polish from the floor below her.

This was her own personal horror movie; she would awake in a second and it would all have been a bad dream. Then she felt his skull vibrate almost imperceptibly against her fingers, then a stronger vibration followed by another. She opened her eyes and looked in fear towards the police officer at her side who was again clearing Paul Trueman's mouth of his tongue with a bloodied index finger.

Paul Trueman began to fit, shaking so violently that his body was clearing the floor, and with each spasm his head crashed back onto the hard tiled floor. Teresa cried out and snatched her hand away from the wound, spraying her face and clothing with blood. She could not however tear her unblinking eyes away from the clear cerebrospinal fluid seeping from his ear and mixing into the bloody pool in which she was now knelt. Frozen by the sudden horror of the blood spattering spasms, the only thing her mind could comprehend was Sergeant Bill Fry talking into his police radio.

"Yes an ambulance as soon as possible, if not quicker it's a bad head injury and does not look good."

Chapter 3 – A Quid Pro Quo

Tuesday 14th January

Dave listened to the sound of the police vehicle fading away, and then the silence that cloaked around him. There was no birdsong, no traffic, not even the sound of wind in the trees. He stood silently, watching the mist of his breath evaporate in the cold air. He sniffed and wiped his nose with his hand, then took three deep breaths, calming himself after the adrenaline fuelled return from the body and the excitement that a murder always brought. He watched the breaths evaporate in the warming air and wrapped himself in the silence before the cacophony that would come with the murder investigation.

Calmed, Dave stated decisively to no-one but himself "Right, Let's get this show on the road." He reached into his pocket, took out his phone and saw there was no signal. Moving over to the wall he had recently climbed over he noticed that only one signal bar came up on his phone. By standing on a jutting out stone in the dry stone wall he was able to get two bars.

An Accidental Death

He tapped in 101. After saying "Derbyshire" into the remote IT Police call system, he waited for someone to answer the phone; the repetitive ringing on his loudspeaker echoing industrially through the surrounding silent countryside.

When no-one had answered after five long minutes, Dave frustratedly exclaimed aloud "Fuck it!" and closed the call.

He tapped in 999 and the call was picked up straight away. He asked for the police and was put through to the police control room.

"Police Emergency, how can I help you?"

"Hi, it's not an emergency, It's DC Baker from Matlock CID, can you put me through to the Control Room Inspector?"

"I can't do that as you could be anyone, what's your emergency caller?"

" I'm not anyone, I'm the DC at the scene of a found body this morning and I need to speak to him."

"I can't just put you through. If you give me the incident number, I can check who you are and might be able to put you through then."

"I have no idea of the incident number as I just got called out about two hours ago to come to the scene."

"I can't help you if you don't know the incident number."

He tried to stay calm but could feel the anger rising in him at the frustration the way the phone call was going.

"How many incidents have you got running with a dead body this morning?"

"I don't know, do you have a post code?"

The calmness that Dave had recently experienced disappeared

"I'm in the bloody middle of nowhere, with no radio contact; if it has a postcode the chances of me knowing it are bloody nil! It's on the A6 north of Ashford In The Water near a village called Sheldon if that's any good!"

"Whereabouts is Sheldon?"

"The Peak District."

"Standby caller."

After about 15 seconds the silence was replaced by a calling ring tone.

"Inspector Willis can I help you?"

Dave let out a sigh of relief. Someone he knew and who knew him.

"Ayup Pete it's Dave Baker, I'm at that body at White Lodge."

"Hi Dave, what you got?"

"Doesn't look good Pete, going to need a police surgeon, Senior CSI, and an SIO to start with, and then probably the whole circus but that's above my pay grade."

Pete chuckled "I'll sort that for you and get them on the way, I'll get everyone else on standby when they come on; if you think it's likely to be a murder that's good enough for me."

"Who is the SIO on call?" asked Dave.

"I'll just have a look…. It's Superintendent Dicks."

"Glad we've done it by the book here then otherwise he'd have had my arse…. seeing as I'm not on his Christmas card list." He laughed out loud.

Pete understanding what Dave meant replied "I'd better do the same or I'll be busted to Custody Sergeant for the rest of my service. Do you need anything else?"

"Bill Fry is sorting out some staff, they should be here soon. We will need more, so give the Divisional Superintendent the heads up. I could do with a direct line into you as I've got no radio and phone signal is poor up here. I'm stood on a wall and only got two bars. You might think about some sort of comms up here as it'll be needed. Other than that, I'll ring you back if I need anything."

Pete Willis gave Dave his direct line number and then continued.

"Leave everything with me, I've got your mobile and I'll update you by message if I can't get through."

"Cheers Pete, I'm glad you're on, I was beginning to lose it getting through to someone."

"It's what's called progress Dave, progress and efficiency."

Dave closed the call and climbed down off the wall. Standing at the side of the lane he realised how cold he was in the shade of the hedgerow and crossed the car park to the sunnier side. The quiet returned although there was now the hum of vehicles passing on the road below as the world woke up to the new morning.

He heard the gear change and then the purr of the powerful engine of the approaching car before he saw it drive onto the car park from the road below. He sighed resignedly when he saw a large black Lexus approaching which then came to halt at the side of him. He could feel a sarcastic "Can you not read police signs!" almost on his lips when the driver's door opened; the driver stepped out, and Dave's heart sank as he saw the flash of scrambled egg on the peaked hat that was being placed on the drivers head. Just what he needed. Brass at the scene of a murder and not a cop in sight.

Dave swallowed the intended sarcasm for the driver and said to himself.

"Fuck, that's just what I needed!"

He checked to himself that he had not blurted the thought out loud.

"Morning Sir "

Detective Constable David Baker greeted Deputy Chief Constable Alan Daley.

"Morning DC Baker, everything in hand?"

At that moment he knew that nothing was in hand at the scene, but that everything would be shortly. The DCC, Alan Daley, was notorious for an extremely short temper for inefficiency, but also renowned for supporting his officers if they deserved it. Dave decided to be straight down the line and hope he got the latter rather than the former.

"I think so sir. The body of a girl was found a couple of hours ago by a local water bailiff. I've been called out and taken a look. I would say it's suspicious to say the least, as there are at least two puncture wounds to the torso. The scene has been preserved as far as possible and we have got a cordon on ….or will have shortly. A witness statement from the person who found the body is being taken together with his clothing and shoes."

Dave's phone pinged, and he glanced at the banner message on the screen of the phone in his hand. The message was from Inspector Willis. He breathed out a large cold expanse of foggy breath

"CSI, Police Surgeon, extra bodies, and SIO are also en-route."

"That's good then, well done. I was notified of the incident when I called in this morning and as it's on my way to the office I thought I'd see how it was going."

At that moment he looked over Alan Daley's shoulder and saw a blue, yellow, and white police car drive onto the car park containing Bod and Curly, and park up on the opposite side to where he was stood. The DCC and Dave watched as Bod and Curly got out the car flasks in hand and with a brief nod towards them, climbed over the wall and scurried towards the body on the track above them.

"I presume that's the cordon."

"That's correct sir, cordon now almost in place."

"Who's the SIO coming out?" asked the DCC getting back to business.

"Supt Dicks according to my pager, boss."

"Big John Dicks."

DC Baker just nodded, not sure if the DCC was gas-lighting him on the nickname or not. Big John Dicks was correct, and originated from his first Sergeant who found that he had two men with the same Christian name on his shift. As one was six feet four and the other five feet four, he had named them Big John and Little John. Dave was aware however that it certainly wasn't 'Big' that the B stood for in many an officer's version.

"There's a rumour going round that you got him and the force out of the shit on the Allestree incident last year…… but of course I don't know anything officially about that" he mused straight faced.

"I'm not sure that Superintendent Dicks sees it that way."

"I can understand that, but because it wasn't made public, as it undoubtedly would have, had it come to light later on in the enquiry, it won't have ruined his career or the forces reputation. I think that you're probably owed a favour DC Baker, so if I'm around and you need one give me a ring and I'll see what I can do."

"Thank you sir, but I just did what anyone else would have done."

"I wouldn't put money on that assertion detective if I were you. Well, I'd better be off and leave you to it before I start treading on toes when everyone turns up. It was nice to bump into you 'Excy?' isn't it?"

"Yes sir" Dave replied feeling uncomfortable at the sound of the senior officer using his nickname.

"By the way tell Bod that the next time he turns up with a flask and doesn't give me a cup I'll have him walking the beat at Glossop for the next six months."

"I will do sir" Dave replied unsure whether he was joking.

Alan Daley got back in the black Lexus, drove around Dave, gave him a wave as he passed, and drove away south down the A6. Dave watched the DCC disappear into the distance and then replayed the last conversation in his head to see whether he had actually been making a joke about Bod and Glossop. He wasn't 100% sure but decided he would tell Bod anyway just in case.

Chapter 4- The Family Of Thieves

Friday 20th December

Like Paul Trueman, Gary Traynor had woken about 7a.m. that morning. Unlike Paul Trueman, it was not to the sound of a £200 electronic Bang and Olufsen alarm, but from the regular raised voices of his parents Ron and Gail, who were downstairs in the kitchen of the semi-detached council house on Leacroft Road in Winster: a small rural village five miles from Bakewell in the Peak District.

"You're a fucking useless piece of shit!" His mother screamed from the kitchen.

Gail Traynor had once been described as 'Five foot two of fire and venom' by Bill Fry. His colleagues who had dealt with her thought that it was an understatement on both points.

Ron on the other hand had spent most of his life dealing with her and knew just how far to push the matriarch of the family and when to make a strategic retreat. Today was not a retreating day

"Well, you go with him if you feel that strongly about it."

"I can't go; it'll kill me if I see him sent down. I couldn't see you sent down or Ron Junior so I'm not going to see our Gary sent down. Why don't you go, you do fuck all for the lad, you've never had any time for him!"

Ron replied calmly.

"If they see me there, they'll give him another six months, he's a big lad now and knows if you can't do the time don't do the crime, we always say that. All I'll say Gail is we don't know he's definitely going down anyway, but if I'm there, you know as well as I do they will definitely send him down."

Ron wiped the last traces of egg and brown sauce from the plate in front of him with a piece of white sliced bread and put it in his mouth. Gail picked up the empty plate, glared at him and looked him in the eye.

"Whatever!"

She put the plate in the sink and went to the kitchen door.

"Gary! Gary!"

His mum called him and then returned to the fat black frying pan, with his breakfast in on the stove.

"Coming!"

The 18-year-old Gary Traynor jumped out of bed, racing down the stairs and into the kitchen, wearing just his blue Y fronts. It was always best to not get on the bad side of his mum in a morning. His dad Ron was sat in his vest and pants at the kitchen table. Gary pulled out a seat from the table and sat opposite him.

"You alright on your own this morning Son?"

"Yeah, I'm meeting Bernie at Court. He says I should get probation provided there's not a Stipe on."

"You alright with that?" his dad asked drawing and then coughing on the cigarette between his amber fingers.

Gary waited for his dad to stop coughing.

"Yeah, if I get sent down, I'll be OK. I know the family motto …If you can't do the time don't do the crime!"

"Fair enough lad, A short one will do you no harm. It'll toughen you up… and smarten you up a bit. You need to stop getting caught, get smart like your dad. I did a six monther at your age and didn't do another till the two year stretch when you were ten, and then only because that weasel Danny MacAleese dropped me for it."

Ron was a big man, six feet four inches of what was once solid muscle, but which was now turning to flab in his late forties. His once bright red curly hair was now turning grey and receding from his large forehead. His ears, like those of Gary, looked too big for his head and were a genetic trait that Ron was pleased to see in all his male children, even though they were not. His daughter Karen was particularly pleased that she had her mother's ears.

Gail poured the contents of the frying pan onto Gary's plate.

"Can't see my boy going away without a good breakfast!"

"Don't worry Mum, I'll be alright either way. Bernie says I'll get probation so stop worrying!"

He grabbed two slices of buttered bread that Gail had already put on the table, stuffed an assortment of fried food from his plate between them and took a large bite out of the makeshift sandwich.

Ron cleared his throat, coughed up some phlegm and then swallowed it and coughed again.

"Make sure that fucking druggie solicitor does his job, tell him you want him to go for probation or else I'll be round to see Holly and Excy, for a chat about cocaine habits!"

All three burst out laughing.

"And another thing don't talk to the cops, they will be trying to get you to have TIC's, don't have anything unless they can prove it. You know the rule!"

"Yes Dad, I know,…admit nowt unless they can prove it."

The back door swung open, and Gary's siblings walked in. Ron junior was identical at the age of twenty four to his dad; six feet four, bright red curly hair and large ears and eighteen stones of solid muscle. His large physique was part genetic and part arduous work. Like his dad when he was that age, he worked in the nearby quarry at Middleton lugging stone around all day and had never been to a gym in his life. What he and his dad did for extra money was not hard labour but might lead to it. It usually involved armoured cars and shotguns.

His sister who came in the door with Ron Junior was a complete opposite; twenty years old, five foot tall, slim, and pretty. Her hair hung in a long bob, the natural ginger hidden in a silver and pink hair colour.

"I don't know why you two left home!"

Gail exclaimed as she carefully laid out three more rashers of bacon into the frying pan and then cracked two eggs into it from the pack at the side of the stove.

"Sit yourselves down, breakfast will be on the table in a minute."

"Thanks Mum!" they both replied simultaneously.

Karen went to Gary and hugged him around his neck

"Aww little Gazza you will be alright won't you. We will visit every week promise you. You know that don't you?"

Gary was swallowing the last piece of his sandwich as her arm enveloped his neck causing it to catch at the back of his throat. He involuntarily started to cough. His brother Ron Junior leaned over to him and hit him hard on his back with his fist causing Gary to fall forward with the force of the blow

"That's it Karen, let's kill him with kindness!" He guffawed.

Everyone in the room laughed, and the Traynor family sat down at the table. Gail laid out two more plates and served out the bacon and eggs from the frying pan to Karen and Ron Junior.

"Sorry, there's no mushrooms, Gary had them all. If you had told me you were coming round I would have got more in."

"Don't worry Mum, I'm alright without them" Karen consoled her and reached for a slice of buttered bread that Gail had just put in the middle of the table.

"She does talk bollocks!" grunted her dad

"You two are round here now more than when you lived here. If you didn't turn up for breakfast she would think you'd got run over or something. We don't mind though, even though you're eating us out of house and home!" he laughed and then coughed as he stubbed out the cigarette in the ash tray on the table.

Gail was now in 'mother-hen' mode as she looked at her family around the table.

"You two want a brew…. of course, you do. Now sit down and I'll get one for everybody."

The siblings quickly finished off their breakfasts and then Ron Junior threw a packet of cigarettes on the table, and they all took one, including Gail as she put the pot of tea and four mugs on the table. Karen passed her lighter round, and they all lit their cigarettes. Gail poured the tea into the mugs and each of them pulled one towards themselves. Gary put his on a coaster.

Ron Junior was the first to speak.

"You need to wise up a bit Gary, stop leaving fingerprints everywhere to start with. There's loads of gloves knocking about, take a pair with you. Try to do jobs when there's no-one about to see you as well, you're as well-known as Father Christmas round here and people recognise you too easily."

"I know Ron, I'm not daft you know!"

"You bloody are or else you wouldn't be looking at some time, just take it on board will you. There's no way you're coming out with me and Dad until you wise up a bit, we will all get locked up if you do."

"He can come when I say!" scolded Ron Senior rebuking his younger namesake.

"He's family and we stick together no matter what."

"I know Dad…" agreed Ron Junior

"If you do get sent down, when you get out, you can come with us, that alright Gaz… give you something to look forward to eh!"

"Thanks Ron!" Gary replied appreciatively to his brother "Means a lot!"

"How you getting there?" wheezed his dad changing the subject.

"Bike" said Gary.

"I'll take you, on my way to work." Karen offered.

"Nah it's OK, I'm hoping to be back by dinnertime, and I don't fancy walking back." Gary reassured his sister.

"What you doing with the bike if you don't come back?" asked Ron Junior.

"I'll get Bernie to drop it off!" Gary laughed, and everyone joined in.

The Magistrates Court at Bakewell was held in the main hall of Bakewell Town Hall every Friday morning. Offenders, witnesses, solicitors, and police were housed or locked up for the day in various smaller ante rooms surrounding it. From experience Gary Traynor knew that the best time to speak to his solicitor was as soon as Bernie arrived at Court, before he disappeared from public view into the small kitchen that police, Court staff, solicitors and Magistrates used on an ad hoc basis. As there was no café in the Court, the communal kitchen was the most popular room in the Town Hall on Court days.

The kitchen gave the place a homely feel as the local solicitors, Magistrates and police would congregate there and sort out the cases and any issues before the Court that day. Once Bernard Marples his solicitor was in the kitchen Gary knew he would not get to see him until his case was called. He needed to be at Court early and collar Bernie before he got to the kitchen.

At just after 9.15 a.m. forty minutes after setting off from his home in Winster, Gary Traynor, otherwise known as Little Shit to the local people of the Dales, arrived at the entrance doors to Bakewell Town Hall. He dropped the bike outside the Town Hall doors and tried them. They were locked, he was too early. Despite his Court hearing that morning, Gary by nature, was always looking for some opportunity that came his way. Drink, drugs, and cigarettes didn't fall off trees and you had to take any opportunity you could. There was a Traynor family rule 'If it's not tied down it belongs to whoever picks it up.' and like all the other family rules Gary liked to follow it to the letter.

He cycled round to the Granby Road car park to see if anyone was leaving their car unlocked whilst they nipped to one of the local shops. People always left some change in the front dash for parking charges and once it was in his pocket, they would not be able to pin anything on him unless they caught him in the act. He positioned himself on his bike at the end of Granby Croft.

The car park was fairly busy with shoppers and workers but everyone he saw purposely locked their car doors after purchasing a ticket when they saw him hanging around. He had been there about ten minutes when the black Porsche with the personalised number plate pulled into the car park and parked opposite the Police Station. He stopped cycling his figures of eight and looked towards it. The driver got out, and Gary recognised him immediately, it was Councillor Trueman, the Magistrate. Gary prayed that he didn't lock the car as it would be a great revenge to steal something from the same Magistrate that was sentencing him. That would definitely take away some of the pain of whatever sentence he was given. His dad and brother would also think it hilarious.

Gary stared at him waiting to see if he locked his car, but as Trueman came back with his ticket he looked his way and Gary couldn't look away quick enough. Their eyes met for a fraction of a second and Gary saw that he recognised him. Councillor Trueman put the ticket in his car, shut the door and pulled his shoulder bag into his side as though protecting it. Gary decided to continue with his figure of eights nonchalantly pretending that he had not seen him.

As Trueman disappeared round the corner of Bakewell Police Station onto Water Street, Gary looked around; there was no-one about, so he cycled up to the Porsche, leant on the door and tried the handle. It was locked. The car park was not paying much dividend at all this morning. He took his door key out of his pocket and nonchalantly scratched the paintwork on the Porsche car door with a single forward stroke of his arm. Gary looked at the deep scratch in the paintwork and felt a sense of exhilaration and so he did it again.

There had been no easy pickings that morning on the car park, so Gary decided to see if the Court was now open. He reasoned that if the Magistrates were turning up it should be. Gary cycled out of Granby Road, onto Bakewell Road, then around the Rutland Square roundabout and onto Bridge St towards the Town Hall. As he approached the Town Hall he saw a police officer reach out and grab Trueman as he slipped on the road. He was still cycling towards the door as events unfolded in what appeared to Gary to be in slow motion.

He saw Trueman finish crossing the road, take a large step onto the pavement and then another into the doorway of the Town Hall. Trueman then slipped and fell heavily backwards. The loud crack reverberated around the square as the base of his skull first hit and then split, spewing blood flecks around his grey hair. At that moment Gary's attention was distracted as the bag Trueman was carrying fell from his hand onto the footpath outside the entrance door to the Town Hall.

Gary pedalled furiously the remaining fifty yards to the town hall entrance, and without slowing down, he reached down and picked up the bag strap in one movement and was gone.

Eighty yards further on, Gary turned the corner onto Bath Street and came to a stop, his heart beating furiously. He looked back anxiously and waited thirty seconds, but no-one had chased him round the corner. He could feel the excitement and adrenalin rush that he loved from the risk of getting caught fading, and he took a couple of deep breaths. He checked again behind him that nobody had followed him, and it was all clear. The bike clattered to the floor as he jumped off it and he placed the bag on the wall of Bath Gardens that separated Rutland Square from Bath Street, making sure he was shielded by a large Holly bush from anyone walking through the Gardens.

He examined the hard black leather shoulder bag and could see it was an expensive one and therefore probably identifiable. He quickly undid the clasp and opened it. In the interior of the bag there were two books and nothing else. He dropped both books over the wall into the back of the Holly bush and shook the bag upside down. Nothing fell out, he peered inside again and saw that it was empty.

Satisfied that there was nothing else in it he dropped it over the wall next to the bush. Disappointed, but with a tale to tell his brother, he picked up his bike and cycled back towards Bakewell Town Hall and his Court appearance.

Chapter 5 - The Girl With A Future

Friday 20th December

Alice Bulman put down her pencil. The numbers in front of her no longer registering through her watering eyes. She sneezed, picked up a tissue and wiped her reddening nose. Her throat felt like sandpaper and every time she swallowed it felt like her neck was blocked by a golf ball hard and unmoving. She wiped her eyes with her sleeve, picked up the tissue and wiped her nose again. Beryl Smith looked across to her from her desk on the opposite side of the accountant's office.

"That's a right cold you've got coming there Alice, have you got anything for it?"

"No not yet. It started coming on last night and it's really hit me this morning."

"Why don't you nip round the chemists and get a Beechams. I'm sure Mr Wildgoose won't mind if you're not gone too long."

"Are you sure?"

"I'll explain to him if he comes back but he's at the golf club so it's very unlikely he will be calling in the office today" Beryl smiled. She liked Alice. She was bright, funny and an extremely diligent worker. Alice had started work at Wildgoose and Wildgoose, Business Accountants, 14 Bath Street, Bakewell, four months ago after graduating from Manchester University earlier that year.

When Alice started work at Wildgoose's Beryl had pointed out to her, that her parent's house in Stoke was too far to commute the forty miles each day to work, and so Beryl had spoken to one of the firm's clients about renting out a flat for her. The client, an estate agent, owned a row of four shops on Buxton Road, just off the Rutland square roundabout. Above the shops were four two bedroomed flats and he had been more than happy, for an accountant with a regular salary, to become one of his tenants.

Alice had moved into the flat at the beginning of October, and Beryl had helped her with some furniture she no longer needed. Together with help from Beryl as well as her mum and dad, the flat was soon turned into a comfortable liveable space for a twenty four year old girl in the centre of the small rural town.

For Beryl, the more time that she spent with Alice, the more she saw how her life could have been. In her younger days Beryl knew she had been seen as good looking, she had never been short of boyfriends and men chasing after her. Alice was the same, all men gave her a second glance, her auburn hair, and lightly freckled face was always complimented by a wide smile and laughing green eyes. She was not so much the girl next door as much as the girl you would want to live next door to.

Beryl like Alice had got excellent 'A' levels and had been persuaded by her headmaster, Mr Morris, to apply for University, achieving a place on a mathematics degree at Durham that September. It was a career move that she never met. The summer she left school at the age of eighteen, her life had come off the rails. She had got happily drunk at Bakewell Carnival, spent the night in the bedroom of a boy who had chatted her up at the end of the night.

Eight weeks later she was no longer going to Durham University and engaged to be married to the boy. Marriage followed four weeks later, to save her the embarrassment of walking down the aisle when the pregnancy was showing.

The boy, John Smith, was a man with a bland name in a bland job at the local lead smelters at South Darley and with no intention of having anything but bland prospects. His only interest was an allotment that over the next thirty three years he had spent an ever increasing time tending and then regaling Beryl with the growth statistics of his prize vegetables.

The wedding took place that November, and her son Simon, named after John's father, was born the following April. A life of domestic drudgery had come with great difficulty for Beryl, especially when Simon had started school, so she had taken a part-time book-keeping job. The part-time bookkeeping job had turned into a full-time one with salary, responsibility and increasing satisfaction for Beryl.

In recent years, her employer Mr Greenwood had retired and been replaced by his son Stephen, who increasingly relied upon her to keep the firm running whilst he played golf and drank beer in the local bars. Her own son had turned into his father, relying on her for food, cleaning, and cooking without any form of stimulating conversation or emotional attachment. At the age of thirty three he remained at home without a girlfriend but with an identical job to his father in South Darley and his own allotment.

Beryl's life was dull; dishwater dull she would have described it. As a distraction from the dullness, Beryl had taken on the role of mothering the students and graduates that came to Wildgoose's on secondment or for short periods of employment. When they left, she watched their blossoming careers through social media and the occasional reunion, feeling a little bit of what she could have been and had in their continuing achievements and happy families.

Although Alice had only been there a short time, Beryl decided that she was the one she liked the best; she was funny and made her laugh with her gossipy tales about the boyfriends she had dated. Alice also learnt quickly and was impressively quick and accurate on the account tasks she was given. More than that she had everything in front of her that Beryl would have had if she hadn't slept with John Smith that drunken night after Bakewell Carnival.

Alice slipped off her sensible flat work shoes and put on her Adidas branded training shoes. She then walked over to the 19th century wooden coat stand, removed her bright red quilted winter jacket and matching scarf. She put on the coat and zipped it up, and then wrapped the scarf around her neck and placed the bright red bobble hat over her bright red tousled hair. Her pale freckled complexion and bright green eyes peering through the bright red mask of coat, scarf, hat, and hair.

She looked across at Beryl for the last acknowledgement that she was alright to leave.

"God! I bet I look like a post box, and a leaky one at that!" She wiped her nose with the tissue from her desk.

Beryl laughed "You do… now get off with you!"

Alice turned and walked out the door. Beryl heard the outside door open and close, and Alice waved to her silently as she passed the window.

Alice walked up Bath Street and turned left towards the chemists. It was the Friday before Christmas, and it was bitingly cold. She was looking forward to going home to Stoke tomorrow for the two week Christmas break. Christmas was always fun in the Bulman household. Her mum made every Christmas special, with loads of presents and there was always Grandma at their house for Christmas Day for 'turkey with all the trimmings.'

Alice smiled to herself, the first thing that would happen when she went home the following day would be that her mum would fuss about her cold and nag her, as mum's do, especially when she would tell her she was going out clubbing. Her dad would then sigh, agree with her mum that she shouldn't go out and then take her to one side and tell her that he would take her and pick her up no matter what time she left the club. When he picked her up he would make her laugh with stupid jokes all the way home.

About sixty yards from the chemist, she looked up to the row of shops on her right and her first floor flat above the greengrocers. The door to the flat was at the side of the greengrocers and once through the door you went up a flight of stairs to the first floor two bedroomed flat. The décor was a bit dated, but it had a new kitchen and bathroom. The old cream décor had been improved with a coat of brilliant white paint by her dad and she had furnished it with bright and cheerful furniture from IKEA together with the old settee from Beryl. Its central location also meant she was only minutes away from shops, pubs, and work so she had little in the way of car expenses. In fact, she realised, her car a Fiat 500 tended to only be used for visiting friends and the fortnightly trip to see her parents in Stoke. The job at Wildgoose's, whilst not well paid, was sufficient to pay for the flat and bills, her car, and her student loan repayments with a couple of hundred pounds a month left over.

For the first time in her life, Alice was able to save money towards a mortgage and her dream of a small house in a small village with a pub and a village shop. There was going to be a loving husband and two red haired children. A boy, and a girl with freckles and of course a small dog.

As she glanced at the door to her flat she remembered that she had left the heating on when she had left that morning and considered nipping across the road to turn it down. She hesitated and then changed her mind. Whilst it would be expensive to leave it on all day at least it would be warm when she got in. Something she was looking forward to, not only to escape the freezing wintry weather, but also the cold virus that was currently attacking her shivering body.

Five minutes later with a packet of Lemsip powders in her pocket, some menthol sweets, a bottle of Vicks vapour rub and a packet of soft tissues in a white paper bag she exited the chemists, stood on the footpath, and put on her bright red woollen gloves. She then turned left towards the square and into Bath Gardens.

It was a slightly longer walk back to the office but a much more pleasant one; she wanted the extra time to think about whether over the New Year she was going to meet her old University friends for a reunion in Manchester, or accept an invitation to go to a party at his parent's house from Darren, who she had met on her last trip back home. He had been on a night out in Stoke with his friends from Derby and they had met up again at the cinema the following night on a 'proper date.' Since then, despite numerous calls and texts from him she had avoided making a second date, in the hope that he would get the message that she was not interested. Something he seemed unwilling or unable to do.

Alice wiped her nose again as she walked through the gardens. It was definitely going to be Manchester she decided, and she was going to have to be honest with Darren. She would tell him it was over that night after work. Decisions had been made she thought and smiled contentedly to herself.

She gave a little skip and became more aware of her surroundings. She noticed the well-kept flower beds ready for planting in the spring. The roses that would line the path in the summer were cut back and bare and the tightly cut summer lawns were now several inches long and patchy where dog walkers and children had scuffed up the wet grass. As she approached the gate onto Bath Street, she noticed something at the base of a dense Holly bush against the wall about ten yards away. Curious she went over and saw that it was a black leather shoulder bag. She put her hand into the bush and pulled it out. It was a shoulder bag, a man's she thought. The clasp was undone, and she looked inside. It was empty. There was nothing to identify an owner. She looked at the outside again and saw the Dior branding. Expensive as well. Alice slipped it over her shoulder and walked back to the office across the road.

"Look what I found in the Gardens!"

Alice declared to Beryl as she walked through the door and put the black calf leather Dior messenger bag down on her desk.

"Someone will be claiming that!" laughed Beryl

"It's Dior! and it's gorgeous, let me have a look!"

Beryl picked up the bag, opened the clasp and peered inside. It was empty.

"Or with a bit of luck will not!"

Alice got out a Lemsip packet.

"Fancy a cuppa Beryl?"

"Do cows make milk!" Beryl retorted back in friendly banter. Alice went off to the kitchen and Beryl shouted after her,

"I'll report it found to the police!"

"Thanks" Alice's fading voice came back down the corridor to her.

Beryl picked up the phone and dialled 101. Waited for the pre-recorded message and said "Derbyshire" into the mouthpiece. She then put the phone down on her desk on speakerphone. The phone started to ring out. Alice came back with her hot Lemsip drink and a cup of tea for Beryl. Beryl thanked Alice for the cup of tea and sat down back to work on the accounts of a local building company. Beryl left the phone ringing aloud on her desk.

Ten minutes later Beryl took the last sip of tea from her mug and looked across at Alice. She was engrossed in her work.

"They really are useless" exclaimed Beryl.

"Who are?" asked Alice looking up.

"The police, you might as well not bother report anything to them. They can't be bothered to answer the phone anyway!"

"I know" Alice agreed.

"My flat at Uni got burgled once and they didn't even attend. I was hoping some hunk in uniform was going to turn up but all I got was some old woman on the phone telling me it wasn't a priority. It was for me; I'd not met a hunky man in uniform for months!"

"You're lucky! I haven't met one for thirty years!" Beryl retorted.

Alice laughed and sneezed Lemsip down her nose at the same time. Both the young girl and the older woman laughed loudly as Alice mopped the papers on her desk and then her nose with a tissue from the pack on her desk.

"What's happening with Darren?" asked Beryl.

"Toast! Tonight, after work he's getting the sad news. He's nice enough but a bit bland. You know there's no spark or anything. It's better to get it over and done with sooner rather than later isn't it?"

"Yes definitely"

Beryl agreed remembering when she had to make the same decision, she had opted for blandness and had regretted it every day since. She did not want to open that particular box especially with herself, so she looked away quickly towards the wall at her side in order to avoid catching Alice's eye and the prospect of extending the line of conversation.

Alice continued. "I've decided that I'm going 'party party' to Manchester as well for New Year with the gang so you never know a new Mr Right might be on the horizon in the New Year!"

"You never know Alice, you never know." Beryl reassured her young colleague distractedly.

Her attention had been caught, when she had looked to the wall, by a fading brown piece of paper sellotaped to it. She had not paid any attention to the piece of paper for years even though it had always been there. It was an old list of local numbers that might be needed in an emergency. Beryl read down the list - Doctors, local hospital, plumber, electrician, and there at the bottom was Bakewell Police Station. Beryl wondered … and into her desk phone 812504 and was surprised to hear a ring tone.

"Bakewell Police Station" answered a voice at the other end of the phone.

"Can I report some found property to you?"

"Not really love. All found property is recorded centrally now, you will have to ring 101."

"I've done that, but no one answers, I've been waiting for over twenty minutes!" Beryl put the receiver next to her still ringing mobile.

"See!" Beryl said to the man on the other end of the phone with a wink towards Alice.

"Well, I'll put it in the diary. What's your name and what have you found?"

"It's Beryl Smith at Wildgoose's on Bath Street. My colleague has found a black shoulder bag, it's leather a really nice one. There's nothing in it as to who it belongs to, but it must be someone local as it was found in Bath Gardens this morning."

"Alright Beryl I've got that, if no one claims it, it's yours in 30 days, but you'll have to let 101 know as well."

"No problem officer will do and thank you."

Beryl put the desk phone down, let her mobile ring twice more and when it remained unanswered by the police, ended the call.

"Well, we've done our civic duty to inform the police and hopefully you might have won yourself a Dior shoulder bag in thirty days' time if no one claims it."

"Ooh that's brilliant! goes well with my trainers and woolly gloves."

She laughed, picked up the bag and jiggled it in front of her, before placing it against the wall at the back of her chair.

Back at the police station Bill Fry put down the phone, walked across to the large blue Station Diary, opened it, and wrote in it his second entry that day.

"Black bag found Bath Gardens, see Beryl at Wildgoose's if anyone reports loss."

Chapter 6 – A Clandestine Meeting

Friday 20ᵗʰ December

Cath Mulvey's feet were cold from the walk up from Wensley Road where she had parked her car. She had parked some distance away as she didn't want anyone to identify her car outside the address that she was visiting. She had also chosen mid-morning to visit as she hoped that there would be few people about on the small estate, and those that were would not be able to recognise her in the hoody that covered her head. Leacroft Road Winster was a mixture of council houses and private ones purchased under the 'Right to Buy' scheme from the council.

The one she was going to was still council owned and was easily distinguishable from the other houses. The uncut long grass, broken picket fence, and rusting pick-ups on the drive stood out like an overgrown wild wasteland from the neat gardens and empty driveways around it. Cath passed the two rusting, but just about roadworthy old Ford pick-ups parked behind the brand new black Navara on the drive and went round to the back of the house. In the back garden there was a range of heavily padlocked sheds and lean-tos that she had spent several hours on several occasions fruitlessly searching. Cath had smiled to herself when she had first seen the expensive locks and chains on the sheds; who would be brave or foolish enough to burgle a shed belonging to the worst neighbours and thieves in the neighbourhood?

Today she was not going to be doing any searching. At the back door she took a deep intake of breath and paused before knocking. She had been stood at this door many times and had never had a warm welcome, so it was with hesitancy she knocked gently on the frosted window of the half painted door.

A small dark-haired figure came to the door and opened it. Gail Traynor looked disgustedly at the woman she knew as Detective Constable Cath Mulvey standing outside her door, before angrily screeching at her.

"What the fuck do you want?" and then turning back towards the living room through the kitchen.

"Ron! It's the Filth!"

Ron lurched out the living room, bare chested but trousered.

"Tell them to fuck off!"

He then hesitated as he saw Cath stood on her own at the door looking towards him. Cath nodded to him, and Ron's hesitation became a lumbering stop halfway across the kitchen.

"Gail, go into the front room!" He ordered his wife.

An Accidental Death

Gail looked at him. She knew that look of her husbands and it was not one to be argued with.

She looked back at Cath and quietly growled to her.

"You had better come in then before someone sees you." Gail looked back at Ron.

"Do you want me to make you a brew?"

Ron looked at Cath "Time for a brew?"

Cath pulled up a chair and sat down at the kitchen table

"Yeah, I've got time Ron."

Ron pulled out a chair opposite her and sat down. Both waited in silence for Gail to put two cups of hot tea in front of them and a sugar bowl. She then went into the living room and shut the door behind her. Ron put three spoonsful of sugar into his tea and stirred it.

"Sugar Cath?"

Cath didn't think it strange that Ron used her first name, she had noticed in her time in the police that only close police friends and criminals called police officers by their first names or nicknames. She put it down to the shared livelihoods and contacts, which broke down the usual social barriers. It was also a particularly clever way of criminal's self-identifying themselves to police as such she had found.

"No, I'm alright Ron,"

Cath picked up her tea and took a sip. It was hot. She put the mug down.

"Gail doesn't know then?"

"No, thought better not tell her, she's likely to lose it if she knows" Ron confided to her.

Cath nodded, "Probably for the best Ron."

Cath reached into her pocket, removed a mobile phone, and put it on the table.

"Wanted you to be sure it's all sorted."

Cath looked across the table and Ron nodded. Cath entered the passcode on the phone and with Ron watching she opened the photos folder "You want to see they're there?"

Ron shook his head and flicked a Marlboro out of the packet on the table. He offered the packet to Cath.

"No, I don't Ron"

Ron lit his cigarette and exhaled smoke into the kitchen.

Cath deleted some of the photos on the phone and the linked cloud. Ron watched as she went through the procedure.

"That it?" asked Ron.

"Yep, all gone"

"Thanks, Cath, how did you find him?"

"I went up there, pulled the CCTV in the pub they had been in and then knocked on some doors."

"Don't suppose you're going to tell me who he was?" Ron asked.

"Don't get me wrong Ron I think he's an absolute shit. I can't do anything against him legally without an official complaint and I understand why Karen won't make one. I've turned him over pretty well and put the fear of god into him. He knows he's likely to lose his job and his wife if he says anything. He is not getting his phone back either."

She looked at Ron and saw he was listening intently to what she was saying, so she continued

"I also know you, and if you know who it is you will feel you have to do something, so I'm not telling you. You came to me and asked if I could sort it and I have done."

Ron drew on his cigarette.

"It's a family thing Cath if you hurt one of us you hurt us all. Karen doesn't want a fuss making and that's the only reason I came to you. He's not local, is he? Karen was worried that he might tell people and it get out?"

"No Ron, He's from York where Karen was with her mates when she got drugged and the photos got taken."

"And then raped her!" snapped Ron temporarily losing control.

Cath saw the flash of anger in his eyes and waited until he had calmed.

"How's Karen?"

"She's a tough one, she will be alright especially now she knows the photos have been sorted, Thanks Cath, I owe you one."

Cath nodded in acceptance of the offer. Ron drew on his cigarette and blew out a cloud of smoke

"A lorry got hijacked two weeks ago just outside Macclesfield near Wildboarclough. It was carrying spirits, Whisky, Vodka and Gin to a distribution centre near Chester. Have you heard about it?"

Cath shook her head.

Ron continued. "The driver was tied up and left at the side of the road. Well, half of the drink is at the home of a bloke called Danny MacAleese. He lives just off Robina Road, in St Helens. It will be on your files. Most of it is in the garage and the rest is under the stairs in his house. He is moving it all to a retailer in Glasgow on Christmas Day, when there won't be any police about. He is taking it to Glasgow in a rented van from Arnold Clark in Ormskirk. It's up to you whether you get him at home or on the road, nothing will come back to me so deal with it as you want. Are we straight now Cath?

Cath nodded.

"Provided it's right Ron."

"It is Cath"

At that moment, the back door opened, and Gary came in. On seeing Cath and his dad sat in the kitchen together, confusion came over his face. His first thought was that someone had seen him steal the bag that morning and his instinct was to run but…. his dad wouldn't have let the detective in the house without a warrant, he certainly wouldn't have made her a cup of tea if she were going to nick him.

"Everything alright Dad?" Gary asked.

"Yes Son, everything's fine."

Gail came out the front room and seeing her son, her face broke out into broad smile.

"You didn't get sent down then Son?"

"No Mum. They cancelled everything when one of the Magistrates fell and got took to hospital. I'm bailed to the end of January so I'm home for Christmas!"

"That's brilliant news!" his mum exclaimed before grabbing him and hugging him tightly.

"You fucking off then Cath?" Ron nodded towards the door. The truce between them was over.

"Yeah, I'm out of here, see you around, especially you Gary!" Cath barbed towards Gary and to let Ron know things were back to normal.

Gail sensed that whatever her husband and Cath had been discussing was now over.

"Yeah, fuck off and don't come round here for my Gary unless you've got a warrant cos you're not coming in here again without one!" Gail shouted after Cath as she stepped out the doorway, and then felt the blast of air and heard the loud bang of the door as Gail slammed it behind her.

"Back to normal then" thought Cath and gave a wry smile.

She would ring Ron's information straight through to a friend in Staffordshire Police. If she put it on a 5x5 intelligence report there would be questions asked about the identity of the source and why Ron had not been registered as Confidential Human Intelligence Source (CHIS) by her. It was much easier to use the normal 'back channels' used by most detectives in relation to information garnered from unofficial sources.

Chapter 7 – The Desolation of Mr Burton

Friday 20th December

Neil Burton had arranged to meet Paul Trueman in the communal kitchen of Bakewell Court in the Town Hall at 9.30 a.m. that morning. He was a solicitor himself but not a criminal one. Neil specialised in Civil Law and in particular Wills and Probate as well as Conveyancing Land and Property. As he did every morning he had woken to an empty house; his wife had as usual gone to the stables to muck out and feed the horses. He had breakfasted on his own and then set off to travel the couple of miles from the large Victorian detached house on the hillside at Matlock Bath, to the small solicitor's office on Dale Rd in Matlock.

Neil Burton arrived at the offices of Burtons Solicitors, 68 Dale Road, Matlock at around 8.30 a.m. The first-floor offices had once housed around seven solicitors with a similar number of administration staff. Following the retirement of the first solicitor named Burton in the practice, his father, the business had moved out of the criminal sphere and concentrated on conveyancing and probate. With the reduced workload the number of solicitors had been reduced to just one, the current Mr Burton. There had also been a similar reduction in employees so that there was now just himself, a Conveyancer Mark Millward, and two part time female secretaries.

Neil Burton was the only one there that early in the morning; the rest would arrive just before nine. He logged onto his emails to check if there was anything that urgently needed his attention. There was nothing. Probate issues never required urgency: the dead don't hurry anyone along, and Neil worked patiently through those that needed any attention before the weekend. Thirty minutes later the sound of cups rattling in the kitchen area notified him that at least one of his employees had arrived and it was nearing nine o clock. He checked that it was 9 a.m. with the clock on his office wall and rang his accountants. The phone was answered on the second ring.

"Hi Beryl, it's Neil Burton, can you get my accounts signed off by second week in January only I've got my annual Solicitors Regulatory Authority inspection at the end of next month and could do with them back by at least the middle of January ... that's brilliant Beryl many thanks see you in the New Year."

Neil closed the call, logged off his computer and went out into the hallway.

"Do you want a cup of tea Mr Burton?" Phyllis one of the secretaries who had been with the firm for over twenty years asked him as he walked down the passageway.

"Not this morning Phyllis, I'm just nipping to Court at Bakewell if you need me, I'll be on my mobile."

"Alright Mr Burton see you later, I'm sure we can hold the fort."

"I'm sure you will Phyllis." Neil smiled at her, carried on to the stairs, and out the front door.

Neil drove to Bakewell and parked next to Paul's Porsche 911. He then strolled towards the Town Hall, the gritted pavements crunching under the soles of his brown brogue shoes.

At the top of Water Lane, he glanced into the window of his favourite shop. Neil had always dressed like his father in the ageless uniform of the Derbyshire Dales, that of country gentleman. Neil Burton purported to be that country gentleman. Brown brogues, brown Peveril tweed jacket and trousers, matching Laksen waistcoat, and gingham shirt finished with a red or green woollen tie. All purchased from Brocklehurst's Gentlemen's Country Outfitters. He didn't have time for any clothes shopping until after he had seen Paul. He bought two croissants from the bakery next door and then crossed the road at The Old Post Office situated in the centre of the one way system that circled the small town centre.

A small crowd of onlookers and an ambulance were outside the doors of the Town Hall, and he crossed the one way system towards them. The back doors of the ambulance were open, and the paramedics were loading into it a blanketed patient. He glanced at the casualty as he passed, and his heart stopped. Even through the blue ice pack to his head and oxygen mask covering his face Neil recognised the patient as Paul Trueman.

Neil Burton froze like a rabbit in headlights. Paul had been shot! Where was the shooter? Why weren't there armed police everywhere? Was he a target as well? The back doors closed and with them his sight of Paul. As Neil Burton stood frozen to the spot, the ambulance drove away blue lights flashing, and sirens sounding, over Bakewell Bridge and away out of his sight.

He was shaken out of his paralysis by a police officer gently shaking his shoulder.

"Are you alright Neil?" asked Sergeant Bill Fry.

"Th…That was Paul Trueman wasn't it?" Neil asked shakily, hoping that he had been mistaken.

"Yes. He slipped and fell, quite a bad head injury by the look of it."

Neil thought "Thank god he wasn't shot" and then relief flowed over him. It was just a fall he would be alright.

"Do you know him, Neil?" asked Bill.

"Yes, I am his solicitor, have been for twenty years."

"That's brilliant. Can I give you his property, they don't like taking it with them to the hospital?"

"Ye..ye..,yes, no problem at all Sergeant," Neil stammered still in a state of shock.

Bill gave him Paul Trueman's jacket, his phone, his wallet, and his car keys. There was no bag and no MacBook.

"Was there anything else...a messenger bag? Paul usually carried one."

Neil hoped he sounded nonchalant and not as worried as he felt.

Bill Fry stroked his chin.

"He did have one with him, must have gone with him in the ambulance."

"Thank you Sergeant. Do you know which hospital he has gone to?"

"No they didn't say but with head injuries like that they usually go to Sheffield's Northern General, so I would try there if you need to find out how he is going on."

"Thank you again. I will try there in an hour or so" Neil mumbled.

He then quickly turned away from the police officer clutching tightly the croissants, as well as Paul Trueman's property, and walked slowly back towards his Land Rover in the car park.

Some fourteen hours later at the Northern General Hospital in Sheffield, in a small private room, Neil pulled the lime green vinyl high backed chair to the side of the bed and sat down in it. Paul lay on the other side of the metal bars of the bed. He suddenly felt a cold feeling at the base of his back rise to his shoulders as though a ghost had passed through him, and he shivered as it dissipated through his shoulders and along his arms. He knew it was fear, fear of Paul dying, his 'partner' for twenty five years in more ways than one, and the loneliness that his death would bring. He knew in his heart that he would never be able to love anyone so much again, a love that could never be open or public. Neither of them could have faced the social stigma that 'coming out' would engender amongst their peers and friends in the town.

His mind was in turmoil, he knew his wife would stand by him. He knew she didn't care about his sexual orientation, never had done. He had done his duty by her. He had provided her with two children, a lovely home, social standing, and her bloody stables. She would be fine, even if there was a scandal so long as the bills kept getting paid.

The thing was, he was no longer sure that there wouldn't be a scandal, and he wasn't sure that his colleagues in London would be too pleased about their money being put at risk as well as not being able to access it in the near future. He needed his bloody MacBook, and he didn't know where it was. The person that knew where it was, lay in the bed next to him and he wasn't saying, in fact according to the doctors he might never be saying anything again.

When he had arrived at the hospital that afternoon, he had expected Paul to be sat up in bed joking about the fall and how he was going to be out in a few days. Instead, he had been asked if he was family and had told the doctor that Paul had no living family, but that he was a close friend and his solicitor. The doctor had then told him that the prognosis was not good. Paul had fractured his skull and suffered a massive cerebral haemorrhage. They had operated to remove several clots on his brain but feared there was brain damage and the possibility of further bleeds due to the damage to his skull and the tissue around it.

Neil looked at the pale green blanket. It had ridden up around Paul's bare torso, Neil reached through the bars and tugged it down hoping that the warmth would comfort him. A tear welled in Neil's eye and then he could no longer hold it back. A low wail developed in the back of his throat, his mouth involuntarily opened and the sobbing cry sirened from his mouth. The tears flooded out along his cheeks and down onto his checked shirt. The silent sobbing that followed wouldn't stop, his heart felt broken, he stood and reached over the metal guards for the lifeless hand and gripped it tightly. He then bent down and raised it to his mouth, silencing the sobbing with the back of Paul's hand. Tears dripped onto the hand and then rolled on downwards onto the white bed sheet. Neil tried to control his breathing, control his sobbing, taking large gulps of air, and holding his breath until he could breathe normally again. He looked lovingly down at Paul. His head was heavily bandaged, fluids dripped into cannulas in his hand, and the broad plastic mask covering his face highlighted his eyes that were open but unseeing.

Neil looked at the clock on the wall. It was past midnight. He had been there over eight hours. There was nothing more he could do tonight, he reassured himself. He would come back in the morning. Neil gave Paul's hand one last squeeze and took one last look into the vacant eyes. He saw a flicker, then another flicker, then recognition in them.

He smiled down at Paul and squeezed his hand.

"I love you!"

Paul's index finger moved gently against the palm of his hand. He squeezed it lightly and felt a return of the pressure. Holding the hand up off the bed, he stood up and looked into Paul's blue eyes over the oxygen mask that covered his mouth and nose. There was still recognition there. The hand that he was loosely holding lifted, released his, and moved towards the mask. Neil realised that Paul wanted to say something. He lifted the mask gently to one side. Paul nodded and looked him in the eyes. He whispered something that Neil could not hear or make out. He squeezed Paul's hand again and bent down closer to his lips.

Paul whispered, "I love you too," and smiled.

Paul then whispered the word "MacBook" and looked at Neil. Neil shook his head.

Paul's eyes suddenly widened he had just remembered something.

"What is it Paul?" Neil asked.

Paul beckoned him closer, and Neil bent down towards him.

"Little Shit…. stole the bag."

"Little Shit stole your bag?" Neil repeated.

Paul nodded.

"With the MacBook?"

Paul nodded again

Neil replaced the oxygen mask and as he did so, Paul looked up at him and a tear rolled down his cheek. Neil squeezed his hand until Paul closed his eyes and fell asleep. Neil then sat at his side as he had done all day going through the lives they had lived and the lives they could have had. He vowed that if Paul came through this, they were going to get out of crime and go public with their relationship.

"Sod Gordy! and sod their homophobic uptight friends!"

He had made the decision. It was time to live the lives they could, no matter what other people thought.

An hour later Paul was still asleep, so he decided to leave. He listened to the electronic devices around him, checking that they continued to beep and whir as they had done since he entered the room. Nothing had changed, Paul had woken up and he was going to be alright. He would divorce his wife; he would marry Paul as they had always promised each other. He felt the relief of decisions made, flow through him. He squeezed Paul's hand one more time and carefully placed it under the warm blanket then walked to the door and took one last look at the love of his life.

"See you in the morning" he whispered towards the figure in the hospital bed and closed the door behind him.

As he walked from the private room along the corridor to the nurse's station, his heart gave a little jump of joy; Paul, was going to be alright and home soon where he could look after him. He also had a starter for the laptop. It wouldn't be a problem getting the MacBook off of Little Shit as he would pay more than enough money for the young Traynor to sell it to him.

He had reached the nursing station at the end of the ward when an alarm sounded. Neil stopped, and watched, as nurses, doctors, and trolleys of equipment assembled within seconds. A doctor and nurse who had been sat chatting at the station stood and ran down the corridor and hurtled through the door he had just closed behind him. A trolley of equipment was pushed by another nurse along the corridor into the same room with a loud bang, as the trolley forcefully hit the door and burst it open.

Neil stood transfixed half-way down the corridor, his heart beating faster and faster, as he stared at the closed door for what seemed hours. Eventually the door opened, and the doctor and nurses slowly filed out. As they reached Neil at the nursing station the doctor looked into his eyes, and he knew.

The nurse with the doctor, took his hand.

"I'm sorry there was nothing more that we could do."

He heard the words and they eventually registered in his mind as he stood there, statue still, immobile. The tears began flowing down his cheeks; he could feel his life like a sandcastle on an incoming tide crumbling around him. The nurse gently took hold of his arm and led him into a room at the side of the nursing station.

"Come on in here love, let's sit you down and get you a cup of tea."

Chapter 8 – The Passing Of The Bad News

Saturday 21ˢᵗ December

The day after Paul's death, Neil went first of all to Paul's office and forced the door when he found it was locked. He did not find what he was looking for and so then went to his house and let himself in with his key. After searching the house he eventually went to Paul's study and tried the desk drawer. It was locked. He went to the bookcase and took down the 'Song of Achilles' and removed the key, went over to his desk, unlocked the drawer, and exhaled loudly. He had found it.

Neil took out the MacBook, and switched it on. He then banged his fist onto the desk and sighed resignedly. As he suspected access was fingerprint password protected. It was something they had always agreed on. He needed the other MacBook the one that he could access.

More importantly he thought that he had better tell Gordy that Paul had died. If he found out from another source he would be in trouble especially if it looked as though he had intentionally delayed telling him. He put the MacBook back in the drawer and locked it. He put the key back in its secure hiding place and returned the book to the bookcase.

Neil sat at the desk and looked around the room. The original modern artwork on the walls, complimented everything from the desk to the real oak flooring. Whilst the room design had been Paul's choice the artworks had been his. It had been something that they had in common, his love of art and Paul's love of design. The house on Eaton Hill was the fruition of the hours they had spent poring over design magazines and visiting art auctions. It was their shared labour of love.

At his own home he had left the decorating and design to Maggie his wife. She in turn had turned it into a home for her and the children. It had always been full of dogs and cats and children and muddy boots. Anything of value would have been broken; anything artistic would have been defaced. This house was as much his as Paul's: it was theirs.

Losing Paul was hard. Losing the house was going to be like losing Paul a second time, he thought, but he had to be strong. It was imperative that he dealt with some of the fallout from Paul's death now and then grieve later.

He went into the lounge and pushed the mirrored glass door of the Credenza. The door sprung open, and he took out the Tamnavulin 1973 from the vintage whisky collection. It was the best and Paul would have approved he was sure. He took a cut-glass whisky glass from the same shelf and poured himself a whisky from the bottle. Taking a sip, he savoured the smooth sweet whisky as the alcohol lingered on his tongue and then his throat. "That was excellent" he thought and raised his glass to his absent lover. He picked up the glass and the bottle and made his way back into the study.

They had discussed at length what would happen if either of them died and had agreed that everything would go to each of their nearest relatives. That would be Maggie for him and Helen for Paul.

Paul's house would go to his daughter, his 'mistake' that had surfaced several years ago. Her mother had told her about Paul being her father when she was about to leave home to go to University. Out of curiosity more than anything she had turned up one day at his office in Matlock. The reception Paul had given her had been frosty, and she had left upset and disappointed. Paul had tried to renew contact over the years but had been rebuffed each time by Helen in relation to any close contact, although she sometimes sent him a Birthday and Christmas card. Paul did the same.

The reasoning behind the decision for family to inherit everything was so that there would be no indication of anything other than a business relationship between them. Not only would that save their families any embarrassment as to their relationship, but it would also hopefully not bring any attention to the main source of their wealth and the criminality upon which it was built.

That did not mean that the surviving partner would get nothing. Both Neil and Paul had also agreed that the surviving partner would inherit the others, offshore wealth, and assets. £100 million in assets and shares was held in their names in offshore company shares, trustee accounts, and property in Antigua. Around eighty percent of these assets belonged to Jill and Martin Gordon and neither Paul nor Neil would ever treat those assets as their own if they wished to see the sun rise the following morning. That still left around £20 million that Neil and Paul owned between them in assets and accounts that were, like the Gordon's money, well beyond the investigative reach of the British authorities.

He needed to make two telephone calls, and both would be very difficult. He gulped down the glass of whisky and poured himself another large one.

The first call, the most difficult, was to Martin Gordon or rather his wife, Jill Gordon who was responsible for the financial side of the relationship. He took out the 'Burner' phone from his pocket and rang Jill. Jill was easier to talk to, as Martin had a habit of 'flying off the handle' at any suggestion of a problem whilst Jill was always much more level-headed. He wanted the level-headed Jill rather than the hot-headed Martin for the discussion they would need to have about Paul, the issues over the MacBook's, and how they were going to deal with things going forward. He also knew that the Gordons would not want to deal with him without Paul and that a smooth transfer of power to new money launderers would be extremely beneficial for his health in many ways. The call went straight to answerphone. He left Jill a brief message letting her know that Paul had died in an accident and to ring him back.

The second call was to Sarah Hall or Sarah Waterman when he had first known her. He decided that he would deal with this one in the capacity of the professional solicitor, that he was. It would be the easiest way to deal with her as he wasn't sure of the reception he was likely to receive. He had last spoken to her around twenty six years ago and at that time she had been quite upset with him. He took out an address book from Paul's desk drawer, looked up H on the index and tapped in a number to his own phone. After three rings it was answered.

"Hello, is that Sarah Hall?"

"Yes, who is that?"

"It's Mr Burton from Burton and Burton Solicitors in Matlock. Is Helen available to speak to?"

"No, she doesn't live here anymore. What do you want with her Neil. I've told Paul she doesn't want anything to do with him and getting you to ring on his behalf won't change that. Gary is her dad, always has been and always will be. It's no good turning up when she's nineteen years old like he did and expecting to take over from the person that's been a father to her all her life."

"I don't think it was quite like that Sarah" interjected Neil.

"She says she's happy to have birthday cards and Christmas cards off him but anything else she can get from me and Gary. We won't have anything from either of you two, you know that!"

"Things are very different for us both since Ibiza, Sarah. That was twenty odd years ago and we are both respectable businessmen now."

"I don't care what you do now! But Helen is mine and Gary's daughter, and we don't want her seeing Paul or having anything off him!"

Neil took a deep breath.

"I'm afraid that the choice for Helen has been taken away from her Sarah. Paul had an accident yesterday and suffered a bad head injury. He died last night in the Northern General Hospital in Sheffield. I'm ringing in the capacity of his solicitor rather than his friend. Paul has left his entire estate to Helen, and she will need to liaise with me in respect of transfers of ownership of property, vehicles, shares and so on."

"Oh my god! I'm so sorry to hear that,….. how did it happen?"

"I wasn't there, but I'm told that he slipped on some ice on the pavement, fell and banged his head, they did the best for him in the hospital but the injury to his skull was severe. There will be a post-mortem, but it appears to have been a bleed on his brain caused by the fall."

"You must be devastated Neil! I know how close you were."

Neil took another deep breath and fought back the tears that were welling up inside him.

"Yes, we were business partners and friends for over twenty five years. Dealing with the probate, will be the last thing I can do for him in relation to that friendship. The reason I need to speak to Helen in addition to the will is that as his only surviving relative she will need to deal with the funeral. It's his wish for cremation followed by the scattering of his ashes at Burbage Edge. It was a place he always loved to walk, and it obviously overlooks the Derwent Valley a place he has always loved since he moved here. I will help of course. I can't see anything happening before the New Year, but she will need to come up for a week or so afterwards to sort things out. As an executor I cannot see any problem with her staying at Paul's house if that will help financially until all the transfers into her name are made."

"Well Neil, I don't know what to say, it's all a bit of a shock, she doesn't live with me now of course, hasn't done since she came back from University three years ago. I speak to her most days though, so I'll let her know and get her to call you back. Will the morning be alright?"

"Yes that will be fine Sarah, sorry to be the bearer of shocking news this close to Christmas. I will be in the office after nine on Monday if she wants to ring me back then."

"Thank you Neil. How much is his estate worth? I know that she will ask me."

"It will depend on the day for things like shares, but I would estimate it in the region of around £2 million with the house."

"Thanks Neil, I'll tell her and I'm sure she will ring you at your office on Monday morning," Sarah ended the call.

He took a deep breath; he was close to sobbing. The loss of Paul was still affecting him deeply and he felt himself wishing he had been the first of them to die. Paul would have dealt with all these issues much better than him. Although Maggie didn't like him, he knew Paul would have been able to put his arm around her, comfort her and wipe her tears …if she had any. She would need it as well he thought. There wasn't very much in his estate other than the house, which had a substantial mortgage and some cash in the bank. His money was offshore where Maggie and her money pit horses had no chance of getting their hands on it.

Neil sat back and finished off the glass of whisky. As he relaxed feeling the warmth of the whisky on his throat and chest, the burner on the desk rang.

He poured himself another large whisky and answered the burner. It was time to tell the Gordon's what he planned to do about the MacBook problem, and he needed another stiff drink before he did it.

Chapter 9 – Mrs Gordon And Her Boys

Saturday 21ˢᵗ December

The three white, and one black man, all looked like line-backers. Each was six feet or more tall and around two hundred and fifty pounds of proportionate muscle. They were sat in a row on the large brown leather Grande settee in the portacabin that also doubled as an office for one of them. Only one of the men was wearing a suit: Martin "Gordy" Gordon. The other three all worked for Martin Gordon.

Worked was the wrong word. There was no contract of employment, no job description, and no salary. They were paid to do whatever Martin Gordon asked them to do, and whatever had a very broad meaning. The 'whatever' was always paid for in cash and the cash was substantial. It was certainly substantially more than all three had received as NCO's in the Royal Marine Commandos.

The oldest, Pete Stevens, had been a friend of Gordy from their days at Mayfield School in Ilford, and after completing his seventeen year term in the marines had renewed that friendship in the Denmark Arms on Barking Road one Friday night three years ago. Six months later his platoon NCOS, Trevor Briggs (Briggsy) and Kwadjo Musa (Kwadj) had bought themselves out of the Marines and were working on the same cash terms as Pete Stevens. As well as size, the three ex Marines were all clean shaven and wore the same closely shaven crew cut hairstyle. It was not a fashion symbol but a badge of who they were. As was the Royal Marine Commando dagger tattoo and the Number "42" each of them wore on their right bicep.

It was the Saturday before Christmas and all four were watching West Ham United play Liverpool on the large TV screwed to the wall in front of them. Saturday Night Football was a ritual, a ritual of beer and Pizza's with Betfred thrown in. In front of them, through a haze of smoke, was a low coffee table on which stood numerous empty cans of beer, an ash tray of cigar butts as well as the half-eaten remains of a pepperoni Pizza. Three more empty pizza boxes littered the carpeted floor around the Grande settee.

"You should have cashed out when you were up Briggsy!"

Gordy the man in the tieless grey suit stated authoritatively, and leaned back into the brown leather settee.

"They let me down every bloody week!" Briggsy replied, putting his mobile phone down heavily onto the cluttered coffee table in front of him.

"You need to bet with your head not your heart, that's the problem Briggsy!. I didn't get where I am by hoping people deliver, I make sure they do deliver, if you know what I mean!"

The three men laughed.

"Take that twat last week who thought that my money was his money, he didn't deliver so I made sure that he delivered me two black eyes and a broken arm didn't you Pete."

"Sure did Gordy! you asked me to deliver, and I delivered. I'm like the pizza man, always deliver no matter the weather!" Pete laughed.

"The Pizza Man! that's you Pete, the Pizza Man!.... Pepperoni Pete!" Kwadj the third man shouted.

All four men leant back laughing into the settee in alcohol induced reverie. Gordy repeated the joke "Pepperoni Pete! Pepperoni Pete!" the three other men laughed sycophantly again.

The crowd roared on the TV.

"He shoots and scores! That's just made me a score as well! Come on you Reds!" shouted Briggsy.

"Bloody Hammers! Can't rely on them, ever!" sighed Gordy.

A ringtone sounded and Gordy reached into the inside pocket of his suit jacket and took out his phone. He looked at the caller and put the phone to his ear.

"Quiet!" Everyone fell silent.

"What do you want? It's Saturday football night love......... I can't hear you …… hang on… turn the telly down Briggsy!"

Gordy put the phone on the coffee table and turned it to speaker as Briggsy muted the TV.

"Right Jill what's up!"

Jill's voice came out clearly from the phone's loudspeaker.

"Well, I thought you would want to know who's going to be in the 'head and shoulders' of the paper this week."

"Not on football night love, unless it's your Mother" Gordy looked around at the three men who all chuckled at his joke.

"It's not my Mother, but it's someone you might be interested in."

"Alright then love who is it?"

"Paul Trueman."

"Paul Trueman!" Gordy shouted angrily, took the phone off loudspeaker, and stood up putting the phone to his ear.

"Who's told you he's died … Burton left a fucking message!"

The table flew into the air depositing its contents in a wave below the TV on the wall.

"Alright, I'm calming down Jill…no I won't ring him in this state… alright you ring him back…let me know what's happened... in fact the football has just become unimportant I'm coming over."

Gordy closed the call and looked back at the settee; the football was still silently running on the TV, but the three men were all looking at him.

"Right, you muppets, I need to make some calls, try not to lose too much eh lads I'll be back in ten."

Gordy checked he had his phone in his hand and walked out of the door of the Portakabin. The PIR flicked on the floodlights in the large yard, illuminating a row of three new white Range Rovers parked outside. By force of habit, he looked around the yard checking that everything was in order. He checked the electronic gate, it was closed. He checked the broken glass topped ten-foot wall that surrounded the four acres of yard, gardens, and bungalow. As far as he could see there was no-one crouching below the PIR activated floodlights that illuminated it. All clear he thought. It was only then that he crossed the thirty yards to the front door of the large, detached bungalow where his wife Jill was waiting for him in the doorway.

Back in the Portakabin Briggsy reached down at the side of the settee and pulled out three bottles of Budweiser from the remains of a twenty four pack on the floor. He handed them round.

"Who's Paul Trueman?" He asked Pete Stevens.

"Fuck if I know!" mused Pete taking a swig from the bottle.

"Me neither" admitted Kwadj.

Pete shrugged "Who gives a fuck, anyway, put the footy back up I think they've just scored again!"

Jill greeted Martin at the door with a kiss and shut it behind him. Even when watching football with the 'boys' she thought he was smart. Not for him tracksuit and trainers but a sharp suit. It had been part of his personality as long as she had known him. They had met at the bus stop on the way to her first school Christmas dance thirty years ago, and she had noticed then that he had stood out from the other boys with his smart clothes and well cut hair. Not only was he smart he was also clean; he had showered and shaved every morning they had lived together. He was what she liked to call well-manicured. His nails were cut and filed at the same nail bar that she visited, and his hair was cut at the same hairdressers in South Kensington.

Looking after himself she knew was a task made easier by his occupation, which meant that he had few actual working hours and lots of time to spend in the gym. Jill likewise spent most of her time looking after herself. Her days revolved around hair, nail, and gym appointments. She was small, thin, and blonde. Facial and breast enhancements gave her a pert figure that drew admiring glances from most men including those much younger than herself.

There were no children. It wasn't as though they hadn't tried hard enough but 'It was just not to be' as Gordy had told her when she had suggested they went to a fertility specialist. In the absence of children Gordy had become the centre of her life and for the last three years the three 'boys' her surrogate sons whom she found herself cooking and cleaning for ungrudgingly.

Both of them knew that they were a perfect partnership, not only in appearance but also in business. They were absolutely ruthless and took equal responsibility for all aspects of their import and marketing operation. The banking and money laundering operation that ran alongside it was completely untraceable back to them because of Neil Burton and Paul Trueman.

They had come across Burton and Trueman when the two boys had crossed them in the early days of their first business venture in Ibiza. A couple of University graduates working as reps, Neil and Paul had decided to sell their own merchandise in competition to Martin and Jill Gordon. Jill, Gordy, and a couple of their 'friends' had paid them a visit one night with the intention of breaking a few bones. Trueman at the thought of avoiding a beating had persuaded Jill that a bent solicitor and someone that knew how to make their illegal money legal again would be a better option. Jill had persuaded Gordy to delay breaking their legs for a few months and paid for two air tickets to Manchester the next day.

The two boys had been as good as their word. For over twenty five years they had run Jill and Gordy's money laundering operation without a hitch and without the authorities making any headway into the source or extent of their wealth. To a significant extent the fact that neither Martin nor Jill had been arrested, never mind convicted was because of those two boys from Ibiza.

Jill looked at him and asked, "Are we in trouble?"

"No, I don't think so, Burton will be able to access everything. Paul put systems in place in case this happened. He always made sure that either one of them could access stuff in case one of them fell ill or something."

"Or died" Jill commented.

"Yes, or died… He planned for this; I just didn't expect it to happen I suppose. I'll call Burton and find out what happened Jill."

"I'll make us a cup of tea. We're going to need a new set up if he's dead you know. I don't trust Burton, without Paul he's too straight Gordy."

"I agree Jill, but let's find out what's happened before we set up anything new. We need two million pounds last week in January for the shipment last month. Let's get that sorted before we make any decisions. This is going to be a fucking nightmare you know, there's a dozen companies at least, and over eighty houses that will need to get sorted. Let's just start putting the feelers out for bent solicitors interested in new business. You're right though, I don't trust Burton, as you say he could be a liability without Paul."

Gordy put his phone on the table and rang Neil Burton putting it on speaker so both could hear. It was answered on the third ring.

"Hi Neil, it's Gordy, sorry to hear about Paul, what's happened and is there anything for us down here to worry about?"

Ten minutes later Gordy was in an even worse mood.

"What the hell does that all mean?" he asked Jill.

"Well, from what I can make out they run the operation off of two MacBook's. He has one, Paul has the other. Paul's crashed and burned for some reason, so he got a new one, borrowed Neil's and transferred everything over. So far so good. Unfortunately, Paul dies from some freak accident, delivering Burton's back to him and it's been nicked by some local low life shit. Paul's is at his house, but Burton can't get into it without wiping everything because it's not set up for his biometric thumb print to access it. He says the options are to get his back from the thief that stole it, get Paul's unlocked by an expert, but it will have to be someone we trust for obvious reasons, and if both those fail you will have to fly out to Antigua with him and set everything up again. The last one we will probably have to do anyway if we dump Burton, but we need two million pounds within four weeks and with Christmas we don't really have time for that option at the moment."

"It's not as bad as it sounded when Burton was bumbling on the phone. We will do option one to start with and get it back off

An Accidental Death

the low life that nicked it. I'll send Kwadj and Briggsy to help him out; he made that twat who nicked it sound like Reggie Kray."

Five minutes later Gordy walked back to the Portakabin. Pete Stevens turned off the TV as soon as he saw his boss's face. He only had that serious look on his face when something was worrying him or there was work to be done immediately. Gordy looked at the three men and took a breath.

"Right lads, I need Kwadj and Briggsy to get off up north tonight, it's only for a couple of days so you will be back for Christmas. Pete you're staying down here with me it's not a big job and these two will be able to manage it with their eyes closed."

"Where you sending us Gordy?" asked Kwadj.

"I want you to give a hand to a solicitor that works for us in a place called Matlock, it's up near Sheffield. Do you know the area?"

"Yeah, I know it, tourist place spent a bit of time round there."

"That will come in handy. Stay low, you're just a bit of muscle, don't get noticed. I'll get Jill to forward you his details to your phones later. Book yourself into a hotel somewhere nearby where you won't stick out. Briggsy I don't want anything happening to him, just keep him company, and see also where he's going and who he's visiting. Finally, make sure I can contact you 24/7 in case I need you."

"OK Gordy, do we need tooling up?"

"Shouldn't think so!" Gordy laughed "But just in case take something small and a couple of bats in case you need to 'deliver' me anything."

"Always at the ready Gordy! Always at the ready!" Kwadj chortled.

Gordy reached into his pocket and took out four £500 wraps of £50 notes and tossed two to each of them. Expenses for you both. Any questions?"

"Other than what's happened? and why we are going?" grinned Briggsy.

"And you know I'll tell you when you need to know" Gordy assured them smiling back.

Both men nodded in acceptance.

"I'll ring you tomorrow when you're set up with him, but let me know if there's anything that you think I might need to know."

"No problem Gordy!" Briggsy replied and threw his empty bottle to Pete who caught it.

"Reflexes still there then Pete! We will get off then, places to go and all that, you can clear up."

"Nothing new there! I've cleared up after you two for ten years!" joked Pete.

The two ex NCOS walked out together into the yard. Briggsy threw Kwadj a set of Range Rover keys.

"Drop me off and pick me up in a couple of hours when I've packed a bag. You book the hotel since you know the area. I'll sort out the bats and guns. I'm not sure what's going off but let's be prepared."

Neil Burton closed the call with Martin Gordon. He knew he was in full panic mode. His hands were shaking, and his heart rate was sky high as he could feel his heart pounding rhythmically against his chest. He knew that the panic he was feeling was irrational because there wasn't a problem. Even if Little Shit had his MacBook, there was still another in the drawer here. Getting his MacBook off Gary Traynor shouldn't be too difficult as he would be prepared to pay any amount to get it back off him and he didn't expect that he would have to reach his limit by any means. Dealing with Gary would not be a problem. Dealing with Gary's father Ron Traynor might be a different kettle of fish. His reputation as a 'hard-man' was well known and a little support would definitely come in handy if getting the MacBook off his son proved difficult.

He had told all this to Martin and Jill. He had expected them to not take the problem well. Instead, they had agreed to the plan and were sending two of their men to help him. He had agreed to the help although he knew he didn't really have a choice. It would be two of the three ex marines that would be coming up to keep an eye on him, as much as help him. He had worked with Gordy and Jill for a long time and knew how they worked.

Neil put the Tamnavulin back in the Credenza and brushed his fingers across the smooth surface. He also had a plan to get the house back if he could persuade Helen to leave the sale to him. He had thought through the legal issues involved and if he used an offshore company with some of the funds from the accounts in Antigua, now that it all belonged to him, it shouldn't be too difficult.

Chapter 10 – The Wretched Gail Traynor

Monday 23rd December

Gail Traynor stood back from the large Christmas tree in the living room. It was Christmas Eve tomorrow and she was all sorted. Ron had just brought a turkey home and she had got the vegetables and Christmas pudding from Sainsbury's in Matlock that morning. She had also seen a maroon scarf that she just knew Karen would love. It was Karen's favourite colour, and she had instinctively bought it. She had just finished wrapping it in the reindeer wrapping paper. She wrote 'Love Mum and Dad' on the label added a couple of 'x' and bent down to put it with the other presents under the pine Christmas tree in the corner of the room.

The addition of one more present caused a snowman wrapped cylindrical box to roll down the pile and stop in front of Ron's red leather Chesterfield armchair. She bent down and returned the snowman wrapped bottle of whisky to the pile under the tree. That was one of Gary's she thought. reindeer for Karen, snowman for Gary, bells for Ron Junior, and Christmas trees for Ron.

Gail loved Christmas, the whole family back together again. Karen and Ron Junior were coming round later and staying till Boxing Day. She had put clean sheets on the beds in their old rooms, although Ron Junior's room was actually now Gary's. He had not complained about his brother sharing his room again although the three day maximum stay had played a part in his enthusiasm.

She had decorated the living room with Christmas stockings on the wall. One for each of her children. She would put chocolate coins and a tangerine in each one tomorrow night, as she had done since Ron Junior was born. It was a family tradition of hers and she had kept it with the arrival of each of her children. The real Christmas tree was adorned with LED lights and various red and silver baubles. There was spray snow on the windows and a battery-operated message of Merry Christmas to passers-by shone from the window. Everything was perfect for Christmas. Gail loved Christmas.

Ron opened the door from the kitchen.

"Cup of tea love?"

"Yes. Thanks Ron, make one for Gary he's been up in his room all afternoon."

Gail went to the bottom of the stairs and shouted up to the top.

"Gary, cup of tea!"

"Coming Mum!"

She sighed and stopped the feeling of sadness that momentarily overwhelmed her. She knew that Gary was not the brightest bulb in the room, but he was her bulb. He would never be street smart like Ron Junior or actually smart like his sister Karen, but out of them all she knew her heart was with Gary. She loved them all dearly, but she always knew as only a mother would, that Gary was her favourite. Maybe it was because he was her last and she knew that after him there would be no more, or because he was more like her than the other two who were just like their dad, quiet, thoughtful, and then decisive. Gary was like her spontaneous, quick tempered, and reckless.

She went in the kitchen and sat with Ron at the table. This was the family table she thought as she sat down. The centre of the family, it had seen thirty years of Christmas dinners, meals, arguments and then make ups, cups of tea and, that once, when Ron came home from prison …. It was showing the signs of age, but Gail loved every polished mug ring where Ron always sat, every small biro scratch that Ron Junior had left as he had done his homework, every un-removable drip of nail polish and the hair curler burn on the far edge that she knew Karen had left but refused point blank to admit to. Nothing from Gary though, he hadn't done homework, he always used a mat for his mug, and he lived in his bedroom watching the TV or playing games on his PlayStation. The kitchen table would not leave a memory of him she thought as she sat down.

Gary came down from his bedroom and sat with his mum and dad. His dad passed him a mug of tea and Gary pulled a mat from the middle of the table and put it on it.

Gail chatted to Gary.

"Well, we're all here for Christmas, I didn't think you would be when you walked out that door last Friday. But I'm glad you're here."

She pulled his head towards her and kissed it on the top.

Gary shook her off.

"Give over Mum! …Hey Dad! did I tell you what happened before I went into Court last Friday, you'll never believe what I did."

There was a knock on the front door. They all looked at each other, no one used the front door that they knew. If it were the police, they would always use the back unless it was six in the morning in which case, they would use the front but wouldn't knock and wait for it to be opened.

Ron turned to Gail "You expecting someone?"

"No... I'll go!"

Gail got up from the table and went through the living room and into the hallway. As she got to the door there were two more loud raps on the wooden door from the other side.

"For fucks sake give me time to bloody open it!" she shouted and hurriedly turned the key in the lock and flung it open.

A middle-aged man in a brown suit and tie stood there in front of her. He took a step back when she opened the door anticipating more verbal abuse after the volley that had been thrown through the door.

"What do you want?" she shouted at him angrily.

The man took another step back.

"Is Gary in?" he asked quietly.

"Yes, what the fuck do you want him for?"

From both sides of the door two very large men came into view and without saying a word pushed her back onto the stairs as they walked purposefully into the house and past her into the living room.

Gail could feel the fear rising in her and she shouted.

"Ron! Ron!" To warn him

It was too late the men were in the kitchen. She ran after the middle-aged man in the suit who had followed the large men through the front door.

She burst into the kitchen to find one of the men holding her husband into his chair by his shoulders and the other one wrestling Gary back into his chair. Gail, for almost the first time in her life, was struck silent with fear. The men carried menace.

She had seen that menace before in her husband and son. Ron looked at her and his eyes requested her to calm down, and not kick off. She suppressed her raging anger and stood silent by the sink, staring like a cornered cat at the man in the suit who was nearest to her.

The large man holding Ron pronounced.

"Right everyone calm down and no-one will get hurt. I presume you're Gary?"

Gary nodded.

"Where's the bag you stole from Paul Trueman?"

Gary looked at his dad for advice. Ron looked at Kwadj stood behind Gary and then back to his son.

"Tell him the truth son"

"I threw it away!"

Kwadj continued "All we want is the MacBook you stole last Friday from Paul Trueman. Hand it over and we're out of here."

Gail and Ron looked at Gary.

"I didn't steal no MacBook!" Gary shouted with a bewildered look on his face.

The man stood behind him slapped him hard with the flat of his hand on his left ear. The thud resounded around the room. Ron went to stand up, but the man squeezed down on his shoulders and held him on the chair.

Kwadj pointed at Gail and shouted "Stay!" as the lioness readied herself to spring forward to protect her cub.

Gary held his ears with both hands to stop the ringing in his head. He couldn't hear anything and then sound came back to his right ear, but nothing in his left ear other than the repetitive pulsing sound caused by the blow.

The man leant in his good ear and whispered menacingly.

"Where's the MacBook?"

The man in the brown suit stood across from his mum watching and saying nothing.

Gary looked at his mum and she saw bewilderment in his eyes

"I don't know what you're on about I didn't steal no MacBook!" He shouted again.

The man unloaded a haymaker at Ron hitting him on the cheek. Ron rocked on the chair but was kept upright by the man holding him. His lip split, and Gail saw blood splatter onto her kitchen table. Ron like a rock sat unmoved staring straight ahead, blood trickling down from the cut on his lip.

Gary, in one movement, took hold of his mug of tea and threw its contents over his shoulder into the face of the man behind him who had hit his dad. Then he was out the kitchen door and running. There was a moment's hesitation and the large men, moving quickly for their size, chased after him, followed much more slowly by the man in the suit.

Ron and Gail chased after them, out of the door and to the front of the house. Ron stopped at the top of the drive at the side of the black Navara, looking down the road, but Gail continued to the bottom of the path. Both saw that Gary was on his bike cycling furiously to the end of the road about a hundred yards away.

All three of the men had given up the chase next to a white Range Rover a short distance away and were stood watching Gary as he rounded the right-hand corner, turned towards them, and raised his right hand in a two fingered salute.

"Fuck off you tossers!" he shouted and pedalled out of sight towards Wensley Road.

Gail smiled: he had got away.

Ron made a mental note of the registration number of the Range Rover. There was a family rule that he had only broken once at the insistence of his daughter Karen. If you attack one member of the family you attack them all.

Gary saw that the men had given up the chase when he turned the corner and freewheeled towards the main road through the village. He was still deaf in his left ear that continued to ring, and he took his hand off the handlebars to rub it. He therefore never heard the approaching vehicle as he cycled into the road in front of it.

Gail had just turned back to join Ron at the top of the drive when she heard a loud thud from the direction of Wensley Road. She smelt the faint scent of the chilly winter wind around her, tree bark and cold pond she thought. Then a metallic scraping and silence.. Her heart beat fast, and then the silence of the darkest pit, no light, nothingness, the silence of the black.

She screamed one word.

"Gary!"

Ron shouted "Gail!" and ran past her.

Then she was running behind him, along the road and round the corner. There was a man stood by the cab of a tipper lorry, staring unblinking to the rear of his truck, his mouth open in a silent scream.

Gail stopped running and looked at the silently screaming man. Khaki oil-stained overalls, black hair, and a mouth that was screaming but no noise was emanating from it. She was close enough to smell him. He smelt of oil and diesel just like the aggregate lorry behind him. She slowly turned to look at what the man's unblinking eyes were staring at behind the lorry.

Her gaze went along the muddy grey truck body to something behind it.

A single black Adidas Samba trainer lay upturned in the road, on its own, solitary in its own space and time. Then there was the twisted remains of a bike. The spokes of the front wheel, broken and bent, lay twisted and flat and then rose upwards at a

90-degree angle from the road. Directly behind the wheel, the frame and handlebars lay flattened to the floor with the rear wheel still slowly turning. Her gaze moved to a denim clad unattached bloody leg flattened under the frame, a large white bone protruded from what would once have been a thigh. Further along the road there was firstly the lower part of the other leg and the remains of a naked torso. A white sock was visible above the black Adidas training shoe on the leg. From the headless torso there was a black oily looking smear that led along the tarmac to a ragged t-shirt and then a flattened bloody mass that she knew had once been someone's head and shoulders but was now a bundle of screwed up rags and bone thrown into the road. Ron was knelt at the side of the raggy bloody mass. He was trying to gather it into his arms, but it kept falling …like half set jelly over his arms back onto the road.

The earlier morbid silence returned to Gail as she tried to take it in but there was nothing other than the smell of diesel and oil… diesel and oil, and … her eyes stared at the carnage, …blood, not oil on the road … it was blood of hers, her Gary's blood. Then the rage took over she was hitting the man in the overalls, spittling him with her rage and her fists and her feet and her head…words screaming out of her mouth, of hate of anger…. and of a loss from which she would never recover.

Chapter 11 – Funerals

Friday 10th January

It had been a cold and dry Christmas and New Year, and the first two weeks of January were no different. The temperature had not risen above freezing since Christmas Eve, but a lack of rain and snow had made the 'Beast from the East' as it was described by weathermen, bearable for most people. The roads and pavements were clear, and every sunny morning gave the indication that if only the temperature would rise a few degrees, spring would be just around the corner.

Dave had put in a few hours of 'time off' with Holly earlier that Friday morning, and then travelled back home to his second-floor apartment at Bradbury Place in Chesterfield. He had showered and put on a black suit, white shirt and black tie and then driven over to Baslow to meet up with Helen and Ella.

He had knocked on the kitchen door, but no-one had answered so he had gone in anyway and was now waiting for Helen, Paul Trueman's daughter and Ella Dawson her best friend, to finish getting ready for Paul's funeral that afternoon at the crematorium in Chesterfield. Repetitive beat music blared into the kitchen from upstairs, and he went over to the sink and picked out a white China mug from the large pile of unwashed pots, rinsed it under the tap, and then looked round for a tea towel before finding one that had been carelessly thrown on the black granite worktop. He gave the mug a wipe and then folded the tea towel and put it into a drawer with the others.

A jar of coffee and open carton of milk stood by the kettle. Dave put two teaspoonful's of coffee into the mug, sniffed the milk, poured some in and added the boiling water. He went over to a stool and sat down at the breakfast bar where his thoughts turned to Helen upstairs in the bedroom. He really liked her, she was fun to be with and very sexy. It was exactly a week since he had first met her and her flat mate Ella.

That night seven days ago Dave had gone out for a drink after work with Cath at The Junction Bar, a short distance from where he lived. Cath was drinking her usual vodka and orange and Dave a half pint of beer as he still had a short distance to drive home to his apartment. They had been sat at a table about fifteen minutes when a drunken Helen had approached, sat on his lap, and kissed him. Ella had then walked up to the three of them and passed Helen a cocktail.

Dave had, later found out that they had bet a cocktail that Helen wouldn't walk up to the handsome guy in the suit, sit on his lap and kiss him. Helen had taken one look at Dave, agreed to the bet and promptly won her cocktail. She had then struck up a drunken conversation with him about whether he was single and free for a date the following night. Dave had noted the drunken state of the blue eyed blonde sat on his lap and had told her that although he was single he was not available the following day because of work. Helen then took his face between her hands, looked at him with her vivid blue eyes and kissed him on the lips a second time. This time she flicked her tongue briefly into his mouth and brushed his tongue with hers before leaning back her head and asking him,

"Are you sure you're not free tomorrow?"

There was really no need for Helen to have asked him again. He had fallen in love the moment she had sat on his lap. He was going to finish work early.

An hour later Dave had been persuaded to drive them both back to Baslow in return for a coffee. Ella had staggered off to her bed and they had not got round to a coffee till the following morning because Helen, sat where he was now, had pulled him towards her by his tie, kissing him hungrily whilst undoing the belt on his trousers.

Since that first night he had spent every night with her at Paul Trueman's house at Baslow. Bit by bit she had opened up to him about herself whilst still keeping lots of her life in Crawley from him. She had told him that Ella was her best friend and that they shared an apartment in Crawley. Ella had come with her to keep her company and give her support if she needed it following the death of her father. He had also found out that they both worked at Gatwick Airport for EasyJet; Helen in HR and Ella looking after the company phone app and website, in the IT department.

Dave took a drink of his coffee. He wished that Ella hadn't come up with Helen or would go home early on her own. He would then have more time on his own with his new love. He wanted to tell her that he really liked her and ask her if they could continue seeing each other when she went back home. He had carefully worked out how they could meet up on his rest days, and how long it would take him to get to her flat in Crawley. He had even been looking at where they could go on holiday together. He dreamed of the idea of them going to a quiet Greek island, walking in the sun, drinking wine, and holding hands at a beach front café watching the sun go down.

The door into the kitchen burst open and Helen and Ella fell through it play fighting over a set of hair straighteners.

"They're mine" shouted Ella.

"No, I bought them" laughed Helen.

"Yes! but you gave them me when mine caught fire and burnt the carpet at home!" laughed Ella back.

Helen let go "Alright you have them then!"

Both then noticed Dave.

"Hi Dave!" Helen walked over to him and kissed him on the lips.

"You look very smart in your suit and tie, oh and you've polished your shoes! Be an angel and do mine for me they just want a wipe."

She disappeared into the lounge and came back with two pairs of black high heeled shoes. Both were muddy on the sides and heels.

"Will you do Ella's as well?"

"Of course," confirmed Dave taking both pairs of shoes over to the sink.

The girls were both dressed in short black dresses with black tights. Ella walked up to Dave.

"We look alright don't we? Neither of us have been to many funerals and we only brought these with us. It's black so it should be alright shouldn't it?"

Dave looked at them both. They would get away with the look at a funeral he thought, or a Christmas party. It was black anyway.

"Yes, you're both fine."

Both Helen and Ella chorused together

"Thanks Dave!."

A few minutes later Dave passed them the now clean shoes, and both bent down and slipped the shoes on; definitely Christmas Party thought Dave as they stood back up in the heels.

There was a knock on the door. Helen picked up a set of keys from the kitchen top near the sink and opened the door. The funeral director Shaun Parker was at the door.

"I have brought the car up the drive if that's alright Miss?"

"Yes that's brilliant come on Ella! It's a Limo! She threw the keys to Dave and shouted over her shoulder.

"Can you bring our bags Dave they're in the living room on the sideboard and lock up. We'll see you in the car, thanks darling."

Paul Trueman's service at the crematorium had been a fairly straightforward affair, although there were a lot more people than he had expected. Trueman had obviously been a popular member of the golf club, as there was a large contingent of his friends from the club that had almost filled one half of the crematorium hall. The other half of the room had consisted of Ella, Helen and himself on the front row and a few men in suits and their partners sparsely filling the seats behind them.

The service went through some aspects of Paul's life. There was nothing about his early life but a lot about his golfing achievements. His year as Captain of the club. Several members stood up and told some humorous stories and incidents he had been involved in. The Chairman of the local Conservative Party took the stand and talked about his contribution to the local area as a Councillor. He mentioned his involvement in moving the local records office. His support for a new graveyard at South

Darley. A renovation of the library garden. It all seemed to Dave very inconsequential. A life less lived he thought.

There were no hymns or prayers in the atheist ceremony and as the coffin disappeared behind the red curtain a tape of "Morning Has Broken" blared out from the speakers. This was the prompt for Helen, Ella, and Dave on the front row to walk out of the service and into the passageway for Helen to shake the mourner's hands and receive their commiserations.

Dave told her that he would stay with her and help her out with Paul's friends as he was sure she wouldn't be able to engage with all these different people talking to her about a father she had only met once, but after a few minutes he realised that he was wrong, she was not fazed at all. Her job dealing with people all day at the airport had made her an expert at communicating with a diverse range of people, and she certainly didn't need any help or support from him.

Finding himself not needed, Dave wandered towards the car park and the waiting funereal vehicles. As he approached the entrance road he was surprised to find, walking up from the car park towards him, Ron Traynor and Ron Junior. They were unmissable with their height, build and bright red hair. Between them Gail in long black dress and hat was dabbing tears from her eyes with a handkerchief. Both men held an arm on each side of her as she walked between them. The male Traynors were dressed in suits and ties and wore them like nightclub bouncers. Jackets open ready for action.

Dave nodded towards Ron when he was about ten yards away. Ron noticed him, murmured something to Ron Junior who looked over and carried on with his mum towards the crematorium door as Ron broke himself off from Gail and walked purposely over to him.

Dave thought "Just what I need, a scene with Ron Traynor at the Crem in front of Helen."

He hoped it wouldn't come to blows because if it did he was almost certain to come second. As he got to him Dave greeted him nervously

"Commiserations about the accident with Gary, Ron."

Ron hitched his trousers up over his waist and looked Dave in the eye.

"What the fuck do you think you're doing, coming here for Gary's funeral?"

"I'm not here for Gary's Ron" declared Dave realising that Gary's service must be the one following Paul Trueman's.

"I've come with a friend for her dad's funeral Ron. It's the one before yours. I didn't know Gary's was today."

Ron looked him in the eye.

"Sorry Excy. Saw you here and thought… well you know how I think about you lot. Look it's not the day for …." He left the last word unsaid and put out his hand. Dave shook it.

"You're welcome to come Excy, if you want to?" remarked Ron.

"Thanks Ron but I will have to go back with my friend." Ron nodded and walked back to re-join Ron Junior and Gail, waiting outside the Crematorium for Gary's coffin to arrive.

Dave turned away to walk back to the gardens where Helen was still talking to Paul's friends. As he did so Karen Traynor scurried quickly up the same path that her parents had come along a few minutes before. As she approached and without slowing down she glanced towards him and whispered

"Excy, can you get Cath to ring me later today it's quite important?"

Dave surprised at the request to speak to his colleague by a Traynor replied quickly.

"Of course, has she got your number?"

"Yes, but I haven't got hers" Karen replied without even slowing and walked on to join her family as though nothing had been said between them.

Dave watched the horse drawn hearse clatter along the tarmacked road. The two plumes atop the black horses bobbing like fishing floats as they cantered towards the Crematorium doors. Dave saw Little Shit's coffin in the clear windowed hearse adorned in a white flowered arrangement that read "Gary" to passers-by. The black horses came to a halt outside the Crematorium doors and Dave waited until the coffin was taken inside. Ron took Gail by the arm, nodded towards the watching Dave, and went through the entrance and out of sight.

Dave took his phone out and rang Cath. It went to answerphone on the third ring, and so he left a voice message

"Hi Cath, it's me, just seen Karen Traynor, Little Shit's was the funeral after Paul Trueman's. I'm ringing to tell you that she says give her a ring. Didn't say what it was about. How come you've got her number?"

Dave put his phone back into his pocket and walked back to Helen. The attendees had made their condolences to Paul's daughter and were now stood in little groups around the car park. Shaun Parker and Ella came across to Helen and Dave.

"Everything go alright for you Miss Hall?"

"Yes, thank you Shaun it was very good. Thank you for organising it all. Did you arrange the free bar at the golf club this afternoon?"

"Yes, they're sending the invoice to Mr Burton as you requested."

"That's brilliant Shaun." Helen smiled and leant across and kissed him on the cheek.

Dave felt a pang in his heart that he immediately recognised as jealousy. It was totally irrational, and he silently chastised himself for it. Helen continued

"Well we are ready to go back if you are Shaun?"

As they turned to go Neil Burton came over to Helen and shook her hand.

"You did a wonderful job Helen; the service was excellent. I'm sure Paul would have approved of it. I presume you're not going to be around for much longer."

"I'll be here till next Sunday as I've got to go back to work on the Monday Neil."

Helen smiled at him, touched his arm, and tilted her head

"Can I ask you to deal with the sale of the house and its contents? I would also prefer it if you arranged for the disposal of his ashes, I know he was a good friend of yours and that you will comply with his wishes. I presume you will charge me by the hour from the estate for doing that?"

Neil appeared to visibly grow taller and brighten up.

"Yes of course I will Helen, it will be my pleasure. Paul was a long-time friend so of course I will not charge you for my time."

Helen smiled "That's very kind of you Neil."

Neil Burton returned the smile and decided to take a chance.

"In fact, Helen I know someone who may be interested in buying the property, without you having to put it on the market and pay estate agents fees."

"That's excellent news Neil. If they are prepared to pay the market value I would certainly be very interested. Can you keep me informed of any developments? Neil, you've been an immense help since I got here last week, I can't thank you enough."

Helen leant across and gave him a hug, she then turned to her two friends and declared unemotionally.

"Come on Ella, Dave, Shaun is waiting to take us home."

Chapter 12 – A Faultless Plan

Monday 13th January

It was the Monday after Paul Trueman's funeral. Neil Burton sat at the large kitchen table two pieces of marmalade covered toast on the plate in front of him and one in his hand. His wife's dogs sat at varying distances around his chair and under the table, waiting for something edible to drop to the floor. Their anxiety was growing as the piece of toast in his hand had not moved for several minutes because he was deep in thought. Those thoughts were about how he was going to get out of his criminal lifestyle. How he was going to get two million pounds for Martin Gordon by the end of the month and how he was going to get access to Paul's MacBook or find his own.

The problems overlapped so he was having trouble getting an overall plan into his head that would solve all three. If he could solve the second or third he was sure that he could solve the first. How to solve the second and third then. Martin Gordon wouldn't care where the two million pounds came from provided it was transferred on time to the supplier. He was confident that if he told him he had transferred it from any of the offshore accounts that Gordon wouldn't delve too deeply as to where it had actually come from.

Separate the issues he told himself and deal with them in importance of urgency. Firstly, was his missing MacBook a problem? Yes in that it had all the companies, accounts, and account passwords on. But the MacBook itself was biometrically pass-coded as were the various files containing the offshore companies and their accounts. The MacBook passcode could be bypassed with some IT knowledge, but any bank transfers needed the authority of both Directors. So far he had not been contacted by any of the banks and therefore whoever had the MacBook was probably not IT competent enough to break the biometric security.

Neil forced himself to look at what he knew. Gary Traynor had stolen his MacBook, and he had seen his face when he had been asked about it and his look of bewilderment told him that Traynor didn't have a clue about any MacBook in the bag he had stolen. That meant it was probably still with the bag. The bags whereabouts were unknown so until something came up it was a dead end and only became a problem if any of the banks notified him of activity or attempts on any of the accounts. He was thankful that he had deleted the photographs of him and Paul on it.

His MacBook, at the moment was a problem he could do nothing about. Neil took a bite of his toast, and all the dogs moved a few inches closer to him. Paul's MacBook was that a problem? He told himself that it was, in that he couldn't access it. He could take it to some geek and get it unlocked but that would involve someone from outside the organisation having access to the money laundering accounts. If push came to shove he decided that he would get it unlocked, he could then make the transfer for the end of the month. The MacBook was still at Paul's house and Helen was there until Sunday so he could get the MacBook on Monday and take it to the Gordon's in Dagenham that evening. There would then be plenty of time to get it unlocked and make the transfer.

The final option he considered was to raise the two million pounds himself. He didn't have access personally to that kind of money, not without access to one of the offshore accounts, and without Paul's signature or flying out to set up a new mandate with his death certificate that money remained out of reach. The only other money he had access to at short notice was the five million pounds in the client account at work. He could 'borrow' the money from his client account as a last resort. The only problem was that he couldn't do that till the last week in January after his SRA inspection. He was sure that he would be able to repay it within a couple of weeks after flying out to Antigua to sort out new mandates on the accounts with the banks.

Neil took another bite out of the toast and dropped the crust to the floor where the dogs scrambled for it. The Jack Russell won and then all four dogs went back to silent watching positions.

He took a drink of his coffee and picked up another piece of toast. He liked the plan. He had good options to get the two million. He then set himself to dealing with how he could get out of his relationship with the Gordons. He came up with another plan for that problem. After the transfer at the end of January had been made he would see Jill and Martin Gordon about transferring his responsibilities to someone else. He also knew they would be thinking about how to get rid of him now that Paul was dead. He would tell them he would do everything he could to make the transfer as smooth as possible and pay for any costs involved. They would accept this offer he told himself and a couple of months later he could just concentrate on being a small rural solicitor in a small rural town... with several million pounds in offshore bank accounts.

He liked the plans a lot. Neil ripped the toast into small pieces and dropped it onto the floor for the dogs. He smiled to himself as he watched the dogs scramble for and then devour the pieces of toast... that was quicker than taking it to the bin he thought. He finished off his coffee and put the mug in the sink. Maggie could wash up when she came back from the horses. Brushing the toast crumbs from his brown tweed suit he walked out into the chilly morning sunshine. He wasn't out of the woods, but he could see a clear path ahead of him.

The SRA were inspecting his practice the following week and he needed his accounts for when they arrived and that is why Neil Burton, as arranged before Christmas, found himself at 2 p.m. that Monday afternoon at the offices of Greenwood Accountants, Bath Street, Bakewell.

Neil loosened his tie and leant on the desk in the warm ground floor office as he waited for Beryl to return.

"Here you are Mr Burton," Beryl came through the door carrying a document box and placed it onto her desk.

"Mr Greenwood has signed them off and I will email you a summary of your tax liability and his invoice later this week if that is alright?"

"Yes of course Beryl."

Neil put his messenger bag on the counter, undid the clasp and opened the leather fold over. He reached inside and removed a bottle of single malt.

"Will you give this to Stephen for me and thank him for finishing these so quickly? I know how busy he is at this time of year."

"Of course. That's very kind of you Mr Burton. What a lovely leather bag. Is it Dior? Only I saw a similar one before Christmas but that one was black. I like your brown one better though."

Neil was suddenly very interested in the subject of the conversation

"There aren't many of these about. This was a birthday present from a friend. Who had the other one?"

"My colleague Alice Bulman found one in Bath Gardens just before Christmas."

Neil could feel his heart racing.

"It had got to be Paul's. It surely could not have been anyone else's could it?" he thought.

"I suppose the owner claimed it. They are quite expensive." Neil tried to sound conversational and not too interested.

Beryl took up the conversation.

"Well there was nothing in it to identify an owner, so Alice took it home. The police haven't been in touch to say that anyone has reported it lost so it becomes hers in about a week."

"Did you look in the Velcro pocket, people tend to put valuable stuff like diaries, and phones in there?"

Neil opened his bag again and lifted the calf skin flap at the back of the bag, revealing the hidden zipped pocket.

"Ooh that's fancy. I don't think we saw that! I'll tell Alice when she gets back She's just out at a clients."

Neil feigned disinterest. He had found out enough.

"Well, I hope you find the owner. I'll get off now will you hold the door for me?"

Beryl held the door open, and Neil walked out the accountant's doorway to his blue Land Rover Discovery parked outside.

He couldn't believe his luck; he had found the bag and the MacBook was probably still in it! He had another option to his plans from that morning, and it was the easiest of them all. All he had to do was claim the bag as his from Alice Bulman, hope the MacBook was still in it and he was home and dry. He smiled to himself. The sun was shining, it almost felt spring like, he could certainly feel a spring in his step. It was a new year and things were looking up.

Neil hatched a new plan on the way back to his office. It was eight miles from Bakewell to Matlock and it took all of the fifteen-minute journey to refine it so that it was flawless. The bag was at Alice's house. He didn't know where she lived so he would park up outside the accountants on Bath St. If she went home in a car he would follow her in his. If she lived nearby and walked home he would leave the vehicle and follow her home from work on foot. When she got home he would wait five minutes then knock on her door. She wouldn't have time to have checked the zip pocket and if she had all the better, because he could confirm that it contained a MacBook that he could access with his thumb print.

When she answered the door, he would say he had been told she had found the bag by the police and that it was his. She would hand over the Dior bag and he would thank her and give her a large reward say two hundred pounds. He practised his 'Thank you so much for finding it' speech. She would thank him for the large reward, and he would then give her an extra £100 because it was of sentimental value...which would be true he told himself. He would take the bag, thanking her again and open it in the car. He momentarily closed his eyes as he drove along savouring the feeling of joy as he unzipped the pocket and removed the MacBook. The other more difficult options he had considered that morning would be redundant. There would be no need for any heavies to threaten her or get her run over. Gordon would be happy and more likely to work with him to enable him to leave his organisation. It was a good plan for a good person he told himself. A new year....a new life. He smiled contentedly to himself. The plan was faultless and couldn't go wrong as far as he could see.

At 4.45 p.m. that evening Neil parked up his Blue Land Rover Discovery about fifty yards from the front entrance of Wildgoose's Accountants on Bath street in Bakewell. He got out of the car and walked along the road to the stone fronted window of the accountants. This was the window to Beryl's office, where he assumed Alice also worked. As he passed the window he looked inside. He could see Beryl sat at her desk, but he was disappointed to see that the desk opposite was empty. Alice wasn't back from her visit to the clients yet. There was always tomorrow if she didn't come back tonight: his plan would be as good tomorrow as it was today he told himself. Trying to appear nonchalant, he carried on walking along Bath street to its junction at Buxton Road.

It was just turning dark, and people were trying to get home to warm houses. Although several people passed him no-one was paying him any attention. He turned around and walked back along the street towards his Land Rover. As he passed the accountants window he again paused. This time there was a second person in the office moving around. It was a young woman with red hair who was just sitting down at the desk opposite Beryl. It could only be the Alice who had found Paul's bag. As he turned away from the window his eye made contact with Alice's as she caught sight of him in the window. Neil ignored it; the glimpse wouldn't have been enough to recognise him. He then turned quickly away from the window and walked briskly back towards his car and got in to keep watch on the office door of his accountants.

After a couple of minutes, he saw Stephen Greenwood come out of the door and walk briskly across the road to a parked Jaguar F Pace. Greenwood got in the car and drove off towards Buxton Road. That just leaves Beryl and Alice in the office he thought. At exactly 5 p.m. Neil saw Beryl Smith come out the office and walk across the road and through Bath Gardens. There was just Alice left in the office. He sat back in the darkness of the Land Rover and waited for Alice to leave.

As Neil Burton had passed the window of the accountants a few minutes earlier, Alice had walked across the road from Bath Gardens unseen by Neil Burton, and noticed him looking through the window. She had then entered the office, hung up her coat and been greeted by Beryl Smith who was waiting for her to return.

"Had a good day Alice?" Beryl asked.

"Yes, brilliant! Mr Liversidge was lovely. Kept making me tea all day and fetching cake and biscuits. I'll not need any tea tonight."

Alice sat down at her desk and kicked off her high heeled shoes.

"That's better!" she exclaimed and rubbed some life back into her squeezed toes.

Mr Wildgoose poked his head around the office door.

"How did you get on at Mr Liversidge's Alice?"

"Alright, Mr Greenwood. One more day should do it."

"Well done Alice. Pop into the office tomorrow morning then go straight there and we'll see you back tomorrow afternoon if that's alright with you?"

"Certainly, is Mr Wildgoose."

"That's the plan then. See you tomorrow, I'm off now. Will the last one out lock up for me?"

"I will Mr Wildgoose!" Beryl shouted after him.

Alice opened her laptop.

"I've got about half an hour work before I can go home so you get off Beryl if you want to. I won't grass you up to Wildgoose for getting away early" she laughed.

"Anyway, your lovers waiting for you, you don't want to keep him waiting!"

Alice was jokingly referring to the man she had seen looking through the window at her as she had come into the office.

"He's still there!" she laughed as she caught sight of the man looking through the window again.

Beryl thought she was referring to Mr Smith her husband

"The only thing that my lover boy will be waiting for is his tea on the table, not me!"

Beryl slipped on her coat and went to the door to leave.

"Don't stay too late and I'll see you in the morning."

" Will do!" announced Alice and lost herself in the figures on her laptop.

"Night Alice!" she shouted as she left the office and waited for Alice to look up and acknowledge her leaving.

"Night Beryl!" Alice shouted back without looking away from her computer screen.

Beryl smiled to herself at Alice's preoccupation with her work and checked her watch as she opened the front door. It was exactly 5 p.m. She dropped the latch and closed the door behind her ensuring to herself that Alice would be safe on her own.

About an hour later Alice looked up from her laptop. At the same time Neil Burton was getting worried that he had missed

Alice leaving. He couldn't be sure that his attention had not wavered for a minute. What if Alice had come out and he hadn't seen her leave? The doubts were nagging in his mind. He needed to make sure. Neil got out of the car and walked up to the Accountants door.

Alice lifted her head from her laptop and sighed. It was time to go home as well as visit the toilet she thought. She had drunk a lot of tea that afternoon. She debated with herself whether she could make it home before having to go, it was only a hundred yards she thought and decided that she could. Alice quickly put on her coat, checked that she had the office key in her hand, turned out the light and opened the latch on the office door. As she did so she was taken aback by man in a brown tweed suit stood in the doorway. Alice nearly jumped out of her skin at the sudden sight of the man appearing in front of her, who appeared to have been trying the door.

"Err Hi!" stated the man in nervous surprise and then looked around as though checking who was nearby.

"What do you want?" asked Alice suspiciously.

Neil Burton decided to transfer his memorised spiel from her home to the office doorway.

"I've come to see Alice Bulman. The police told me that she found a bag just before Christmas and I've come to claim it." He smiled at Alice.

Alice was still startled by the man at the door, there was something that wasn't right about him, stood in the doorway waiting for her at that time of night and what he had just said didn't ring true.

"Are you sure the police told you that Alice Bulman found the bag, only it wasn't Alice Bulmen who told the police she had found it but Beryl Smith?" challenged Alice, taking a step back from the door and remembering the phone call reporting the found bag to Bakewell Police Station.

The man's face seemed to show confusion and he stepped forward through the doorway towards Alice

"Well it wasn't the police that told me, but can I come in and explain?"

Mr Brown Suit moved to push open the door.

Alice was now frightened and as he stepped towards her tried to shut the door on him.

"I will pay a reward!" he shouted and pushed back against Alice on the other side of the door.

The door flew back forcefully at her, causing Alice to stumble backwards into the stairs. Alice screamed. Neil started to panic.

He stepped into the hallway and shut the door behind him putting his finger to his lips to tell Alice to stop screaming. Alice stopped screaming and looked at him firstly with fear, and then hatred and anger in her green eyes.

She stood up, getting off the stairs, and taking her shoe off as she did so. Alice faced Neil shoe in hand with the sharp heel pointing towards him. This was not what Neil had planned, his flawless plan had developed some issues. He knew he needed to get away from this situation but how without getting arrested by the police for harassing Alice?

His mind raced through his options, if only he could explain to her that he meant no harm….. it was too late. Like a cornered cat she came at him swinging the heel of the shoe at his head. He ducked and her knee came up into his face. He felt his nose explode and was momentarily stunned. She was on him in an instant raining blows with the heel of her shoe on the back of his head. Feeling the lightness of her body on his back, Neil stood up, pushing upwards, Alice caught off balance fell back heavily onto the stairs. Neil followed her; his vision blurred from the blow to his nose. His hand went to her small thin neck, and he pinned her to the stairs.

"Stop it! I won't hurt you!" he shouted trying to see through his watering eyes.

As his eyes cleared he watched the blood from his nose drip onto his hand then around her neck below him. Alice continued to struggle underneath him.

"Calm down!" he pleaded.

He felt her body go stiff and then to his relief she stopped struggling. He looked into her eyes to see if she was calming down but all they showed was anger…then confusion and then

…. panic. She went to grab his hand on her neck, but her hand never made it and it fell motionless at her side…. her eyelids closed on her panicked eyes and then opened for the last time. Her eyes like Alice herself were lifeless…she was dead.

Neil let go of her neck… he couldn't have strangled her; his hand had only been there a few seconds.. she must be acting….,he shook her by her shoulders, but he knew as she stared past him with those unemotional and lifeless eyes that she was not acting. He froze with a fear and dread that he had never felt before as warm urine flooded down her legs onto his suit trousers and polished leather shoes.

Chapter 13 – Help From Dagenham

Monday 13th January

"Turn the lights off, lock the door and don't answer it till Briggsy and Kwadj get there. Do nothing, don't make a phone call, stay still, and don't walk about either. They will be there in.."

Gordy looked at his watch…

"…4 hours. You got that?. … Good …don't panic we will have everything under control when Briggsy gets there…. Alright …. If it's important ring me back but only if it's important. Don't worry Neil, we can sort this out, but you will need to do your part…good, you understand… the boys are setting off now…hang tight till they get there Neil." Martin Gordon closed the call.

"For fucks sake!" He shouted at no one in particular but himself.

Problems with Burton?" Jill asked him.

"He's only gone and killed some girl!"

"I thought he was gay, whys he killed a girl?" asked Jill, showing no surprise at the news whatsoever.

"Fuck knows babe, he's becoming a right liability. I'm sending Briggsy and Kwadj up to sort it out, get them on the phone for me while I finish my dinner."

Jill picked up his phone and sent a text to both of them. She put the phone down and said to Gordy.

"Let's get Paul's MacBook, and get it unlocked. It's got to be easier than waiting for Burton to sort things out. He's becoming a liability now Paul's died."

"I think you're right babe. Can you get somebody trustworthy to do it?"

"Somebody more trustworthy than Burton... I would hope so. You get the MacBook and leave the unlocking with me."

"I will, don't know what I'd do without you babes."

At that moment, his phone rang, and Jill answered it for him. She waited until he had swallowed a mouthful of pie and then passed it to him.

"Briggsy….urgent job mate. Pick up Kwadj and get your arse back up to the Peak District. That twat Burton has only gone and topped some girl …. accidently strangled her he said….no idea …yes he is gay….. for fucks sake Briggsy I don't know if it was a game… they're in an accountant's office … hang on I wrote it down…. Wildgoose's, Bath Street, Bakewell. Google map it on your way there. He's waiting for you with the body. At this time just look after him. Thanks, Briggsy, I'll wait up till it's sorted so ring if there's anything you think I need to know... I think you're right but hold fire on that till I give the OK....you're a star Briggsy. Speak later."

He finished the call and took another forkful of pie.

"Briggsy says he's a fucking liability."

Jill sat down at the table with her plate of shepherd's pie and broccoli and began eating. She thoughtfully chewed on the first portion, looked at her husband and observed

"I think you will need to do something about him. He's not the sort to be able to deal with killing someone. The police will be over him like a rash and then us."

Gordy nodded and in silence finished off the shepherd's pie, pushing the broccoli uneaten to the side of the plate. He didn't answer Jill: she knew he was thinking about what he was going to do with Neil Burton.

Back at the accountants Neil Burton was sat on the stairs above the body of Alice Bulman. He knew now that when he thought that Paul's death was the worst thing that had happened in his life, that it had been untrue. This was the definitely much worse than that. Much, much, worse. He was going to prison for murder. He imagined himself being arrested, standing before those same Magistrates that he had sat with at the Rotary Club and Masonic Lodge dinners. His business friends talking about why he had killed some random young girl…he would be called a sexual predator in the newspapers, his picture circulated nationwide and then the Court case and spending the rest of his life in prison. Neil held his head in his hands, he was in anguish, his life was over he grieved to himself. He never gave a thought to Maggie his wife or his children.

Neil wiped his eyes with the sleeves of his suit. It was hopeless, what could Kwadj and Briggsy do to save him from this nightmare. He had a flashback of what was left of Gary Traynor behind the truck, from the last time they had tried to help him.

There was only one thing for it. He would kill himself. He looked around him. How do you kill yourself in an accountant's office? It was unlikely they would have a rope with which to hang himself. He thought about throwing himself down the stairs and breaking his neck. That was a good plan he thought, quick and painless. He looked at which stair above him he could throw himself down from and then realised that it was a stupid idea. He might not break his neck, just seriously injure himself or even not injure himself at all and just end up with lots of minor painful injuries.

Neil leant his head against a metal staircase spindle and looked down at Alice's body illuminated by the moonlight through the window halfway up the stairs; the arms at her side, legs straight out like a wooden doll, her red hair now black in the darkness falling over her pale white moonlit face.

"It's all your fault! If only you had taken the reward, and handed over the bag none of this would have happened. You deserved this!" he angrily said to the body on the stairs.

Neil held his head in hands he needed a new plan.

Could he get away with it? Neil brightened up he didn't need to kill himself if Briggsy and Kwadj could sort this out.

He would go home to Maggie, tell her that the business meeting went on longer than expected. There would be nothing to link him with this body if he cleared the scene up with Briggsy and Kwadj. Everything would be alright, he just had to wait until they arrived. They would need to get rid of her body somewhere he thought. He was local, and he could be useful to them if he could think of somewhere to dump it where it wouldn't be found. Neil, now feeling positive, set about thinking where a body could be dumped without it being found for a long time… if ever.

Three hours later his phone lit up and a banner message read. "We are outside." Neil stood up, stepped over Alice, and went down the stairs. He jumped over the pool of urine on the floor at the foot of the stairs and unlocked the door. Briggsy and Kwadj came silently through the door, which he locked behind them. He was about to speak when Briggsy held up his hand and handed him a spray bottle of disinfectant and a cloth and intimated to him to clean and polish everywhere he had touched. Neil took the cloth and cleaner and started with the entrance door. Kwadj put a black canvas bag on the floor and took out a packet of nappies from it.

He mouthed to Neil "Any blood?"

Neil pointed to her neck.

Kwadj looked at the pool of urine and started to mop it up. Briggsy took out a knife from a sheath on his belt and cut Alice's skirt up the middle and then her cotton top. He removed her outer layer of clothing and put it in a black plastic bag. He then removed her underclothes in a similar fashion before laying her small pale body naked on a plastic sheet on the floor and scrubbing the blood from her neck with a disinfectant wipe. She was then wrapped in the sheet, and it was secured by adhesive tape. Kwadj wiped the last of the urine off the stairs and whispered to Neil who was still stood with the cloth and cleaner in his hands.

"Anywhere else need cleaning?" Neil shook his head.

"Alright, put that stuff in the bag and fetch your Land Rover to the door, we need to dispose of her where she won't be found for a while."

"No problem."

Neil gave them a thumbs up.

"I have an idea where we can dump her."

Chapter 14 – The Jealous Poacher

Monday 13th January

It had fallen dark about an hour ago. Dylan Oxley had waited for nightfall before staking out his quarry. Under cover of darkness, he had scuttled silently along the row of back-to-back terraces and into the yard of 15 Railway Terrace Rowsley. Taking the key from his camouflage trouser pocket he unlocked the padlock of the small wooden shed in the yard, silently slid over the latch, and let himself in. Once inside he closed the door behind him so that he could see anyone leaving or entering the yard through the window, especially anyone entering through the back door.

After a couple of hours he had seen no-one come into the yard or go into the house through the back door.

Dylan knew that two children lived there but that they would be staying at their grandmothers on a Monday night as they had done for the last six months. The light in the kitchen went out. Dylan crept out of the shed and secured the padlock. He crept across the yard and put his ear to the white UPVC door. There was no sound. He stood back and looked through the kitchen window. Standing in the back yard he could just see that the lights were on in the lounge from the sliver of light underneath the door. There were pots draining on the side of the sink. Dylan took a closer look. Two large plates in the stack. That's all he needed to know. He pushed the handle down on the door, it was unlocked. The latch clicked and he slowly opened the door and gently stepped into the kitchen. His high laced black Doc Martin boots hardly making a sound on the linoleum floor.

He silently closed the door behind him and then waited, listening for sounds in the house. The only thing he could hear was the sound of the television in the adjoining room and so he moved towards it. As he did so the living room door opened into the kitchen.

He stood there five feet four inches tall in his black boots, camouflage fatigues and bush hat looking at his wife who stood a good four inches taller than him backlit in the doorway. He felt the anger rise in him. Two plates and her dressed like the tart that she was in her black tights and short skirt, a white open necked blouse hardly keeping in her large breasts.

Dylan exploded "Where the fuck is he you fucking tart!"

"Where's who?"

"The bloke you've got here! It's Graham from next door, isn't it, I'll kill him if it is. I've seen you eyeing him up, where is he?"

An Accidental Death

Dylan pushed past her into the living room. Emmerdale was on the television and his two children Texas and Arizona aged four and six respectively sat apart on the settee separated by the gap where their mother had been sat a few moments before. Seeing their father, the two children huddled together looking at him with frightened eyes.

The children might as well not have been there as Dylan's eyes cast round the room looking for the man he knew, Jackie his wife, was hiding. Seeing no-one in the room, he ran through into the hallway and then up the stairs slamming the living room door behind him. Jackie Oxley heard him leaping up the stairs three at a time and then the thudding on the ceiling as he stomped and ransacked hers and the children's rooms.

She looked at the children and consoled them reassuringly.

"Sssh, it's going to be alright" and smiled at them. Then she turned round and went into the kitchen. She opened the drawer underneath the draining board and took out a large, pointed chopping knife. Feeling the weight, she adjusted it in her hand into a stabbing grip and waited for her ex-husband to come back downstairs.

Eventually she heard Dylan walking slowly down the stairs and hid the knife behind her back. Dylan walked through the living room door into the kitchen where he stood looking at her.

"Shut the door behind you!" she hissed slowly through clenched teeth. Dylan closed the door.

158 | P a g e

"Me and you finished six months ago. You don't own me, you never owned me... I will fuck whoever I want but the one person it won't be is you!"

Dylan took one look at his wife and knew he was in danger. He had gone too far. He took up a defensive position and raised his right arm to fend off any attack from her. Jackie drew the knife from her back and held it shoulder high as she came up to her ex-husband. They circled each other in the kitchen until Dylan had his back to the outside door. He reached behind him and opened it.

"You're just a slapper, you were a slapper when I met you and are a slapper now!"

"Well, I have to get it where I can when my husband can't get it up, so fuck off out of my house and if you sneak in here again I'll cut off something that you don't want to lose!"

Dylan turned quickly away from his ex-wife and the threatening knife. He cleared the steps into the yard with one jump, turned back to the kitchen door and slammed it behind him.

An audience in the windows of the overlooking terraces had gathered at the shouting including Graham Potts the next door neighbour, who was looking through his kitchen window at him. Dylan reached down and picked up a small half brick from the floor of the unkempt yard and threw it at Graham who was clearly illuminated by his kitchen light. Graham ducked as the brick thudded into the double-glazed window and bounced harmlessly onto his yard.

Frustrated, Dylan ran towards him fists raised and then realised that he would not be able to get over the five foot wall between the properties. He stopped waved his fist at Graham over the top of the wall and then turned, ran five yards across the yard and drop-kicked the gate, knocking it off its hinges and falling with it in a heap in the roadway between the houses.

Embarrassed at his fall, he quickly got up and looked around to see if anyone had seen him. They had. He gave an angry two fingered salute to a watching neighbour in a window opposite, and then ran between the terraces to his black Ford Ranger pick-up.

The black Ford Ranger was his pride and joy. He had customised it with an array of five floodlights on the roof and had resprayed the bonnet with a picture of a hunter. Everyone knew Dylan Oxley's Ranger. He felt the diesel engine turn over and then gunned it back along the narrow roadway between the terraces, turning right towards the A6 and then towards Bakewell.

An hour later, after retrieving his rifle from a hollow tree in woodland at Stanton in The Peak, Dylan Oxley pulled up against a metal farm gate about a quarter of a mile south of White Lodge Car Park on the A6. He got out of the Ranger, opened the gate, and drove it into the field. The icy ground crunched under the 4-

wheel drive wheels as he parked the Ranger behind the dry-stone wall and trees that would shield it from the road.

He was still angry, but he knew that would dissipate in the fresh air and excitement of the next few hours. He would drive past the bitch's house later, about midnight, and see if there was a light on. It would prove she was shagging about if there was a light on in her bedroom at midnight.

He reached across to the passenger seat, opened a tin of shoe polish, and smeared it on his cheeks. He then stepped out of the pick-up, gathered up his camouflaged bag containing his nets out of the back of the Ranger, and slung his silenced .22 rifle over his shoulder. About fifty or so trout would be good tonight, but a deer would be even better if he came across one. He looked around him, everything was quiet.

He locked the Ranger and set off across the field to the pond above White Lodge Car Park. He knew that Stan Moore might be looking for him. It was a small community, that of gamekeeper and poacher, and he liked to think that he was always one step ahead of him. Dylan had chosen this night as it had given snow, and he thought that Stan Moore would not want to be out in it.

Dylan climbed over the nearby dry-stone wall and like the accomplished stalker he was, moved silently through the trees towards the flooded quarry. He was about twenty yards from the track leading up to the pond when he heard voices.

Dylan froze and then went to ground, hidden from anyone moving along the track. It was a three-quarter moon and with his eyes now clearly adjusted to the night he could clearly see three men moving along the track. One was shining a torch in front of them. His initial thought was that it must be Stan Moore and two of his gamekeepers, but he quickly dismissed that as they were making too much noise; one was also dressed in a suit and the other two in jeans and jackets. Definitely not gamekeepers. One man was carrying something slung over his shoulder, like he would a deer, and as he watched, the man dropped it to the floor.

"Bloody hell she's heavy for a young un!" the man exhaled loudly as he dropped the bundled package to the floor.

Dylan Oxley slung the rifle to his shoulder and peered through the attached night-sight. The bundle appeared to be an unconscious young girl wrapped in plastic.

"She's your problem it's about time you carried her a bit."

The man who had dropped her groused to the man in the suit who was stood looking at him.

"No problem Kwadj I think I can manage it for a bit" the man in the suit replied.

The third man laughed.

"You're getting old, I remember a time when you would do ten miles across Dartmoor with a load like that."

"That was ten years ago Briggsy, I like to delegate now if there's help about. How far we got to go Neil?"

"Not far now, just to the top of the hill, I can carry her to there, give me a hand to get her onto my back."

"First thing we do when we get there is make sure she doesn't float so we need to get some rocks and put them in that bag, and we'll tie it to her with the rope. We also make sure she doesn't float when she starts airing out by putting some holes in her lungs. Are you sure this pond is deep Neil?"

"Yes, it's an old quarry. I used to swim here when I was a kid. It's deep and got steep sides. It should be perfect."

Dylan continued watching through the night-sight on the rifle as the first man took out a dagger from his belt and dropped astride the plastic bundled girl and stabbed downwards into her chest with the knife and then again in two quick motions.

Dylan Oxley thought that if the girl wasn't dead before she certainly was now. He moved ever so slightly as he pulled the gun further into his shoulder, so that he could get a better view through the night-sight of the two men and the plastic wrapped body.

Briggsy caught sight of the movement at the side of the track and lifted his own night-sight binoculars that hung around his neck to his eyes and focused on where the movement had come from. There was a man with a night-sight and rifle laid in the undergrowth aiming at Kwadj.

Dylan Oxley now had a more comfortable view through his night-sight of the two men and the plastic wrapped body. He then scanned ahead of them for the third man. As he did so, he heard something crashing towards him. He looked away from the night-sight to see what it was. All he saw was a blinding flash, and then his right eye went black, he thought it was really weird because he could not feel or hear anything. Then through his good eye he saw the third man stood over him with a gun. It was the last thing that Dylan Oxley ever saw as everything turned to black forever as the second.38 went through his other eye.

"What the fuck just happened!" shouted Kwadj.

"Fuck knows but he's dead now, double tapped him" pronounced Briggsy.

Kwadj flicked on his torch and looked down at the military camouflaged figure at the side of the track as Briggsy turned him over with his foot.

"Fucking ammo! Neither's gone through him" Briggsy angrily exclaimed.

Chapter 15 – Trapped

Monday 13th January

"What just happened?" groaned Neil cowering against the wall.

"No idea, who the hell is he? It looked like he was about to take a shot at one of you. Do you know him Neil?"

Neil looked down at the eyeless body of Dylan Oxley and thought that even his mother would have been unable to recognise him.

"No, I don't know him"

"Alright then. Those shots might have the police here soon so keep an eye out for blue lights, I'll need to sort this out with Briggsy."

Kwadj waited for Neil to walk down the track until he could get a view of the A6 and more importantly until he was out of earshot.

"What you reckon we do now then Kwadj? What's he doing here?"

"From his outfit he's either a poacher or a gamekeeper. Either way he's got two bullets in him that might link him back to us at the end of the day. I suggest we dump him where we were going to dump the girl."

"What about him?" Briggsy nodded towards Burton.

"Not sure, I don't like leaving witnesses" confided Kwadj.

"Me Neither, but first off let's see who our shooter is."

Briggsy searched through the dead man's pockets and discovered a wallet and bank cards.

"Cards say Dylan Oxley and his nets and gun say more likely poacher than gamekeeper"

Kwadj removed a mobile phone and a set of car keys from Oxley's camouflage jacket pocket and passed them to Briggsy.

Briggsy pressed the unlock button on the car keys and yellow indicator lights flickered through the trees about a hundred yards away.

"Bingo!" proclaimed Kwadj.

Briggsy pulled Dylan Oxley onto the track and up towards the pond whilst Kwadj picked up Dylan Oxley's bush hat and pushed it into his bag, together with some fallen rocks from the dry-stone wall. Briggsy took out the dagger from its sheath on his belt for the second time that night and stabbed Oxley in both his lungs, opening the wounds out with a sawing motion. Using the rope, they bound the rifle and his bag full of rocks to him and rolled him into the pond, and then watched as his body slipped into the water slowly sinking deeper down into the black depths of the water filled old quarry.

"What are we going to do with her?" asked Kwadj.

"We need to get her weighted down so we will need some more rope and bags to start with, so I suggest we leave her and come back later with some more gear if the police haven't been alerted by the gunshots. What you think?"

"Sounds like a plan, What about him?" Kwadj asked, indicating towards Neil Burton forty or so yards down the track.

"Not our decision. I'll ask Gordy later" Briggsy replied quietly.

Kwadj whistled, and then gestured for Neil to come back and join them.

Neil walked hesitantly back up the track to Briggsy.

"We are going to get some more gear in order to dump the girl in the quarry. It's in the back of the Range Rover in Bakewell Neil, so we need to leave her here for a while."

Briggsy stepped over the naked girl on the track, bent down and stripped the plastic from her with his dagger.

"Don't want to leave our fingerprints everywhere if things don't go to plan, Grab this Neil we are going to have to get rid of your clothes anyway,"

Briggsy threw the plastic bundle to him. Neil caught the plastic and screwed it into a tight ball. The three men then set off back to the Land Rover that was parked out of sight on the car park below. They had gone about forty yards when they saw blue flashing lights illuminating the night sky in the distance.

Briggsy turned to Kwadj "Get to the car with Burton and then follow me. I'm going to get rid of our shooter's car. We need to get it well away from the body. Come on let's move!"

Briggsy disappeared into the darkness towards Oxley's pick-up and Kwadj half dragged Burton quickly towards the car park. As they got to the car park the lights of the ambulance came into view and Kwadj and Burton watched from the darkness as it drove straight past the car park and along the A6 towards Buxton. Seconds later a Ford Ranger pulled into the car park and Briggsy wound down the window and shouted to them.

"Come on!, get a move on! There might still be police on the way."

"I think I've twisted my ankle!" moaned Burton.

"We will sort it later! First thing we need to do is get our stories straight about why we are about at this time of night and a back story for you with the girl Neil. Any idea where we can park up to sort our stories and dump this pick-up in a place where we won't have to kill someone else" joked Briggsy.

Neil thought for a moment. He had thought of two good places to dump Alice's body when he had been sat on the stairs in the accountants office. He had gone with the pond, as it would hide the body from any random walker stumbling across it. The other option was also remote and a good place to dump a body if you didn't want it to be found for a while, but there were walkers who, rambling off the beaten track, might have come across it.

"There's an old spa mine towards Calver, it's no longer used, and you can't see it from the road."

Ten minutes later the three of them were parked up on the old Long Rake Spa opencast mine just outside Calver. As Neil had promised it was well off the beaten track.

Kwadj watched the first flurries of snow as they settled on the windscreen. Nothing was going right that night and snow was the last thing they needed. He let out a long sigh and then said reassuringly to Neil Burton who was sat next to him in the driver's seat of the Discovery

"Wait here I'll be back in a minute I just want to have a quick word with Briggsy, about what we are going to do now it's snowing."

Kwadj got out and went round to the driver's window of Oxley's Ranger. As he got there Briggsy put his phone down from his ear onto the dash in front of him.

"I've spoken to Gordy. He's up to date with what's happened, and he agrees it's all going tits up. We can't go back to the girl in the snow because we will leave footprints everywhere. He has decided that Burton is only useful until we know where one of two MacBooks are. He's become too much of a liability, he's seen us kill a bloke and killed someone else himself. I've told Gordy that he doesn't know where one of the MacBooks is because he killed the only person, the girl, who knew where it was. So, he wants us to find out where the other one is and text him back."

Briggsy got out of the Ranger and walked back with Kwadj to the Discovery. He gestured for Neil to wind down the driver side window whilst Kwadj got back in the passenger seat.

"Looks like we aren't going to find your MacBook Neil, you do know where the other one is don't you?"

"It's at Paul Trueman's house in Baslow."

"Does anybody else live there, housekeeper gardener or someone?"

"No-one lives there, although his daughter is staying till Sunday."

"Could you be more specific, whereabouts in the house is it?"

"It's in the drawer of the desk in the study, the keys are in a book on the bookcase."

Kwadj smiled.

"That's great Neil. Now we need to get your story straight, you need a story as to where you have been all night and why you cannot have been anywhere near Bath Street when the girl got murdered."

Briggsy's phone pinged, replying to the message he had just sent Gordy.

Kwadj, hearing the ping, got out of the Discovery, and walked to the back of it where Briggsy joined him.

"Gordy says that's good enough. He's coming up Sunday to pick up the MacBook himself. In the meantime, everything needs sorting." He nodded towards Neil Burton in the front seat.

"The car, the lawyer, the girl, everything. Let's get started."

He walked over to the driver's door and opened it. Burton looked across at him and Briggsy hit him square on the jaw with his leather gloved fist. Burton slumped forward unconscious.

"Still got it!" Briggsy grinned towards Kwadj, as he flipped the bonnet and moved to the front of the vehicle to open it.

Kwadj poured petrol from a jerry can, which they had put in the back of the Discovery earlier in case they needed to burn Alice's body, over the engine and then over the bundle of plastic wrapping and Alice's clothes in the boot, before throwing the empty jerry can into the back of the Ranger.

At the front of the car Briggsy tossed a match onto the engine, putting the bonnet down as the petrol ignited. Then they both got in the Ranger and reversed down the track, until they were a hundred yards away and watched as the Discovery became engulfed in flames.

Neil was dreaming that he was running, his feet were getting heavier so that he was straining to lift them, his leg muscles were refusing to work, and his feet were beginning to feel hot against the ground they were struggling to lift from …and then he breathed in and was immediately awake as the acrid smell of burning plastic hit his nostrils and burnt the back of his throat. He coughed, held his breath, and opened his eyes.

The pungent smoke seared his eyes but not before he could see that he was in the driving seat of his car and that he was in an inferno of smoke and flames. The pain in his feet was excruciating. He was not in a dream.

He was going to live he told himself…as long as he didn't breathe in the fumes and could get out. He was sitting next to the door; it would only take him an instant. He tried to raise his legs from the flames, but they were trapped by the steering wheel. His chest was exploding with the urge to breathe. He needed to get out of the vehicle and fast. He pulled the door handle towards him and felt the skin on his hand burn away on the hot metal handle as he pushed it open. He was free…he would live…. but he couldn't move, he was trapped by his seat belt. His trousers were burning, and he could see the skin of his thighs blackening in the fiery furnace of the footwell. His left hand went instinctively to the seat belt fastening and flinched away as the metal seared his fingers. Neil knew he was going to die if he didn't get out of the vehicle; he forced himself to grip the release button one last time. He still could not release the seat belt as his skin melted with the contact on the hot metal. The flames licked at his face; he knew he had lost. There was nothing but flames in front of him as the heat burnt his eyelids away, he looked resignedly down and watched his now bare legs and arms blacken and crack. There was no longer any pain, but he smelt his burning hair and then the searing heat in his mouth, throat, and lungs as he took his last breath, just as the petrol tank exploded with a loud thud and the Discovery and its sole occupant were enveloped in a ball of fire.

"That's Burton and the Discovery sorted but what about the girl?" asked Kwadj, as the fireball lit up the grey walls of the opencast mine.

"I've been thinking about her. We don't need to do anything now Burton's gone. There's nothing for the police to link Burton to her and they will go round in ever decreasing circles if they find that guy in the lake. Let's pick up the Range Rover and then dump the Ranger somewhere well out of the way in Sheffield. We can get something to eat while we're over there. I haven't eaten since lunch and there's bound to be somewhere open even at this time of night."

Kwadj nodded.

"We will be back home by the time anyone comes across any of this shitshow in the morning."

Chapter 16 – DC Mulvey & DS Hollins

Tuesday 14th January

DC Catherine Mulvey known to everyone as Cath, parked her car against the stone wall in the back yard of Matlock Police Station. The two paracetamol and can of Red Bull had started to clear her head from the previous night's vodka, and the low winter sunlight was no longer burning the back of her dry reddened eyes. Cath took out her eye drops from her bag and squeezed several drops into both eyes and blinked them until they felt clear and refreshed.

"Time for work!" she uttered to herself and with a sigh opened her car door just as a silver Ford Mondeo pulled up alongside her.

Both drivers got out the car at the same time.

"Morning Sarge!" Cath cheerily greeted her boss Detective Sergeant Kevin "Holly" Hollins over the top of her red BMW Mini.

"Morning Cath, you seem happy this morning"

"Well, it's Tuesday, and that's only three days to the weekend. Seeing as I've had one night out since New Year, and that was with Dave after work last week, I want to go out with the girls and get drunk as a skunk this weekend, happy days are here again and all that."

"Whereabouts are you going out with the girls?" chatted Holly, joining her as they walked together across the yard.

"Start off down Brampton as usual, few cocktails, then into town till late." Cath looked up at the now greying sky.

"Provided it doesn't snow."

"That's if you can get off work of course, talking about which I've got some good news and bad news on that front today," Holly teased and then paused as though thinking about something else.

"Bit like your home life then!" Cath quipped back.

"Sorry, what did you say?" Holly asked coming back to the here and now.

"Nothing, it was just a bad attempt at humour. I said a bit like your home life then."

"No that's always bad news and bad news, you know that!" Holly shrugged.

"Yeah, sorry Sarge, not called for. You alright?"

"Yeah, not bad actually. She was in a good mood this morning."

"That's a lie isn't it Holl. You can't hide that plaster on your forehead, it's bleeding through it."

Holly put his hand to his head where a plaster on the side of his forehead was showing a red blood stain and smiled at Cath

"I might actually have walked into a door this time!"

"Oh look! a flying a pig…can you see it?" Cath pointed upwards to the sky.

Holly went quiet and went back to his deep thoughts as they walked across the yard into the garage and to the bottom of the stairs leading to their office on the next floor.

As they reached the stairs Holly came out of his deep thoughts and said to Cath

"Bad news first then Cath, might as well get it over with Excy got called out this morning."

Excy was the office nickname for DC Dave Baker. He had been christened Excy by an exasperated Holly two years ago shortly after being appointed as a detective at Matlock. When the newly appointed Detective Constable Baker had asked why 'Excy' he had told him that it was because you just had to point him at the target, and he would relentlessly focus on it just like an Exocet missile. DC Baker had taken it as a compliment and liked the comparison and had not objected to his new nickname.

What Holly or Cath didn't tell him was that his nickname came from his tendency to totally focus on one target at a time, and like the French missile, he was named after he would usually hit his target but be oblivious to the damage he caused to those around him. Although he was a likeable work colleague, he had a tendency to occasionally piss off everyone who worked with him.

"What was he called out for?"

"Body of a woman up at White Lodge north of Ashford, Comms let me know about ten minutes ago, on my way here."

"Serious?"

"Looks like it, naked dead woman apparently, BJ is on his way to run it with the Murder Team."

"Excy's going to love that!" Cath laughed.

"Now the good news....there isn't any more bad news!" Holly laughed loudly.

Cath smiled back at him but didn't see the humour as much as Holly. Eventually Holly stopped laughing when he realised he was the only one laughing at his joke and assumed a much more supervisory tone with Cath.

"Much on today Cath?"

"Think I've cleared up that sneak in burglary on Lime Tree Road at the beginning of December. Fingerprints turned up Little

Shit of all people. That was such a surprise!" she observed sarcastically.

"It's going to be an easy detection for our figures now he's dead."

They were now near the top of the stairs and Holly's forty eight years of bad diet, long hours and general lack of exercise was catching up with him.

"Don't know whether I'm happy or not now he's no longer with us…..He was bad for our crime rate but brilliant for our detection rate…….I don't think I've ever come across a worse thief though …….I don't think he knew what a pair of gloves looked like, and he's certainly never heard about DNA and crime scenes," he gasped as he exhaled the last bit of oxygen from his lungs.

Cath waited for him to get his breath at the top of the stairs before replying

"Well, he left enough DNA at his last one, about thirty yards of it all along the road."

Holly looked at her and shook his head.

"Bloody hell Cath that's bad, true, but very bad taste…Seeing as you've brought it up, has Professor Graham sent you the result of the post-mortem for the Coroners file."

Cath chuckled

"Yes, got it in despatch yesterday. Multiple traumatic injuries each of which would be fatal was the Pathologists verdict. Personally, I think being run over by a 32-tonne wagon would have sufficed seeing as there was just about enough to put him in a bin liner. The size of his coffin was never going to be an issue."

"How's the driver?"

"Don't think he will be driving wagons again in the near future. When I interviewed him last week, he couldn't even light a cigarette."

"What's left to do on the file?"

"Statement from Pathologist, and Accident Investigator, CPS file can then go in, there's not enough for a reckless but he was breaking the weight restriction taking a shortcut. I've left it to CPS and Traffic to sort out motoring charges as I was never any good unless it was a bald tyre or a duff tax disc. None of the Traynors will make a statement. Ron told me in no uncertain terms that it's part of their family 'Honour' to not assist the police in anything, even apparently the death of their own son."

Cath didn't like holding things back from Holly. She certainly could not tell him Karen Traynor had told her something had gone off in the house before the accident involving a man in a brown suit and a couple of heavies, without a lot of questions that she was unsure that she wanted to answer.

"My honest opinion is it's not going anywhere; there's two witnesses say he just cycled in front of the wagon and there was nothing the driver could do. Coroner's file can go in at the same time, so I've just got a covering report to do really."

"How long do you reckon?"

"About two weeks is normal for the Accident Investigators report so it will be done by the end of the month. That should be fine as the Coroner's not pushing for anything yet."

They had now turned left at the top of the stairs, walked past the gent's toilets, and then left again into the CID office. Holly walked through to his office and Cath went over to the corner desk facing the door, pulled out her chair and sat down. As she did so Holly's voice boomed out from the office behind her.

"Brew would be nice!"

Cath sighed, stood up and made her way to the kitchen upstairs shouting back as she did so.

"That will be two teas and 'four coffees' if you ask me again this morning Sarge."

"I'll not ask again then, in fact, I'll make the next one" bargained Holly.

An hour later both had caught up with the daily urgent computer and telephone enquiries. Holly came out of his office and sat opposite Cath.

"You caught up?"

"Yes, there's a pile of overtime and expenses here for you to sign off and then I've just got Little Shit's burglary 'mark off' to finish. Other than that, I've still got a statement to do for Excy's Coroner's file for Paul Trueman."

"Where's Excy on that one anyway, it should just be a couple of statements and pathologist's report isn't it?" asked Holly.

"Well, there might be a bit more to it actually," Cath replied with a broad grin.

"Bloody typical! I'm still a bit pissed off we won that one, he only fell over on us, and he died on South Yorkshire in the hospital. The fact that he was some bloody member of a secret society Lodge in Bakewell that the Divisional Commander is in shouldn't come into it," Holly suddenly angrily exclaimed.

The outburst was so unexpected to Cath that she was temporarily speechless. In the four years she had worked with Holly she couldn't remember him getting angry about anything. He was generally calmness personified. Cath tried to calm him down.

"I agree that the fact that he was a mate of our Divisional Commander shouldn't come into it Sarge, but you know the politics of these things. I'm sure it will level out next time we want something back off the Chief Superintendent he knows he owes us one."

Holly went from anger to calmness in an instant.

"What's the hiccup in the case?" asked Holly.

"There isn't one really Holly. Excy says it's done apart from some statements that need picking up from the Northern General Hospital. However, knowing Excy and his love life, I reckon he will spin it out a bit now that Councillor Trueman's daughter has turned up. We bumped into her up Brampton last Friday."

"He hasn't mentioned anything to me," mused Holly.

"Knew you would take the piss probably, I think she took a shine to our Excy, she was all over him at the end of the night."

"Bloody hell that's all we need! I hope it's not going to be another broken heart when she goes back to wherever she was from. I still have recollections of him moping around like a lovelorn schoolboy after that holiday romance he had with that woman from Leeds last year who turned out to be married" laughed Holly.

Cath continued with the story.

"I would have loved to have seen his face when he turned up at her house with a bunch of flowers only for it to be opened by 6-foot 4inch oil rig worker back home for a few weeks."

Holly joined in with her laughter.

"I would have loved to have seen the husband's face as he stood there with a bunch of flowers that Excy had shoved in his mitt and watching a smartly dressed bloke legging it down the road. I'm not sure who would have had the most explaining to do, him or his missus!"

After a few seconds Cath realised that she was laughing at the reminiscence on her own and looked across at Holly. He was back in his deep thought place again.

"Are you sure you're alright Holly?"

His expression didn't change, and he appeared to have not heard her. Then he suddenly jolted awake and brought the conversation back to work.

"If you've not got much on this morning, shall we have a run out to Buxton. We could call into the incident room, pick up an Action or two and we might get co-opted onto the murder for a few weeks I could do with a couple of weeks overtime in March's pay-packet. The missus wants a new kitchen and I've got a horse to pay for."

"A horse! You never mentioned a horse before! When did you get that?"

"Donna bought it for Georgia for Christmas. Well, I suppose I did as she doesn't work. It's stabled down at Two Dales and needs new shoes already. But it will keep Georgia happy she's been horse riding a couple of months now and been hankering after a horse of her own."

"Bloody hell Holly! You're going to need a promotion or two at this rate. If I were going to give anybody in your family an expensive Christmas present it would be a divorce for your Donna. She will always spend whatever you earn and more. You know the more you give, the more she will take, so you might as well give her half your pension now as all of it later."

Cath realised she had gone too far by the sad look that came across Holly's face, so she changed the subject.

"Is Donna still battling with Georgia?"

"Yeah, it's like a war zone every time I enter the house, a hormonal teenager and an angry woman. It's not a good mix," Holly sighed.

"I presume you told her no to the kitchen by the plaster on your head?"

"No, that was a flying plate when I told her we couldn't afford to buy new shoes for the horse."

Holly's face fell to sadness again and he went again to his faraway place.

Cath decided to give up on talking about Holly's home life. She was going to be with him all day and didn't want to spend it looking at him being sullen and miserable as well as silent.

"Tell you what Holly. I'll have a run out, but let's avoid the murder enquiry. If BJ is running it, the only Actions we will get will be Trace, Identify and Eliminate red car seen on A6 sometime in last week or search all drains within a five mile vicinity for unknown weapons. I don't fancy either of those, so, let's have a run out to the Northern General and pick up those statements, then on the way back get lunch from the Pudding

Shop in Bakewell, and see if Excy is in the office. We could grab a cuppa with him and see if he wants a chuck with anything that's currently in his 'In' tray until he gets back. What do you think?"

"You're driving detective," instructed Holly a smile brightening up his face.

Cath gathered up her bag off the back of her chair and the keys off her desk.

"Come on, let's get off then Sarge. I'm getting hungry and a bit of sport later, with Excy over his new girlfriend, will cheer us both up."

Chapter 17 – The Murder Team Arrives

Tuesday 14th January

By 8.30 a.m. Bill had got back at the scene with the morning shifts from Ashbourne and Bakewell, two officers from each station. The two from Bakewell, PC Graham Walker and PC Keith Billings, Dave knew well. The two from Ashbourne Dave had seen a few times but he had not worked with them before.

Bill put the Bakewell officers doing vehicle checks Northbound and the two Ashbourne officers doing vehicle checks southbound. The rationale was to get some idea of who was travelling along the A6 and whether they may have been around earlier in the day or the previous evening. All the information would be inputted into the HOLMES Major Incident System later, and hopefully, identify suspects as well as generate "Actions" to develop lines of enquiry or compile evidence towards prosecution of the case.

Information from the "Golden Hour" was often the most important, and both Bill and Dave were aware what was done in the early hours of an incident could be vital in its later stages. The imminent arrival of 'Big John' Dicks was also a factor in ensuring that things were done efficiently and expeditiously as far as Dave was concerned. To say that he was not BJ's favourite detective would be an understatement.

Bill offered Dave a coffee from the flask and then a Marlborough. Dave accepted both.

"I'll pack up again tomorrow!" Dave joked as Bill lit the cigarette.

"Bod says the DCC paid you a visit, while I was away." Bill drew on his cigarette.

"Yeah, was on his way to work, and thought he'd just check we had got everything covered."

"Must have been disappointed then!" Bill joked.

"Only that Bod didn't give him a coffee, other than that clean bill of health" Dave retorted back to Bill.

"That's a relief, last thing you want is him turning up and bollocking everyone all morning." Bill blew out lungful's of smoke.

"I know…he was alright though. BJ is on his way to take charge, so I'll be back at Matlock in a couple of hours. He'll have you and your lads running round like blue arsed flies though for the next couple of days,"

Dave stamped his cold feet on the snowy ground.

"I'll look forward to that and the done nowt know-alls he will be bringing with him. He's not forgiven you yet then?" Bill asked.

"Is a cod's head wet? He thinks what I did was to embarrass him on purpose, which is the opposite of what I intended. I had to tell someone and didn't know that he was on duty, so I told the Chief Super. BJ made a big issue about it and then blamed me for everyone finding out,"

"I'm your friend Excy and known you since you started. I can tell you I wouldn't have been happy if someone had gone over my head like that. It was either inexperience or ruthlessness. Knowing you as I do, I would put it down to inexperience. You will learn from it. My advice for what it's worth is put up with the grief for a while, it will pass. BJ will be promoted to Chief Superintendent soon and he's being fast tracked to ACPO so get on his good side. Hanging on to his coat tails would be a good career move."

"Thanks Bill, I always appreciate your advice. I'll keep my head down for a while and hope it blows over."

"It will. BJ will do whatever it takes for an ACPO post and bearing grudges against your staff is not a good look for a senior officer. Being nasty to them all is fine, but just to one is severely frowned upon."

"Understood Bill, but I don't think BJ is ready to bury the hatchet just yet. I'm pretty sure I will be back on section CID later this morning, which I don't mind as I have got more than enough work anyway."

"Speak of the devil and all that."

Bill looked down the car park towards the main road.

A lime green Mercedes saloon pulled onto the car park. Following in convoy was an assortment of other vehicles. The vehicles parked up in a line at the side of the green Mercedes and out of each stepped two suited or skirted detectives. Superintendent Dicks waited until all the Detectives had parked up and gathered around his car before he got out of it.

Dicks was unmissable. Six foot four and seventeen stone. He had the appearance of, and had been, a rugby forward. This vision was embedded through his large cauliflower ears and crooked nose as well as the large scar on his forehead that he had told everyone was the result of a collision with another player. The opposing player in the tale, he joked, had spent a week in hospital as a result, whilst Dicks had continued playing with a blood soaked bandage and had led his team to victory.

Dave saw Dicks break into a smile, and set off walking towards him, with the crowd of detectives in tow. He stopped a few feet in front of Dave, legs apart and arms folded.

"Right then, top teams arrived so you can stand down now. Anything I need to know other than what's on the incident?"

"I wouldn't have thought so, think it's up to date boss," Dave reassured him.

"Sir, if you don't mind detective!" Superintendent Dicks loudly reminded him for his audiences benefit.

"I wouldn't have thought so…. sir!" Dave emphasised the 'sir.'

"Good let's get started then. Turning to the cohort of detectives behind him Supt Dicks addressed them.

"Right then, let's show the locals how Murder Team detectives do it. I want this wrapped up quickly lads… and ladies. There's a dead woman wanting some justice, and we are going to give it her aren't we!"

Looking round at the audience in front of him he received the acknowledgement he was looking for.

"First job is house to house in a one mile area and then we will meet up at the incident room being set up at Buxton for a briefing at 12 a.m. I'm going to have a look at the body so let's get on it gentlemen… and ladies."

Bill looked at Dave and correctly read what he was thinking. House to house within a mile radius wouldn't take long as there were only a couple of farmhouses, and it was doubtful whether without some local knowledge they would be able to find them.

Dave turned to Detective Superintendent Dicks.

"Shall I get off then…sir… now you have everything in hand?"

"No, you're on exhibits until Saturday when Jack Bainbridge gets back from his holidays."

Dave felt his heart sink. The role was the most unpopular one on any murder incident team, especially in the first few days when thousands of exhibits would need checking, re-bagging, identifying, inputting, and storing. He would also be liaising with all the CSI's, the pathologist, and the rest of the detectives on the murder team.

Dave took a deep breath.

"No problem … sir, I'll get on it straight away."

"Good. It's only for four days. I'm sure you can keep out of trouble in that brief period of time detective."

Dicks turned and walked away down the car park with the other detectives. Dave had identified at least two other trained exhibits officers amongst the other detectives as they had been on the same HOLMES Exhibit Officer course as he had. Dave sighed resignedly, Dicks was just yanking his chain, but he would follow Bill's advice. It was only four days, it would be an exceedingly long four days, and a lot could happen in four days especially on a murder enquiry.

Dave turned to Bill and with a wry grin quipped

"Sucking it up Bill. Sucking it up."

"It's for the best Excy. Where you setting up?"

"Bakewell I think. In the old CID office if that's alright?"

"It's alright by me. It will be good to have some company, the place is like a mausoleum since they moved everyone out."

"Right, I'll get off then before he makes me family liaison as well. Can you tell the CSI's where to drop any exhibits off when they turn up, and I'll make a start with Curly and Stans clothing back at the police station. See you back at the nick later."

Dave gave Bill a friendly nod and walked to his car, put his fluorescent jacket back in the boot and drove away towards Bakewell.

Two hours later Dave was just finishing his third cup of coffee of the day in the old CID office on the first floor of Bakewell Police Station. At one time each of the three police stations on the sub division had a CID office with at least a DS and two DCS but under efficiency reorganisations that had been reduced to two DCS and a DS at just Matlock but covering the other two stations at Ashbourne and Bakewell.

Luckily, the IT systems had been retained at each station and he had been able to log into the Holmes Major Incident system at Bakewell without having to have a desk in the incident room at Buxton. If BJ wanted him up at Buxton, he would go, but not until that order came. The last thing he wanted was being under the nose of Superintendent Dicks all day and his vengeful tongue.

He found a key in one of the empty desks in the CID office to the walk-in stationery store in its corner. The key had unlocked it, and Dave was satisfied that the store would be big and secure enough for an exhibits store.

He had then inputted the clothing and footwear seized from Curly and Stan Moore into the HOLMES system and secured them in his new exhibits store. He would put his in tomorrow when he had bought another pair he decided.

Dave, up to date with exhibits from the scene, realised that he had not eaten anything that morning; it was time for a late breakfast bacon sandwich, before the deluge of exhibits from the CSI's at the scene came into him for logging later that afternoon.

It was on his way back, white paper bag in hand containing the foil wrapped sandwich, that he remembered that Dicks was holding a briefing at Buxton at midday for the incident team. Dave checked his watch it was nine miles away and he had ten minutes to get there. He walked quickly to his black BMW A3 parked outside the police station, got in, threw his sandwich onto the passenger seat, and set off with a squeal of wheels, for the briefing.

Fifteen minutes later Dave slowly opened the door and crept into the briefing room. He found an empty seat by the door, and sat in it. As he sat down the door closed behind him with a loud click.

"Good of you to join us officer!" Supt Dicks voice boomed towards him.

"I hope we haven't interrupted your milking or some sheep shearing with our briefing DC Baker?"

Laughter echoed round him as everyone turned round and joined in the joke. Dave could feel the colour rising in his face.

"Sorry I'm late…sir.."

"Don't sit down! Stand up and tell us where the exhibits store is and where we can find you," Dicks continued.

Dave feeling very embarrassed, stood up and took a deep breath

"The Exhibits Officer and Exhibits Store is on the first floor of Bakewell Police Station."

Dave sat down.

"Thank you, officer, it's probably better you're on your own down there as you're not much of a team player I hear. Now for those of us who could be bothered to turn up on time, the post-mortem is scheduled for 9 p.m. tonight at Chesterfield Royal… try not to be late for it will you DC Baker. I've been to the scene and although I will not pre-empt the findings of the post-mortem, the victim has obviously been stabbed to death, so this is now a murder enquiry. John do you want to brief everyone on what we have found out so far?"

John Casey a Detective Inspector on the Murder Team that Dave recognised from the Allestree murder earlier in the year stood up.

"The victim we think is…may be…Alice Bulman, white female, twenty four years old, trainee accountant at Wildgoose Accountants, Bath Street in Bakewell. She lives on Buxton Road, Bakewell in a two-bed flat above a Greengrocers. Single according to her work colleague Beryl Smith but had a boyfriend she's just finished with from Derby. Beryl Smith rang the police this morning reporting Alice missing when she failed to turn up for work and then didn't answer her door when she went round to her flat to find out why. Alice Bulman fits the description of our victim, but we have no positive ID yet. We've contacted Alice's, parents who live in Stoke, and they are being brought up to identify her. once the body is released from the scene later this afternoon. We have a warrant for her flat and are going with the CSI teams soon as the briefings over. Boyfriend is suspect A. Two teams led by DS Annie Patel are going to grab him from work this afternoon, I want him in or out as a suspect Annie before he sees a solicitor, so you know what to do, no custody till he has coughed it!"

"No problem sir." Annie replied to laughter from the rest of the detectives in the briefing room.

"Everyone else this afternoon and this evening is house to house where she lives, someone must have seen something so let's get this one cleared up quickly."

Supt Dicks took over "Thank you John. If it's not the jilted boyfriend it will be someone else that she's dumped. She's a bit of a party girl so I want boyfriends, lovers, and anyone she's slept with in the last twelve months Traced, Identified,

Eliminated. Together with any locals who might have taken a crush on her since she landed out here in the sticks. Right pick up your Actions from Tina unless you're on the search. Debrief here at seven tonight."

The briefing room emptied, and Dave stood up to leave. DS Annie Patel came up to him and to Dave's surprise stopped in front of him.

"You shouldn't have dropped Dicks in it like that, he's not a bad boss but it's difficult to get on the right side of him when you have undermined him. Rumour is he's off the Murder Team soon and being made up to Chief Super so my advice would be make it up to him and get on his right side or wait it out till he's gone."

Dave sighed, he had only a few hours earlier had similar advice from Bill Fry.

"Thanks for the advice Sarge, but I'm away from here on Saturday so I will brave it out till then, and then I will hope I don't bump into him on another incident for the rest of my career."

Annie Patel shrugged.

"Probably not the best plan as you will definitely bump into him again. He is odds on favourite to be ACPO in a couple of years and Chief in four according to the Headquarters bookmakers. So good luck in avoiding him."

An Accidental Death

"Thanks for the heads up Sarge, I will bear it in mind," Dave replied and the two of them made their separate ways to the door.

Chapter 18 – Help From Friends

Monday 13th January

Back at Bakewell after coming back from the briefing at Buxton, Dave made himself another coffee, put his bacon sandwich in the microwave and then took both up to the CID office. He took a bite of his sandwich followed by a sip of his coffee, and relaxed back in his chair. The afternoon was going to be hectic, and he needed to get food, drink, and some downtime when he could. In a few hours CSI would be back and booking in any non-scientific stuff they had seized at the scene. The murder team would be handing him anything they had picked up from that day's enquiries and searches. Then he would have to get off to the post-mortem at the mortuary at Chesterfield Royal Hospital. That would keep him busy till the early hours of the morning. He would get out of the briefing tonight because of having to attend the post-mortem. But he would have to make the next briefing around eight in the morning and then there would be more exhibits to book in. With a bit of luck, he might get a couple of hour's shut eye tomorrow afternoon, just a thirty six hour shift then, he smiled to himself.

Dave's thoughts then turned to his home life. He had also better let Helen know he wasn't seeing her tonight or tomorrow. She would be going home at the weekend, and he needed to tell her that he loved her and that he wanted them to continue being a couple after she went back. He also needed to get some time off work at the weekend, one way or another. That was vital he thought if he was going to spend enough time with Helen to get their relationship sorted.

The front door of the police station downstairs opened, and he heard two sets of shoes clattering up the stairs. Dave's heart sank. Just what he needed more exhibits and he waited for the door to open and a pair of Murder Team detectives to walk in. The door flew open, and into the office walked Holly and Cath.

"You two are a sight for sore eyes!"

"Thought you might need some company," Holly explained and sat down heavily in the opposite desk to him.

Cath pulled up a chair and sat angled to him on the corner of the desk.

"Pack in with the caring attitude, I know you've just had a ride out for a sandwich or to find out about the body up at White Lodge....in view of the Pudding Shop bags I'll go for the former."

"You're not a detective for nothing are you!" Holly laughed as he bit into the ham salad cob.

"We have also picked up your statements from the Northern General so a thank-you wouldn't go amiss,"

Holly tossed a buff folder across the desk. Dave opened the folder and glanced at its contents.

"Thanks, Sarge, appreciated,"

"No problem at all Excy, me and Cath fancied a run out this morning anyway. So, what's the crack with the body? I see BJ is running it, so I presume you're back with us after today?"

Holly brushed the breadcrumbs he had dropped onto his brown plaid jacket and black corded trousers, with the back of his hand.

"No such luck, he's dropped me for exhibits till Saturday morning."

"Serves you right Tomcat, you shouldn't have dropped him in it on that last murder!" taunted Cath mischievously.

"Less of the Tomcat, and I didn't drop him in it, as you well know, he dropped himself. Not searching the victim's house was hardly my fault"

"Anyway Tomcat, where were you last night? Grapevine says it didn't take you long to get to the scene this morning!"

"Bloody hell, who needs 5G when we've got the Dales gossip brigade!"

Dave looked seriously back at Cath, checking whether she was fishing or actually knew where he was when he had been called out.

"So, you have cracked off with that daughter of Councillor Trueman then! What's she like… in the sack?" Cath laughed continuing to tease him.

Dave coloured up as she knew he would and through his obvious embarrassment muttered

"Never you mind, I'm saying nothing other than she's very nice."

"I'd second that, she's a right catch! Any chance she's gay only I'm single and available if she is?"

Cath was now enjoying Dave's embarrassment.

Dave, still unsure what Cath actually knew about himself and Helen, decided to take a defensive approach to her teasing

"She's not your type Cath, she's not a one-night stand slapper. I'm taking her out again at the weekend if you must know."

Cath knew 'the slapper' jibe was aimed at her and also went into defensive mode.

"Bill says you got up to White Lodge in less than an hour this morning."

"Doesn't take me long to have a shower and shave and get going in a morning Cath."

This time Cath knew Dave was aiming a jibe at her drinking.

It was Cath's turn to redden angrily.

"You carry your superman shower and shaving kit everywhere with you then. Seeing as Bill saw your car parked up at Trueman's house. Divisional Commanders asked section to keep an eye on it since he died. So, you've been ratted out Mr Tomcat."

Holly saw that things had gone from gentle teasing to friction between the two detectives and intervened.

"You two pack it in, you only get your chance when she dumps him Cath, till then she's Excy's squeeze, just don't get to marrying her Excy before you've seen her mother, they all grow into them in my experience. Can we get round to the body…? and not that of Trueman's daughter…. Is it definitely a murder?"

"I reckon so, naked young woman in the middle of nowhere with what appeared to be two stab wounds in her chest so yes, I reckon so. I'm going to the post-mortem later today, so I'll be the first to know"

Cath smiled at him and playfully flicked a paper spit-ball at him; it hit him just below the eye. Dave picked up a pencil rubber from his desk and threw it hard at Cath hitting her on the back of her head as she turned away.

Holly decided to stop the childish behaviour before one of them went too far …. Again.

"Right let's have a brew and sort out what we can do to help out till you're back on Friday Excy," He stated forcefully at them both.

Dave thankful for the escape route from Cath's teasing stood up and disappeared down the back stairs to the kitchen, returning a few minutes later with three fresh cups of tea.

"Right Excy what you got on ……. that can't wait till Friday?" asked Holly taking a sip of his lukewarm milky tea.

"I've got a burglary, the one at the stone centre at Middleton, it will be local, but I've not done anything on it yet. I've got the affray from Christmas Eve at the back of the Hurst Farm Club as well. There are six suspects, and all are answering bail tomorrow morning but there's nothing back from CPS on a charging decision so they will need re-bailing. The file has been done for the assault on the doorman outside The Crown at Matlock on New Year's Eve. The offenders just need charging with assault and affray when they also come back on bail at Buxton tomorrow and the file can go in. That's about it on the urgent front."

"I'll sort all those out for you. Are the files on your desk?" Cath asked amicably, with a smile to Dave, signalling to him that her teasing was now over.

"Thanks Cath" Dave thanked her and decided to reciprocate.

"Do you want me to get some historic background on Paul Trueman for the Coroner from his daughter? She's called Helen Hall by the way…she's told me she only met him once…she says, her mum knew him better."

Cath and Holly guffawed loudly at the faux pas and Dave realising the humour of what he had just said started to laugh as well.

"Bet you got more than some historic background from her last night!" Cath playfully teased Dave.

"I'm strictly a foreground man Cath!" Dave replied with a laugh this time.

Holly finished his sandwich and then continued his conversation with Dave in his supervisor role.

"Alright Excy get what you can for the coroner when you next see her, it can't do any harm."

"I won't get anything till the weekend though Cath,"

"Neither will I." Cath gave him an exaggerated wink.

Cath and Holly stood up to leave and Dave realised the visit was over.

"Thanks, you two, I'll keep you updated on the murder and hopefully see you Saturday, if all goes to plan."

Cath picked up the three empty mugs.

"Right then, we're off! I'll wash up Excy."

Holly following Cath out of the door added

"We'll get out of here and give you the chance to catch forty winks, Excy. It's going to be a long day. Any problems give me or Cath a bell."

Dave smiled. He knew they were a good team, and it was good that they had each-others backs

"Will do, and thanks for calling in. It has been good to see some friendly faces."

Dave listened to them going downstairs and into the kitchen with the mugs and then went back to his chair and rested his head on his arms across the desk. He was asleep before the front door of the police station closed behind his colleagues.

Chapter 19 – "It's Not Going To Be Her"

Tuesday 14th January

Dave stood outside the trolley battered fire doors of the mortuary at Chesterfield Royal Hospital. The small parking area below the ramp was empty of cars, other than his and Billy's moped, as was the access lane that led from the circular road of the sprawling site. Night had fallen some four hours before and the temperature had fallen with it. With the darkness had come an exodus of staff and day patients from the hospital. It was cold; the snow flurries from the previous night were now starting to freeze into a hard carpet on the grass, where they had been shaded from the sun by the hospital buildings.

The cold vapour of his breath reminded Dave that he had been at work from seven that morning when he had been called out to White Lodge. He knew it would be many hours before he would slip into bed and catch up on some much needed sleep. His mind went back to the previous night and the warmth of Helen's body. He closed his eyes remembering the smell of her hair, her perfume; the way she took control of the sex, tutoring him in how to bring her to climax before sitting on him and bringing him to climax as well. The way that she snuggled into the crook of his arm before falling asleep, motionless other than for her rhythmical breathing. He had laid there awake, with her warmth until a contented sleep had taken him.... until the ringing of his mobile phone had woken him.

He wanted to be back there now; with Helen asleep in the crook of his arm and her shallow breath taking away the stress of his job. He could feel the stress now rising within him. He didn't like post-mortems. He disliked the smell and taste of formaldehyde that clung to his throat and every fibre of his clothes and hair, so that every breath he took for the following couple of days reminded him of where he had been. He disliked the sight of people's bodies being cut and dissected like meat on a butcher's slab, but most of all he hated the sounds of the mortuary, or rather the silence and then the crescendo of bone saw and then the silence again. It was that silence, the noise, and then the silence that Dave knew he hated the most.

He was woken from his thoughts by the sound of footsteps behind him. Dave turned and saw the friendly face of Billy Mercer the mortuary assistant.

"I've done my best, but I can't take her out the bag. There's enough of her face to ID her though. Whose coming to identify her?"

Dave paused a moment trying to recall through his tiredness "Her dad I'm told, at least the Family Liaison team will be with him, and I won't have to do the ID, I hate doing that."

An Accidental Death

Like most police officers Dave hated having to be the one that knocks on the door to pass on the news that a loved one has died. Even worse was to actually show them a cadaver and get them to identify it as their loved one, especially if it was a young son or daughter. The reaction of the mother or father was something that you never, ever, forgot.

Both men fell silent, Billy had been in that position many times himself and knew what Dave was feeling. Billy eventually broke the silence.

"Want a coffee?"

"Yes please Billy, I'm falling asleep here," confessed Dave and exhaled a frosty cloud of breath as he tried to rid his body of the tiredness into the night.

At that moment, he saw a silver Toyota saloon driving along the road that circled the hospital. Dave followed it under the road lights as it indicated to no-one and then turned left into the mortuary access road and came to a halt in a parking space at the bottom of the ramp. A male and female got out.

Dave recognised them as two of the detectives who he had seen earlier in the day at the briefing. The female detective opened the rear nearside door and a man got out. He was a tall, large, bald man, about fifty years old, and weighed around twenty stone. The bright external security light reflected off his shaved balding head as he stood up and turned to face the mortuary. The female detective took his arm and led him falteringly to the bottom of the stairs and then towards the

208 | P a g e

wheelchair ramp. His large head was bowed and his step reluctant and shuffling. The male detective took his other arm in support and helped him to the bottom of the ramp where the female detective looked up at Dave and explained.

"This is DC Baker he will be doing the identification. If you go with him now, we will wait here for you and take you home afterwards. DC Baker he's all yours now."

Dave stood there shocked, for what seemed an eternity to him, as he tried to rationalise what the two detectives had just dumped on him. Then his brain and professionalism kicked in and he walked down the ramp to the man and took his left arm. He introduced himself as he led Mr Bulman up the ramp and through the doors to the mortuary. Dave looked back as they went through the doors to see the female detective give him a sympathetic shrug and the male detective lighting a cigarette and trying to avoid any eye contact with him.

"If you just sign here and here, thank you Mr Bulman." Dave took the pen from the trembling man's hand.

"Ready?"

The man nodded and slowly stood up from the white plastic chair in the mortuary corridor. Dave took Mr Bulman slowly along the corridor, holding onto his elbow. The previous tall and well-built man seemed now bent and harrowed. His breath kept catching in his throat, his sobbing was like incessant hiccups as Dave led him back through the exit doors and to the ramp. The two detectives stood at the bottom of the ramp and Dave walked him down to them.

"Mr Bulman has identified his daughter Alice as the deceased. Can you look after him now? Thank you officers."

"Thank you DC Baker"

The male detective nodded, and the female detective mouthed "Sorry" towards him. She then turned to Mr Bulman

"I'm so sorry Mr Bulman, let's get you home."

The rear red lights of the Toyota shone brightly against the wet tarmac road and snow-covered grass, before flickering as it met the circular road and then drove out of sight.

Billy again joined Dave on the top of the ramp.

"It's Alice Bulman then. Do you want that coffee now…. and a cigarette before we start, the Prof has just rung he won't be here for another half an hour."

Dave paused tasting the formaldehyde mixed with the day's stale coffee around his mouth and then remembered that it could be a long night and the caffeine might come in helpful.

"Yes. Thanks Billy, milk no sugar if that's alright?"

A couple of minutes later Billy came back with the coffees. He handed one to Dave and then offered him a cigarette which Dave took and put in his mouth. Billy lit it. Dave stood at the top of the ramp staring into the night and taking the occasional drag on the cigarette and then a gulp of coffee. He was deep in thought reliving the previous twenty minutes of his life. Twenty minutes he knew he would never forget.

The black bag containing Alice's body had been laid out in the viewing room, an ante room in the morgue with a soft upright chair and small occasional table with a cheap white vase and some plastic forget-me nots in it. Its straps had been undone and tucked under the bag. The heavy black fabric had been unzipped about a foot and framed the pale dead face of Alice.

Dave had walked into the room with Mr Bulman holding tightly onto his elbow; the fear of the man was palpable.

As they had entered the room, he had looked up at Dave with eyes that were red and rheumy with grief and fear.

"It's not going to be her you know. She's gone to a friends and lost her phone…." and then the need for comfort for his thoughts.

"Do you think that's possible Officer? It might not be her…do you think?"

Dave had just nodded. In that moment he knew he wanted Alice Bulman to be sat watching TV in a friends front room, her broken phone on the floor at the side of her, laughing at something funny with her auburn hair, green eyes and freckled face lit up in happiness. That Mr Bulman would take one look at the face in the bag and shake his head, his bent body would straighten, and the grief stricken eyes would clear. Dave knew in his heart that this would not happen. It was Alice in the body bag, and they had just reached it.

Dave indicated with his head for him to look away from him to the face in the bag. Mr Bulman let go of Dave's elbow and grabbed his hand, squeezed his fingers tight and then made himself look. He took a glance at the face in the bag and turned back to look at him. The face was expressionless and his eyes vacant. There was nothing there, no emotion just nothingness.

Dave waited feeling his own sadness in empathy for this poor man. Then it came, the moment of realisation in Mr Bulman's eyes. Dave saw Mr Bulman's heart break in them. His legs gave way and the man fell heavily to his knees. A cry of pain started in Mr Bulman's throat and then gained momentum through his now broken spirit and body. Tears flowed relentlessly from his tightly closed eyes onto the shiny white tiled floor.

Dave smelt the mud on Alice's hair.

Mr Bulman's grip on his hand weakened and he began to fall forward to the floor. Dave clasped his shoulder to keep him upright on his knees, feeling the weight of his body and grief transfer to him. Mr Bulman just kept repeating his daughter's name

"Alice… my Alice….my Alice."

Dave took another drag on the cigarette and a swallow of the now cool coffee. A tear ran down his cheek for the grief of the man whose would never, ever, stop.

An Accidental Death

Dave had helped him to his feet and then the nearby plastic chair. He had written out the short one paragraph statement at the side of the forget-me-nots, checked the date and time were correct and then got Mr Bulman to sign it. Professional to the end.

Chapter 20 – The Cause Of Death

Tuesday 14th January

Billy Morton stubbed out his thirtieth Marlboro of the day under the sole of his white rubber boot and the movement brought Dave back to the cold dark night. Dave stubbed out his second Marlboro of the day, under his black brogue shoe.

Dave turned to him.

"Thanks Billy I needed that, time to get the show on the road."

"Yeah, no problem, you know where the changing room is don't you?"

"I should do by now."

Dave walked down the corridor and took the second door on the left into a small changing room. The room was about twelve feet square, with a line of hooks on opposing walls to hang clothes on. All around the spotless bleached green tiles reflected the ceiling fluorescent lights. It was this room that opened out into the mortuary from which the smell of formaldehyde grew stronger. Dave checked that he had his menthol rub and smeared some on his nostrils, immediately negating the chemical smell. He then checked that he had his mints to clear the taste from his mouth over the next few hours.

Dave undressed and put on the blue coverall fibre forensic suit, taking care not to rip it as he put his arms into the sleeves and over his shoulders. He then picked out a pair of white rubber boots from the line under the bench that looked about his size. They were a size too big but would be comfortable enough for him to walk the short distances required for the following three or four hours. Fully suited and booted Dave picked up his exhibit case and walked into the mortuary.

The mortuary was a large, fully tiled, windowless square room. The three body trays, on which post-mortems were performed, were lined up centrally to enable a pathologist 360-degree access. To his left was a bench area with scales, plastic containers and an assortment of knives and electrical equipment. Above the bench was a large window that allowed observers to view what was happening in the mortuary without having to be inside.

Dave took out an array of different sized plastic exhibit bags, plastic containers, paper exhibit labels, brown windowed paper bags and two black Biro pens. He arranged them precisely in a line on the body tray, furthest from the one on which the body bag that Alice was in had been laid by Billy while he was changing.

An Accidental Death

The process would be that the pathologist would take samples and evidence from the body. He would pass them to a CSI who would place them into the correct type of container or bag and pass it to Dave. Dave would then correctly record what the exhibit was, give it a consecutive scene number for the mortuary and a consecutive exhibit number for the person producing it. At the mortuary it tended to be the pathologist and he would be relying on Dave to have got the descriptions and numbers correct for his eventual statement for the Court. Dave looked at the line of bags and labels and went through in his mind if he had forgotten anything. Satisfied that he hadn't, he walked back out through the mortuary and changing room to the small rest area where Billy had just finished making another pot of coffee.

Billy asked, "Another fag?"

"Yes, why not I'll be bumming one off you again, if that's alright?"

"I thought so, but we might as well while we can," laughed Billy.

As they walked towards the fire doors at the ramp, they burst open and two CSI carrying large cooler boxes stumbled through. Dave recognised them straight away as Senior CSI Sally Brooks and CSI Simon Metcalfe.

"Evening Sally, do you need a hand with the boxes?" asked Dave.

"Thanks, Excy, wouldn't mind. I'm not late, am I?"

"No, there's plenty of time, Proffs not even here yet."

"Good, it's been a mare of a day!"

Dave handed his coffee to Billy and took one cool box off Sally Brooks and one-off Simon Metcalfe. He carried the boxes through the main doors of the mortuary and put the cool boxes on the second body tray between Alice and where he had neatly laid out his own bags and labels.

"I'll leave you to get set up. There's a brew in the back and feel free to join us outside when you're ready," Dave suggested to Sally Brooks.

"Thanks, Excy." Simon thanked him on behalf of them both and started to unpack the boxes on the body tray.

Dave re-joined Billy outside, took the proffered cigarette and coffee for the second time, and then both, in silence, drew on their cigarettes and sipped the hot coffee.

After about ten minutes Sally Brooks joined them holding a fresh mug of coffee. She was also suited up with a pair of obviously oversized white rubber boots.

"I wish you'd get some smaller boots Billy, there's enough room in these for another pair of feet and they're the smallest I could find, Simon Metcalfe is waddling about back there like a duck with a broken leg trying to keep his on!"

Billy laughed and quipped to her.

"Cutbacks Miss, it was cheaper to get a job lot of large sizes!"

At that moment, all four looked towards the access road as a green Mercedes came around the red bricked block followed by two more cars and parked up in a line in the reserved parking spots for the mortuary.

"That's all we needed" observed Sally Brooks as Supt Dicks and Insp Casey got out the first car followed by two more detectives from each of the other cars.

"Professor Graham's not going to be impressed, they have parked in his parking spot."

Dicks walked up the ramp and casually remarked to Dave.

"Hope you're all set up detective? We don't want any mistakes on this enquiry."

"Like you last time you mean!" Dave replied under his breath, but unfortunately a little too loud.

"What did you say?" queried Dicks.

"I think he was chelping back at you sir, not very nice to a senior officer," smirked DI Casey who was a few steps behind him.

"What did you say DC Baker?" repeated the Superintendent.

"I said it's getting on in time sir, and Professor Graham's not here yet," Dave lied.

"I bet you did officer." Dicks gave him his false smile.

"Right where can we get changed. I hope you've got some spare suits in your van Sally."

"To the end of the corridor to change sir and I'll get the suits out of the van."

Sally Brooks went off down the ramp to the access road to get some forensic suits and returned with six plastic packs of suits and shoes a few minutes later.

Sally raised her eyebrows as she passed Dave.

"What are all these doing here?"

"No idea"

As she disappeared down the corridor, Billy looked towards the access road.

"Professor Graham's here."

The pathologist's Volvo estate pulled into the access road and stopped momentarily by the three vehicles parked in the reserve parking spots and then drove onto the mortuary ramp.

Professor Graham got out of his car. Dave took one look at his ruddy face and decided to not be the first person to suffer his wrath, so he turned on his heel and shot off to the mortuary to 'check' on his exhibit table. Sally Brooks was already there as Dave started to busy himself shuffling bags and labels, she grimaced and pronounced,

"He's not happy is he?"

An Accidental Death

"He's not happy at all. Have you got a spare box of gloves?"

Sally Brooks went into a cool box and threw him a box of surgical gloves.

"I want the unused ones back!"

A few minutes later six forensically clad detectives entered the mortuary. Sally Brooks and Dave had already staked their positions in the mortuary at the two body trays together with all their equipment. Dave avoided eye contact by writing into the exhibit book the essential forensic items from the body that would be taken, if the exhibits started to come thick and fast.

He tried to recall each one from memory: Plucked hair, cut hair, nail clippings, nail scrapings, stomach contents, blood for DNA, blood, body bag, mouth swab, vaginal swab, anal swab. As he wrote each one down in the exhibit book he was aware of the six detectives gathering around the third body tray with Alice's body bag on it.

Billy walked in and put on a full-face visor that he carried with him. He was closely followed by Professor Graham who marched in nodded at Dave and Sally Brooks and then approached Superintendent Dicks and the detectives gathered around the third body tray.

"And what are you six doing in here?" he growled at the group.

Superintendent Dicks turned towards Professor Graham.

"We've come to observe the PM."

Professor Graham pushed past him.

"That's fine. Please go to the observing area of my mortuary on the other side of the glass window and observe from there, off you go then, quick some of us have got work to do,"

Professor Graham ushered the detectives out through the main doors and towards the viewing area. A few seconds later he came back into the mortuary nodded in turn towards the expectant CSI's, Dave, and Billy, and stated to himself.

"Now we have got the sightseers out of the way let's get started."

Professor Graham unzipped the bag exposing the bloodied body of Alice. He then walked around the body and directed Simon Metcalfe to take pictures of various wounds, abrasions, and marks. Numerous swabs and samples were taken and handed to Sally Brooks, who then bagged and containered them before handing them to Dave, who labelled them up and recorded them in the exhibit book.

Eventually, after about an hour, Professor Graham got down to the stab wounds in Alice's chest. After they had been cleaned Dave could see there were two clear incisions, both about two inches long. The detectives peered closer on the other side of the glass window. The wounds were measured for width and depth and photographs were taken that showed the damage done to the lungs and arteries that had been severed by the instrument that had caused the wounds.

Superintendent Dicks tapped on the window of the viewing room to gain Professor Graham's attention.

Without looking up Professor Graham shouted

"What?"

Superintendent Dicks came to the double doors, he had recently been ushered out of, and opened them but stayed in the corridor.

"I've got to go, but all I need to know is... has she been sexually assaulted, and has she been stabbed, is it a murder?"

Professor Graham replied without looking up

"There's no evidence she's been sexually assaulted, but you will have to wait on DNA for possible recent sexual activity. As to whether she's been stabbed I can confirm that, but I will need to do more to tell you what sort of knife or implement was used. As to cause of death I'm not sure at the moment."

"So, it's a murder then?"

"Can't say that yet, but you'll get my report soon as I've finished. Leave me your email address if you don't want to wait as we could be here for a couple more hours."

"I'll leave it on your desk," Dicks replied, and as the door shut behind him, everyone in the mortuary heard him say

"The Prof says she's been stabbed so we are up and running. Briefing at nine get some sleep and be ready for a long day in the morning."

As the door closed shut, the detectives disappeared from the glass window and Dave heard the fire doors close loudly behind them as they left the mortuary and returned to their cars.

Professor Graham looked up from his work and turned to those that remained in the mortuary.

"Right then everyone let's take a break, we've been going a couple of hours and I need to get my head around something."

A few minutes later Simon Metcalfe, Sally Brooks and Dave were in the kitchen drinking coffee. Billy was outside having a cigarette. Professor Graham had gone to his office.

"Can't believe BJ turned up with all that crew," observed Simon.

Sally joined in the conversation "I know. There's a rumour going round you're not on his Christmas list Excy."

Dave smiled "You're right on that one but I don't really want to talk about why."

"You don't have to, everyone knows" she laughed. "He forgot to search the victim's home for a week on the Allestree job. You really pissed him off when you went to the house and found blood and money everywhere."

"I thought it had been covered up by the Chief Super," confided Dave.

"Don't be daft, you can't cover up something like that, everyone in the force knew within ten minutes of it coming to light, but no one obviously admits to knowing, especially around BJ or his team who have all taken it as some sort of personal affront."

"Well, they've got it in for me, so I'm going to be happy to be off the investigation by Saturday."

At that moment Professor Graham came back in.

"Right lets go. I've just checked on something and need to have a close look for some particular injuries."

The next half an hour went extremely quickly as Professor Graham incised Alice's chest and neck removing her trachea and then her heart. He took both over to the bench, weighed them and examined them closely. He asked Simon Metcalfe to take photographs at various points whilst Sally Brooks and Dave caught up with labels and catalogued them in the exhibit book.

Eventually he called them over

"I think we have solved the problem."

When he had their attention, he carried on.

"There is no blood in the trachea and if the stab wounds had been inflicted pre-mortem it would have been full as she bled to death from the internal wounds. I would also expect the lungs to have been full of blood but there is only a limited amount. My conclusion is that the wounds were inflicted post-mortem with a six to eight inch straight double-bladed knife similar to a dagger. It would be about an inch or so wide at its widest point going down to a point. It looks like the knife was inserted with considerable force and then pushed forward and backwards in a sawing motion. Both wounds are almost identical so I would say they are intentional and not frenzied. They were done for a purpose, but I do not know why. The problem now is that we do not have a cause of death."

Professor Graham returned to the body examining it closely starting at the toes and working his way up to the head. At the neck he took out his glasses and cleaned an area.

"Ahh, there's some light bruising here, let's have a swab for DNA. Professor Graham then made an incision.

"That's interesting"

He called over Simon Metcalfe to take a photograph.

"There's some tissue crush and infiltrating haemorrhages here on the Vagus nerve."

Forty five minutes later Professor Graham was signing exhibit labels at Dave's body tray. Dave was helping Simon Metcalfe and Sally Brooks to pack their cool boxes. Billy was stitching up Alice. Professor Graham announced to no-one in particular.

"I'm pretty sure death was caused by vagal inhibition."

"What's that?" asked Sally.

"The Vagus nerve has an important task in regulating blood pressure and when over stimulated, for example by strangulation type pressure, the brain can interpret it as extremely high blood pressure and stop the heart beating almost instantaneously, causing death."

"So, was she strangled to death?" questioned Dave.

"Basically yes, somebody strangling her caused her to die"

"It is a murder then," observed Dave.

"Well that's for the police to determine. All I can say is that an outside force caused her death. I'll e-mail superintendent Dicks and tell him."

Professor Graham then finished signing the labels and went out of the mortuary.

"Not bad, 3 a.m." noted Sally Brooks looking at her watch.

"I'm ready for bed. My beds calling, and I've got to book all this lot in." yawned Dave

"Well, me and Simon are off once we have packed up. I'll see you tomorrow. We're back on at 11 a.m. where will you be?" Sally asked Dave.

"Old CID office at Bakewell, where are you taking the forensic exhibits, I'll need to book them in on the system?"

"Freezer store in our office at Chesterfield."

"Thanks Sally have a couple of hours sleep for me will you!" joked Dave.

It was 6 a.m. in the morning when Dave, back at Bakewell, had booked all the exhibits into the HOLMES system and secured them in the stationery cupboard. Eventually, with a sigh, he rested his head onto his crossed arms on the desk and despite the images of Alice rebounding around his mind and the strong smell of formaldehyde emanating from his suit, he fell fitfully asleep at his desk for an hour.

Chapter 21 – Mrs Burton's Missing Husband

Tuesday 14th January

Cath and Holly had been back at Matlock about an hour after their visit to see Dave at Bakewell, when Comms rang Holly. A Mrs Margaret Burton was reporting a missing person. Her husband had not returned home the previous night and failed to go into work that morning. Mrs Burton would not be available until later that evening. Holly, after taking the call, asked Cath if she would take the report as he had to go home on time to sort out a problem.

It was just after 8 p.m. that evening when Cath turned into the driveway, of a large red bricked, double fronted Victorian house on Temple Road at Matlock Bath. The driveway was semi-circular, and Cath parked between a mud spattered green Range Rover Vogue and a large horsebox. The pebbled driveway to the oak porch scrunched under her black boots, and a white LED security light clicked on as she reached the door and activated the PIR. The formidable looking arched oak door had a large brass knocker in the form of a lion's head which she rapped three times. The police officer's knock.

The door was opened by a woman Cath presumed was Mrs Burton. She was about fifty, quite tall… a good four inches taller than Cath's five feet two inches. Her dyed blonde hair was grey streaked and had been tied back in a red ribbon. Her heavy build was hidden in a pair of loose-fitting black slacks and a cashmere sweater.

"Hi!" Cath introduced herself as she flashed her warrant card.

"DC Mulvey from Matlock CID. You asked to see the police about your husband. You reported he was missing last night, and you had concerns about him?"

"Yes, thank you for coming so late but I had to sort out the horses," Mrs Burton explained.

Cath entered the oak panelled hallway behind Mrs Burton and sat down on a hall chair. She unlaced and took off her boots placing them next to a pair of heavily muddied Hunters. Cath looked worriedly down at her socks and wished that she had taken more care that morning when getting dressed as she saw that her vividly striped socks were not a matching pair. One was bright green and black and the other red and yellow. Both contrasted loudly against her black tights. Mrs Burton had noticed her odd socks.

"I've got an identical pair at home Mrs Burton."

"Don't worry about it, I haven't got a pair without a hole in. By the way, it's Margaret but you can call me Maggie, everyone else does."

"I'm Cath if we're not standing on ceremony." Cath smiled.

"There's no ceremony here Cath, just cats, dogs and horses. The dogs are in the utility as I wasn't sure you would be alright with them, and the cats are god knows where. I've just put the horses to bed, but they're not allowed in the house anyway," Maggie Burton joked as she led Cath into the kitchen.

"I'm alright with dogs," Cath reassured Mrs Burton, hoping that they were not big angry ones.

Cath followed Maggie into the farmhouse kitchen at the end of the hall and saw at least two dog baskets up against a large oil-fired range. In the warm kitchen, thick pine work surfaces surrounded a large oak table, which was covered in scattered letters and their empty envelopes, horse magazines, Sunday supplements, and books…. Cath could only see horse fiction of which there were at least two Jilly Coopers. In an almost clear corner of the table was a pot of jam and the remnants of a loaf of unsliced bread. Cath glanced further round the kitchen. The sink under the kitchen window was an enormous Belfast one with a pile of unmatching mugs and plates waiting to be washed. Along the walls were photographs of Mrs Burton and two children. A boy and a girl, of differing ages, standing with horses, or jumping them over hedges and fences, as well as graduation photographs of the two children, now adults, wearing mortar boards and capes and holding rolled graduation certificates.

An Accidental Death

There were a few pictures of someone she presumed was Mr Burton, but these were all of him on his own, posing at formal dinners or other social events. She recognised him from the photographs, as someone she had passed regularly in the streets around Matlock town centre.

Mrs Burton beckoned Cath to sit down on a large brown leather settee that had been squeezed into the far side of the room. A black cat lay fast asleep on one end, so Cath sat on the other end, so as not to disturb it. Mrs Burton went to a door at the side of the settee and opened it. A pack of dogs of varying sizes poured through it and jumped and fussed around Maggie Burton. At her shout of "Down!" the dogs, that Cath could now see comprised of some sort of giant Irish wolfhound that she could have ridden if it had been saddled, two springers, a pug, and a Jack Russell. At her command all of them dropped obediently to a sitting position in front of their mistress.

The dogs, seeing their mistress glance over to the settee behind them, turned as one and noticed Cath sitting on it. Having missed the stranger coming into the house they all immediately turned their friendly attention to her. The springers jumped together onto the settee, oblivious of the startled cat that shot across the room in indignation at being woken from its sleep. They then bounced around at Cath's side, trying to get in front of each other to be the closest to her. The wolf hound buried its face in hers from the side of the settee and through the melee Cath saw that the Jack Russell was eyeing her suspiciously from a seating position behind the fussing springers.

Cath looked quickly around her for the fifth dog, whilst fighting off the largest three with her arms and hands and saw that the Pug had wandered off to get the warmest position by the range. Cath, like all police officers, knew that the most dangerous dog in the world is a Jack Russell, and so that was the one she kept her eye on.

Maggie shouted "Basket!"

At her command, the dogs ambled over to the baskets by the range, where they sat waiting for any further instructions. All that is except the Jack Russell that remained eyeball to eyeball with Cath.

Maggie shouted "Della! Basket!"

The Jack Russell looked at Maggie, looked at Cath and then at Maggie again. Deprived of its prey it dropped off the couch and sauntered over to the basket where it lay staring unblinkingly at Cath, curled up next to the Irish wolfhound.

Having been introduced to the occupants of the house Mrs Burton asked if she would like a cup of tea or coffee.

"Coffee… no sugar please."

She then playfully scowled at the still staring Jack Russell as Maggie put a kettle of water on the hob. The Jack Russell accepted defeat and dropped its gaze, snuggling itself into the warmth of the wolfhound that was already asleep in its basket.

Cath took out a pen and a small, lined notebook from her black leather handbag and pulled up the small coffee table closer to where she was sitting. She looked at her socks and considered whether she should take them off and put them in her bag. She decided it was too late to hide them so sat back and listened to Mrs Burton rattling cups and saucers as she made their coffees.

Mrs Burton eventually returned to the settee, put down two cups of coffee on the small coffee table, and sat next to her. Cath took a sip of coffee and put the cup back down on the table. To business she thought and leaning towards Maggie, looked directly into her eyes, and stated quietly,

"I understand you have reported that your husband failed to come home last night, and you have some concerns as to his safety. Do you want to tell me what's happened?"

Mrs Burton clasped her black slacked knees together.

"I feel I should be more upset, but it just won't come. We've not been close, in a marriage sense for years, but I do really care for him, and I'm quite sure he cares for me. We do talk, you know about things like the kids and the dogs but not about serious stuff…"

Her hands went to her face and covered her eyes. Her shoulders began to shrug up and down and then tears poured down her face as she removed her hands and tried to speak, words came out between great gulps of air.

"I'm so… I'm so… I'm so sorry, I didn't think I would be like this …"

Cath smiled and waited for Mrs Burton to regain control.

Maggie Burton got off the settee, went over to a box of tissues on the kitchen table and removed a handful. She dabbed at her eyes and nose with them, scrunched them into a ball in her hand and sat back on the settee next to Cath.

As she sat down Cath reassured her.

"That's alright, it can't be easy to talk about your husband when he's missing, and you are concerned for his safety. Tell me why you think he's gone missing and why it makes you worried about him."

Mrs Burton calmed a little and began her story.

"Well, can I start at the beginning?" Maggie dabbed her eyes with her jumper sleeve.

"Yes, start at the beginning, It's usually the best place" Cath suggested and smiled encouragingly at her.

"Well, I met Neil in 1992 after he came back from Ibiza where he'd been working for the summer. He'd qualified as a solicitor earlier that year. You know he's Burtons Solicitors on Bank Road, don't you?" Cath nodded and Maggie continued "His father was Bryan Burton, who set the firm up. Well, when he came back from Ibiza he started working for his daddy, and he ended up doing the conveyancing for me on some land I had bought to graze my horses at Tansley. I was working for my father at the time and so had my own money. Anyway, I had to call in the office a few times to sign documents. Neil asked me what I did, what university I had gone to and seemed genuinely interested in me. I was very flattered as he was very handsome. Anyway, he asked me to go with him to the Ashbourne Hunt Autumn Ball. I said yes and that was it, we were a couple. We got married about a year later and then we had Marcus and Laura. He was a good father.... but there were problems. He was what I would call a bit distant, you know in the bedroom, it was sometimes very difficult....then he wanted his own room. We told the children it was his snoring and made a laugh out of it, but it was difficult, very difficult.........anyway about him going missing…...well you have to know this I suppose to understand …...well how can I explain it … the beginning I suppose… Sorry Cath, I've never told anybody any of this so it's probably going to sound very disjointed. Do you know Paul Trueman, the Councillor who died before Xmas?"

Cath nodded "Yes I know of him."

Maggie continued "Well, he was a friend of Neil's. I think they had met when they worked together as Reps for some holiday company in Ibiza that summer before he started working for his daddy. Anyway, before Paul bought the house in Baslow, he lived in the flats at the top of Bank Road . Paul moved up here just after Laura was born … must have been about 1993. Paul and Neil were good friends, …well more than good friends if you know what I mean and that's why Neil wanted his own room. I was hurt at the beginning but the kids and his family you know… he didn't want them to know… shame and all that I suppose…. looking back shortly after we met, I should have known, he wasn't very interested in you know what and the two children only came about because of my persistence. Anyway, I'd got the stables and my horses, and he'd got his work. After Laura was born, he would go drinking with Paul at the weekends and occasionally stop over because he was 'too drunk to drive.' It just became more regular especially after he moved to Baslow, until he was stopping over with him once or twice a week. Neil just carried on pretending that they were good friends and business associates, and they were incredibly good at it. ……I don't think anyone knows…. Marcus and Laura probably suspect but we've never talked about it. Anyway, when Paul had his accident and died, Neil was terribly upset …he went to see him in the hospital you know. He was there when he died. It affected him badly."

Cath nodded and indicated with her pen for her to carry on. She was sure Mrs Burton would get to why he had gone missing eventually.

"Well, I just thought he was grieving for Paul but after Christmas he started to get stressed and short tempered. I asked him what was wrong, and he just kept telling me that it was nothing for me to worry about. He wouldn't talk about anything, but I could tell something was wrong. We might not have had much of a marriage, but I knew him well enough to know when something was wrong with him. I had a bit of a go at him, and he told me that he had left his computer thingy…. laptop…but smaller.." Maggie struggled for the word.

"iPad?" suggested Cath.

"No like a laptop but thinner" Maggie responded.

"MacBook?" suggested Cath.

"Yes, that's it."

Maggie continued "How much of this will be public? It's difficult to talk about."

"To be honest Maggie, I won't know until you have told me. If it's any help we wouldn't ever publicly release anything about Neil unless it was important that we do so."

"Thanks Cath. Well, I didn't want anything to do with Paul as I thought of him as a slimy toad and told Neil that. There was something about him… I didn't like him at all."

"How long have you known Neil was gay Maggie?" Cath asked trying to get Maggie back to why she was concerned about Neil going missing.

"Since just after Marcus was born. You're going to ask why I stayed with him?"

Cath just wanted to know why Neil had gone missing.

"Probably later. Just carry on telling me why you think he's gone missing and why you're worried."

"Alright Cath, as mummy used to say to me, keep to the subject girl and stop dithering." She smiled towards Cath and carried on.

"I asked him what was so important on the computer thingy, and he told me it was personal stuff....well I know for sure that there were compromising photographs on it of them both as he left it unlocked on the table in the kitchen when he went to the loo about a month ago. I had a quick look at the e-mails and pictures on it,...curiosity I suppose... maybe even a bit of jealousy but you would have a look wouldn't you if you had the chance?"

Cath nodded. Maggie was in full flow again, so Cath indicated for her to carry on.

"I'm no prude but a couple of the pictures were pretty what I would call depraved, ...anyway I know it was very naughty to look but I suppose I just wanted to know for certain.... well, any wife would.... wouldn't they. You want to know who your husband is sleeping with don't you?"

Cath nodded.

"Was it definitely a MacBook?."

"Yes, one of those new MacBook things, I think Neil has kept the box in the garage. I'll have a look later for you if that would help?"

"Was there anything else on the MacBook that was important to Neil? There's the photographs you have mentioned but do you think there could have been anything else that could have caused him any concerns?"

"I don't know for sure, but I think it was just the photographs"

"Just the photographs then. But why has he gone missing now?"

"Well, that's what I don't know. After Paul died he was quite stressed but after the funeral last week he seemed a bit better. He was still obviously concerned about something though as he has been more thoughtful and quieter than usual. Yesterday he got up early and had gone off to work by the time I came back from the horses. He was at work in the morning as I rang him to ask if he could let the dogs out at lunchtime. He told me that he would let them out on his way to the accountants at lunch time. He then rang me about four saying he was meeting a client and would be home late. Well, that was odd as he never meets clients outside of office hours, other than Paul of course. …He must have come home and let the dogs out at lunchtime as there was no messes when I got back from the stables that afternoon. But he didn't came home after meeting the client last night. When I got up this morning and went to his bedroom he wasn't there, and his bed hadn't been slept in. So that's what's got me worried. He's been stressed and upset since Paul died, his laptop thingy has gone missing with those photographs on, and I think he's really worried about those photographs getting into the wrong hands."

"Anything else worrying him that you know about?"

"He's got an SRA inspection at the firm next week, but he doesn't usually worry about that at all…. he can't be at Paul's, can he?" Maggie asked herself and then answered her own question.

"That girl his daughter is stopping there isn't she?" and looked at Cath for confirmation.

"I don't think he's there."

Cath knew this with some certainty as she knew Dave was there last night with the new 'love of his life.'

Mrs Burton carried on "I just hope he hasn't done anything stupid."

"Like what?" Cath asked.

"Well, you know anything stupid ……… killed himself or something."

"Do you think he might have?"

"I don't know, he was very stressed and worried, the meeting clients thing was very strange, and when I rang his office this morning to see if he had gone into work, his secretary told me he hadn't been in and had missed appointments with clients. There was also nothing in his diary for last night, and she hadn't arranged a meeting with anyone. That's when I got really worried. His car's gone as well."

"What sort is it?"

"A Land Rover, a blue Discovery."

"Registration number?"

"B02 TON… it's sort of a personalised plate, that's why I know it."

"Do you know what he was wearing?"

"I'm not certain, but probably a brown tweed suit from Brocklehurst's, he's got a few that he wears all the time for work. You know the country gentleman look, brown tweed suit, cloth tie, check cotton shirt, brown brogues…I can check his wardrobe but I'm pretty sure that's what he would have been wearing."

Cath made a note for the missing person form.

"That's fine, what about friends and his children have they heard anything?"

"I've rung Marcus and Laura and they've not seen or heard from him."

"Mobile phone?"

"It won't connect not even a recorded message."

"Friends?"

"Just Paul really and he's dead. The others from the Rotary and Masons are just business friends really and I can't see him staying over with any of them. I'm pretty sure he would have gone in or at least rung work if he had just stopped over somewhere with somebody. That's why I think something's happened to him."

Cath put her pen down and took another sip of the now cool coffee. She thought, she had better ask the question.

"Maggie, there's a dead girl been found just north of Bakewell on the A6. Do you think Neil could be involved with her in any way?"

"Girls weren't really his thing, so I doubt it. Do you know her name?"

"No not yet, we're still trying to find that out," Cath confided.

Cath decided that she had heard enough to make out a missing person report. In her experience if Neil hadn't walked back through the door by tomorrow morning, the chances were that he would be found in some back lane with a hoover pipe from the exhaust through the window.

"Have you got a hoover?"

"Yes. I've already checked, and the hose is still attached to it."

Maggie is a smart lady Cath thought.

"Maggie, I will need a list of the clothes he was or might have been wearing. I will need his mobile number and social media accounts, his bank accounts, as well as vehicles he has access to.

A list of friends and relatives he may have gone to or contacted, and we will need to search the house and outbuildings to make sure he's not hiding here. We can then broaden the search out. Can you get the details together for me for the morning?"

Maggie nodded.

"In the meantime, I'll get a uniform officer and CSI to join us, and we can start the search of the house and grounds. We will need to take some samples for DNA and something he's touched for fingerprints, as well as your own for elimination purposes. I'll put out an alert on him and the car in case he's out on the roads or parked up somewhere."

"Can you write the list down for me? and I'll get it done for you by the morning."

Maggie looked down at her clasped hands holding the scrunched up tissues and then back to Cath.

"He's dead isn't he, …I know he is…. how am I going to tell Marcus and Laura?"

Chapter 22 – The Long Rake Discovery

Saturday 18th January

It was Saturday morning, four days after Alice Bulman's body had been found, and Neil Burton had been reported missing. Holly was stood on the frozen track to the Long Rake Spa Mine in Calver, in a forensic suit. CSI Simon Metcalfe stood next to him also gowned up in a forensic suit.

"How long ago do you reckon the fire started?" asked Holly.

"Well, the vehicle is cold to say the least. There's not been many people up here with the weather so it's hard to say. I would reckon a couple of days at least. If that dog walker had not come across it could have been here till the spring, this place is well out the way" replied Simon.

"Just the one occupant?" Holly looked for confirmation from the CSI.

"Yes, just the one. Not a lot left of them to be honest, post-mortem might give you the sex and rough age but at the moment it's too difficult to tell you anything other than it was human."

"What about the vehicle then? Discovery I reckon from the shell," Holly speculated about the burnt out vehicle.

"Well done Mr Clarkson!" retorted Cath with a smile, joining them from the direction of the burnt out Discovery. She was fully forensically suited up as well.

"Well, anything other than just a Discovery?" Holly asked CSI Metcalfe with a wry smile towards Cath.

"Blue probably," Simon Metcalfe confirmed.

"Puts Burton as more than a probable then. He's still missing and the car matches" Cath commented.

"Number plates and glass have gone, but I think we can get something off the VIN plate. I have bagged it up and I'll see what I can recover when I get back" offered the CSI.

"Anything more to do here Simon?" asked Holly.

"No, it's going to be a job for Professor Graham and the lab now. We're going to recover the vehicle as it is and take it back to the garage at the nick. We'll see what other evidence we can get off it back there. We have decided to cut out the body and the seat it's on, back at the garage as well. Professor Graham at the post-mortem will hopefully be able to figure out whether it's a suspicious death or not. There's nothing here to help us either way."

Thirty minutes later, an unsuited Holly and Cath leant against her red Mini, watching the Matlock Green Garage car transporter take away the tarpaulin covered burnt out Discovery.

"You reckon it's Neil Burton in the driver's seat don't you?" concluded Holly.

Cath nodded "Yes, it all fits, Blue Discovery, right area, Mrs Burton said he was quiet and stressed. Lover just died, SRA inspecting his practice, fits the circumstances although I would have thought pills or hoover pipe to the exhaust would have been a better choice. You don't get many that send themselves up in smoke. I suppose he might have thought he could save money on the cremation costs; you know killing two birds with one shot so to speak." Holly smiled resignedly at Cath's dark humour.

The recovery vehicle turned left onto the main road and out of sight. Cath looked at Holly and stood up away from her Mini. "Come on Holly, jump in! We will have to see what Professor Graham thinks before we know what happened for certain."

Holly looked at his watch "I'll call Excy and tell him to get the kettle on, he should be off the murder and back at Bakewell by now."

Chapter 23 – Saturday Briefings

Monday 13th January

Dave had been at the 10 a.m. briefing for an hour, and it was dragging on interminably. He wanted to get away but after his rebuke from BJ for entering the briefing late a few days ago he was not going to make the mistake of walking out half way through one. Dave yawned, he was having trouble focussing on the speaker, as so far, he had only covered what everyone in the room already knew.

There was one suspect Dylan Oxley and Superintendent Dicks wanted him caught as soon as possible. At that moment Superintendent Dicks was listing the evidence linking him to the crime scene as though persuading himself that he had the correct suspect. Dave didn't know whether Oxley was the right suspect or not, there was plenty of evidence linking him to the scene but no evidence linking him to Alice's body or a motive for her murder as far as he was aware, but he was not going to be the person to point this out. He was on the incident hopefully for another thirty minutes at most and then it would no longer be his problem.

He let his mind drift to his problem at the moment, namely, how to get some 'alone time' with Helen that evening and how he was going to persuade her to meet him again once she left.

The sound of the Christmas carol blared loudly from his jacket pocket, Dave jumped suddenly awake from his thoughts and fumbled frantically in his inside jacket pocket to find his phone, before muting the sound and ending the call. Superintendent Dicks stopped speaking and looked around the briefing room to see who had so rudely interrupted his soliloquy. His face lightened from a scowl into a smile when he saw that it was DC David Baker. Dave saw the look and switched his phone onto record.

"Good to see that you are still in Christmas mode DC Baker. 'The Holly and the Ivy' eh... so, what of all the trees that are in the woods do you bear the crown DC Baker.... I suppose it should be the wooden crown to go onto your wooden head!" he looked round the room for the laughter at his joke.

As he had expected the room found it extremely funny and laughed loudly. Dave put the phone back in his pocket and tried to avoid any eye contact with his colleagues who had turned to look at him. He then waited for the laughter to die down and everyone to turn back around. It was only then he looked towards Superintendent Dicks and apologised,

"Sorry sir, it won't happen again."

"No, it won't detective! Because you're leaving us today to go back to your sheep shearing, aren't you DC Baker?"

"Yes sir" Dave replied.

Not getting Dave to rise to his jibe, Superintendent Dicks turned to a detective stood at the side of the dais from where he was delivering the briefing.

"For all of you who don't know him this is DC Jack Bainbridge. He will be taking over from DC Baker as Exhibits Officer today. DC Baker, as I have just said, is off the incident and going back to division."

Dicks made it sound as though the move was a punishment rather than a previously agreed course of action.

"Has everything been passed over this morning by our rural carol singer Jack?"

"Yes sir. All transferred to Buxton, and everything is up to date. Everything now comes into me in the old CSI office, on the ground floor here."

"Any problems?" asked Superintendent Dicks.

"Not that I know of" affirmed Jack Bainbridge.

"Well it will be a surprise if we don't find any," quipped Superintendent Dicks giving a wide false smile to Dave.

"You won't find any no matter how hard you look" thought Dave. He had double and triple checked everything before handing it over.

"Right then, lets recap, before we get interrupted again by DC Baker's carol singing. As I was saying we have one suspect Dylan Oxley. We are hoping to have some result from the Garda today to see if he's crossed into Ireland to see his parents. Forensics have linked him to the scene through some spots of his blood that we think were caused by wounds inflicted by Alice fighting for her life. We need to make sure when he gets caught, and he will get caught ladies and gentlemen, that we check for scratches cuts etcetera. It would be a travesty if she fought to leave us this evidence and we failed to use it. His Ford Ranger that was abandoned in Sheffield has been wiped clean according to CSI. South Yorkshire have got nowhere so far on CCTV at the station, there's just too many people for them to conclusively say whether he caught a train or where to. They're now doing house to house for us in the vicinity of where he dumped his Ranger to see if there's any indication where he went. They aren't hopeful though as it's an old industrial area and there aren't many cameras around. Any luck on Sheffield taxi companies he asked the room.

DI Casey in front of Dave stood up.

"Nothing yet boss but there's a lot of them and some are still checking their records."

The DI sat back down.

Superintendent Dicks continued. "Keep on it and let me know immediately if we get a breakthrough. We've got TV coming this afternoon, for the evening news slot. Mr and Mrs Bulman are going to be here together with the press and TV so best behaviour from everyone and no chatting about the case in earshot of the Bulman's or the press. Let's keep everything tight. I don't want any awkward questions at the press conference because somebody has blabbed something to the press they shouldn't have. Everyone understand?"

Superintendent Dicks looked round the room and was met by a unanimous "Yes sir!"

Dave thinking the briefing was over took his phone back out of his pocket and checked whether it was still recording, it was. He smiled to himself and then stopped the audio recording.

Superintendent Dicks however, carried on with the briefing.

"Anybody got anything they think may be relevant that they want to share with the team, that's come up since yesterday that might help us with Oxley?"

Superintendent Dicks looked round the room. DS Annie Patel on the second row of seated detectives stood up.

"We were doing house to house on Buxton Road in Bakewell yesterday and there was a youth walking down towards town. He's got learning disabilities and works in the pet shop, likes feeding the animals. Says he was walking back home about 5 p.m. after work on the night that Alice died and there was a bloke in a brown suit hanging around the top of Bath Street. Might be something… might be nothing."

Superintendent Dicks furrowed his brow as if in thought.

"Learning disability, you say. He's probably mistaken…Go back and see him and take a statement, It was dark, there's street lighting and it's difficult to identify colour so I suppose it could have been a brown and green suit he saw… like a camouflage one that Oxley was wearing. I reckon if you see him again and talk to him properly that it will be a camouflage suit he saw, don't you? That would then tie Oxley into near the place we think she went missing as well as where she was found."

"No problem sir." Annie Patel agreed and sat down.

"Bloody hell! Talk about getting fitted up," thought Dave.

He was glad he was getting off this enquiry even if it was turning out to be a successful one.

"Finally, Division are attending a burnt-out Discovery this morning with what may be a body in it. According to CSI it's likely to be a local missing person, a solicitor with personal and business problems who has topped himself. It's nothing to do with this enquiry and local CID are dealing with it. There's nothing to suggest our suspect has access to any such vehicle and we are ruling out any connection at this stage. Does everyone understand?"

A consensual murmur went around the room.

253 | P a g e

"Right, everyone get out there and get some justice for Alice Bulman. As it's Saturday, debrief at 6 p.m. and let's get away for an early night. Apart that is from the volunteers manning the phone lines after the TV appeal."

Superintendent Dicks smiled towards the seated detectives, picked up his file of papers and walked out of the room. As he did so the room full of people stood up and stretched themselves, picked up their own folders and papers, and then also made their way out of the briefing room.

Dave joined the throng moving towards the back doors of the police station and felt his phone vibrate in his pocket. There were two messages. One from Holly, (he vowed to himself that he must change Holly's ring tone on his phone) saying that he was coming with Cath to Bakewell for lunch and would he be there. He looked at his watch 11.15 a.m. plenty of time… and texted back "See you there."

The second was from Helen agreeing to go for a curry and stop over at his apartment for the night. Ella was coming for the curry as well but was getting a taxi back to Baslow after. That's brilliant thought Dave. He was only slightly disappointed that Ella would be on their date, but he understood that Helen couldn't leave her on her own on a Saturday night. Off the murder and most of the night on his own with Helen. He was so happy that he had to stop himself skipping to his car, the embarrassment of the phone call in the briefing was now completely forgotten.

253 | P a g e

Chapter 24 – The Team Meet Up

Saturday 18th January

An hour later he was sat back in the old CID office at Bakewell with Holly and Cath.

"Well, it's good to have you back Excy" announced Holly tucking into a sausage roll, and dropping pastry crumbs onto his un-ironed shirt.

"Good to be back Holly, BJ made it quite plain I was there under sufferance. Nice thirty hour day Tuesday and Wednesday though, so that's a week in the sun in August paid for," replied Dave.

"Everything handed over or have you got to go back?" asked Cath.

"No, handed everything over to Jack Bainbridge this morning. They searched her flat Thursday and seized everything that wasn't screwed down. They were just trying to wind me up with all the exhibits. There was at least a dozen pair of shoes and the same number of handbags, they even booked in her gym bag.

None of it was relevant as far as I could see, but they kept coming in with it every fifteen minutes all afternoon. I was here till eight last night booking it in. Anyway, I have handed over everything to Jack Bainbridge this morning. Books and exhibits have all gone to Buxton with him so Bakewell's clear of everything. I know that will please Bill Fry, he was getting really pissed off with everyone off the murder calling in to drop stuff off and using sections tea and milk as well as leaving the kitchen a right mess."

"What's the latest on the murder?" Holly asked.

Dave summarised the earlier briefing.

"BJ has put all his eggs in the Dylan Oxley basket. He hasn't been seen since the same night that Alice was killed, and there are tyre tracks matching the type of tyres on his pick-up in a field nearby. South Yorkshire police found his pick-up yesterday near to the railway station in Sheffield and are going through CCTV from nearby to see if they can spot if he's took the train somewhere. His missus says he was wearing Doc Martins and they've found matching shoe marks from the field where they found the tyre tracks to near to the scene where she was found. To top it off they found a trace of blood in some flattened ground nearby that's come back to him as well. So, BJ reckons she must have put up a bit of a fight. Too much traffic on the car park to get anything off there of course and the snow ruined any footprints on the track where they found her body. Nearly forgot, when they spoke to his wife she told them he'd tried to strangle her the same night and then shot off in a right temper. He's got family in Ireland, so BJ has sent a team over there to see if he's stopping at relatives. Basically, it's Oxley. Everything is geared up to finding him. BJ is strutting round like a cock pheasant, having cleared it up in a few days."

Holly having finished off the sausage roll, took a bite out of his bacon sandwich.

"We heard that Oxley was the suspect yesterday. Bod reckons that the strangling his ex-bit, is a right load of old crap. He says Jackie would kill him before he got anywhere near her neck, and that they have had violent rows every day for the last ten years without him going out and killing someone. Having said that though, Bod also told me he wouldn't put it past him to have killed the girl as he's a nasty bastard and reckons that he's quite capable of killing someone. Bod says Stan Moore told him he's took a few pot shots at gamekeepers on the estate in the past."

"Has he got firearms then?" asked Cath.

Holly continued "None officially but both Stan and Bod reckon he's got a silenced .22 rifle and that it's in a hollow tree somewhere up Stanton. Neither of them has found it yet though it's not for the want of trying."

"Do the incident room know about the firearm?" asked Cath.

"Yes, Bod rang it in but there's nothing but rumour, so it's not gone very far especially as she wasn't shot. Finding it doesn't take them anywhere. Nearly forgot to tell you that BJ is going on the TV later, national and local with Alice's mum and dad.

He's going with an appeal for info on Dylan Oxley. Armed and dangerous so public not to get involved and all that type of stuff."

Cath laughed loudly.

"He will be loving that! National TV, identified murder suspect, armed and dangerous it's his wet dream."

"Does BJ know we might have found Neil Burton?" Asked Holly

"Yes, CSI have told him. BJ has him out of the picture for the murder… if he was ever in" mused Dave.

"I hope our body isn't Dylan's and Burton's done them both then" joked Holly.

"Yeah gay mild-mannered solicitor sets fire to armed and dangerous murderer in fight over girlfriend… can't see that one running very far" quipped Cath.

Holly's mobile phone rang. Holly checked the caller and went out of the room to answer it, shutting the door behind him. Cath mouthed "Donna" towards Dave.

Dave mouthed back "Problems?"

"Always!" confirmed Cath loudly, confident Holly wouldn't hear them on the other side of the closed door.

"I don't know why he doesn't leave her: she makes his life hell. He came in with another cut on his head last week. It was bleeding down the side of his of his face."

Dave slowly shook his head towards Cath.

"Oh and don't mention pets whatever you do. Donna's bought Georgia a horse. I think he will need a lottery win to keep himself going soon" sighed Cath.

"How are you doing Excy? Alice's post-mortem must have been awful."

" It was, and the bastards dumped me with the ID by the dad as well. You get through it though and put it in the box marked 'Do not open' with all the other shit and fasten the lid down."

Dave looked down at his desk trying to avoid Cath seeing the sadness in his eyes as he remembered the grief of Alice's father.

"Yeah I know. We just put it in the box, slam down the lid and forget about it. I helped clear up what was left of Gary Traynor and put it in a bag just before Christmas with Holly, as well as going to the post-mortem just after Christmas. There wasn't much to post-mortem mind. It was hard though when you've known him since he was a kid."

Cath stared through the window, trying to avoid any eye contact with Dave. Both fell into silent lonely thought as the two memories came out of the box they had been put into.

"Did you speak to Karen?"

An Accidental Death

Dave eventually asked Cath breaking the silence as he remembered the conversation with her at Paul Trueman's funeral.

"Yes, she was rambling on a bit about Gary's death that's all"

Cath lied; she didn't trust him to understand the informal nature of the arrangement she had made with Ron and Karen. Karen had actually told her that on the day that Gary was run over and killed, a man in a brown tweed suit and two heavies had forced their way into Ron's house and threatened Gary about a stolen computer. Gary had run off, got on his bike, and cycled into the lorry. She thought that there was more, but her mum and dad were fairly tight lipped about what had happened. Cath was unable to do anything with the information Karen had given her without corroboration from Gail or Ron, and there was no chance of that according to Karen. Without their evidence it meant there was nothing she could act on, even though it probably meant that his death was at least manslaughter.

The other intelligence she had got from Ron Traynor, about the lorry hijack, Cath had put through Holly and then directly to a police colleague in Staffordshire. It had turned out to be accurate as Ron had promised her. Danny MacAleese had been stopped on a 'routine check' by a traffic unit in an Arnold Clark hired van, on the M6 on Christmas day. A quarter of million pounds of stolen spirits from a lorry hi-jack at Wildboarclough had been surprisingly found by the traffic officers in the back of the van.

"How have Ron and Gail taken Gary's death?" Dave asked breaking Cath's chain of thought.

"I've not seen them since before the funeral, but Gail is broken, there was none of the usual hostility from her. I can tell you she's not going to get over it quickly. It didn't help that she went to the scene and saw the carnage, it wasn't something as a mother I would think you can live with easily"

"Ron?"

"He was quiet. He's not said that much to me at all. He has refused to give a statement or help the investigation in any way. For a big hard bastard, I think it even shocked him seeing what was left of his son like that."

The phone rang on the desk and Cath answered it.

"Hi Simon .... He's on the phone......yes, I'll tell him.....OK thanks for that and thanks for getting that done so quickly.....bye."

Cath looked up at Dave "VIN plates come back to Burton's Discovery."

Holly came back into the office, looking red faced and flustered.

"Who was that Cath?" he asked.

"Simon Metcalfe, VIN plates come back to Burton's Discovery."

"Right, that's good then….. for us." Holly went out the office looking at his phone and shut the door behind him.

"Definitely just spoken to Mrs Hollins, he only looks flustered like that when he's been given a tongue lashing" quipped Cath, and then changing the subject.

"You still shagging Trueman's daughter? what's her name… Helen?"

"You still shagging anyone with a pair of tits?" Dave hit back hurt at her crudeness about his girlfriend.

"Ooh touchy!"

Cath recognised that Dave was smarting at her comment. He had obviously fallen in love with her.

"Don't get too involved Excy, she will be gone once she's sorted Paul Trueman's stuff out, and I don't like seeing you hurt."

"I know she will, but I can go and see her on my rest days, and she can come up here at weekends….. she might even move up here now she's got Paul Trueman's house to stay in."

"You do this every time Excy. You meet a girl and go all in on a pair of twos. I'm not saying she's not nice or anything, but you know nothing about her. She might be married for all you know. I just don't want you to get hurt, I look at you as a good mate and I do care about you, even though I tease you sometimes."

"I'll take the advice on board Cath, though it was a bit below the belt … the married bit anyway after last year."

Dave smiled good humouredly at Cath remembering how she had ribbed him for several weeks about his relationship with the married woman from Leeds and her oil rig worker husband.

"Yeah, I'm sorry, it was a bit below the belt. But find out a bit about her before you start thinking about marrying her. Girls aren't fluffy kittens, sugar and spice and all things nice. I should know I'm one and I've have had my heart broken by a few as well."

"I won't Cath, I'm seeing her and Ella tonight. I'm taking them both for a curry at the Gulab, then Helen's stopping over at mine and Ella's going back to Baslow. I should have some alone time with her tonight to find out more about her. If you and your mates are down Brampton tonight we might bump into you later."

Cath nodded and smiled at Dave's suggestion.

"Highly likely if I get off in time to get out. I'm in dire need of a night out with the girls and a bit of debauchery afterwards if I can pick someone up."

"Cath, you get worse! Don't ever call me a Tomcat again," he laughed.

Holly came back into the office. He was not looking as flustered this time.

An Accidental Death

"I've told Comms that we have identified the burnt out Discovery as belonging to Burton. They have told me Professor Graham is doing the post-mortem on the body found in it at nine on Monday morning at Chesterfield, so we will hopefully know whether it is Burton that died in it then. He can't do it any earlier as he's got another murder in Birmingham that he's got to do the post-mortem for. That's you two brought up to date and because I am the best Sergeant in the world I've decided that I'll deal with anything that comes in tomorrow so you two-night animals can have tomorrow off. I'm sure that a good curry night with your girlfriend…"

He looked towards Dave.

"…or a night of alcohol and debauchery…" he smiled towards Cath who felt herself blushing

"…is calling you both."

"Well one of us is looking forward to getting pissed, Holly. The others got some wedding books to look through!" teased Cath.

"That's not funny!" Dave good humouredly retorted back.

"Right then, you bugger off Excy, and pick some bedding and curtains before I change my mind. Cath, you can come with me to see Mrs Burton and give her the sad news about the Discovery and the burnt body, and then you can get off as well. I'll let you know if there's any change of plans to the post-mortem on Monday tomorrow night, so have your phones on at about 6 p.m.

Other than that, give my love to Billy Morton and Professor Graham first thing Monday morning and I'll see you about mid-day in the office at Matlock. Let me know the result of the post-mortem as soon as you know. If it's suspicious at all I don't want Alan Daley jumping all over my arse because we didn't tell him straight away. Right let's all bugger off before any more dead bodies come in, it's like god's waiting room round here the last week or so."

Chapter 25 – Cath and Ella

Saturday 18th January

Cath drove Holly back to Matlock Police Station, parked her Mini in the yard and turned to Holly. She was worried about him.

On the journey from Bakewell, he had received two phone calls on his mobile that he had let go to answer phone after checking the caller. This was unusual even if it was Donna…especially if it was Donna. Holly had also been silent and contemplative, a mood that was becoming common over the last few weeks. Cath decided to confront him about what was going on. He was not only her boss he was a friend as well.

"Was that Donna on the phone… trouble at home Holly?"

"No, no trouble Cath. Just family stuff, I'll deal with it later when I get home."

Holly brushed her concerns off too quickly, and she realised he was covering something up. Cath decided to probe a little deeper.

"Are you alright Holly? I'm only asking because you have been a bit quiet for the last month or so, not yourself so to speak."

There was a silence as though Holly was thinking what to say and then he looked earnestly towards her.

"I'm fine Cath, just been a bit busy that's all, what with Christmas and all these deaths over the last couple of weeks. I'll be alright."

He smiled.

"I'm quite cheerful actually. Look you get off I don't think it will need two of us to tell Mrs Burton about the vehicle and the body in it."

"Are you sure?"

Holly opened the car door and got out.

"Yes I'm sure. You get off Cath, I'm fine honestly. Have a night out, get drunk, have some fun and I'll see you Monday lunchtime."

"Well, if you're sure you are alright?" Cath looked up at him from the driver's seat.

"Yes perfectly sure, Go out and get drunk with your mates!" he smiled at her and shut the door.

Cath drove the twelve miles home to her terraced one bed house at Walton in Chesterfield. On the way her thoughts were still with Holly. He was definitely not himself she thought. As a team they had been very busy since Christmas especially with the sudden death of Paul Trueman, the fatal accident of Gary Traynor and the murder earlier that week, but that didn't explain Holly's mood swings. She had been with Holly for most of the last few weeks and had noticed that he was unusually quiet for lengthy periods and then his mood would change suddenly to one of false jollity, like he had when she had dropped him off at the police station that evening.

She shrugged, there was only so much she could do. She had asked him, and he had affirmed he was alright, but…. She decided she would ask Dave on Monday when they got back to work what he thought they should do. She knew that she over-thought things sometimes and her worries were possibly just her thinking too deeply about her colleague.

Having eaten a drive-thru Big Mac in the car on the way home, Cath walked through her front door and turned on the TV, before collapsing onto the IKEA lounger in her small kitchen/lounge. Cath closed her eyes and wondered whether she would be better off getting a good night's sleep. The image of the badly burnt body still in the car seat in the Discovery flashed up in her mind…Sleep would be out of the question. It was a night to go out, get drunk and get laid. Cath checked whether her friends were going out by logging into their WhatsApp 'Girlynightsout' group.

Cath scrolled down the messages. There were seven of them in the group. Two of them were married, Mandy and Bev. Both had messaged that they were not out. Alison was single, a nurse, and was working nights. That left Sarah, Pip, and Becky. Cath read the messages that revealed they were out and meeting at nine in Maison a cocktail bar on Chatsworth Road and that they were going clubbing in the town centre later. Cath messaged that she would see them in Maison at nine.

Cath looked at her watch not much time to get ready, but she could make it if she hurried. Thirty minutes later she had showered and done her hair and nails. She picked out a short plain red dress, with heels, (her legs were her best assets she thought, and the outfit showed them off.) She went to the coat rack… sensible long zip up because of the cold or red light woollen wrap-over, no brainer she thought as she modelled the wrap in the mirror by the door, the vodka would keep her warm.

The WhatsApp group pinged again. It had been non-stop with what they were wearing, and where they were going. Cath took a selfie of her in her red dress and cardigan and then posted it to the group. Three pings followed in close succession all with thumbs up emojis. Good enough, red dress and wrap it was.

Cath had known Sarah, Pip and Becky since her early schooldays. They had been in the same class throughout their school years at Brookfield Academy. University, Jobs, boyfriends, and in Pip's case one ex-husband had not diluted their friendship and Saturday night drinks was the ritual that bonded them together every week or so.

An Accidental Death

It was a strange relationship; none of them ever talked about work. Becky worked for the local council, but Cath had no idea what she actually did. Sarah was something to do with Social Services for children, and Pip worked in logistics whatever that was. She knew that her friends were aware that she was a police officer, but they had never asked what she did, the jobs she went to or the things she had seen or experienced, and Cath didn't want to talk about such things with her friends either. It was an unwritten code between them, never to talk about work, religion, or politics. Men, marriages, affairs, and sex were on limits though and their drunken nights out always revolved those issues.

Cath also knew her three friends going out that night would all be drunk by midnight. Pip would be sick in the toilets about 1 a.m. and need putting in a taxi home shortly after. Sarah would be on her way home by 2 a.m. in the morning with a man she had met in a club. Becky would last till 3 a.m. before either finding one of her regular 'friends with benefits' or staggering to a taxi on her own and leave without telling Cath she was going home.

They all knew how the night would work out having lived it most Saturdays for many years. The only person who never knew the actual ending tended to be Cath. She struggled to get drunk and could down copious quantities of vodka without any noticeable signs of drunkenness, and being gay, she often struggled to find potential partners in the places they went to. The gay scene was a small one for women of Cath's age and tended to involve casually sleeping around at weekends with the same women, before going back to her single weekday working life.

Cath looked at her watch …. 8.30 p.m. she had half an hour, and it was a fifteen minute brisk walk to the bar. Time for a preload she thought, and she made herself a large vodka and orange in the small kitchen overlooking the lounge. She drank it in one and poured herself another one. She checked that the kitchen and lounge were presentable if anyone came back and looked up at the mezzanine bedroom above the kitchen and mentally checked that she had made the bed. She had she confirmed to herself, recalling that the bed sheets had been changed the day before. She downed the second vodka and orange, took one last look in the mirror on her way out, and set off on the short walk to the cocktail bar and her friends.

Two hours and three bars later the four girls arrived at The Junction Bar on Chatsworth Road. Cath noticed Dave through the window on her way in. He was sitting at a table in the window area, looking miserable, with two women she recognised as Helen and Ella that she had met a fortnight before in the same bar. Dave had a full half pint in front of him and the girls had a large number of empty cocktail glasses. Cath smiled; they had not made the meal.

The bar was packed and after a cursory nod and smile to the doormen, who knew Cath was a police officer, she headed for the bar, whilst her friends headed as a group to the upstairs toilets. It took Cath ten minutes to get served, but eventually four cocktails were ready for collection. Cath scanned her bank card to pay for the drinks and looked behind her for her friends.

They were directly behind her, so she passed their three Pornstar Martinis back to them, helped by a man, who wanted to take her place at the bar. Cath kept hold of her own vodka orange and as she fought her way through the throng to join them, the table, next to Dave about ten yards away became free, and she indicated to her friends to grab it. They all surged towards it, spilling the drinks of two men in the line of their path as they pushed past them. Cath, apologised to the two men who were brushing beer off their coats as she went past, and joined her friends at the table.

The four of them pulled up stools to the high table and jumped up onto them. They then went into their 'night out' modes. Pip and Becky had seen a couple of men stood nearby that they knew and beckoned them over to the table. Sarah was updating her social media with some photos she had just taken in the toilets as the girls had revitalised their make-up, and Cath was people watching and wishing she had gotten two vodka and oranges, as the one she had purchased was almost finished, and she did not fancy having to go back to the throng at the bar to get served again.

She looked across at Dave. He was still looking quite miserable. Helen and Ella looked the opposite; they were laughing and joking together. It was too loud to be heard above the music and general noise in the bar so when Cath caught Dave's eye, she mouthed silently to him.

"Good meal?"

Dave shook his head and pointed to the assortment of cocktail glasses on the table in front of him. Cath couldn't help laughing. It was as she thought when she had entered the bar and seen them at the table through the window, the girls had come out to get drunk… not have a meal.

Cath looked more closely at Helen and Ella. He could see why Dave would like Helen. She was five foot four inches of girly blonde. Blue eyes and an extremely attractive figure. She was leaning and laughing on the shoulder of her friend Ella who looked very different from the last time she had seen her. Ella who had her back to her was a lot taller than she remembered. She was nearly five feet ten inches tall in her high heeled shoes and her tanned legs below the short dress she was wearing revealed long legs that Cath would have died for. Her straight brown hair was cut in a straight line just above her waist and hung like a curtain across the backless dress. As she admired Ella's figure she turned and looked at her. Cath caught a fleeting look at Ella's brown eyes as they met hers and embarrassed at being caught looking her over quickly looked away.

The two men Sarah and Becky had been talking to put their empty glasses on the table in front of her and walked out the bar. Cath saw Becky whisper something in Sarah's ear. They both burst out laughing, with Sarah screaming loudly to her friend

"You didn't!"

Cath realised that she was admitting to recently having a fling with one of them and burst out laughing as well. The two men had been in the same year as them all at school and had been known by the girls as undatable geeks. That Becky had slept with one of them was quite funny as she had a reputation of only sleeping with muscular gym types.

Cath looked at Becky and shouted at her over the noise in the bar

"No!"

Becky shouted back "Yes!"

They all broke into laughter at the disclosure.

Hearing the screams of laughter from her friends Pip put her phone down on the table and confusedly looked around.

"What did I miss?"

"We will tell you later," shouted Becky as the girls picked up their drinks and finished them off.

Helen had seen that Cath and her friends were getting ready to leave and walked over.

"Hi Cath, it looks like you're moving on. We're off as well. Dave's taking me back to his apartment, I think he's feeling left out."

"Your right, he looks as miserable as sin. Look after him Helen, we are off clubbing."

Helen turned to Cath's friends at the table and asked

"Any chance Ella can join you? It's only eleven and I'm having an early one" she winked at Cath.

Cath looked towards her friends to see if they would be alright with a new girl in the group, but it was too late, Ella had been gathered up and was being hustled out the door towards the line of waiting taxis outside.

Another six Vodka's later Cath was sitting on her own under an outside heater in the beer garden of Association Club in the town centre. Her hopes of casual sex had been dashed earlier when the only two gay women that Cath knew there had told her that they were now a couple. Cath had wished both of her ex and potential partners that night her best wishes for the future and had decided to take some fresh air in the small outside area of the club.

She sat down on the concrete step and closed her eyes. With every scratching beat that blared from the speakers in the outside chill down area she was reminded of the sound of the shovel on the tarmac as she scraped up the remnants of Gary Traynor from the road. She tried to close her ears to the music, but her mind went straight to memories of a burnt Neil Burton. Cath shook her head wanting the images and sounds to go away. She knew it was too much alcohol and took some deep breaths to get oxygen back into her system.

Her mind began to clear a little and she was about to make her way to the bar for a last straight vodka, when she saw Ella walk into the chill out area. Cath watched her long tanned legs step confidently through the entrance and then pause. Long fingers and painted nails pulled the hem of her short skirt down. Cath's eyes lifted to Ella's head and met the brown eyes that recognised her own. Ella flicked her long brown hair from her shoulder, walked over, and sat down alongside Cath.

"Thought I'd tell you that everyone's gone home apart from me and you," reported Ella.

"I'm usually the last to leave. In fact I'm always the last," she laughed.

The two women sat on the step in awkward silence. Eventually Ella took a deep breath of the cold night air and speaking straight ahead said,

"Becky told me you're gay."

"Yes. It's not a secret," Cath confirmed into the night sky.

"I didn't know, it's just that you don't look…dressed as you are."

"You mean I've not got a skinhead haircut and wearing dungarees!" Cath laughed.

"Well yes, you're very like… girly, hair, make up, dress…you know what I mean?"

Cath would normally have made some wise crack retort, but for some reason felt like being truthful with this attractive stranger who she would probably never see again

"Being gay for me isn't about how I look it's what I am sexually. I'm still a woman, I like womanly things I just sleep with women rather than men."

"So, do I." Ella turned and looked seriously at Cath.

"Fancy a cuppa? Helen's stopping over at Dave's, so we've got the house to ourselves."

Cath woke up slowly. Her mouth tasted of alcohol, and she needed a drink. She mentally checked for a hangover and then whether she was going to be sick. She was alright on both fronts. Thank god she had stayed on vodka last night and not mixed her drinks. Although she hadn't opened her eyes yet, she was aware she was not at home. The bed was much more comfortable, and the duvet was luxuriously thick and silky. Her right breast was cupped by someone's hand, someone who was spooned up against her back, and instinctively snuggled into the warmth of the body behind her. Cath opened her eyes she could see that it was still dark through the blinds in the bedroom window; she hadn't been asleep very long.

Cath went mentally through the events of the previous night. Unusually it came back without much searching or blank spots. Couldn't have been that drunk she thought to herself. She then remembered the sex.

"Definitely not that drunk!"

Cath gently took Ella's hand from her breast and slipped out from beneath the duvet. She turned back to see if she had woken her, but Ella's rhythmic breathing told her that she was still asleep. Cath tiptoed into the hallway and tried to remember where the toilet was. The door at the end of the hallway was open and she recognised the black and white tiled floor and headed for it.

Cath sat on the toilet. Looking around her the bathroom was an absolute mess. It was the sort of mess that only two women sharing a bathroom could make and reminded her of the shared bathrooms on holidays with her friends.

Cath stood up and headed into the large walk-in shower picking up a half full bottle of men's sandalwood shower gel from the bathroom floor that had been abandoned on a damp towel. The shower was refreshing, and she dried herself on one of the large white bath towels from the pile in an alcove at the entrance. Cath found a well squeezed tube of toothpaste, she squeezed the remnants into her mouth, and brushed it round her teeth with her tongue. That felt much better she thought as the taste of alcohol disappeared into the minty freshness.

Cath turned and looked at herself in the backlit full-length mirror that covered almost one wall of the bathroom. I must get one of these she thought and then thought better of it as she remembered her tiny bathroom had hardly enough room to turn round in, never mind stand five feet away from. She appraised herself. Her legs were alright she thought but her feet were too pudgy to be attractive. She was pretty she decided, and her fine naturally wavy light brown hair was one of her better assets as well. She didn't like her breasts they were too big for her body and although still firm were now hanging looser and needed more support than when she was younger. As if to reinforce the point she pushed them up and together, as she looked at herself. Cath smiled at the image that reflected back at her, she was going to need a bigger bra in the future.

Cath walked back into the bedroom, recognising her own underwear amongst the piles of discarded clothes on the floor. Ella was still asleep. She looked beautiful asleep. Her long hair lay across the pillow and flowed onto the duvet behind her. One of her tanned legs lay outside the duvet where Cath had pushed it back to get out. Cath loved those legs and recalled them circling and tightening around her back as Ella had orgasmed a brief time ago. She knelt on the bed at the side of the exposed leg and ran the back of her hand along the smooth skin. Ella turned sleepily onto her back at Cath's touch, exposing the short soft brown down of her pubic hair. Cath paused for a second and then slipped under the duvet, crawling up the bed until she was between Ella's legs and gently waking her with slow rhythmic flicks of her tongue.

The next morning Cath and Ella were sitting up in bed with Cath resting her head in the crook of the taller girl's arm. Cath's eyes scanned the bedroom in the morning light.

"It's a lovely bedroom."

"I love this house. If I had the money I would buy it. It's been like staying at a posh hotel," Ella replied stroking Cath's hair.

"Aren't you here for another week?" Cath asked.

"No, it's back to work tomorrow, back to the grind of crashing apps and recovering lost customer data. My job's really boring. I wish I were a police officer; it sounds like a really exciting job. Do you ever get fed up with it?"

"Yes, lots of times."

The clank of the shovel on the road flashed through her head. Cath closed her eyes and leant further into the crook of Ella's arm. The warmth drove away the image that followed the sound in her head. Ella felt the increased pressure and squeezed her comfortingly with the arm that she had around her.

"Who do you talk to?" asked Ella.

"About what?" whispered Cath hesitantly.

"Anything, being gay, the horrible stuff at work, girlfriends, anything really?" asked Ella comforting Cath with a gentle squeeze of her arm.

"I tend to speak to Mrs Vodka."

Cath opened her eyes. Had she blurted that aloud. She waited to see whether Ella had heard her.

There was a long silence then Ella asked her.

"Have you ever wondered why you sleep around?"

Cath closed her eyes. The image of the burnt body in the car from the previous day came to her mind. She opened her eyes again.

"I think I like it, the searching for someone new, I think it makes me feel that I'm still attractive."

"Or, you don't have to talk to them. They come and they go, in and out of your life like a light switch. I'm going this afternoon so before you turn this light switch off tell me what makes you happy."

"This does," said Cath.

"What the wild sex with someone you hardly know!" laughed Ella.

"Of course! But the hugs afterwards are important, it drives the demons away for a while."

" Tell me about a demon, what's the latest one?"

"It's a bit gory are you sure you want to hear it?"

"I'm a big girl, hit me with your worst."

"Well, this lad got knocked over and he was in bits all over the road. I scraped most of him up with a shovel whilst a colleague picked other bits of him from underneath the chassis of the lorry that ran him over. I keep hearing the shovel on the road. Also, we think we found Neil Burton yesterday, he was in a burnt-out car. There wasn't much left of him, but I can keep smelling the burnt body. There you are… the two latest demons. There are a hundred more, but they disappear after a while."

"Is that where Mrs Vodka comes in?"

Cath thought I did say it and she was listening.

"I suppose so. It seems to work."

"Why not talk to your colleagues?"

"I don't know, it's just there for everyone. We have to cope or else you wouldn't come in the next day. Everyone just copes with it and gets on with life, you have to."

"How does Dave cope with things?"

"Alright I think. Better than me," Cath replied thoughtfully.

"But you don't know though?"

"I suppose not," confirmed Cath.

"I don't get it. If you and Dave are friends why you don't talk to each other about personal stuff it doesn't make sense," Ella observed.

"Do you talk to Helen about personal stuff? You know like being gay and relationships?" Asked Cath.

"Yes all the time. She listens but I don't think she understands any of it. She's very self-absorbed really. She is the sun and everyone else are like planets or moons, just orbiting around her. I'm sure for example that we are best friends because when we go out she knows there's no competition for the men that try to chat us up. But if I had a problem she would listen and say the right things and I'm pretty sure she would be there for me if anything really bad happened."

"What's she going to do about Dave?" asked Cath nestling further into the warmth of Ella's arm around her.

"She's going to tell him it's over before we go. He's been a bit of a distraction whilst we are up here really. She's seeing a guy called Matt and has been for a few months. Trouble is he's married and won't leave his wife, so Helen's giving him the run around to get him to leave her."

"It's serious with Matt then?"

"Who knows. Helen tends to get what Helen wants…. If he leaves his wife she will probably dump him, but while he won't she will make him chase after her. We agreed when we came up here that 'What happens in Baslow stays in Baslow.' To stick up for Helen she's not led Excy on at all. From the first night she's made it plain that it's just a fling while she's up here."

"I don't think Dave is seeing it that way, he tends to fall in love pretty quickly and out of it very slowly," remarked Cath.

"Maybe being in love is his way of coping with the stuff you go through, love's a strong emotion and maybe he uses it to mask everything else, a bit like your one-night stands and Mrs Vodka."

Cath closed her eyes. Ella was very insightful. She put her arm round Ella's waist and rested her head against her breast. Ella kissed the top of her head.

"I'm glad I came home with you last night," Cath whispered.

"I am glad you did as well" Ella whispered back.

Ella felt wet tears dropping onto her breast and embraced Cath even more strongly as the tears flowed silently from Cath's eyes. Cath didn't know why she was crying she just knew she wanted to stay in Ella's arms and didn't want them to stop.

A couple of hours later they were parked outside Cath's house in Ella's car.

"Will you be alright Cath?" asked Ella.

"Yes, I'll be fine," confirmed Cath with a smile.

"You've got my number give me a ring…. if you need to talk to someone." Ella kissed her awkwardly on the cheek.

Cath quickly opened the door and went to get out the car but before she was out, turned and blurted out to Ella

"I don't suppose you fancy coming back up next weekend ?. We could maybe go for a walk in the Peak District somewhere…… you can stop with me if Helen doesn't want to come."

"Of course, I would, I'll come on my own though. I'll ring you, and we can do the details then. Take care Cath and keep away from Mrs Vodka."

Cath closed the car door and faced the front door of her house. She took a deep breath. She was twenty nine years old and for the first time in her life she didn't feel as though she was an outsider and on her own. She didn't want to turn her back on Ella as she drove away. She had done that too often with girlfriends on a Sunday. She turned round and waved slowly as she watched Ella drive away down the road.

Chapter 26 – Remembering

Saturday 18th January

The PIR activated the lights and Holly banged the brass knocker three times. The sound of barking dogs sounded from a room deep inside the house and then went silent. Holly shuffled his feet nervously as the light in the hallway came on and Maggie Burton opened the door.

Holly took out his wallet and showed her his police warrant card.

"DS Hollins from Matlock CID Mrs Burton. Can I come in a minute?"

"Yes of course, come through to the kitchen. It's about Neil isn't it?"

Maggie turned and led him through to the kitchen where she sat down at the kitchen table. A small dog barked once and then went quiet from behind a door at the far end of the room.

"Can I get you a cup of tea Mrs Burton?" Holly asked trying to avoid both eye contact and also delaying telling her that her husband may have died.

"No, it's fine Sergeant. I was expecting a visit but thought it would be Cath Mulvey that came. How did he die?"

Holly was taken aback by Maggie Burton's straightforward approach to her husband's death. He had expected the shock to cause her to break down crying. That he would then make her a cup of tea and call a close friend or relative to comfort her. He started to feel uncomfortable.

"We don't know whether it's your husband yet, but we have found a body in a Land Rover that may be Neil's."

"Was it an accident or did he kill himself?"

"We don't know yet, we will have to wait for the fire investigators report and the post-mortem, but I have to tell you that we may never know."

Holly had a flashback to the blackened skinless eyes of Neil Burton staring accusingly at him from the front seat of the burnt-out Discovery.

"If it is him, it will have been an accident of some sort. Neil would never have the guts to kill himself." Maggie loudly affirmed to herself.

She then turned to Holly.

"Thank you Sergeant. It must be a horrible job to tell people about these things. I don't think I could do it."

Maggie got up to escort the Detective Sergeant out of the house. DS Hollins however remained seated, vacantly staring at the wall behind her. She sat back down.

"Are you alright Sergeant?"

Holly woke from the image of Neil Burton.

"Yes, Yes.. sorry I don't know what happened there."

"That's alright, Do you want a cup of tea?"

Holly didn't know if he did or not. That's weird he thought to himself. I need to answer that question. Holly tried to remember the question ....was it "do I want a cup of tea?"

The noise of a mug being placed in front of him brought him back to the kitchen. He stared at the mug on the table and realised it was full of hot tea. He must have made a decision but couldn't remember telling Maggie he wanted one. He looked across the table at Maggie as she sat down with a mug of her own.

"What do they call you when it's not Detective Sergeant?"

She watched as his eyes closed again and his chin slowly fell to his chest as though he was sleeping. Maggie put her mug down on the table.

"Are you alright?"

There was no reaction from her sleeping visitor. Concerned, Maggie repeated the question. The police officer raised his chin from his chest and opened his eyes.

"Holly," he calmly stated and took a sip of his hot tea.

Maggie leant onto the table towards him and smiled

"You're not very well Holly. You need to see a doctor. Shall I call one?"

"No I'm fine just had a lot of work on recently, I'll be alright when I've had a good night's sleep."

"Are you sure Holly?"

"Yes, I'm sure."

Holly put his mug of tea back on the table. He suddenly felt very tired and stood up to go.

"I'm really sorry about your husband Mrs Burton. Is there anyone I can contact who can come round and sit with you for a while?"

"No, you get off, I will be fine I've got the dogs and they will be the best company I can have at this time. Let me know when you know for sure, whether it's him or not."

Holly walked out the kitchen to the front door with Maggie following him. At the door he stepped to the side so she could open it. Maggie stood in front of him and looked into his eyes, then stepped forward and put her hands on his shoulders.

"Holly promise me you will see a doctor?"

Holly felt something inside him break. The close contact and warmth of someone who actually cared about him was something that he had avoided for a long time, and tonight was not a good night for it to happen. Holly's eyes erupted in tears, and he felt any hope and happiness he carried in his soul sinking into the ground around him. He softly disentangled himself from Maggie's arms and walked through the open door without looking at her, so she didn't see the rivulets of tears running down his face as he hurried out the door.

Chapter 27 – Mr and Mrs Hollins

Saturday 18th January

By the time he had reached his home three miles away Holly had regained most of his outwardly normal appearance. Everything had gone alright at Mrs Burton's he told himself. She had not seen him crying and he had delivered the message to her in a professional way. Everything would be fine tomorrow if only he could get some rest and a good night's sleep.

Holly pulled into the driveway of the 1970's detached house on Megdale Road at Matlock. There were tufts of grass sprouting from between the broken paving on his driveway. He needed to get the drive re-laid he thought. That would be several thousand pounds that he didn't have. There was little chance he would ever be able put that sort of money together in the near future either, he sighed resignedly.

Holly turned off the engine and sat silently in the car. He wanted to cry for some reason but didn't know why. After a while he took a deep breath and got out of the car, walked to the front door, and let himself in. The lights were on in the hall and landing, and he could hear music coming loudly from Georgia's bedroom. Bobby, his Golden Retriever, poked his head round the kitchen door saw him and waggled excitedly down the hallway to greet him. Holly reached out, bent down, and took the dogs face in his hands.

"Good Boy Bobby, Good Boy!"

"Is that you?" a voice shouted from the living room.

"Yes it's only me!" he shouted back.

There was a pause and he stroked Bobby's ears. The living room door opened and his wife, a short muscular woman came out.

"Why are you so late?" she asked accusingly.

"I had to tell someone that their husband might have died."

"Wasn't there anybody else in the Derbyshire Constabulary that could do that? Why does it always have to be you?"

Bobby looked at Donna and trotted past her back into the kitchen. Holly took a deep breath and wished he could follow Bobby.

"There wasn't anybody else tonight and it's part of my job, I can't just walk away, things have to be finished before I can come home from work."

"I suppose Cath,"

She emphasised the 'Cath.'

"….was with you, she usually is when you're late."

"No, she wasn't, and she isn't always with me. It depends who's on and what the job is. I have to work with her as she's the only woman on my team. Can you give it a rest with the jealousy Donna? I've just walked through the door."

"Give it a rest!" Donna shouted at him.

"I wish I could give it a rest! She's been a right little bitch all afternoon! She's done nothing but chelp back at me every time I've asked her to do anything…. and she's not cleaned up her bedroom as we agreed. I told her that you would be having a word with her when you came in…. Georgia! Georgia! ….come down here! ….your dads' home and wants a word with you! ….Georgia! ….I told you to come down here! …..Get down here now!" Donna screamed angrily to her daughter upstairs in her bedroom.

Georgia's exasperated voice replied over the music.

"In a minute!"

Holly saw Donna's face explode in rage, she raced up the stairs and then he heard Georgia's door crash open followed by screaming

"Get off me!... Get off me!"

"Shit!" Holly thought and raced up the stairs after his wife.

When he got to his daughter's bedroom he saw through the open door, that his wife was on top of his daughter slapping her face and grabbing at her hands as she tried to fight her off. It was an unfair fight. As he watched, Donna pinned Georgia to the bed, slapped her hard across her cheek and red faced with anger, screamed into her face.

"Don't you ever tell me to wait a minute you ungrateful little cow!... I'll knock you into next week!"

Donna raised her right hand and slapped her hard across her cheek again. Georgia looked across to him, the cheek reddening as she glared at him, the anger in her eyes not towards his wife but towards him. He knew it was his fault, he should have left years ago but that would have meant leaving her with Donna and he couldn't do that. Holly grabbed his wife's arm as she went to strike his daughter again and pulled her off the bed.

"Come on Donna, there's no need for any of this!" he pleaded.

"What do you know what there's a need for!.... you're never here! .....you don't see what I have to put up with! You're a useless husband and a useless father!" Donna screamed at him.

She had worked herself up into an absolute rage. He knew from years of daily experience that it would not stop there. Donna had no 'off' button she just kept going until she blew herself out and she was nowhere near that point yet.

Georgia glared at him.

"She's mad! Why can't we leave her!"

He couldn't think what to say to his daughter, he knew the courts would never give him custody over her mother, but didn't know how to explain that to her. His head wasn't working, he couldn't think. He couldn't face this anymore and he turned to get away, as Donna in a rage got to her feet. He was on the second step going down the stairs when the punch caught him on the top of his head causing him to stagger and then fall down into a heap at the bottom. His ankle had twisted, he could feel it swelling up, but it wasn't broken. He rubbed his head where Donna's punch had landed, there was no cut so no-one would know.

Donna barged him into the wall as she went past him into the kitchen her phone in her hand. In the kitchen doorway she turned to him as he got to his feet.

"You love your job eh! Let's see how much you love it when you're arrested for domestic violence then!" she screamed and punched herself hard with her right fist on her right cheek, once and then again leaving a bruising red mark.

Holly stared at what he had just seen. The punches weren't pulled. He had not thought it possible that anyone could actually punch themselves so hard. She showed the phone to him and pressed the "9" button twice, and then screamed menacingly to him.

"Let's see how your so-called friends think about you when you're arrested for domestic violence, let's see how many come and see you when you're locked up in a cell and suspended."

Grinning triumphally at him Donna went to press the last '9'. Holly rushed forward and went to grab the phone from her hand and close the call. Donna head butted him on his cheek as he grabbed the phone and Holly stunned, staggered backwards onto the floor. He looked up at the hate filled face of his wife above him as she mouthed obscenities at him. For some reason Holly realised that he could no longer hear anything. He could feel his cheek swelling, he had tried to stand up to her but knew now that he was beaten, he slumped slowly against the kitchen cabinets.

"You are mad, you really are mad!"

He was not sure if he was referring to Donna or himself.

"…if I lose my job we lose everything."

The kick to his midriff caught him by surprise and then his wife's spittle flecked face came up to his and snarled,

"I lose nothing Holly, I get your pension and I get Georgia, and I'll make sure you never see her again. The only person who will lose everything is you, you pathetic man!"

Holly knew that she was right. He just wanted to get away, get out of the house, go anywhere, away from this hell he was in. Holly got unsteadily to his feet.

"I'm taking the dog out, if that's alright," he asked Donna.

"That's it run away, don't hurry back, nobody wants you here anyway!"

Holly picked up the dog lead and Bobby, who had been cowering in the corner, trotted over to him. He slipped the lead on the dog and limped towards the door. He noticed he hadn't even got to take his coat off. He opened the door and turned to look back at Donna.

"Just once I'd like to come home and not be faced with this madness!"

"I don't care!" Donna hissed and very slowly, arched her neck and spat into his face.

"The only person that cares about you is that whore you work with!"

Twenty minutes later Holly was sitting in the bandstand in Hall Leys Park in the centre of Matlock. His cheek was smarting. His fingers picked out a chip from the tray on his lap and he offered it Bobby. Bobby sitting eagerly in front of him wolfed it down and waited for the next one. Holly put a piece of fish on his fork and raised it towards his mouth. Then sat silent and motionless. Holly sat there haunted by the image of Gary Traynor being shovelled by Cath into the bag he was holding and the blankly staring eyes of Neil Burton. Most of all he was haunted by the feeling of Maggie Burton's considerate touch on his shoulders.

In the distance a skateboarder was trundling through the park. Eventually he rumbled past Holly causing Bobby to bark a warning that woke him from his stupor. Holly looked down at him and put the fish back in the tray with the remaining chips and peas.

"Good boy Bobbie…Good boy" Holly stroked his ears and then put his tea on the floor, and watched as Bobby made the contents of the tray disappear. There must be more to life than this, thought Holly, and sat back on the bench. He felt so…so tired.

Much later he looked down at the big brown eyes looking up at him expectantly,

"Come on Bobby let's not sit moping around here, carpe diem and all that, she will have blown herself out by now with a bit of luck."

Bobby stood up and they were off on their way home.

Chapter 28 – Dave and Helen

Saturday 18th January

Dave laid on his bed with his hands at the back of his head. Helen's blonde tousled hair rose from under the duvet.

"What's happening Dave, things aren't working down here!" she smiled up at him.

"Sorry Helen must have had too much beer," he explained looking into her blue eyes.

He knew it wasn't the beer he was distracted by something, but he couldn't figure out exactly what it was. His mind was restless, there was something about work that was bugging him, but he couldn't put his finger on it. It was there but just out of reach, like a name on the tip of your tongue that you can't quite recall. The more he thought about it the further it seemed to drift away.

He broke away from his dreaming. It was Helen's last night. She was going back to Crawley tomorrow, and he was going to be sad to see her go. He had been disappointed that on her last night Helen had preferred to drink cocktails with Ella rather than go for a curry with him, but they had eventually waved goodbye to Ella when she had gone off with Cath and her friends. He would buy Cath breakfast for that favour on Monday he resolved to himself. Helen was, however, stopping over at his apartment tonight and he didn't want anything to get in the way of her not wanting to see him again. A failure to perform caused by his work distraction could well fall into that category.

"Doesn't mean that I can't sort you out though!" he laughed and flipped her onto her back.

Kneeling above her he began playfully biting her sides, first one side and then the other, making her squirm and flail at him with her arms as the tickling sensation rippled through her body. He continued lower down her body until she was able to raise her legs around his broad muscular shoulders, and give an ecstatic groan as his kisses found the right spot.

The following morning Dave woke late into the morning. Helen was sleeping soundly at his side in a foetal position. He turned over towards her and rested himself on his elbow to look at her. She was beautiful he thought. He loved how her natural blonde hair curled over her pale shoulders, how her manicured eyebrows shaped her eyes, how her nose was perfectly formed for the size of her face. Not too big, not too small just perfect. Helen opened one blue eye and looked at him.

"I knew you were looking at me," she grinned.

"Coffee?" he asked.

"Yes. But not yet. I want to see whether that beer's worn off from last night first. I think I owe you something."

As she slid under the duvet, Dave knew from his reaction that this time he wasn't going to be distracted.

They had fallen asleep afterwards and it was mid-day when he became aware of Helen moving around the bedroom. She was showered, her hair wrapped in a towel like a turban and dressed in one of his shirts. He felt her sit on the edge of the bed, putting last night's clothing into her overnight bag.

"Morning!" said Dave sleepily.

"Afternoon." Helen replied smiling at him.

"I've made you a coffee." She indicated to the bedside table at his side.

"What time is it?"

"About 1.30 p.m. Ella will be here in about an hour."

"Are you getting off straight away?"

"Yes. We've both got work in the morning and it's a three hour drive back home at least."

"You've got time for some breakfast then …. Or lunch?" Dave grinned hopefully.

"Yes, I'm just going to dry my hair first."

An Accidental Death

Helen took out a travel hairdryer from her overnight bag and disappeared into the other bedroom. Dave clambered out of bed, put on a t-shirt and a pair of shorts, and made his way to the kitchen. There was an uneasiness between them. He knew it was around what would happen next; both were putting off the inevitable conversation. Dave busied himself around the kitchen making coffee, toast, and scrambled egg, then shouted to tell her that breakfast was ready.

Eventually Helen hurried into the kitchen, dry haired and in a pink tracksuit from her overnight bag. She sat down opposite him.

"Well, Dave…" Helen put a slice of cold egg and toast into her mouth.

"I've really enjoyed the last couple of weeks, but it's time for me to get off I'm afraid."

His heart was telling him to plead with her not to finish with him or at least for them to carry on seeing each other on his days off.

"Is there anybody in Crawley you're going back to?"

A split-second hesitation.

"No, Dave. But we are going to be too far apart to carry on what we have had. I've really enjoyed the last couple of weeks and think you're a great guy, but I think things should end here."

Helen looked at his disappointed face.

"Don't be upset, I'd rather it happened now while we are friends rather than later when we have just drifted apart."

He was heartbroken but would not let her see it.

"Yes, I agree it's probably for the best. It's been a brilliant couple of weeks. We both might feel different tomorrow though Helen."

"Yes we might, but we probably won't." Helen smiled at him.

Helen's phone pinged and she looked at the message.

"Ella's on her way, she will be here soon."

Dave grabbed at the chance they might not be breaking up permanently. He needed to change the subject in case Helen rowed back from what she had just said.

"Who is going to sort out the house and Paul's Will if Neil's dead?"

"I was thinking about that lying in bed this morning, so I've googled it. Someone takes over the practice by the look of it. I'm in no rush for the money so I'll leave it a couple of weeks and then chase it up. I fancied driving the Porsche back, but can't change the name over yet, so it looks like I'm not going to be doing any posing in it till the summer."

"How much do you think his estates worth, the house must be nearly a million?" asked Dave.

"Neil told me around two million. So, I will be a millionaire soon, it sounds really weird Helen Hall the millionaire. Mum's not happy but hey-ho, it's better in my pocket ."

"Why is your mum not happy?" Dave asked.

"She didn't like Paul after what happened in Ibiza. In the early nineties, she was a rep for Thomson Holidays in Ibiza and Neil Burton and Paul Trueman were on the same team. Near the end of the season she told me all the reps went out in a group one night and according to mum got quite drunk. She ended up with Paul and apparently I was the result."

"That's some admission from your mum, when did she tell you?"

"Just before my 18th birthday. It's never really bothered me, Mum always loved me, and my stepdad always treated me like he was my real dad so if anything, it was quite exciting finding out I had another dad. I used to think he could be quite famous, a footballer or a singer or something. Anyway, I did a bit of a social media search on Paul Trueman, and a picture came up of him and a Neil Burton at some Rotary thing in a newspaper. Well, the chances of it being another Paul Trueman with a Neil Burton were quite slim. It was a short search then to find Paul Trueman's business in Matlock and I turned up at his office one day. He was quite obnoxious, denied at first knowing my mum and I thought he was ever so snobby. I told him what my mum had told me, and he eventually realised that he could have been my dad but didn't want me to tell anyone because of his 'reputation.' I thought if you don't want to know me publicly it's your loss not mine, so I decided never to see him again until he would. He sent Birthday and Christmas cards and I sometimes sent him a Christmas card if I remembered, but that was it, until Neil Burton rang Mum and told her that Paul had died. I rang Neil the following Monday and he asked me to come up and sort out his funeral and estate."

"I wish some mysterious relative would turn up and leave me a couple of million. My notice would be in, and I'd be off to the south of France like a shot!"

Helen looked at him seriously.

"You wouldn't Dave. You love the job you do. You have just lost your ambition. You told me that when you left university you wanted to make Superintendent by the time you were thirty. You're twenty seven and have not even made Sergeant yet. Even if I did want us to make a go of it together there's no way I would want to marry a detective. There's no order in your life, I would have no idea when you were starting or finishing work or if you were going to have days off. You did a thirty six hour shift last week when that girl got murdered and have been preoccupied with it ever since. You've been here physically but that's all. You have no life Dave, just a job."

"You noticed," agreed Dave.

"Dave that's the choice you have made. Have you ever given any thought as to why you are stuck as a detective and that you have given up on your planned career. You told me that both you and Cath passed your Sergeant exams last year but have not taken it any further. I've only known you a short time but I'm sure that it must be worrying you, and that you know it."

Dave was taken aback by Helen's insightfulness.

"I am going for promotion Helen I just want to get some more experience on CID first. I don't know why but I feel as though it's the right thing to do. It's something that I can't put my finger on. Like whether you really did lock the door or leave the oven on when you go out."

Helen reached across the table and took Dave's hand.

"Think about what I am saying Dave, you are a really nice bloke, but I don't think you're ever going to get anywhere in the police staying in CID, or for that matter settled down with a nice girl, as a detective."

"You're saying I need to get promoted, and get a nice 9-5 desk jockey job at Headquarters for the next twenty years."

"No, I'm not saying that. I'm saying that you joined the police as a career not to be a career detective. You should be going up through the ranks before it's too late. You can have a home life as well as a work life, but not in the job that you do at the moment. I work in HR and see this all the time, people stuck in a role thinking they are 'making a difference.' They don't really, the job spits them out at the end of the day and things just go on without them. We are all pebbles thrown in a bucket; we make a few waves, but the surface goes back to as it was after a while."

Dave listened to what Helen was saying and knew it was true. He wasn't sure if he was ready to give up his job as a detective though or no longer work with Cath and Holly. It was a decision he knew he had put off for a long time and it was one he would think about after Helen had gone home.

"Just going back to your mum why didn't she tell Paul she was pregnant?"

"Well according to her they all went back to England about a month later and it was only then she found out that she was pregnant with me."

"She could still have contacted him and let him know," remarked Dave.

"She says they had a big fall out just before she came back, and that as a result there was no way she was going to let him have anything to do with me."

"Did you know Neil Burton's wife told us Neil was gay and was in a relationship with Paul Trueman," confided Dave.

"Mum told me he was gay. She told me that she found out he was gay when she called in on him a few days after they had done the business to surprise him, and surprised herself. When she walked through the door he was actually having sex with Neil on the bed!"

"What did she do!" exclaimed Dave.

"Well, nothing really, they were facing the other way and didn't see her, so she went back out and shut the door quietly behind her," Helen laughed.

"Ella will be here in a minute, so I'll cut it short. The reason she didn't want him to have anything to do with me was because it came out that him and Neil had been dealing drugs to the holidaymakers all summer. They were very good at hiding it though because all the reps were very close, and Mum says she never had a clue. She used to joke with me that she didn't have a clue about them being gay either and that was much more difficult to hide with some of the holidaymakers they had to look after. Anyway towards the end of the season it appears their drug dealing ended up treading on the toes of some people who didn't like what they were doing. The rumour amongst the reps afterwards according to Mum was that they were both visited by some large blokes who had a quiet word with them. The next morning Neil and Paul were on a plane back to the UK. Mum and the other reps followed a few weeks later at the end of the season. It came as a bit of a surprise to her that Neil turned out to be a solicitor and Paul a business consultant. She says she never trusted them after the drugs thing."

Dave sat back in his kitchen chair.

"Well, that's quite a story. At least you have come out of it alright. If you need anything doing up here you only have to ask……if only as a friend nothing else. I don't want to come across as a bit intense I know that we have probably finished, but I'm not daft, stalker like."

"I know that Dave, I wouldn't have stuck with you if you were. Come here you daft thing, I'm going to miss you."

Dave stood up out of his chair and Helen threw her arms around him. She hugged him very tightly and he smelt the almonds of her newly washed hair probably for the last time. There was the honk of a car horn on the car park below the apartment and she let go of him. She turned to the door and took a step towards it before looking back.

"Dave would you…."

He finished the sentence for her laughing "…bring my bags down."

Chapter 29 – That Monday Morning Feeling

Monday 20th January

Cath turned over, leant on her elbow, stopped the alarm on her phone which was on the bedside table and then laid back on the bed. "That came around quickly!" she mused to herself and then realised that for the first time as long as she could remember she had slept through the night. The whole night. From the moment her head hit the pillow to the moment her alarm had gone off. No lying awake for hours trying to get to sleep, not suddenly waking up in the middle of the night wide awake with some horrendous mutilated body vision fading into the blackness of the room and then hours of restless sleep until the alarm went off. The whole night she thought to herself, and she realised that she felt happy about it; the sort of happiness that you have when you wake up on the first day of the school summer holidays and it's a sunny day and you feel like it's going to be like this for the whole of the holidays even though you know underneath it won't be. But just for that one minute of that one day you feel that there is the possibility that it could happen, that sunny summer days could last for a whole six weeks.

Cath jumped out of bed; the large Quicksilver t-shirt she was wearing swirled loosely around her as she ran down the mezzanine stairs to the kitchen diner. It was cold and she turned up the thermostat on the wall at the bottom of the stairs and made herself a cup of coffee. Morning strong with a drop of milk just as she liked it and then raced back up the stairs with it to her bed where she rewarmed herself in the still warm thick duvet. She took a few sips of the hot coffee and put it down on the bedside table and picked up her phone.

Here goes nothing she thought and texted Ella. "Hope you had a good trip back x." She then paused and deleted it. She typed, "Have a good week at work see you Saturday xx." Cath read it back several times and deleted it again. Neither text expressed what she wanted to say. She took a deep breath and typed, "Are we alright?" Thoughtful emoticon. and pressed send.

The reply was almost instantaneous. "I hope so XX" - smiley face emoticon.

Cath's heart jumped with happiness, and she sent back "Heart" emoticon.

Ella immediately sent back the same emoticon. Cath put her phone down and picked up her coffee. She felt so happy that she started to cry.

Holly an hour later was sitting, silently crying, on a park bench in Hall Leys Park in Matlock, with Bobby asleep at his feet. Holly did not know why he was crying, he just felt intolerably sad. He was however aware that he was having trouble concentrating on anything and that his memory was failing. At that moment he couldn't remember what had happened between Maggie Burton asking him whether he wanted a cup of tea, and her taking him by the shoulders as he left and asking him if he was alright, no matter how hard he tried.

He wiped his eyes with the sleeve of his jacket and took out his phone. He had just remembered he needed to tell Dave and Cath that Professor Graham had moved forward the post-mortem that morning to 8 a.m.

He checked the time on the phone, it was past 8 a.m. There was no point in ringing Cath and Dave about the post-mortem, they wouldn't make it. He stood up and then straightened himself to his full height and took a deep breath.

"Come on Bobby…Carpe Diem" and limping slowly set off home to get ready for work.

Chapter 30 – The Beginning Of The End

Monday 20th January

At 8.15 a.m., bang on time to the minute, Dave pulled up outside Cath's house and pipped. For the fifth time that morning he checked his phone to see whether there had been any messages from Helen. Nothing. It was still early he told himself and maybe she would text him later. The previous afternoon when she had finished with him, she had not ruled out getting back together or at least being friends and at least if they were friends he would see her again and you never knew what might happen in the future, especially if he left CID and got promoted.

He needed to see her picture and opened the 'photo' folder on his phone. He had no photographs of the two of them together, in fact he didn't have a single one of her. He realised that she had been very careful that any selfies of them both had been taken on her phone and although she had promised to share them she hadn't done so. He checked his Facebook account. She was no longer on it and had unfriended him.

His heart sank. He had been well and truly dumped. He put the phone back in his pocket sat back in his seat and closed his eyes. He always had his career, he thought, Helen had given him good advice about that. Girlfriends might come and go but his career was always there, and he had got that back up and running before setting off to pick Cath up that morning.

The car door opened, and Cath plonked herself down on the front passenger seat. He could tell by her body language in that split second that she was full of life and energy that morning. He wanted her to be down and hungover, her miserableness would have made him feel better. Her good mood was confirmed when she turned to him as she fastened her seat belt.

"What a brilliant day! Come on let's get going we don't want to be late."

Dave started the car, looked in his mirror and sighed.

"You will never guess what. Helen's dumped me."

"Well, I wasn't expecting that!" she mockingly exclaimed.

"She seemed such a nice girl as well. Are you alright ?"

"Yeah I suppose so, we were only seeing each other for a couple of weeks, I'll get over it."

"I hope you do," thought Cath, or the next few weeks were going to feel very long indeed.

"I'm glad that you have decided to move on," Cath empathised.

"Especially as my ears don't want to hear about Helen this and Helen that all day, I don't think they could take it! Are you sure she's history?"

"Absolutely sure, I've unfriended her on Facebook and everything."

Dave drove in thoughtful silence the three miles to the mortuary. At the mortuary Dave told Cath he needed to check his phone, and walked out of earshot to make a phone call. Cath watched patiently from a distance trying to catch the conversation. The person on the other end did most of the speaking but she heard Dave say,

"Thank you, it's much appreciated. I won't let you down."

Dave walked back to the car and Cath, intrigued, asked him

"What was that about?"

Dave's face flushed red in excitement.

"I can't tell you yet but it's really good news."

Cath sighed and hoped it wasn't Helen telling him she was coming to see him next weekend.

Billie Morton came out of the double doors of the post-mortem room as Cath and Dave were walking along the corridor towards the mortuary office. Dave glimpsed Professor Graham and Sally Brooks by a mortuary table upon which was a black wizened mound.

"Has he started then?" Dave asked Billy.

Billy laughed.

"He's nearly finished, can't you detectives get out of bed in a morning?"

Dave checked his watch.

"It was scheduled for nine o clock Billy and it's only just past eight thirty so we're actually early."

"Nope! Changed yesterday to eight didn't Holly tell you? I rang him up in the afternoon and told him."

"Nope, back at you" retorted Cath.

"Have we missed much?"

"Nope!" Billy laughed.

Cath and Dave got suited up and entered the mortuary. What was left of the car seat was laid on the floor leaving a rusty brown sprinkling of ash around it on the polished tiles. Professor Graham was leaning back onto the body tray that held the remains that had been in the seat of the Discovery. He was in a good mood and going through what he had uncovered with Sally Brooks and another CSI.

"In the absence of evidence, of which there is very little on such a badly burnt body, circumstantial evidence has to be considered in ascertaining any cause of death. In the case of Mr John Doe here I can tell you that the weight, build, sex, and age would match those of Mr Neil Burton the owner of the vehicle. I would be very surprised if a DNA match in a few days did not confirm that the body is that of Neil Burton. There is smoke damage in his lungs and trachea, and this gives a strong indication that he was alive when the fire started, and I would say with some strong opinion that at some time after the fire started he fell into an unconscious state from inhalation of toxic fumes caused by the fire. I base this assumption on the premise that if he were conscious I would have expected him to make some attempt to exit the vehicle, but his seat belt was still in place. It is very difficult for even the most determined person to commit suicide by fire and not change your mind when the body begins to experience the pain caused by such extreme heat. There is no evidence that I can find at this time to suggest foul play of any kind, although there is very little of the body left to examine for it. As you can see the best-preserved area is the torso itself. Both legs have gone which suggests that the hottest part of the fire was in the footwell. I am not a fire investigator, but it would suggest that the fire entered the cabin of the car from underneath or the engine compartment of the vehicle. I can't find any evidence from the burning patterns on what's left of the body that he was doused in petrol or some other flammable substance. In a nutshell, there is no evidence that he was murdered, and neither is there any evidence to suggest that he killed himself. I can tell you, that I am fairly confident that cause of death would have been by inhalation of toxic gases although trauma injury caused by fire cannot be ruled out. Any questions or anything you think I've missed."

Dave and Cath looked at each other and shook their heads and then looked towards Sally Brooks. Sally shook her head at Professor Graham.

"No, I think you have covered everything."

Sally then turned to Dave and Cath.

"Luckily, I'd got Nick, whose on work experience from university, to help out with the labels seeing as you two couldn't get out of bed this morning."

Sally's smiling face told the two detectives that she was having a joke at their expense.

"Professor Graham did manage to get some skin from the finger ends of his clenched fists that I'll run through against the lifts we got from Neil Burton's house. It might identify him quicker than DNA and save us some money."

Dave asked, "Can you run it against Dylan Oxley as well…just in case."

Sally Brooks chuckled.

"If it comes back to Dylan Oxley you're telling BJ not me…. but can I be there when you do."

"Right then!" remarked Professor Graham.

"If we're all done let's get a brew. Billy should have boiled the kettle by now."

Chapter 31 – Breakfast In The Peak

Monday 20th January

Martin Gordon walked into the breakfast lounge of the Peak Edge Hotel. He looked as though he was on a summer holiday in Cuba rather than in a hotel on the outskirts of the Peak District, in late January. His multi coloured parrot themed cotton shirt clashed wildly with his brilliant white flared trousers and white un-socked espadrilles. As he entered Gordy looked around the lounge looking for any potential threat.

A group of four men of differing ages sat at a table against the window. All wore identical grey polo shirts with red sleeves that he assumed were a corporate uniform of some sort. The young man facing him at that table, looked up and caught his eye. He blushed as Gordy held the stare, and then looked away.

No threat there he told himself. He transferred his gaze to the only other occupied table. Loud laughter erupted from the corporate table, and he glanced back to see the three men, whose backs had been turned towards him, quickly looking back from him to their breakfasts in front of them. "Twats!" Gordy thought to himself and again looked back to the other occupied table.

The three large muscular men were also uniformly dressed… although there was no way that he would have called it corporate. Sockless black flip flops accompanied by loose navy-blue weightlifters' shorts and faded loose fitting cream t-shirts appeared to be the order of the day. He walked over to the table and took the empty fourth chair and sat down. A young brown-haired girl walked over from the breakfast buffet area.

"Would you like some toast sir, brown or white, and some tea or coffee. The cold buffet is over to your right, and we have an array of cereals, fruit juices and fresh fruits. If you want a hot breakfast, that is served by chef at the hot buffet counter to your right," the young girl spieled.

She then pointed to the hot buffet area from where the mingling smell of bacon, sausage, beans, and fried eggs wafted across the dining room.

Gordy, without looking up towards her, recited loudly,

"Toast, brown, Tea, pot of, and milk. Could chef make me a bowl of porridge, water not milk." Gordy dismissed the girl with a wave of his hand.

"I'll ask chef sir."

The Waitress turned and walked towards the kitchen.

Gordy looked round the table at the heaped piles of 'Full English' on the plates of the three men.

"You lot will die of heart-attacks before you're forty. You should look after yourselves. Did you know that you're sixty per cent more likely to die of coronary heart disease at the age of sixty five if you have bacon for breakfast every day…I bet you didn't? You should try porridge every morning, it will reduce your cholesterol as well as reducing your chance of cancer at seventy by twenty eight percent."

Pete cut a piece of bacon from one of the rashers on his plate, forked it with half a sausage then dipped it in the yolk of one of the three eggs, before smearing it in the brown sauce at the side of the pile of fried mushrooms. The mass of dripping food was then pushed into his mouth and as he chewed on it he agreed with his boss.

"You're right Gordy, we need to look after ourselves more don't we boys."

Kwadj and Briggsy chewing on similar amounts of fried food nodded in agreement. Gordy glanced round the room checking that no-one was listening to them.

"Right lads straight forward day today. First job is to go down to Trueman's house at Baslow. If Burton is right it should be empty as his daughter should have gone home yesterday. Recce it first and if no-one is in let's get in and out without anyone noticing us. The MacBook should be in the desk drawer, that's all we want so let's keep it neat and tidy."

Kwadj finished chewing, swallowed, and confirmed he had understood.

"No problem boss. Are we straight back after, or do you want me and Briggsy to stay for a few days?"

"No, we all came up together and we can all go back together soon as we've got the MacBook. I don't think we will ever need to come up here again."

"That's fine we'll check out this morning then. Are we taking both cars?" asked Briggsy.

Gordy thought for a few seconds.

"Yes, you and Kwadj go in one Range Rover and me and Pete will go in the other. I don't fancy sharing a car with you two farting bacon and eggs at me all morning."

All three nodded and grunted in assent of their boss's plan. Pete clattered his knife and fork down on his empty yolk and sauce smeared plate, wiped his mouth with the back of his hand and asked Gordy the question that had been bugging all three of them for the previous four weeks.

"What's the issue with the MacBooks boss?"

At that moment, the girl returned with Gordy's porridge, toast, and tea on a tray. She removed the bowl of steaming porridge from the tray and placed it heavily in front of him. She then removed the rack of toast and pot of tea and put it to the side of his bowl of porridge, before polishing a spoon on a white napkin she was carrying and laying it at the side of it.

"Is everything alright sir?"

Gordy looked at the breakfast in front of him and nodded

"Yes, thank you."

Gordy picked up his folded napkin and tucked it into his parrot shirt as he waited for the waitress to disappear back into the kitchen. He then looked round the table at the three faces looking expectantly at him.

"I'll tell you, but not a word outside the four of us…apart from Jill of course."

Gordy looked conspiratorially around him and continued.

"The MacBook's are important because they contain all the companies and bank accounts we launder our money through. Trueman and Burton laundered all our money out of the country and then invested it in property, mainly in London. You three take the cash to the Isle of Man on the ferry and deposit it into the Swiss bank in Douglas. That Swiss account is for a Delaware company. The Delaware company then buys non-existent yachts and planes in the West Indies from an Antiguan brass plate company. With the proceeds that company provides loans to other offshore companies owned by us, with which we purchase property, mainly in London. Burton and Trueman are the trustee directors of all the companies involved. Burton did all the legal work off his books and Trueman administered the accounts and companies as our Business Consultant. Rental and sale proceeds from any properties or investments go back to the loan companies through the companies that own the properties. When we want cash for product, Trueman transfers it as a share dividend to themselves from one of the loan companies to an escrow account run by him and Burton in Mexico and then it's transferred to our suppliers in South America."

Gordy took a spoonful of porridge and looked at the three others around the table. Their silent glazed look told him all he needed to know, he smiled, swallowed the porridge, and went on.

"As you can understand, it's not fool proof, but nothing whatsoever comes back to us, and it's complicated enough to dissuade plod from finding out how our operation runs and where our assets are."

Briggsy joked, "I got lost after Isle of Man Ferry."

"You're lucky!" retorted Pete "I got lost after the MacBooks are important!"

Kwadj took a drink of coffee and laughed.

"What's a MacBook?"

The four men burst out laughing.

Gordy stopped laughing.

"In a nutshell we've got loads of offshore companies with their own bank accounts. Each bank account has got lots of money in it that looks legit, and we own millions of pounds worth of rental property in London that is not traceable back to us either. To ensure that nothing comes back to me or Jill the only people who are named or have access to the accounts were Burton and Trueman. They both kept everything on two MacBooks, and each had access to everything on both in case something happened to one of them. That access was by biometric password but according to Burton on the day Trueman died, due to some cock up between them, Burton hadn't got access to Trueman's, and Burton's was in a bag that Trueman was carrying, and the bag got nicked. The trail on the nicked one is dead so that leaves us with just the one belonging to Trueman that is at his house. We need it so we can authorise a payment to our suppliers and also get the various company details when we go over to Antigua to set up new trustee directors."

Pete looked across at Gordy.

"Sounds complicated….but how are you going to access Trueman's MacBook without the biometrics?"

Gordy took a spoonful of porridge.

"It's not apparently a long job and we can get round the biometrics, but we need some geek to do it. Problem has been finding some geek I can trust to do it. I don't want someone making off with the information on it and nicking all our money or running off to the police with it. Anyway, Jill's pretty sure she's found someone we can trust now, so we just need to pick it up and I can get the money to our South American friends by the end of the month sorted. Then we are all going to Antigua for a few weeks in February to set it all up again. Jill's sorting out new bent solicitors to replace Burton this morning. If the other MacBook ever turns up you three will deal with the people who are in possession of it."

"I won't say I understood all that Gordy but be good to get some sun after this winter," Briggsy observed, as he finished off his breakfast.

"Didn't follow a word of the company thing Gordy but like Briggsy I like the idea of Caribbean sunshine next month. You going this morning?"

Kwadj made fun of Gordy's attire and all three ex commandos burst out laughing.

"You piss taking twats! At least I get dressed for breakfast you three look like you've just walked out the sweat room of some boxing club! Go get showered and changed we will meet up at ten in the car park."

Chapter 32 – Consequences

Saturday 18th January

At 10 a.m. that morning Briggsy climbed into driving seat of one of the white Range Rovers whilst Kwadj threw their bags into the back, and then climbed up into the passenger seat. Briggsy started the engine and pulled out of the hotel turning left towards Darley Dale.

"Scenic route I think Kwadj, may as well make the best of our rural holiday."

Briggsy fastened his seat belt.

"Why not, be good to get back home though, the ex is playing right up about me missing little Charlie's birthday party yesterday."

"Not got that problem. Hope you told her to think of the money. Gordy will pay us big style for this week's work. What you reckon ten grand each?" asked Kwadj.

"At least. I can't believe the cops haven't found that guy we dumped in the pond though, numpties or what. The girl was what fifty yards away."

Briggsy shook his head at the uselessness of the police.

"Is Pete behind us or have they gone the other way?" asked Kwadj looking over his shoulder.

Briggsy checked his mirror.

"They're about three behind us." Briggsy drove past the turn off for Stanedge Golf Club and then half a mile further on turned right towards Beeley.

Three vehicles behind the first white Range Rover, Pete and Gordy were discussing the route to Baslow as well.

"Where the fuck is he going! The Satnav says we should have turned right when we came out the hotel!" exclaimed Gordy.

"Fuck knows. I reckon they think they're on their holidays... hang on Satnav now says were back on route. What's the plan when we get there Gordy?"

"Park up nearby, Briggsy and Kwadj can then break in. It should be empty so they should be in and out in a couple of minutes. The ram's in the back if they need it."

"Sounds like a plan...bloody hell look at this twat!"

A black Nissan Navara had pulled out from behind them and went past them at speed and then also overtook the white Golf in front. The Navara was still on the wrong side of the road when a grey Micra came round the bend a hundred yards in front of it and swerved to its nearside to avoid a head on collision. The white Golf in front of Pete was forced to brake sharply to let it into the line of traffic. Pete anticipating the sharp braking manoeuvre of the Golf had already braked sharply throwing Gordy forward and whiplashing him back into the seat.

"Fucking idiot! Nearly wiped that car out!" shouted Gordy getting his breath back after the blow to his chest by the seat belt.

"There's some absolute wankers on the road nowadays, no patience some of em, look he's going again!" observed Pete.

The road was now a series of narrow winding bends dropping down into Beeley village and the black Navara was pulling out, taking a look and then pulling back in tailgating the black BMW in front of it that was following Briggsy.

"He's an accident waiting to happen," pronounced Gordy.

Pete fell silent and clicked on the Range Rover's Media voice control.

"Ring Kwadj"

The voice control repeated the instruction. "Ringing Kwadj."

In the Range Rover three vehicles in front of him Kwadj answered the call.

"Hi Pete, everything alright?"

"Not sure mate, there's a Navara behind you driving like a right twat with no plates. Keep an eye on him."

Kwadj looked behind him.

"Yeah got him, he's all over that Beamer. Hang on… two up…both masked up!"

The Navara pulled out approaching a sharp left hand blind bend and accelerated past the BMW, going round the bend on the wrong side of the road, and then pulled in sharply in front of it behind the Range Rover containing Briggsy and Kwadj. The BMW braked sharply and went into a skid, understeering into the bank on the bend and then ricocheting at a ninety-degree angle across the road. Pete seeing the skid, pulled sharply to the right, and braked heavily coming to a sudden stop a few inches from the side of the BMW. He heard the screech of brakes of the car behind as it came round the corner and braced himself for the collision that never came. After a few seconds he checked the nearside mirror and saw that it had avoided colliding with him by driving into the hedge on his nearside.

Kwadj's voice came over the speaker.

"He's right behind us. Any idea what's going on?"

Pete turned to Gordy "Hold on!"

He put the Range Rover into first and hit the back end of the BMW that was straddling the narrow road, pushing it along the road and then a further ninety degrees so that the road ahead was clear. He could see the driver waving angrily at him as he completed the manoeuvre. Pete then went through the gears and sped down into Beeley after the Navara.

"Where are you?" Gordy shouted down the phone to Kwadj.

"At speed towards Chatsworth. Navara's behind us, they are definitely after us. We are tooling up. We'll take him somewhere out the way in the park and deal with them. Any ideas who it is Gordy?"

"None whatsoever. We are…"

Gordy held onto the strap above the door as Pete swung the Range Rover at speed towards Chatsworth from the Beeley junction

"…we are about half a mile behind you, tooling up as well."

Gordy reached below the seat and removed the .38 automatic from the webbing under the seat. They hit a straight stretch of road and Pete doing eighty mph reached under his seat and removed another .38 throwing it to Gordy.

"Check the safety for me."

Kwadj was looking back at the Navara, it was close behind them now.

"Think the passenger's got a shotgun," he observed to Briggsy.

"Right then, let's take them out in the open and deal with them out of sight."

Briggsy approached the lights on the bridge at the entrance to Chatsworth Park at speed. The lights changed from green to amber, and he accelerated even faster. The Range Rover accepted the instruction and plunged forward towards the bridge, Briggsy felt the wheels leave the ground as they reached the pinnacle of the humpback on the bridge, waited, and then braked as the tarmac met the rubber again steering sharply to his right into the ninety degree turn into the park. The tyres slid and then bit into the road surface. Briggsy came off the brakes and back onto the accelerator and the Range Rover shot forward under control into the park. Briggsy checked the mirror. The Navara had followed them over the bridge but had dropped back behind them about fifty yards.

" Get ready!" he shouted to Kwadj as he drove over the cattle grid and off the road onto the muddy parkland, engaging the four-by-four drive as he did so.

In his wing mirror he saw the Navara follow them.

"I'm going over the hill and then turning so you can get a shot at them. They will hopefully not be able to use the shotgun head on."

"Good Plan!" agreed Kwadj lowering his window and readying himself for the turn and then the shot at their pursuers.

Pete sped away from the bridge, up the incline into Chatsworth and through the park gates.

"Over there!" shouted Gordy, with a .38 in his hand and one on his lap.

He pointed towards the white Range Rover and Navara four hundred yards away heading towards the brow of a hill in the distance. Pete swerved off the road after them and watched as both vehicles in front of them disappeared at speed over the hill.

"Let's go!" announced Briggsy putting the Range Rover into a 180 degree sliding turn and then accelerated forward.

Kwadj leant out of the window and took aim at the windscreen of the Navara as it came into view and Briggsy accelerated the Range Rover towards it. He fired four shots in quick succession that patterned the windscreen, where the masked driver's chest would be.

"Got him!" shouted Kwadj.

The Navara slowed and veered to the right of the Range Rover and out of the firing line of Kwadj. Briggsy picked up his .38 and keeping his left hand on the wheel, took aim through his open window to get another shot at the driver, as the Navara passed on his side. The driver's window in the Navara had been lowered, and he saw a glimpse of a shotgun resting on top of the door in the open window, and then he saw that it was held by the passenger as it passed level with him. He felt a chill of fear pass through him and fired a shot at the open window of the Navara, and then everything disappeared as the saboted hollow point slug hit the side of his head.

Kwadj was watching the Navara go past and had seen Briggsy fire at it when he was suddenly blinded. He smelt the blood first and rubbed his eyes with his arm. His senses checked for injury and felt none, but he felt more than blood on his arm, there was hardness and a jelly like mass. His eyes cleared and he realised he was being thrown first to the left and then the right as the Range Rover careered at speed out of control. He looked towards Briggsy to see what he was doing to control the car and he wasn't there. Or rather his head wasn't. Where his head should have been there was just a lower jaw. His left hand still held the wheel, and his foot was still on the accelerator driving the car forward, but he was certainly not in control of it.

Kwadj was transfixed at the sight. He fell back against the door and then onto the half grinning corpse as the Range Rover swayed one final time, before falling onto its offside and rolling. Kwadj felt like a rag doll as he hit the roof, his leg shot out of the shattering windscreen and then was crushed between the bonnet and ground. The Range Rover rolled right over itself, bounced on its tyres and landed upright silent and smoking. Kwadj's body hung out of the vehicle, his head trapped at a ninety degree angle to his shoulders between the steering wheel and the dashboard, and what was left of his left leg lay squashed, bloodied and like the rest of what had been his body, useless on the Range Rover bonnet.

The pickup came to a stop and Kwadj saw a large man, six foot four inches, wearing a boiler suit, black leather gloves and a full-face woollen balaclava get out of the passenger side. He began to walk over to the stricken Range Rover. As he closed, he put the shotgun to his shoulder and fired at Kwadj's body on the Range Rover bonnet. The front of the vehicle exploded in a cloud of smoke, sparks metal and blood, as one slug hit the bonnet and the other hit Kwadj's exposed right leg, blowing it off at the knee. Kwadj though conscious, felt nothing. His body and nervous system rendered useless by his broken neck.

The only sense that remained was his sight, which was fixed on the open driver's window and steering wheel still held by Briggsy's lifeless hand. As the gunman walked towards him he reloaded the 12-bore side by side shotgun with a fresh round of saboted hollow point slugs, locked the shotgun with a flick of his arm and brought it up to his shoulder and took aim through the window at the trapped head, Kwadj could do no more than blink and stare as he looked down into the dark tunnels of the shotgun. The last thing he saw was the fire and gas explosion from the left barrel

At that moment Pete and Gordy came over the brow of the hill. Pete saw the shattered Range Rover and the balaclava clad gunman at the side of it in the same instant. He aimed the speeding Range Rover towards him. A split second later the gunman heard the vehicle and turned towards the sound, swivelling the gun with him as he did so.

"Too late muppet!" Pete shouted, as the Range Rover hit him.

Pete felt the thud as the body hit the grill and then the chassis underneath his feet. The metallic clattering of the shotgun reverberated along the underside of the vehicle as the vehicle dragged the man along, trapped between the chassis and the muddy ground.

"Got him Gordy!" he exclaimed loudly and looked towards his boss in the passenger seat.

Gordy's pained eyes looked back at him. Then Pete saw the single hole in the windscreen and what had once been Gordy's left shoulder was now just a mosaic of bone, blood, and lung. Arterial blood was spurting metronomically from the bloody mass onto the roof above him and back down onto his tilted head. Gordy shook his head slightly, and slowly closed his eyes as the spurting blood diminished to a trickle and then stopped completely.

Pete looked away from Gordy, refocused on the danger to himself and brought the vehicle to a stop. He jumped out of the vehicle, grabbing his blood-soaked .38 from Gordy's lap and crouched against the open Range Rover door. Twenty yards behind the Range Rover he saw what was left of the shooter. The balaclava on his head, like the boiler suit that covered his torso, was now a squashed muddy bloodied mess and his right arm, still holding the shotgun, lay a further five yards away from the dismembered corpse.

Pete kept the Range Rover between himself and the Navara and shouted back towards the other Range Rover.

"Briggsy! ....Kwadj!"

He waited…. there was no reply. He looked again towards the Navara to see what had happened to the other gunman. He could hear that the engine was still running but couldn't see inside the cab of the vehicle. Pete took a breath, ducked down and crept round to the front of the Range Rover, shielding himself all the while from any occupant of the Navara's cab. From this position he could see a black balaclaved figure motionless in the driver's seat. Pete waited a few seconds, but the driver didn't move at all.

Pete took aim and sent two .38 bullets through the door of the Navara towards the driver and then another two. The driver didn't move. Pete left his cover and zig zagged towards the Navara and took new cover by the front wheel, watching and listening for any movement. Nothing. Pete jumped up and took aim at where the drivers head should have been but there was no movement from the person sitting there. Pete saw the ring of four shots in the windscreen and thought, 'Good shooting Kwadj!' Briggsy wasn't good enough for that sort of grouping. He then focussed his eyes on the bloodied boiler suit, and the puckered bullet holes in it. All four rounds through the windscreen had hit the driver in the left side of his shoulder. His eyes moved to the right side of the driver's torso and saw that he had hit, with at least two of his shots, through the door.

The driver's eyes moved through the slit in the mask to his, and his lips grimaced to a smile. Too late. In his peripheral vision Pete saw the barrels of the sawn off shotgun move up from a pivoted position on the driver's thigh. Pete depressed his finger on the trigger of the .38, that was still pointed at the drivers head and felt the recoil of the gun as it sent the bullet towards the side of the driver's head. He never saw it hit. Pete's headless body stood upright by the driver's door for several seconds before it crumpled at the knees and then the ankles, falling lifelessly backwards from what was left of the door of the Navara.

Chapter 33 – Fresh Starts

Monday 20th January

Holly knew he wasn't feeling very well. He didn't know what he was coming down with, but he felt ill. He had also forgotten to do something again, but he couldn't remember what it was. His head didn't feel very well at all and although he tried to focus on what he could have forgotten: his mind wouldn't let him. He felt drained both physically and mentally. Climbing up the flight of stairs to the CID office at Matlock that morning had seemed liked climbing a mountain. Each step was laboured and stamina draining.

Holly made it to his office and sat down behind his desk. There was a pile of buff files from Cath and Dave to review, as well as some end of month overtime and mileage forms. 'Annual Reviews,' he thought. He had forgotten to do their Annual Reviews. They had to be to be completed for the end of the week. He opened the first buff folder. It was the mark off for the burglary on Lime Tree Rd by Gary Traynor that Cath had put in for a detected 'mark off' now that he was dead. He read the first two paragraphs and then realised that he hadn't comprehended any of what had been typed, so he read it again. By the time he got to the third paragraph he was thinking about Donna arching her neck and spitting in his face. He pushed the memory away. He knew he was struggling emotionally. His mind was wandering and so he started the report again from the beginning.

The phone on his desk rang.

It was a full ten minutes later that he calmly put the phone down. He realised that he should be angry. Angry with DC Baker for not discussing the subject of the phone call with him first. He should be very angry with DC Baker for going over his head. He should also be angry at himself for agreeing with Superintendent Dicks as to what to do with him. But he wasn't annoyed, he didn't feel any emotion at all. He just wanted to get out of the office, somewhere away from this paperwork, away from people, away from work just for an hour.

A realisation came to him. He knew what was wrong with him. He was having a breakdown. His mental state was crumbling but if he could get an hour away from everything, he could recover he told himself. Then he could do the paperwork, he could go home to Donna, he could deal with everything like he always did. Just an hour and he would be alright. Holly put the buff folder back on top of the pile, picked up his keys and set off for his car. He would go to Monsal Head, grab a coffee from the café there and re-set himself. Clear his head. Get back his energy and deal with everything the day had to offer.

He had got as far as Darley Dale driving north on the A6, when he saw the blue flashing lights in his mirror and pulled over to let the ARV pass him at speed. I hope they're heading north onto Buxton section he thought to himself and then his phone rang. He checked the caller; it was the central communications room. He had a sinking feeling that the ARV and the call would be connected and pulled into the side of the road again. It was. He closed the call a few minutes later telling the operator

"Get DC Mulvey and DC Baker to the scene and tell them I'll meet them at the rendezvous point at Chatsworth House Car Park."

Holly could feel the adrenalin surging through his body, clearing his head of the fog that had prevented him from concentrating that morning, and also felt it clearing his body of the crushing lethargy he had been experiencing. "Come on Holly, let's get cracking Carpe Diem" he encouraged himself. He checked his mirror to pull back out into the traffic and saw the yellow and green of a paramedic Volvo estate speeding towards him, blue lights flashing and siren blaring. He waited for it to pass and then pulled out after it and sped away in fast convey towards Chatsworth Park.

As Holly was leaving Matlock Police Station to go to Monsal Head, and thirty minutes after leaving the mortuary, Dave and Cath were sitting in the kitchen/lounge at Cath's house. Dave was sitting on the two seater cream settee looking at the photographs on the wall of Cath, in various stages of her police career: a class photo at training school, one of her in uniform on the day she 'Passed Out' of training, a Commendation with the Chief Constable, and another of her, Dave and Holly hanging off each other drunkenly on the Christmas night out from the previous year.

Cath handed Dave a coffee and then jumped up and sat on the kitchen worktop that separated the two rooms, with her odd socks over her black tights swinging loosely below her.

"Did you think Holly sounded a bit weird on Saturday?" she asked.

"No, not really. You worry about him too much. He seems fine to me. Donna is a nightmare, but he seems to cope with her, and he is doing alright at work. He even did that death message on his own and gave us Saturday night off. He wouldn't do that if he was struggling. Some stress is part and parcel of the job," Dave stated disinterestedly.

"I don't know, I've been with him more than you for the last couple of weeks and he keeps going quiet and thoughtful all the time," stated Cath, with a worried look on her face.

"That's probably you noticing you've stopped talking! You don't half rabbit on, he's probably enjoying the silence, giving his ears a rest," Dave joked.

Cath picked up a plastic coaster from the worktop and playfully threw it in Dave's direction.

"That's good coming from you! You promised you wouldn't talk about her this morning and that you were over her. My ears have gone numb on the way back from the mortuary this morning with the sound of you droning on about some girl called Helen… Do you think I should call her…should I text her…why doesn't she want to see me again…do you think she still likes me….god Excy! I had less grief off my teenage mates when they got dumped than I do off you."

"Yes but do you think…"

"No!" Cath shouted at him with a smile

"I've had enough. She's gone back, she made it plain that it was a short term fling. The best and only advice I will give is, get over it, it was fun while it lasted but it's time to move on."

"I'm sorry, I just thought we had something that's all, I promise you I am trying to move on though," Dave smiled.

"When was that then? You've been going on about her all morning."

"Alright, not quite over her, but nearly. I've got something new to think about after that call I made this morning. I'm leaving Matlock and going on the Murder Incident Team."

"What!, you're leaving us… when?" Cath looked at him in astonishment.

"I think fairly soon. I realised what was bugging me the other day, you know the thing I couldn't put my finger on?"

Cath thought about it but couldn't remember him saying anything to her but decided that whatever it was she was going to find out anyway.

"What was it?"

"Well, I was thinking what if I did wrong in going over Superintendent Dicks' head with that cock-up on the Allestree murder. It's not going to help my promotion chances if he makes ACPO rank at some time in the future is it?"

"No," agreed Cath, unsure where this conversation was going.

"Well, I have decided I want to get some promotions under my belt. I'm not going to get them on the wrong side of Dicks so I have called in a favour, and I think I will be going on the Murder Incident Team soon."

"Bloody hell Excy! Dicks is going to have you for dinner. What makes you think that he's going to bury the hatchet with you?"

"I think he will, but I don't know for sure yet."

"Does Holly know?" Cath asked.

"I don't think so, you're the first person I've told," confided Dave.

"So you're leaving us?" asked Cath, feeling suddenly sad "I'll miss you, you know."

"I know Cath, but I need to make my next promotion and whilst Superintendent Dicks has got a down on me it's not going to happen."

"How are you going to get him onside? Working for him isn't just going to do it, even if he will have you on his team."

"I think it's being sorted Cath. I can't tell you any more than that."

At that moment both of their mobile phones rang simultaneously.

Dave answered his as Cath searched her handbag for hers. She stopped searching when she heard him say,

"Yeah she's with me," and then waved silently towards her, intimating to her that he would take the call for them both and put the phone on speaker.

"We have had a report of a shooting incident at Chatsworth Park, there's some suggestion of a couple of deaths. Can you make your way to the rendezvous point which is the car park at the side of the house. Entry is through Golden Gates. The road through the park has been closed as part of the cordon. Firearms officers are at the scene. DS Hollins is on his way and will meet you there."

"We are on our way, and can you let him know we will be there in about twenty minutes?" Dave closed the call.

"Our good run of bad luck on sudden deaths looks like it's continuing Cath, I'll see you there."

Dave stood up and waited while Cath slipped on her boots and picked up her bag.

"After you.. by the way you smell of the morgue."

Dave stepped past her and out the door

"So do you." He held his nose between his fingers and then smiled towards her and set off for his car.

Chapter 34 - Changes

Monday 20th January

Twenty minutes later Cath followed Dave through the open Golden Gates entrance of Chatsworth House. A House Security officer on the gates was checking that only emergency service personnel were admitted. Cath knew the House Security were nearly all retired police officers from Bakewell, and recently retired ex PC Wallis recognising them waved them through. The two cars then sped along the mile long straight drive towards the car park, at the side of the house.

At the car park Dave couldn't see Holly's car and so he parked up next to one of two ambulances that stood in line in front of the house. Cath pulled in alongside. He looked around to see if he could get some idea of what was going on. The forces two ARV's were parked up but empty of any occupants. He looked around and saw their occupants, automatic rifles slung over their shoulders walking over the bridge that straddled the Derwent towards the Car Park.

The DCC Alan Daley, Superintendent Dicks and a senior ambulanceman were huddled together at the side of Dicks'

Green Mercedes. Some of the murder squad had also parked up at the side of the Mercedes and were gathered together looking towards a wisp of black smoke that rose from behind a small hill in the distance. Just before the hill he could see a paramedic Volvo and Holly's car. A senior fire officer pulled up at the side of him and the accompanying fire engine circled the car park and pulled up alongside the ambulances. This was a big job thought Dave. Cath jumped into the passenger seat.

"Looks like this is a big job," remarked Cath as she shut the door behind her.

"Where do we go? Or shall we just wait here until someone notices us?"

"I think we just hang around till someone notices us and tells us what to do. Holly's up at the scene," observed Dave and gestured towards Holly's car half a mile away in the distance.

"Well, if we are waiting around, I'm going to use some local knowledge," said Cath as she pointed towards the gatehouse where there was always a hot cup of coffee or tea waiting for any passing local police officer.

"Good idea," agreed Dave.

They both got out of the car and began walking towards the gatehouse.

Halfway there a shout of "Excy!" came towards them.

They both turned in the direction of where the shout had come from. It was DCC Daley.

"Make that two more coffees Excy!" he shouted towards them and then carried on talking to Detective Superintendent Dicks.

"I suppose telling the DCC to 'four coffees' is not going to be appropriate on this occasion," Cath quipped quietly towards Dave.

"No sugars in any of them!" Dicks shouted behind them as they walked to the gatehouse.

Five minutes later, Cath and Dave returned from the Gatehouse, Cath carrying a tray with four mugs. Dicks took the tray of drinks off Cath and put it onto the roof of his car. He passed Cath and Dave a coffee and then gave one to Alan Daley. Cath and Dave turned to go, but Dicks called them back

"Hang on you two, I've just been talking with DCC Daley, we need to have a chat about what you two are doing today and going forward."

Dicks then turned to Dave.

"I know I've given you a bit of a tough time DC Baker…Excy…can I call you Excy?"

Dave nodded.

"Well after your call this morning to Alan, we think it would be helpful to your career if you had some time working with me on the Murder Incident Team. So, as of today, you're joining us. We are also starting with a clean sheet if that's alright with you?"

Alan Daley interjected.

"What Superintendent Dicks is trying to say Excy, is that he has reviewed how he may have come across in some of his previous dealings with you, in the light of the Derbyshire Police Fairness at Work Policy, and he now realises that some of his comments and actions may have been open to misinterpretation, is that correct Superintendent Dicks?"

"Yes, that's correct sir, so I apologise for any inadvertent upset that I may have caused," Dicks replied.

"Thank you Superintendent Dicks. Obviously there has also been some misunderstandings as to the way that you have acted, in relation to investigations conducted by Superintendent Dicks, which have resulted in him feeling that you have actively sought to undermine, his authority, and the investigations he has been conducting. I am sure that this was not the case, but it would be helpful if you could confirm that to Mr Dicks."

Dave took his cue.

"Sorry Superintendent Dicks."

"Apology accepted Excy."

"I have already spoken to DS Hollins and informed him of the transfer subject to your agreement. Me and Alan have just been discussing what we need to do today with this incident, and the Bulman murder. DS Hollins, when he gets back from the scene, is going on the Bulman murder. That's going to be run by DI Casey now that it is just about sorted, other than dealing with Oxley when he turns up. I am going to run this incident as we think there may be at least six dead from initial sightings at the scene by the ARV's. That leaves me with a supervisor short on the murder incident team so Alan has decided that you will be promoted to Temporary Detective Sergeant, Excy."

Superintendent Dicks offered his hand to Dave, who in acceptance of the agreement shook it.

Cath felt a wave of sadness come over her. She was going to be working on her own for the foreseeable future. Dave would be gone for good and Holly for at least six months on the Alice Bulman murder. The chances of her seeing Ella on a regular basis had just taken a massive downturn. She took a deep breath and exhaled slowly with the realisation.

"DC Mulvey."

Cath jumped, DCC Daley was talking to her.

"I understand that you have passed your Sergeants examination as well, is that correct?"

"Yes, sir, me and DC Baker took it together last year."

"Well in that case how do you feel about being temporarily promoted to Detective Sergeant as well and running the subdivision CID whilst DS Hollins is attached to the Murder Incident Team ?"

Cath didn't have to think twice. If she was going to run the area CID on her own she might as well have the extra money.

"Yes, sir, I think I'm up to it!"

"Well, that's settled then. Just for today hang around a bit as we might need the help. It will also give you time to think about who you want appointing to Temporary DC to work with you. Let me know and it will happen no matter what objections come from their supervision; you alright with that?"

Cath nodded.

"Right I'm off back to Headquarters to deal with the press. It's all yours here John and good luck, we are going to need it."

The three of them then watched him stride off back to his car, get in, and drive away. As they watched DCC Daley go out of sight towards Golden Gates, Dicks turned to Dave.

"Don't go away!"

He then walked off to the line of CSI vans parked against the perimeter wall of Chatsworth House.

"Well, I didn't expect that when I walked out of the mortuary an hour or so ago. You and Holly gone, both of us promoted. How did you manage that Mr Exocet?"

"Helen told me I wouldn't be able to have a proper relationship with anyone whilst I was a DC. I've thought about it, and she is right, CID is no place to work if you want a good relationship with your partner, it's also a dead end if you want promotion. Last night I decided that I'm going to be a Chief Inspector in the next five years Cath and I had a plan as to how to start it off. As they say, the first step is always the hardest and I took it this morning."

"So, you made a record of Dicks giving you some grief, took it to the DCC and threatened to embarrass the force and Dicks unless you got your own way! I thought you were better than that Excy. Blackmail is not an effective way to get things in my book and I didn't think it was yours."

Cath looked sadly at him.

"Cath it's not the how, but the result that matters. I did record him, but it was when I thought he was going to wreck my career and I needed it to protect myself. I haven't blackmailed anyone. DCC Daley had told me that I was owed a favour and I just pulled it in. I'm planning to get on the right side of Dicks now that I'm working with him, especially as everyone knows he's going to make ACPO in the next couple of years and if I do alright he might be inclined to take me up with him. You know how this works Cath you've been in the force long enough."

"Excy, Helen is not likely to go back out with you no matter what rank you get to, so if this is about getting back with her I would forget it."

"It's not. If we do get back together that would be a bonus, but I joined the police to have a career and I want to get it back on track. We were a good team, but nothing lasts forever Cath, it would have ended some time. I just decided that I would leave on my terms not someone else's. You should do the same Cath, take control. Look what's happened in the space of a morning I've got us both promoted. Stay friends with me and hang on to my coat tails Cath and I'll take you with me."

Cath looked up at him. His beaming face looking down at her waiting for her to agree to his plan. His mind was focussed now he had persuaded himself that his plan was working out. She had seen that look a number of times in the last few years…when he met a woman and fell in love.. when he decided that a colleague had not followed procedure or policy…. It was a look that told her that he knew he was right and that no matter how much you pointed out any flaws in his plan that he would not listen, he had focussed and set his sights on the target like a guided missile. Holly had named him well she thought.

"Thanks, Excy, I might just do that," she lied.

Dave had a ruthless streak, and she was not going to be collateral damage she thought to herself. It was time to step out of his way. Dicks came towards them carrying two sterile suit packs.

"Come on Excy lets go and look at the scene together."

Dicks threw one of them to Dave who caught it one handed.

"We need to talk, and it will also get the others on the team off your back if they see you're my new favourite."

Dicks gave Dave a genuine smile and they both ripped open the cellophane packing of the suits.

Cath decided she needed some time to think. She put her mug on the tray that was still on the roof of the green Mercedes, picked up the other three from the ground at the side of it and whilst Dave and Superintendent Dicks climbed into their sterile suits, she set off for the gatehouse with the tray and empty mugs.

"That looks heavy!" remarked Sally Brooks joining Cath as she was half way to the gatehouse.

"Do you think I could blag another with you when you take those back?"

"I reckon that's a certainty, just walk in with me, they always have the kettle on for the locals."

Sally Brooks dropped into step at the side of Cath.

"I did a quick check on the skins we lifted when I got back to the office this morning. I ran it through NAFIS and didn't get any hits so it's not Oxley. I've also had a quick look against some of the prints we lifted from Burton's house, and I would say they matched his, but it will need an expert opinion of course. I don't think Professor Graham mentioned it, but we got some brown tweed material from underneath him when he was cut off the seat. That would match the brown suit that his wife claimed he always wore for work."

"Thanks Sally appreciate it."

Tumblers in Cath's mind spun and clicked into place.

"Brown suit!" she exclaimed loudly.

Sally looked at her surprised.

"What did you say?"

"Sorry Sally, it was nothing, I'm just glad it isn't Oxley. Superintendent Dicks says there are six dead over the ridge. That's going to be quite some incident for you and the other CSI's. Look Sally I'm just going to be a spare part round here for a while, I'll get another tray of teas and bring it over to you while you get set up. I still owe you for the mortuary this morning and a few teas will go some way to pay you back."

"Thanks, it's appreciated Cath."

Sally walked back towards her CSI van and Cath carried on to the gatehouse for another tray of drinks. She needed to get straight in her mind a link involving Neil Burton and a man in a brown suit.

Cath leant against the wall next to the CSI vans, watching them getting suited up and took a sip of her hot brown tea. She was deep in thought. Burton could have been the man at the Traynor's house when Gary ran off and was killed.

Cath went over her conversation with his wife. The only thing she had disclosed he seemed to be worried about, other than Paul dying, was a MacBook that had incriminating pictures of him and Paul on. She could see why he might have gone to see Gary Traynor if the computer Karen had told her about was in fact his MacBook. But was there a connection with Alice Bulman? Who were the two 'heavies' that Karen had told her about and where had they come from? What if the Traynors had taken revenge on Burton for Gary's death and had killed him? The brown suited Burton could be the key, which might unlock the recent serious crimes the police were investigating.

As Acting Detective Sergeant in charge of the deaths of Trueman, Gary Traynor and Neil Burton she had some free reign to do some investigating without treading on the toes of the Murder Incident Team. The first thing she would do is to speak to Holly before he went on the Bulman Murder. He would give her the best advice, she decided.

Cath looked up towards the smoky hill in the distance. Dave and Superintendent Dicks were almost there. She saw that Holly's car was still parked up by the ridge, but the paramedic Volvo was making its way back down the park towards the road. She watched as the Volvo reached the road and then continued slowly towards Chatsworth House, over the bridge and into the car park and came to a halt at the rear of one of the ambulances parked next to Dave's car. She saw that Holly was in the passenger seat and set off to walk the thirty or so yards towards him, and then stopped. Something didn't look right.

A Paramedic got out of the Volvo and opened the passenger door. At the same time, another paramedic opened the rear doors of the nearby ambulance and lowered the ramp with a wheelchair on it. Cath was suddenly stricken with a sense of foreboding for Holly and hurried towards the Volvo. The second paramedic helped out of the passenger seat a bowed and shuffling Holly, who slumped awkwardly into the wheelchair.

Cath shouted

"Holly!, Holly!"

He didn't register any recognition towards her.

She broke into a run towards him. The first paramedic however blocked her path as Holly was loaded, vacant eyed and with chin on chest, into the back of the ambulance.

"I'm sorry love, he's not well, I think he's had some sort of a breakdown. It's pretty horrific up there. We were checking to see if any of them were alive, and he just sighed quietly to me "I'm sorry" and sat down. He hasn't said anything since. We are taking him up to the Hartington Wing at the Royal in Chesterfield to get him seen by the Mental Health Team. I'd ring there later when they have had a look at him, Miss."

Cath looked at the catatonic Holly and worriedly asked the paramedic,

"Is he going to be alright?"

The paramedic slowly shook his head.

"I'm not sure, love, he's not good."

The doors of the ambulance closed shut, and Holly was driven away towards the Golden Gates.

Cath looked around her at the multitude of detectives, uniform officers, CSI's, ambulances, and fire vehicles in the car park. Each one grouped together in their respective disciplines.

No-one was going to miss her if she left. She was a group of one, on her own she thought. An outsider. She took out her phone and tapped in "You won't believe the morning I have had! Can I ring you later…replacement for Vodka?"

The reply came back immediately. A thumbs up emoticon and a heart.

Cath's heart skipped a beat for the umpteenth time that morning.

"Sod this! I'm going to see if Holly is alright!"

She announced loudly to herself and got in her car and set off for the hospital at Chesterfield for the second time that morning.

Chapter 35 – The Scene

Monday 20th January

Dave put on his sterile suit and slipped the mask over his hooded head, letting it hang limply around his neck. He looked across to Dicks who had just done the same and walked over to him.

"Are we driving some of the way?" asked Dave.

"No. I think the walk will do us good. It will also allow the CSI's to catch us up when they are ready. You alright for a walk?"

"Yes boss, no problem at all."

The two men set off at a brisk walking pace out of the car park and over the bridge. At the end of the bridge and out of the hearing of the gathering emergency personnel in the car park, Superintendent Dicks turned to Dave.

"Now we are out of earshot. You could have had me busted down to Inspector with that recording, but you went to the DCC and used it to get on my team. I have been trying to make sense of what you did, but I suppose I might as well hear it from the horse's mouth. What's your angle Dave, what do you want?"

Dave took a few steps in thoughtful contemplation before replying.

"Well, I started out in the police on the Graduate Entry Scheme. I went on CID thinking I would spend a couple of years on it and then get off and get promoted. I have been on CID three years now and I have realised that my career would come to a dead end if I stayed there. So, I want out, and I want to make at least Inspector in the next three years and Chief Inspector in five."

"Nothing wrong with ambition Excy, but I still don't get what it is that you want from me?"

Dave took a deep breath,

"Well sir, I have also considered the best way for me to make that come about. I had a look around and out of all the up and coming senior officers it seems pretty obvious to me that you will be the most likely to make ACPO in the next couple of years. So, I want to hang on to your coat tails if you will allow me."

Dicks gave Dave a wry smile.

"I hope you're right about ACPO, but the flaw in your plan as I see it is that now you have used your trump card of the recording what is in it for me to help you out? I've got half a dozen officers on my team that deserve a leg up more than you.

I'm not saying I won't help but there's got to be something in it for me as well. Scratching backs is a mutual activity in the police, Detective Sergeant Baker, especially if you want my assistance."

"Well Boss, if we are being straight with each other, I could argue that I am one of the few police officers who has actually helped your career in the last year. I discovered that you hadn't searched the victim's house on the Allestree job last year. If it had been found out later, either by the press or at Court, it could have been pretty bad for your ACPO prospects. I agree I could have dealt with it better and not told the Chief Super, but I didn't know what to do. I thought you were off, and he was cover. It was sorted out alright for you at the end of the day though. The bullying I recorded has gone nowhere either, but anyone in that room could have recorded it and made a complaint and your ACPO would have been dust. Me going to DCC Daley and telling him I wanted nothing doing about it, takes that off the table as well. So, if you look at it from that point of view I don't think there's much for you to be too angry at me about."

"It's a point of view Excy but I'm not sure I would agree with it. However, as I agreed back in the car park, I'm happy to start again with you, but if you want me to help you plan out your police career you have still not told me what's going to be in it for me if I help you?"

"Well sir, I can say I want to do lots of things for you but how about if actions speak louder than words. Give me a chance over the next few weeks and see if I help you out at all. If I'm useful let me hang on to your coat tails if I'm not send me back to Division. What have you got to lose?" suggested Dave.

Dicks remained silent and carried on walking towards the approaching ridge and the wisps of smoke rising above it. As they started to climb the incline to the ridge Dicks looked at Dave.

"I will go with that suggestion Excy. If you are as ruthless as you seem to be, you may be useful to me. I don't know you well, but let's start from scratch this morning and see what happens over the next few weeks. I want you at my side though. Trust is earned not given and that goes both ways. I'll show you what you need to know about Major Incidents, and you show me you're useful to me. Are you alright with that?"

"Definitely sir!" Dave beamed and almost gave a skip of joy. He was in.

Dicks stopped just before they reached the top of the ridge

"We are coming up to the scene now, the ARV lads who were first here disclosed it's not pretty, Excy. We will stay about fifty yards away and get a first look at the scene. It helps when you're reading statements later because you can put them into the context of what you have seen yourself."

The two light blue sterile suited officers walked the last few yards to the top of the small hill that hid the scene and stopped at the crest.

"Bloody hell!" announced Superintendent Dicks loudly through his face mask.

Dave's gaze was drawn firstly to the severed tattooed arm, still holding the shotgun, in the open ground between a black Navara and two white Range Rovers. His eyes then went to the remains of what was once presumably a body half way through the windscreen of the still smoking white Range Rover. There looked to be another body in the driver's seat of the same Range Rover, but he couldn't see a head. Dave looked away, blinked a few times, and looked back hoping to refocus on the interior of the Range Rover and peered over the remains on the bonnet. It was definitely a body in the driver's seat, but it still didn't seem to have a head. There was a balaclaved body in the driver's seat of the Navara hanging limply out of the shattered window and below it, on the ground, another headless body, from which an expanding spray of blood and matter, probably the remains of what had been its head, spread for around twenty yards towards the second Range Rover.

"I see one…two...three...four…five dead," Dave counted out loud.

"Let's move round a bit," instructed Superintendent Dicks.

Both men circled the stationary vehicles, keeping around the agreed fifty yards from them.

"There's another one in the second Range Rover," Dicks pointed out.

"I think that's the six dead that the ARV lads mentioned. It's a right blood bath. Are you alright Excy?"

"Yes Boss, I'm alright. How are we going to deal with this?"

"First thing is check whether its terrorist related, if it is, the investigation goes straight to the Met, and we play a secondary role to them. The Navara's got no plates on it, but the Range Rovers have. Make a note and we will PNC them when we get back. It might give us some angle whether it's terrorist related or not if SO15 in the Met have got any intel on them or the occupants."

Dicks looked slowly around the carnage at the scene. "What do you reckon has happened here then Excy?"

Dave looked around. The Range Rover had finished emitting steam and smoke from under its wrecked bonnet.

"Well, it looks like the occupants in the white Range Rovers have been involved in some sort of gun fight with the occupants of the Navara. I'd hazard a guess that our guy on the floor over there, without the arm, is from the Navara as he is dressed like the driver hanging out the door. So, I would go for some sort of fall out between criminals."

"I'll agree with you on that. Let's leave it to the CSI's now though, we have got an incident room to pass over to John Casey and another one to set up. It will give you an idea of what's involved in setting up the administration side of a murder. If you're hanging on to my coat tails you might as well stay close enough to reach them."

The two men turned and walked back towards the car park, passing a convoy of CSI vehicles making their way to the scene.

Chapter 36 – Hanging On To Coat Tails

Saturday 18th January

An hour later Dave was back at the Alice Bulman Incident Room at Buxton Divisional Headquarters. The first thing he had done was to find the registered owner of the Range Rovers at the scene on the PNC database. Both came back to a Martin Gordon of The Paddocks, Cook Road, Dagenham in Essex. Dave, as instructed by Superintendent Dicks, then passed the vehicle and owner details to SO15 Counter Terrorist Command at the Metropolitan Police to ascertain whether they had any intelligence that might link the incident at Chatsworth to terrorism.

While he was waiting for a reply, he watched as the incident room staff packed up the Alice Bulman murder documents into boxes and then moved it into the old CID Administration Office, on the ground floor of the old building across the yard. Dave thought to himself it was only a week and a half since he had been called out to her body at White Lodge and it was already old news. A fact that seemed confirmed by the investigation being moved into an old office in an old building where it would age away until Dylan Oxley was caught.

DI John Casey who was taking over control of the enquiry had been trying to get a new Detective Sergeant to assist him once he had been informed that DS Hollins had been taken to hospital. Dicks had told him that he couldn't spare anyone to cover the loss and the DI was now in a bad mood as he realised he had only a few officers and administration staff to run the investigation. As the evidence of the Bulman enquiry was removed, the remaining administration staff from the Bulman Murder were setting up the databases and document folders for a new incident room for the murders at Chatsworth.

Dave had spent half an hour. firstly watching Dicks rebuff DI Casey's request for a new Sergeant and then organising the setting up of the two incident rooms. He had been impressed with how calm he was dealing with everything, and he could see why people who had worked with him closely would respect him. Dicks was an island of calm in a sea of disruption. He made decisions quickly and calmly. Dave had noticed the same calmness and use of tone that morning when he had been talking to him.

An hour after the call to SO15 Dave received a call back. The Counter Terrorist Command had no intelligence linking the Range Rovers or Martin Gordon to any terrorist activity and had forwarded his enquiry to the Serious Crime Directorate. They had a lone source of information graded A3 that Gordon was involved in the importation of Class 1 drugs, namely heroin and cocaine from Columbia. The intelligence had not been acted on, as it was not corroborated by another source. Gordon paid all his taxes overseas and there was nothing to identify any sources of income in the UK.

Dave went into Dick's office to tell him the news, and also that the Metropolitan Police were taking out a search warrant on Martin Gordon's home address on behalf of Derbyshire Police and would be there within the hour. Dicks listened thoughtfully to the update and sat back in his chair.

"Well, you wanted to learn by hanging onto my coat tails. Here commences the first lesson. This will be high profile as you can see from the news." The TV on the wall of the office tuned into Sky TV was showing a loop of drone footage of the scene.

"These murders will generate huge media interest and be very high profile. The TV people in particular will be wanting almost hourly briefings so, whoever will be turning up on the TV screens the most will get the most political benefit from it. So, do you think it will be me Excy?"

"I would have thought so. You will be leading the enquiry won't you?"

"I will be lucky if the TV gets a passing shot of me entering the police station on the news. The Chief and the Police Commissioner, as we speak, will be arm wrestling each other as to who from this force gets most coverage on the telly today. After today, now that the Met is involved, we will be lucky if Derbyshire Police even gets a slot on the local news. They will be up here and over us like a rash by tomorrow morning Excy and you won't be able to move for Met Commanders elbowing us out the way to get their faces on the telly."

"I don't follow boss, it's a Derbyshire job surely the Met don't have any sway up here, the Chief won't allow it."

Dicks laughed. "Excy, these murders are now about who can make the most political capital out of them. The Met backed up by the Home Office hold a Full House, three aces and two kings against our nine high. There isn't much of a downside for anyone who takes it on, as it looks like all the main offenders are dead, so it's not going to be an expensive enquiry. The key sign for me is that the Met are turning over Martin Gordon's address. That means some Commander down in London has already decided that he wants this job on his CV or else we would be being given a straight bat back to us, to send a team down. The Met don't generally help anyone out unless there's something in it for them. You will see what I mean over the next few days. That's tomorrow's news however, today we have got a briefing in ten minutes, and I want everyone out there finding out who the dead are, where they have been and why they have ended up shooting each other. You will be delivering some of the briefing so get yourself up to date from the CSI's at the scene and anything that's come in from the public. The DCC is opening up a call centre at Headquarters that should be operational by mid-afternoon so keep an eye on information from there and also keep an overall view on any important Actions going out to the detectives from the incident room. I want you as my eyes and ears Excy don't let me down."

"On it!" announced Dave as he picked up his phone off the desk to make the calls.

"By the way Excy, don't expect anything from the Met. Watch the news if you want to know what they are doing and whatever you do don't tell them anything that you don't want on the telly or the villains to know five minutes later. They leak like a sieve."

Dave paused, took in what Dicks had told him and started talking to Sally Brooks at the scene.

The mid-afternoon briefing was a very short affair. Dicks gave a short outline of what he and Dave had been able to see at the scene and then introduced him to the room.

"We have a new member to the Murder Incident Team that I want to introduce to you today. Detective Sergeant Baker, or Excy as most of you know him has been transferred to the team and promoted to Temporary Detective Sergeant at my recommendation. I believe that he will be a terrific addition to the team and hope that you will also come to that belief as well. Detective Sergeant Baker will be acting as liaison between yourselves and me. So, anything that comes in that is important and that you think I need to know about, you put to me through him. This is a large enquiry, and I will not have time to have everyone coming and going in and out of my office. Everybody understand the chain of command for information?"

An assenting murmur went around the room. Dave took over the podium and took a deep breath. He needed to make an excellent job of this if he were to get the detectives back onside.

"Good afternoon gentlemen and ladies of course." Dave cleared his throat.

"As Superintendent Dicks described earlier, it looks like we are probably dealing with a fall out between two criminal gangs. What we know so far is that Martin Gordon and three others were staying at the Peak Edge Hotel at Stanedge just outside Chesterfield. They booked in yesterday evening for one night and left there this morning about 10 a.m. in two white Range Rovers. A black Navara seems to have chased the first Range Rover from near to where they set off in an erratic manner causing an RTC with the second Range Rover and two other vehicles just outside Beeley. The Navara has then chased the first Range Rover from Beeley into Chatsworth Park. The second Range Rover has removed itself from the RTC and chased down the Navara into the park where a gunfight has taken place, killing all those involved. First jobs are statements from employees at the hotel, and drivers at the RTC who saw the vehicles on the way to Chatsworth Park. That's five Actions that need completing today."

Dave handed them out to five detectives on the front row.

"Just in from CSI is that we have identified the two occupants of the Navara. NAFIS has identified them as two locals Ron Traynor and Ron Traynor Junior. We have addresses for both at

Winster. The rest of us are going to both addresses and arresting any occupants as well as searching both addresses for evidence. We will pick up the search warrants on the way. I will lead one team of seven and DS Wickham the other team of seven. CSI will meet us at both scenes. Expect trouble from Ron Traynor's wife at the Leacroft Road address as she is anti-police. All prisoners go to Derby. Nothing that I've told you goes outside this room. Everyone alright with that?"

"Yes Sarge!" went up around the briefing room. Dave carried on.

"Everyone get a brew and a sandwich they are on a table at the back of the incident room before you go. Exhibits to Phil Bridges in the old typists office on the first floor. No debrief tonight but there will be one at 9 a.m. in the morning. Let your partners know that you don't know what time you will be home tomorrow. Tomorrow is going to be a long day. Let's get cracking!"

The Murder Incident Team in front of him, stood up as one and headed for a cup of coffee and a sandwich at the back of the incident room.

Chapter 37 – News Travels Fast

Monday 20th January

Jill Gordon loved Mondays. It was her day. It was the day she went to the gym at 8 a.m. for her aerobics class and then following a sauna and a shower, she got the tube to South Kensington for her 10.30 a.m. appointment for her hair. Today she should have been having her long blonde hair cut and then blow dried. She would then have walked to the nail bar fifty yards further along the road and have her nails manicured and , and polished. Lunch in Soho with Carol her friend and then home for 4 p.m. in the afternoon, slightly squiffy, to cook Martin's tea.

This Monday however was not a Monday that she knew she would love. She had cancelled the aerobics class at the gym, cancelled her hair appointment and unsuccessfully tried to rearrange it for later in the week, and to top it all she had been forced to cancel lunch with her friend Carol, who she had been looking forward to telling that she was going on a sunshine three week holiday to Antigua the following week.

An Accidental Death

Just before 11 a.m. on this unloved Monday, Jill found herself in an empty pub known as The Swan on a side street off Russel Square in Bloomsbury. It was too early for any regular lunchtime drinkers and the Australian bartender had looked up surprised at the early customer as he restocked the bottle fridge at the back of the bar.

He was early twenties she thought, and she had been flattered in the way he had looked her up and down as she had confidently entered the pub on her own. For her meeting that morning she had chosen to wear a black mink hat that revealed just enough of her blonde hair, a matching mink fur coat that ended just above her knees, and a pair of designer black suede knee knee-high boots. The look was meant to show wealth and power and she thought that she carried it off very well.

The coffee and biscotti was brought to the table by the barman and Jill handed him a five pound note and told him there was no need for change. The barman returned to the bar, put the large TV on the pub wall to Sky News and disappeared back to restocking the fridges below the bar. Jill waited at the table for Harry Singh to arrive and considered her morning so far.

She had woken up alone at 6 a.m. that morning: she could never sleep without the comfort of Martin at her side. In all the time they had been together she had only spent a handful of nights without him. Unable to sleep Jill had lain awake for around half an hour thinking about how she was going to approach this meeting later that morning, and what she was going to wear. Having made those decisions she had then walked to the kitchen and made herself a cup of peppermint tea which she had taken back to her bed. At quarter to seven she had rung Martin at his hotel. Martin of course was already up and waiting for her to call.

"You alright Babe?" he had answered her call.

"Yeah, I'm fine Gordy. Missing you though. I don't like not having my big tiger at the side of me in the morning. I'm not used to it."

"I don't like not having my baby bear next to me either. I'll be home later today though babe and we will be back to normal tonight," comforted Gordy.

"I know, I'm not complaining. These things have to be done sometimes. Is everything alright up there?"

"Yeah no problems, me, Pete and the boys got up here about seven last night. The rooms really nice and the meal was excellent. The plan is we will go over to Trueman's about ten, get the MacBook, and hopefully be back home about three this afternoon. Is all fine with you babe? You still seeing Harry Singh this morning?"

"Yes all sorted. I've got the cash. I'm meeting him at a pub called The Swan at Russell Square about 11 a.m. It's public enough and the tube is just round the corner, so I'll be fine."

"That should get the accounts sorted. Is the computer guy still coming round later?"

Jill laughed. "Yeah, he's a right geek, about five foot two, specs, spots and stutter. He says that he should be able to unlock the MacBook in an hour or so. That will be about four hours with you and Briggsy watching over his shoulder!"

Gordy laughed down the phone with her and when he had finished laughing he told her seriously.

"I'm going to go and get ready for breakfast then babe, one of us has to make an effort to uphold standards. I'll be lucky if I'm not sat having breakfast with those three muppets in their underwear."

Jill closed the call. "You go and get ready then Gordy. Have a good day and I'll see you later. Love you."

"Love you too baby bear." Martin Gordon closed the call as well.

A blast of chilly air blew through to her table as another customer came into the bar. She looked towards the door and saw that it was Harry Singh. He looked around the pub and saw her sitting at a table on the far side of the wooden floored pub. He raised a hand in greeting, ordered a pint of Stella lager at the bar, brought it over to the table and sat down opposite her.

Harry Singh's blue pin striped suit was showing its age she noticed, as was his once white cream shirt that was also frayed around the neck area. His face showed a day's growth through a bad case of acne and his swept backed greying hair had been gelled down to disguise that it had not been washed in several days. He looked in his early fifties, but Jill knew he was at least ten years younger.

Harry looked around him conspiratorially.

"I told you no-one would be here at this time."

Jill looked at him disdainfully.

"We didn't need to make this meeting so cloak and dagger Mr Singh. It's a straightforward business arrangement between me and my business associates and a solicitor acting on their behalf, do you understand?"

"Yes, I understand but in my position I have to be careful who I am seen with."

He looked around him conspiratorially again. Harry Singh was a solicitor with his own small firm based in an office above a convenience store at the side of the Blue Lion pub on Gray's Inn Road. He dealt with debt recovery evictions on behalf of landlords who wanted tenants out of their properties for assorted reasons and was not averse to by-passing the Court process with friendly bailiffs willing to work 'off the books' and outside the law, where necessary. As the so called 'bailiffs' often worked for the Gordons in the same type of work with their unwanted tenants, Jill had been put on to Harry Singh as the type of solicitor who may be able to assist them in other 'off the book' activities.

Harry drank half of his Stella and placed the glass back onto the wooden table, then wiped the froth from his mouth with the back of his hand. He leant across to Jill and in a muffled voice, whispered to her.

"So, you need the directors of some brass plate companies in Antigua transferring into new names because the current ones are now deceased. I can arrange this, but I'll need to travel there with you. I will also need death certificates of the deceased directors. It's Antigua so provided you have enough cash it should not be a problem."

Jill leant away from the malodorous breath and body odour mingled with a faint whiff of Brut that encompassed her as he leant in towards her. Jill coughed it out from the back of her throat and confided to him.

"That's all we are looking for to start with Harry. Now, is twenty grand alright?"

Harry Singh licked his lips.

"I'll need twenty five plus expenses Mrs Gordon if I'm going to be away from work for three weeks."

Jill was desperate to get away from the now overpowering body odour emanating from Harry Singh.

"No problem Harry, that seems fair to me if you have to cover yourself at work."

At that moment, the Barman shouted out to no one in particular in the bar

"Bloody terrorists have struck again, they ought to shoot the bastards when they catch them!"

Jill and Harry turned to the TV tuned to Sky News on the wall, and the bartender turned up the volume. Cath watched as the yellow banner headline showed "Suspected Terror Attack at Duke of Devonshire Home in Chatsworth Derbyshire." Drone footage showed a scene, from height, of two white Range Rovers and a black pick up abandoned on parkland in the park. Some areas had been blurred from the footage. A news reporter in the background was enthusiastically reporting that the police were on the scene and that there were reports of numerous fatalities.

Jill stood up, picked up her handbag and walked closer to the screen leaving Harry Singh at the table. She watched as the drone footage looped back to the Range Rovers and the pick-up abandoned on the park. Her Gordy and the boys were a few miles from there and they had two white Range Rovers. She could feel a worried panic coming over her. She watched a third loop of the footage and there was nothing that could identify the Range Rovers as those that belonged to her husband. Stop worrying she reassured herself, just give him a ring he will answer, and everything will be alright. Jill looked back at Harry Singh and saw he was watching the news footage. She turned to her left and walked into the ladies cloakroom fumbling in her handbag for her mobile phone.

She had rung Gordy ten times without success and then Pete, and then Briggsy, and finally Kwadj with a similar result. She could feel her hands growing clammy with worry and she could hear and feel her heart beating fast against her chest. Jill told herself to stay calm. It would not do anyone any good if she started to panic for no reason. Deal with the issue at hand she told herself and then find out what had happened to Gordy. They were all together and probably in an area where there was no reception.

Jill straightened her hat in the mirror, applied a new layer of her pink lipstick and walked out of the cloakroom. She walked up to the table where Harry Singh was still sitting, took out a brown envelope from her bag and placed it onto the table.

"I've got to get off Harry, but we have a deal. We fly to Antigua on Wednesday. There's five grand there for you and twenty for the other 'expenses' over there if its needed. I'll text you your flight and hotel details later today when I've spoken to Mr Gordon."

"Thanks. We have a deal Mrs Gordon," Harry Singh replied smiling up at her, and pocketed the envelope into his shabby suit pocket.

He finished off his pint of Stella and walked over to the bar and ordered another Stella.

"Bloody terrorists!"

Harry struck up a conversation with the barman and indicated to the looping drone footage of the Range Rovers.

Meeting over, Jill walked out of the pub, turned right, and emerged into Bloomsbury Road where she paused, fighting down the wave of panic and dread that was rising within her.

Her phone rang, she sighed with relief; it would be Gordy ringing her back. She opened her bag and frantically looked for the ringing phone. Jill found the mobile and looked at the screen, it wasn't Gordy. She didn't recognise the number but still answered it in case it was Gordy ringing on a 'burner.'

"Mrs Gordon?"

She recognised the voice as Detective Sergeant Glyn Munroe. He was a police officer in the Metropolitan Police Specialist Crime Department that had been on their payroll for many years.

"Hi Glyn, problems?"

"Yes Mrs Gordon, SO15 the anti- terror unit have just passed us the job at Chatsworth that's on the telly have you heard about it?"

Jill could feel her legs going weak in dread and leant against the cold iron railings at her side.

"Yes I've just seen it on the TV."

"Well they have decided already that it's not a terrorist incident and it's been passed to us. The two Range Rovers involved come back to Gordy and there are a number of people dead. I've tried to ring him but he's not answering so can you pass him a message that the police will be all over you in about an hour or so."

"Thank you Glyn, he's here with me now I'll tell him," Jill lied and closed the call.

She slid down the railings until she was sat on her haunches looking down at the pavement, her bag at her side. She wanted to cry, to bury her head into a cushion, to lie on her bed wrapped in the white duvet smelling of Gordy. She couldn't do any of that at the moment, now wasn't the time. She took a deep breath and stood up straightening her coat. She needed to get organised. They would need to get out the country if Gordy hadn't been arrested. The police would be at their house in a couple of hours. She needed to clear the house of anything incriminating and be away by the time the police arrived with a search warrant as she would be arrested just for being the wife of the owner of the Range Rovers involved. These things she knew would happen and needed to be dealt with.

More importantly if she were being tipped off by their contacts in the police, the Columbians that supplied them with merchandise would also be tipped off by similar sources and they would become concerned about their payment. With Trueman, Burton and now Gordy arrested…. or dead they might believe they would not be getting paid. She saw a taxi approaching and waved it down.

Back at home Jill pushed the rolls of £50 notes into the false bottom of her hairspray and deodorant cans. Their false British

Passports lay on the bed with a small make up bag and a spare set of underwear. She pushed another roll of £50 notes into her panties and the articles on the bed into an overnight bag. Neither Gordy nor the boys had answered any calls yet. She told herself that Gordy wouldn't be dead, he would have been arrested or laying low having escaped from the police. He was too smart to have been shot or arrested. She looked at her watch it was an hour since DS Monroe called her. She wouldn't have much time before the police arrived. She sat on the bed and rang Harry Singh. He answered on the third ring and sounded like he was still in the pub.

"Harry can we still put the directors in our names without the death certificates?"

There was a pause at the other end of the phone and then Harry replied.

"Yes, but it will really cost, maybe over fifty thousand. Everything is possible it's just whether the person who acts for us over there knows the right people who will help you at the right price."

"Money's not a problem….provided that Gordy had got the MacBook," Jill thought hopefully to herself.

"Right Harry book a flight on Wednesday and if you get everything sorted I'll pay you double."

"I'm booking the flight once you put the phone down," confirmed Harry.

Jill hung up and rang the geek.

"Get yourself on a train to Manchester Airport first thing in the morning. You're going on a holiday with me to Antigua and I'll pay you fifty grand if you unlock that MacBook when we get there. I'll be paying for your flight and don't forget your passport."

"Al… Al… Alright Mrs G..G..Gordon," the geek stuttered.

"See you there."

Jill closed the call, and put her phone in her bag.

Passports – check, Money – check, phone – check, set of clean clothes and underwear – check. She looked around the room and made sure that she had not left anything that might let the police know where she had gone. There was nothing.

She threw the overnight bag over her shoulder and went out of the front door. No point locking it she thought, the police will just force it. She then turned and walked to the taxi she had instructed to wait for her, after dropping her off. Its engine was still running and so would be its meter she thought as she approached it. She opened the rear door threw her overnight bag in it and instructed the driver sat in the front.

"St Pancras please."

The vehicle did not move and neither did the driver. The glass of the driver's door window lay shattered on his shoulder and on the back seat of the car where she had thrown her bag. She looked closely at the back of his head and saw a spray of blood on the back of the passenger seat in front of her. Jill was perplexed, she could not understand what she was seeing. She looked at her hand, there was blood dripping onto it. She looked up, the roof was covered in blood that was dripping onto her and her clothes. She looked again at the still forward facing head of the driver and saw the trickle of blood running out of a large hole where the drivers left ear should have been and into the blue crew neck woollen jumper at his shoulder.

Jill's felt the same panic that had afflicted her earlier that day rising within her as she took in the scene. She needed to get out of the taxi and run, just run … there was a knock on the window at her side and Jill turned slowly with dread towards the sound. There was a young dark skinned boy about fifteen years old sat astride a pedal cycle looking at her through the window. As she watched, the boy raised a silenced automatic handgun, pointing it to her head and smiling. Jill was thinking "What is such a small boy doing with such a large gun?" when she stopped thinking anything at all, ever again.

The small boy on his pedal cycle released the gun from his hand and let it fall to the floor. He then casually rode out of the open gates of the compound where he stopped, dropped the cycle to the floor and waited for a black BMW SUV to pull up at the side of him. The young boy opened the rear door, got in and the BMW drove away, just as the first of a line of marked police vehicles pulled into the compound and came to a stop at the side of the blood splattered taxi.

Chapter 38 – The Commander From The Met

Tuesday 21ˢᵗ January

It was just after 6 a.m. and Commander Colin Foxley-Jones looked at the full five foot nine inches of himself in the hotel mirror. He had been chauffeured up to the five star Peacock Hotel late the previous night after a woman called Jill Gordon and a taxi driver had been found murdered at her home address in Dagenham. Her husband, ,Martin Gordon and three associates had been identified as both victims and offenders to six murders the same day in Derbyshire.

The image in the mirror was perfect he thought to himself. The starched white shirt beneath the spotless black police uniform. At Bramshill Police College he had once been complimented on the ironed creases in his uniform trousers and sleeves. He had never forgotten the compliment and ever since had prided himself on his ironing prowess for uniform creases. His bulled plain leather Loake's reflected glass-like in the mirror.

Foxley-Jones then practised a couple of stances from the Amy Cuddy TED talk; a wide 'At Ease' stance, arms crossed, and then uncrossed. He liked the uncrossed better and then the 'Power' stance. In the TED talk Amy Cuddy had explained how people could be successful if you believed in your own successful future and could transfer that belief to other people by how you looked and your body language. He had watched the TED talk, memorised it and then put his interpretation of it into practice. That practice Foxley-Jones believed had been instrumental in his rise through the ranks of the Metropolitan Police. One day he would be Commissioner of the Metropolitan Police through his own willpower and the projection of it to others.

He also knew that media incidents such as the "Chatsworth Massacre" came along once in a career, and he was not going to miss the opportunity to increase his public profile through it. There was a knock on the door of the hotel room, Foxley-Jones took one last satisfying look at himself in the mirror, made the "Power Pose" and held it for five seconds. He was ready. He put his gold peak braided cap on his head, took a final look in the mirror and picked up his leather briefcase on the way to the door where his driver was waiting to take him the fifteen miles to Buxton, and the waiting media.

Dave pulled out of Clifton Road and onto Silverlands in Buxton. The Divisional Headquarters, once a bustling society of police officers and administration staff was now reduced, by a succession of budget cuts, to an almost abandoned building of empty offices. The police station across the yard at the rear of the building however retained some life as a base for the dwindling number of police officers who covered the area.

It was just seven in the morning and Dave had wanted to get to the incident room early so that he could go through all the information that had come in overnight and the previous day. He would then be in a position to quickly update Superintendent Dicks before the briefing that morning. As he turned into the road he saw in front of him a line of media vans on the road and TV cameras and journalists on the lawned area in front of the Headquarters.

"Media's here early," he said to himself.

He sounded his horn to move some of the throng off of the access road and turned into the police station, parking up in the almost empty car park in the rear yard.

By 7.15 a.m. Dave was sitting at his desk in Dicks' office and was reading through the statements and interview summaries of the previous day. The statements from a number of witnesses gave a commentary of the chase between the Navara and the Range Rovers from Stanedge to Chatsworth. Statements from the Peak Edge Hotel had been obtained identifying that a Martin Gordon, Peter Stevens, Kwadjo Musa, and a Trevor Briggs had booked in the previous day for one night. All had given Martin Gordon's address at The Paddocks in Dagenham. The hotel rooms had been sealed pending a forensic examination that morning once the CSI's had been released from the scene at Chatsworth.

Karen and Gail Traynor had been arrested and their houses forensically searched together with Ron Juniors rented cottage in Winster. Nothing had been found at any of the addresses that gave any indication as to why the Traynors had been involved in the shooting. Both Gail and Karen had asked for a local solicitor, Bernard Marples, and had remained silent in interview even when told on tape about the death of Ron and Ron Junior.

Dave put the papers to one side, picked up the remote control, and turned on the TV. He needed to put all that he had read into a short briefing report for Dicks before 9 a.m. and he had plenty of time to do it. He picked up his still warm coffee and sat back in the black swivel chair to catch up on the news on Sky.

On the screen was a uniform senior police officer. The yellow banner at the bottom of the screen identified him as Commander Colin Foxley-Jones of the Serious Crime Command of the Metropolitan Police. Dave turned the volume up.

"Following the incident at Chatsworth yesterday The Metropolitan Police Serious Crime Command followed up on information held by the Metropolitan Police and attended the home address of a Martin Gordon on Cook Road in Dagenham. The Metropolitan Police believe that Gordon and three of his associates were four of the people found murdered in Chatsworth yesterday. At the home address of Martin Gordon two further people were discovered to have been killed. A taxi driver and Mrs Jill Gordon appear to have been murdered in cold blood. The Metropolitan Police are linking these murders with the ones in Derbyshire and due to the substantial London connections to both incidents have today put at the disposal of the Derbyshire Police substantial resources to assist in the linked investigations. I will now take a couple of questions from the media. Linda at Sky news…"

"Do you think that the murders are terrorist related?"

"No. The likelihood is that the murders are related to a dispute between rival organised crime groups in London, but I do not want to go into too many details at the moment Linda. I want to take this opportunity to reassure Londoners that the Metropolitan Police is putting all the resources at its disposal to ensure the safety of the residents in Dagenham. They will see a lot more officers on the streets today to reassure them that the streets of Dagenham are safe to walk on. It is still early days in the enquiry Linda and as you know I will give you a fuller update once we know more about the incidents…. Harry from the BBC."

"What resources are you giving to the Derbyshire Police to help with their side of the investigation?"

"Well Harry, as much as they need really. I can have a hundred detectives here by the end of the week. In addition, we can have support services such as specialist search teams and CSI's here within twenty four hours. These incidents are of national importance, people must feel safe from the tentacles of violent organised crime groups. Whilst the Metropolitan Police has specific experience and expertise in these matters we are aware that some of the smaller provincial forces do not. The residents of these areas should be able to feel reassured that the expertise of the Metropolitan Police will be available to them in their hour of need and that is why I am offering the Derbyshire Police the resources that they will require to continue their investigation today. Thank you everyone I will give a further update at twelve in time for your mid-day news bulletins."

The news camera panned round to the reporter. Dave immediately recognised the background road and drive as the one he had driven down around half an hour earlier. Commander Foxley-Jones was outside Buxton Police Station. Dave exhaled loudly there were another two murders yesterday linked with the six in Derbyshire. Neither he nor Dicks had been told anything about them and so they were obviously out of that information loop.

The door to Dicks' office burst open, and Dicks came through it, a mobile phone at his ear. Dicks shut the door behind him as he listened to the person who was speaking to him at the other end and made a cuppa gesture to Dave. Dave pointed to one already on his desk. Dicks sat down, still listening to the person talking to him on the phone. He took a sip of coffee, gave Dave a thumbs up, and carried on listening until he eventually replied to the caller.

"Right, got all that!" Dicks closed the call.

"You up to date with the stuff from yesterday and overnight Excy?"

"Yes sir, apart from the murders in London I've been through it this morning but not done a resume yet."

"Good. Nip next door and get the first detective that walks in to get hold of Commander Foxley-Jones who is wandering around somewhere in this establishment and sit him in the old Chief Superintendent's office across the way, together with anyone who has come up here with him. Tell them to keep him happy with coffee and biscuits, but on no account is he to be allowed in this side of the nick. In fact, get a second detective or uniform to stand on the door downstairs and make sure that no-one comes in that he doesn't know especially the bloody media and particularly the Commander or anyone from the Met. Got that, Excy?"

Dave nodded

"And a hot cup of coffee would be welcome on your way back."

Dave gave a thumbs up and shot out the room to ensure the Superintendent's instructions were complied with to the letter. Five minutes later Dave walked back into the room with two hot cups of coffee, he gave one to Dicks and sat with the other at his desk.

"One detective taking Commander Foxley-Jones and his entourage to the Chief Superintendent's office and another on the door downstairs. Do you want updating on what's gone off overnight yet?"

"Yes, get me up to date and then I will get you up to date with what's happening at Headquarters."

Dave ran verbally through the information he had read earlier, to Dicks.

"Thanks, Excy, can you get that down on paper for this morning's briefing? It's going to be hard going today. We have got six bodies or what is left of them which have got to have post-mortems, the Traynors are in the cells and are saying nothing, and we have to make a decision whether to keep them another twenty four hours or not. We have also got to do a forensic search of the hotel rooms but I'm not hopeful we will find anything. To make things even more complicated the Chief wants us to concentrate on finding out what the criminal association is between the Traynors and Gordon. So, I want everyone who is spare on that today."

"Why is that the Chief's priority boss?"

"The answer to that is sitting across the way in the old Chief Super's office. We are now in the politics of policing, Excy, that I told you about yesterday. That was the Chief Constable on the phone to me when I came in. He's had to cancel his press conference today following Mr Foxley-Jones's bombshells to the media this morning. The reason for Commander Foxley-Jones coming here and making that press announcement, when and where he did this morning, is because the Met or more correctly the Commander has decided that they want this job on their CV. As a result, whether it's true or not the Met have tied in the two murders down in Dagenham to the gunfight up here and are using that as a means to get involved in our enquiry. The offer of resources he made on TV this morning is a slam dunk that we didn't want or ask for and the Chief has gone ballistic. He hasn't liked the Met since they turned up in the miners' strike in the early eighties and showed, in his view, what a corrupt lot of undisciplined thieves they actually were. Unfortunately, he cannot now be seen to turn the offer of mutual aid away."

"The murders are on us so we would still be running it wouldn't we?" queried Dave.

"It's not that simple, we have got thirty detectives on this job, and they can send a hundred. The basic maths denote that with all those resources they are going to want to run the case. If the Chief is forced to give the Met the role of lead force it may mean that we are going to have Met personnel and detectives all over us by the end of the week. The Chief wants us to occupy Commander Foxley-Jones till tomorrow to give him time to think what to do. In the meantime, we have got to keep him away from the incident room, so brief a pretty policewoman to butter up his ego, drive him to the scene, one of the post-mortems and then round some local beauty spots to pass the time today. Tell her I'll pay her double time and a rest day thrown in for her trouble. The Chief has also asked that we get something that will give him a media opportunity to highlight the role of the Derbyshire Police on the investigation, preferably the reason for the gunfight or why our local family called Traynor are involved before he is forced to hand it over to Foxley-Jones. We have got twenty four hours to get some answers and credit for the force before the Met probably walk in, take it over, and walk away with the media plaudits. Any ideas what they were into or ways to get the Traynor women talking would be helpful Excy. You're local, any ideas?"

Excy slowly exhaled between his teeth in thought, he had only had involvement with Gary Traynor, and he was now a 'dead end' in more ways than one. Cath had dealt with the accident....

"My colleague Cath Mulvey dealt with the death of the son just before Christmas, I can ask her if she knows anything. They weren't very helpful even with that investigation though. The whole family is very anti-police."

Dicks stroked the scar on his forehead.

"Is there anything in the death of the son that's likely to link to what happened yesterday?"

"I don't think so. It was a straightforward RTC. Witnesses saw the son cycle straight in front of a truck. It's with the coroner at the moment but I can't see him deciding that it was anything other than an accidental death. The driver's a local bloke with no previous convictions who is being prosecuted for some minor motoring offences."

Dicks thought for a few seconds.

"Get a copy of the file just in case Excy. We need to make sure we don't miss anything, and then get on with that briefing paper. I've got some calls to make to Sally Brooks and the pathologist re the post-mortems later today. Let's see what comes up today from further interviews with the Traynor women, the searches at the hotels, and the post-mortems. If nothing helpful comes up, as a long shot see Cath Mulvey tonight and see if she has got anything."

Dave noted everything that Dicks had asked him to do.

"On it sir,"

He would give some thought about what he would say to Cath later if it became necessary.

Chapter 39 – Detective Sergeant Mulvey's First Day

Tuesday 21ˢᵗ January

Cath sat at Hollys desk, or as of 9 a.m. that morning her desk. A Detective Sergeant with no detectives she thought. There was no way that she was going to get one in the near future either, not with seven murders being investigated on the patch.

She picked up the first buff folder from the pile on the desk, opened it and saw that it was her file on the Lime Tree Rd burglary by Gary Traynor. She went straight to the back page signed it off and put it in the 'Out' tray.' This is easy she thought, picked up the next file, it was another one of hers. She went to the back page signed it off and put it in the 'Out' tray. Next was her mileage claim, signed off and in the 'Out' tray. Dave's expenses… he was gone now, signed off and 'Out' tray. Ten minutes later she had an empty 'In' tray and a full 'Out' tray. She picked up the contents of the 'Out' Tray and carried it through to the Despatch Office where she put it all in the tray labelled Divisional Admin and then picked up a blank piece of paper from the copier and went back to her desk.

"Right then" she said to herself. Trueman dies, she wrote 'PT dead' then drew an arrow to the word 'MacBook' and another to 'Brown Suit.' She leant back, pen in mouth, it was easier in the movies she thought, screwed the piece of paper up and hit the inside of the bin first time.

Cath looked at the clock on the wall, it was only 9.30 a.m. She took the screwed up piece of paper out of the bin and smoothed it out on her desk. She didn't have any evidence to link Neil Burton with the man in the brown suit seen near to Gary Traynor and Alice Bulman before they died. The nagging feeling in her mind was that there could be a link if there was a Traynor connection to the 'Chatsworth Massacre' as the press were now calling it. She decided to give the itch a scratch. She opened a call to Dave on her mobile and he answered it on the third ring.

"Is that Temporary Detective Sergeant Baker?" asked Cath.

"Is that Acting Sergeant Mulvey?" Dave playfully replied.

"Sure is, how is it going?"

"Great, BJ has got me running as his personal batman, I think he's decided to keep me on a short leash for a while. In all honesty Cath he's been alright. He's been showing me how to run an incident and keeping me in the loop of decisions and why he makes them and all sorts. How's things with you?"

"Piece of cake Excy. Got rid of the admin in thirty minutes can't understand why Holly always makes such a big issue about it!" she laughed.

"How is he, have you heard?"

"No, I went over to the hospital after he was taken there yesterday but I couldn't see him as he got sectioned. I rang this morning before coming to work and he's on the Hartington Wing but because I'm not family they wouldn't tell me anything."

Cath then changed the subject to what she was ringing him about.

"Any idea who our dead shooters are yet?"

"Cath, it was carnage up there. According to the news this morning the Met reckon that one of the victim's was a bloke called Martin Gordon and they have discovered his wife was murdered yesterday as well, together with a taxi driver. As to the rest there wasn't a lot to identify; some of them had been almost blown to bits. Two of them have been identified through fingerprints, although it's only informally of course, so not a word to anyone else till it's released."

"Stop teasing… who were they?"

"The Traynors, Ron and Ron Junior."

Cath took a slow intake of breath and tried to stop herself from sounding excited at the news.

"That's a surprise. Any idea what it's all about?"

"Not really Cath but we are looking at some sort of gang killings probably, at least that's what the smart monies on at the moment. Look Cath I can't say much more as I'm going into the briefing soon and Dicks wants me to lead on some of it. I've got to go, briefings starting in a minute, speak soon," He closed the call.

She put her phone down on the desk. Dave had just politely blown her off. The old team of Holly, Excy and herself had gone. Holly was in hospital and might never come back and Dave was off on his promotion mission. She was now a team of one, and felt a little sadness at the thought that the office next door would never bounce with the playful banter between the three of them again. They would never get drunk together after work in the pub or sit around eating bacon and egg sandwiches in a morning. She sighed. She had been here before, when she had left uniform shifts and it was always a sad time when the almost close family bonds of a police team finish. You get over it though thought Cath to herself.

Cath shook herself out of her maudlin mood and forced herself to think about the links in the investigation. As she had suspected there was a Traynor amongst the dead from Chatsworth. Two of them in fact. The man in the brown suit, when Gary had got run over, was going to be Neil Burton she thought to herself, and the two men who had chased him under the truck would probably be amongst the other dead men she was certain, but she had no evidence.

Cath looked for a motive. The only incriminating thing in relation to Burton that she was aware of were the photographs on the missing MacBook that Maggie had told her about. Gary Traynor was an opportunistic thief.....what if Burton had thought Gary Traynor had nicked his MacBook with the photos of him on its hard drive and had taken a couple of unknown heavies to get it back off him. Then the Traynors had been killed getting revenge on the heavies that had chased Gary under the truck. She realised that her imagination was getting ahead of her, there were too many evidential pieces missing for it to make proper sense.

Her thoughts about Neil Burton reminded her that she did have something to do that day. She had to confirm the sad news about her husband to Maggie Burton that Sally had given her yesterday. It would also be a good opportunity to see if Maggie Burton could fill in any of the missing gaps in relation to her husband.

Cath knocked quietly on the door of Maggie Burton's house at Matlock Bath. A crescendo of dog barking and scurrying arose down the hallway, as each of the dogs vied for pole position of 'nearest the door and loudest bark competition'. From the other side of the door there was a loud shout of "Quiet!" followed by silence and then a single bark. That was the Jack Russell thought Cath. Then a shout of "Basket!" followed by a scurrying sound that disappeared down the hallway towards the kitchen. The door opened and Maggie Burton recognising Cath, smiled, and invited her inside.

"Ah DC Mulvey…come in… come in," she urged.

"For some reason I was expecting the police this morning. I thought it would be DS Hollins, is he alright, I was worried for him after Saturday... of course, he is…for goodness' sake Maggie stop wittering on… come into the kitchen, can I get you a cup of tea or coffee?"

"Coffee please," replied Cath.

She bent down, unzipped her boots, and placed them with the line of Hunter and riding boots in the hallway. She had odd socks on again! Cath walked through to the kitchen and sat at the table whilst Maggie made two cups of coffee and then sat down opposite her.

"Before you say anything Cath, it was Neil in the car wasn't it?"

Cath nodded.

"That's alright, I accepted that it would be after DS Hollins came on Saturday. It's strange really isn't it?"

Cath queried what Maggie was asking.

"What is?"

"Death" pronounced Maggie taking a sip of coffee.

"It feels like the end, but it's also really a beginning. Since Saturday I've really only thought about what happens next now Neil's gone. You know things like, how will I pay the bills, what will happen to the stables and horses, will I have to sell the house? I should be grieving about Neil dying, but I'm angry with him for leaving me in this position. The bank accounts have got hardly anything in them, he always let me believe that we were quite well off but like the rest of his life it turned out to be a lie. I'm sorry Cath I'm going off on one again, you must be busy and eager to get off."

Cath gave Maggie her winning smile.

"Actually, I'm not. I've got what you might call a fairly empty day."

"In that case Cath I was about to make myself some breakfast, do you want to join me? I was going to make pancakes if you fancy some?"

Cath had as usual skipped breakfast.

"Yes I'd love some, but only if you let me help you, I'll feel awkward just sat here."

"Do you know how to make pancakes?" asked Maggie.

"No," replied Cath.

Maggie threw her a red and white check apron and laughed "Young people nowadays! Put this on, I'll show you, you might get a bit messy though."

Half an hour later Cath finished off her third pancake rolled in orange juice and sugar.

"That hit the spot!"

"You've got flour on your face,," observed Maggie as she chewed and swallowed the last of her own breakfast.

The dogs deprived of any scraps, disappeared from under the table and back into their baskets by the range. Cath rubbed her face with the back of her hand, smearing more flour on her face and across her nose.

"Fancy another coffee? I'll make it," suggested Cath.

"Love one," said Maggie.

Cath got up and began making the coffees.

"So how is DS Hollins? I could tell he wasn't right on Saturday; he kept going into some sort of trance. I told him that he needed to see a doctor, I was that worried that I nearly rang for one while he was here. I ended up giving him a hug, he seemed to need one," said Maggie thoughtfully.

Cath decided to be truthful with Maggie.

"He's not well at all. We think he's had some sort of breakdown."

"That's so sad, I think Neil was on the point of one before …. You know…"

"Yes, you told me about the MacBook and the photographs. He at least shared that worry with you. I don't think Holly… DS Hollins felt he could talk to anybody about what was worrying him. I thought we were close, but he wouldn't ever talk about his worries at work or at home. I think it's a police thing, looking mentally strong to colleagues and the public, no matter how you're actually feeling."

"I suppose I had better ask how you are then!" Maggie laughed.

"I'm fine Maggie, I'm not just saying that either. I've just been temporarily promoted. I've got no staff yet so I've no HR problems whatsoever, I've got a new girlfriend and I've just learnt how to make pancakes. What more could a girl want?"

"In my case to have enough money to keep the house and stables, and to be truthful, a sex life again! Oh god! I can't believe I just said that! For goodness' sake, I've just been informed my husbands died and I'm complaining about not having a sex life. You must think I'm such a bad person?"

"No, you're not Maggie, you're looking ahead, a beginning as you told me earlier. On the money front did you not think it strange that Paul Trueman didn't leave Neil anything in his will? Neil was his partner for so many years."

"I did," confirmed Maggie.

"But Neil wasn't bothered at all. It was as though it was irrelevant. I get everything from Neil's will; he didn't leave anything to Paul either, so I think it was something they had discussed and agreed on. Neil's not left very much, I should be able to keep going for a year or so, but the house and stables will have to go. I'll have to downsize a bit, but I'll keep the dogs and a couple of the older horses."

"Can you work at all?" asked Cath.

"I've done nothing work wise since working for my dad after university. So, unless you know someone who can cook, bring up children and spend most of the time mucking out horses, I don't think I've got much prospect on the work front."

"Ideal material on the wife front round here though!" laughed Cath.

"What did you do for your dad?"

"He had a company formation business in Sheffield. I got a degree in accountancy and started working for him when I left Uni. I was there a couple of years but then met Neil and we got married, dad retired about a year afterwards and I didn't fancy running it on my own, so I became a housewife."

"What did you do at your dad's company?" Cath asked

"Just the normal stuff. It was setting up limited companies mainly, although I did set up some offshore ones as a one off for Neil just after we got married," Maggie explained.

"You said on the day when you reported him missing that he was going to his accountant's, why didn't you do them for him?"

"I did offer, but the Solicitors Regulatory Authority demand that they are done by a proper accountant not someone who never even qualified. He's used Greenwoods since I've known him, and his dad used them before Neil took over the business."

Cath's heart skipped a beat. Neil was at Alice's office the day she went missing. Cath took the last gulp of her coffee.

"Look Maggie, it's been great talking to you and breakfast was lovely but I'm going to have to go soon."

"Yes I know, thanks for coming round to tell me about Neil. If you want to call again for a chat or breakfast please do. I've enjoyed chatting with you, I don't get to talk to many people now the children have left. That's what I will miss most about Neil, our occasional chats."

"I promise I will, I've got your phone number and you've got mine so call me if you want to talk, and I promise I'll be back round for pancakes in the next week. That's a proper promise as well."

The dogs got up as one and walked towards Cath in anticipation of her leaving. Cath stood up and walked down the hall followed by the dogs and Maggie. She slipped on her boots and zipped them up as Maggie opened the door.

"Thanks Cath,"

Maggie gave her a hug which Cath reciprocated. Then Maggie let her go, picked up the corner of her apron and motherly wiped some flour off Cath's nose.

"Can't have you going out, meeting the public looking like a dough girl!"

Cath gave her a genuine smile and walked off to her car. She took a quick glance at her watch. It was twelve o'clock. She would have a trip to Bakewell, but first she wanted to speak with Bill Fry and made the call to see whether he was on.

Chapter 40 – The MacBook

Tuesday 21st January

Cath went through the blue painted door that closed with a click behind her and walked into what used to be the public enquiry office of the police station in Bakewell town centre. She had arranged to meet Bill Fry there, but the eerie silence meant that he had not arrived yet. The reason she wanted to talk to Bill was to find out the local gossip on Greenwoods before she went round to their office. She walked quickly through the old public front office and turned on the light in the dark kitchen at the back of the police station.

There was milk in the fridge and so she switched the kettle on. It was such a shame, she thought, that the police station was now no longer operational. It had an atmosphere of an old 'Nick,' the two small cells in the back was no Custody Suite just an old fashioned 'lock up' where prisoners could be stashed away for days without their solicitor finding them and a small passage led to a flight of stairs to the CID office. Designed for old fashioned policing and prisoners falling down stairs.

An Accidental Death

She looked at the old oak farmhouse kitchen table that was probably older than the station itself. How many cups of tea had been drunk on it she thought as she put her coffee down on it and put Bill's tea on the other side of the table. The two mugs creating two more circles amongst the thousands of mug rings that decorated its surface.

The big blue station diary sat closed at one end of the table. Another throwback to earlier times she thought, when everything that happened on a section would be written down in it so that the next shift or visiting police officer could immediately find out what had happened in the preceding day, week, or month just by looking through it. There was little recorded in it nowadays because everything went through a central control room and was fed into electronic briefings.

Cath opened the big diary to pass the time whilst waiting for Bill. She recognised Bill's handwriting on nearly all the notes. The last two pages dated from Christmas and concerned day to day sightings of local criminals, most of which ended with the words "Could be a suspect in case anything happens."

She turned to the previous page and the name Gary Traynor jumped out at her. "Gary Traynor hanging around car park at front of police station seen 9.10hrs - 20/12. could be a suspect in case anything happens." That was the day he was at Court she thought when Paul Trueman slipped and died. Directly underneath it was written "Black bag found Bath gardens, see Beryl at Wildgoose if anyone reports loss."

She was still staring at the two notes minutes later when she heard the front door open, and Bill shout out her name.

"In here Bill!" she shouted back.

"Tea's on the table!" and closed the diary.

Bill came in and sat down.

"I hear that it's Detective Sergeant Mulvey now. How's the dizzy heights of supervision going so far?"

"First day Bill. Cleared all the admin in half an hour, not got anyone to supervise, there's no prisoners anywhere and no recordable crime happened in the last twenty four hours. So actually, it's a piece of piss so far. Don't know why you sergeants make such a fuss about it."

"You're not on that recordable multi murder massacre crime then?"

"No! that's why I'm driving around rural stations drinking tea" laughed Cath.

"How's Holly?"

"I don't know Bill. He's been sectioned on the mental health wing at the hospital. That's all I know at the moment."

Cath shook her head slowly and sighed sadly.

"Sorry to hear that Cath. Let me know if there's any change will you? Changing the subject a bit, have you heard anything on the grapevine about the murders?"

"Nothing official Bill and I don't want to add to the rumour squad as what I've got was on a sworn to secrecy basis."

"That's alright Cath, no problem as far as I'm concerned. Now what did you want to grill me over. Bear in mind anything I tell you will be on the same sworn to secrecy basis."

"Well two things Bill. Firstly, I need a Temporary DC. Have you got anyone who could do with an attachment for a couple of months? Secondly Greenwood Accountants, what's the low down gossip? The guy we found in the burnt out Discovery up at Long Rake turned out to be that missing solicitor from Matlock. Neil Burton. Apparently Burton was in the accountant's the afternoon he went missing."

Bill looked at her.

"That would be the same day that Alice Bulman disappeared from the same office. Half the police forces in the country are looking for the one and only suspect in her murder, a certain Mr Dylan Oxley, who has also not been seen since the same night. I hope you're not going rogue young Mulvey, there will be hell to pay if you start buggering up Dylan Oxley as a suspect."

"No Bill, I am very aware of that. I just wondered if you knew anything about the firm that's all, solely in relation to the potential suicide enquiry of course."

"Well whatever I tell you is under sworn secrecy, so it had better not come back to me if you end up throwing shit into the fan, I'm too close to retirement! Greenwood accountants on Bath

Street is run by Stephen Greenwood who took over the business when his dad retired. Clients are nearly all local and he probably does about half the businesses in the town and a few from Matlock. Used to have two employees now just the one for obvious reasons. The remaining one is Beryl Smith. Been there years. He spends most of his time up at the golf club, either on the course or in the bar and only pops in to sign accounts off after Beryl has done all the work. That's it in a nutshell really."

Cath got up, picked up the empty mugs and started to wash and dry them.

"Will Greenwood be in now? I just want to ask him about Burton's accounts, see if there was anything in them that might have caused him to top himself."

"You would be better speaking to Beryl she actually does the accounts. She is also more likely to be in than Greenwood. It's medal day up at the golf club and I would reckon he will be playing this afternoon in view of the weather."

"Thanks Bill, I'll nip round and see her. Don't forget the Temporary DC post!"

"I won't, I'll just nip round the back and unpack another officer, I think Amazon delivered a few this morning…"

Bill paused when he saw Cath's face fall in disappointment.

"Don't worry Cath I'll ask around for a volunteer and if no-one comes forward someone will be pressed into service, let you know Friday?"

Cath's face lit up "That would be brilliant Bill!"

Cath cheekily kissed him on the side of his face making him blush, and set off walking to Bath Street.

Cath pushed open the door to the accountants and walked into the hallway. The black and white tiled floor and jade painted walls gave the hallway an Edwardian appearance that was enhanced by the cast iron spindles and handrails of the staircase leading to the first floor. A polished wood panelled door with a sign identifying it as the 'Office' was on her left and she opened the door and stepped inside. A woman about fifty years old, with short grey hair, a high necked dress that was button tied at her neck and a hand knitted cardigan, looked up from her computer screen. "Hello there, can I help you?"

Cath had her wallet in her hand and opened it to show her warrant card.

"Detective Sergeant Mulvey, I'm looking for Beryl Smith."

"That's me. Is it about Alice again?" asked Beryl.

"No, I'm looking at the sudden death of a solicitor from Matlock called Neil Burton and I understand he was here on the afternoon he went missing," Cath explained to her.

There was only one other chair in the office and that was behind the desk opposite to Beryl's. Cath thought about taking it out and sitting on it but decided to lean back against the desk instead, so that she faced Beryl.

"Yes, such a nice man. He came to pick up his accounts. He's been with us for years. You don't think he had something to do with Alice's murder do you?"

"No, not at all, I am nothing to do with the murder enquiry but I'm certain that the investigating team believe that it was Dylan Oxley," she reassured Beryl.

"I am looking at a possibility that Mr Burton may have been depressed or upset about something on the day he went missing, and as you saw him that day I was wondering whether you noticed anything unusual?"

Beryl leant back in her chair.

"No nothing at all. He seemed quite normal. He picked up his accounts and we had a chat about a Dior bag that Alice had found, he had an identical one, but brown rather than black and then he went. He wasn't here for more than a few minutes."

"Was there anything in the accounts that could have caused him to be upset?" Cath continued with her questioning.

"No, he makes a good profit. It's not life transforming but there was nothing in the accounts that I saw to make him worried." Beryl shrugged.

"Must have been the bag then!" Cath joked.

Beryl broke out into a smile.

"No!" she chuckled.

"He was quite happy talking about that. I don't know if I should tell you this, but he was a bit gay…if you know what I mean. We have been doing his accounts for years and he always talks to me about stuff that men don't generally talk about. I live with two men, my husband and grown up son and in all the time I have known them I have never heard them talk about what colour a bathroom should be, or whether a plain shirt went better than a checked one with a tweed suit, never mind knowing about the usefulness of secret pockets in Dior shoulder bags."

"Dior bags have secret pockets!" laughed Cath.

"Well according to Mr Burton, they do. I mean do you know any straight blokes who would know that?"

Cath thought for a second.

"No, can't say I do, …. was there anything in the secret pocket in the bag that Alice found?"

"I don't know, Alice took it home and she wasn't here when Mr Burton picked up his accounts. I forgot to mention it to her when she got back, and then she was murdered that night ……it was just so unfair. She was such a live wire, full of fun, she was going to do so much, travel the world, visit places and then it was all snuffed out by someone."

At that moment, the office door opened, and a middle aged man popped his head round.

"I'm off to the golf club if anyone wants me I will be on my mobile. Will the Baxter's accounts be done for tomorrow?"

"Yes Mr Greenwood,"

"That's fantastic! I don't know what I'd do without you. See you in the morning."

Mr Greenwood shut the door behind him. If he had seen Cath he had neither given her eye contact nor acknowledged her presence.

"That your boss?" asked Cath raising her eyebrows.

"Yes for a little while longer," Beryl smiled conspiratorially to Cath.

Cath took up the offer, jumped her bum onto the desk behind her and encouraged Beryl to tell her more.

"Oh do tell, and it's Cath if we are sharing secrets!"

"Well, I've decided to leave. It's all been a bit sudden. I'm leaving my husband as well. There I've said it, so it's got to happen now."

Beryl took off her wedding ring and placed it symbolically on the desk.

"That's bombshell drastic!, Am I the first to know?"

"I'm afraid so Cath, I decided just before you came in and I suppose I had to tell someone, or I wouldn't be able to do it… and you were the first person…and you looked like a good listener. It's Alice's fault. I've been sat here looking at her empty desk for almost a week and thinking about the life she lost and the life I live. I'm going to live her life. I'm going to travel and visit interesting places like Paris, Rome, and Australia even. I'm going to get divorced and fall in love for the first time in my life, I'm going to marry someone I can talk to and with whom I've got something in common."

Cath smiled at Beryl's glowing face. She could see the determination in it and believed her.

"What are you going to do for money?" Cath asked.

"I'll get half the house, half our savings, I can cash in my pension, I've thought it through, and I will not have a lot, but I think I will have enough to get by. I will get a life though and there's no price on that."

Cath was grinning broadly now. The second time in one day she thought. Maggie Burton this morning and now Beryl Smith both looking forward from a death that had impacted them either emotionally or financially.

"Well, this stranger will keep your secret for you Beryl. What's the first thing you're going to do after you have left your job and your husband?"

"I'm going to change my name from Smith to something interesting and dye my hair that modern pink and silver colour. Have it done properly as well, and get rid of this old grey middle aged fuddie-duddie look" she laughed out loud.

"I haven't felt this happy since I was a teenager."

Cath slipped herself off the desk.

"Come here."

Beryl stood up and came round the desk. Cath put her arms around her and gave Beryl a hug. When she broke away and looked at Beryl's face it was a picture of joy and sadness at the same time.

"Go get em girl and let me know how you get on."

Cath gave Beryl her business card and turned to leave.

The last thing she heard as she walked through the door was Beryl shouting after her.

"I will put your number in my phone…and thank you for listening!"

"Well, I wasn't expecting that" thought Cath as she walked back through Bath Gardens towards the police station. She had got what she wanted though. The links were coming together. Traynor was hanging around the morning that Paul Trueman had slipped on his way to court, and it was likely that he had stolen Trueman's bag. If Neil Burton thought the MacBook with the incriminating photographs on it had been stolen by Gary Traynor, it might link him to the man in the brown suit with the two heavies at Ron Traynor's house. Burton could also be a link to Alice's death as Beryl had told him that Alice had found a similar Dior bag to the one that had been stolen. That information would give Burton a motive for contacting Alice on the night she disappeared. Did he kill her for the bag containing the MacBook? It was an alternative to Dylan Oxley she thought, but she was certainly not going to start making waves with half-baked theories. She needed the Dior bag and the MacBook needed to be in it, otherwise she had nothing.

Her phone pinged a notification. She checked it and it was Ella. "Looking forward to the weekend. Missing you" Heart Heart emoticon." Cath's heart leapt with joy, and she texted back. "Missing you too. Can't wait till the weekend" Heart emoticon.

Cath did something she hadn't done since she was a girl and took a skip and then did a hopscotch. She realised that she just felt happy. Beryl's optimism was rubbing off on her... I'm not dying my hair pink though she thought. She checked her watch. It was 2.30 p.m. She still had some of the afternoon left and decided that whilst her luck was in she would roll with it.

Dave had told her the murder team had seized all of Alice's bags when they searched her flat. They would be in the store at Buxton. She wondered if she could blag her way into the exhibit store and see if there was a Dior shoulder bag amongst them?

Half an hour later, with a plan she had not really thought through other than it might get her access to the exhibit store, Cath walked through the open door signed 'Exhibits Office' for the Alice Bulman Murder. DC Jack Bainbridge was sitting behind a desk that was full of brown paper bags with yellow exhibit labels attached to them. Jack was typing one fingered, transferring the details from a yellow exhibit label on one of the bags into the computer screen on the desk.

Cath introduced herself.

"Hi DS Mulvey from Matlock CID. Are you busy?"

Jack Bainbridge looked up at her.

"No not really, everything is winding down now that the shooting murders are taking precedence. Can I help you Sarge?"

"I was hoping to help you. I presume you signed for all the exhibits when you took over from Excy?"

"Yes why?"

From behind her back Cath pulled a brown paper bag containing a handbag.

"I found this in the old exhibit store at Bakewell that Excy was using. I presume the exhibit label's come off it."

Jack Bainbridge tapped in a search.

"There's about a dozen handbags from Alice's flat. It could be one of them."

Cath put the bag containing her own handbag on the desk.

"Can we check if it's one of those? I'll help you and get the others if you want."

Jack Bainbridge pointed to a large store room at the side of his desk.

"Exhibits from the flat are on the bottom two shelves, round the corner. The bags should be there Sarge."

Cath went into the exhibits store and found the shelves with the exhibits from Alice's flat. They were piled loosely on top of each other as she suspected they would be. She searched through the piles of brown paper bags on the next to bottom shelf and found six of the handbags that according to the exhibit labels were from Alice's flat. Looking through the windows of the bags she could see none of them were the black Dior shoulder bag. She picked the six bags up and took them through to Jack Bainbridge.

"I've found six," Cath declared and put them on the desk.

"I'll go and find the others."

Cath went back into the store and began looking through the assorted paper bags on the bottom shelf. She found a brown paper bag containing a red handbag and put it on the floor. Underneath it was another large brown paper bag containing some sort of bag. She manipulated the window in the bag and saw the Dior logo. She put it back on the shelf and carried on looking for the other bags. Cath found the other four handbags and put them on the floor with the first one, and then took the five bags through to Jack Bainbridge. He was checking the exhibit reference on the last bag from the first lot she had brought through. The ones he had checked had been removed from the desk onto the floor.

"Shall I take these back?"

Cath intimated to the brown paper packages on the floor.

"Yes put them on the shelf where you found them, it helps if I need to trace them."

"Should there be any more?"

"Yes one more," replied Jack.

"I'll check again when I take these back, but the one I found might be the missing one."

Cath went back into the store, picked up the brown paper bag containing the Dior bag and ran her nail along the sealing Sellotape. She took out the bag undid the clasp and looked inside. It was empty.

Cath felt around it looking for a hidden pocket. Nothing. She looked back inside it and noticed a leather flap. She lifted it up unlocking the Velcro strip that sounded like a roll of thunder in the small, enclosed storeroom. Cath froze and listened expecting Jack to come in and challenge what she was doing at any moment. He didn't come in, so she slowly unzipped the pocket. Clearly visible was a silver and black MacBook. Cath's heart raced with excitement. She took a breath…she had not made any plans about what she would do if she actually found the MacBook! In a panic she removed the MacBook, stood up, pulled her blouse out of her skirt, and then pushed the MacBook down the front of her tights pulling the top of her tights over it. It was bigger than she had expected. She should be alright she thought so long as she didn't bend down. She put the Dior bag back into the brown bag folded the top and took it out to Jack.

"Found another, but the seal's come off it."

"Should be a Dior Shoulder bag. No contents." Jack shouted through the open door.

Cath brought the bag to Jack and put it down on the desk. The top of the paper bag containing the Dior Handbag unfurled open. Jack took the bag out, checked that it was the Dior and that it was empty.

"Pass me the tape Sarge."

Cath looked to her right and saw a Sellotape dispenser with a full roll on it. Cath picked it up and passed it to Jack who expertly resealed the paper bag and its contents.

"Well, the bag you found isn't one of ours. I've cross referenced with all the statements and we aren't missing a handbag Sarge."

Jack Bainbridge sat back in his chair relieved.

"You don't want this one then Jack?" Cath joked and waved her own bag in the brown paper bag at him.

"No, definitely not, I've got no statement for it, and it will just bugger up the system if it looks like we've got duplicate exhibits knocking about," Jack chuckled.

"I'll take it back and see if it's from a local job then,"

She turned round and felt the elastic on the top of her tights start to slip along the MacBook, and she put her hand to her chest to keep it inside her blouse.

Jack seeing her quickly clutch her chest asked,

"Are you alright Sarge?"

Cath pushed the MacBook against her chest, looked at Jack and lied.

"I get twinges sometimes… you know ladies stuff …that's all."

Jack reddened and awkwardly stood up to help her

"Oh, right Sarge, my wife's the same, ….I'll bring the bag to your car if you want?"

"Thanks Jack it's appreciated."

Cath walked back to her car accompanied by Jack Bainbridge, carrying her handbag in the exhibit bag and opening doors for her on the way. At her car she opened the boot with the electronic key and Jack put the bag in the boot.

"Thanks, Jack. Sorry to have wasted your time,"

"No, it's fine, I would rather have made sure, than get to court and find an exhibit missing. It was good of you to check" Jack reassured her.

Cath opened the door with her free hand and sat down gingerly in the driver's seat. The MacBook moved up her chest painfully trapping the skin under her bra. She started the car and drove to the barrier where she pulled her blouse out of her skirt, undid the bottom two buttons, and slid out the MacBook onto her lap with a sigh of relief as the trapped skin was released. She then fastened her seat belt, waited for the barrier to rise up, and set off back to Matlock through the media throng that was gathered on the lawn at the side of the driveway.

Chapter 41 – Broken Chains

Tuesday 21st January

Cath was shaking with adrenalin.

"What the hell did you just do! what the hell did you just do!" she kept saying to herself as she drove back to Matlock.

It had been a rubbish plan but somehow it had worked.

"What a day!" She mused to herself.

She had left the office that morning with one aim; try and link Paul Trueman, the man in the brown suit, and the MacBook. Everything had fallen into place. She had been lucky with the desk diary at Bakewell, but the rest had just been good police work.

Back at Matlock, Cath put the MacBook on her desk. She had some decisions to make. Did she call Superintendent Dicks, or her own Detective Chief Inspector?. Before she did either, she needed to work out what it was she had actually found. She sat down and looked at the MacBook. It had been a good day, a great day for a detective. She had tied Burton into both the Gary

Traynor death and Alice Bulman's murder, as well as the probable murder of Dylan Oxley. It was highly likely, with the Traynors being killed in the shoot-out at Chatsworth, that it was also linked with those murders as well, if they were in revenge for Gary's death. The MacBook belonging to Neil Burton was the motive or a link for all the deaths. Cath ran through the timeline of events that she now thought had happened.

The MacBook had been in a Dior messenger bag that had been stolen from Paul Trueman by Gary Traynor. Traynor had not found the MacBook in it and thrown the bag away in Bath Gardens where it was then found by Alice Bulman who also had not discovered the MacBook in the hidden pocket. Neil Burton had found out somehow that Gary Traynor had stolen it and gone to see him to recover it with a couple of heavies. Gary Traynor had then been chased under the truck that had killed him by Neil Burton and probably two of the men who had been killed in Chatsworth. Alice had almost certainly been killed by Neil Burton trying to retrieve the MacBook from her. That meant that Oxley, if he didn't kill Alice, must have stumbled on them at White Lodge. In view of the evidence at the scene he may have been killed by whoever was dumping her body there as well. That meant Neil Burton was probably killed by the Traynors, or the same people who had killed Oxley. It sort of made sense she thought. All the deaths were linked or likely to be linked.

Cath picked up the phone to tell Superintendent Dicks and then replaced it, as the reality of what she had done hit her like a brick wall. There was no way around the fact that she had just stolen an exhibit from the exhibits room of a murder enquiry. No matter what she did, if she disclosed how she had got the MacBook, she would probably be sacked and possibly even prosecuted for theft. She also realised that if she disclosed she had found the MacBook anywhere but in the Dior messenger bag from Alice's flat, any evidential links to Neil Burton, Gary Traynor and Alice Burton would be lost. Cath could feel herself starting to panic.

Cath took a deep breath. The Dior bag had been originally labelled up as empty. No-one would ever know she had stolen the MacBook unless she told them. There was never any record that it was in the Dior messenger bag in the exhibits store and the only person who even suspected that it was, Neil Burton, was dead. She was in the clear, the theft could never be proven. Cath exhaled and then banged her fist on the desk.

"How could she have been so stupid!"

All that work she had done today had been for nothing. She couldn't tell anyone about the evidence to clear up the Bulman and other murders without losing her job, and the evidence she had recovered was of no use unless she could get it back into the bag in the Exhibits Store.

She glared at the MacBook.

"You haven't half caused some upset for a piece of tech."

There was only one thing left to discover she realised. What was on the MacBook? It must be more than photographs if it led to so many people being killed, but even if she found out what was actually on it she knew it would not now help in the detection of the murders. Cath picked up the MacBook. She would take it home with her, what was on it could wait, she had had enough of the darn thing for one day.

Later that evening Cath closed the empty pizza box and put it on the floor at the side of her settee. She then picked up the MacBook from the floor at the side of the discarded pizza box and placed it on her lap, opened the case, and switched it on. The screen lit up and a pop up showed that a biometric fingerprint was needed to log on.

Cath's heart sank. She was not technically minded and didn't even have a laptop of her own. She would never find out what was on the MacBook unless she could log on to it. She wondered whether the skin lifts taken yesterday by Sally Brooks from Burton would open it. That's how someone would do it on a TV detective programme she thought and gave a fleeting thought to doing a similar theft to the one she had done at Buxton, to get the samples and access the computer. She dismissed it as quickly as she had thought about it. She had been lucky today and wasn't going to take the same risk twice.

Cath looked at her watch, it was 6.30 p.m. and she had promised she would ring Ella at 7 p.m. She closed the MacBook and put it on the floor. She would do some tidying up before she rang her.

Chapter 42 – Too Late

Tuesday 21ˢᵗ January

Just over three hours later Cath was asleep in a short nightshirt, on the settee in her lounge. Her first day as a detective sergeant had been an eventful one and after the adrenalin rush of that afternoon she had felt drained. She would normally have poured herself a large vodka and sat on her settee thinking about what had happened at work, until the alcohol had so numbed her senses, she could eventually stagger upstairs to bed and find some drunken sleep. Today, however, Cath was on her second no vodka day. Although the bottle was still clearly visible on the kitchen counter top, she was proud of herself that its contents remained at exactly the same level since Saturday night. She had chatted to Ella for over an hour on the phone, and then had a relaxing soak in the bath before settling down on the settee for an evening watching the television and an early night.

Cath woke with a start. The Ten O Clock News was just finishing, and she realised that she must have fallen asleep. A loud knocking at her front door caused her to almost jump off of the settee a second time. Cath instinctively looked at her watch, it was just after 10.30 p.m., and she had no idea who would be calling on her at this time of night. She was also only wearing her nightshirt.

Cath got up to go to the door.

"Coming"

She looked around; her work clothes lay on the kitchen floor where she had undressed for her bath. Cath pulled her panties from her tights and slipped them on. She picked up her work clothes and went through to the front door, opened the bathroom door that led off the small hallway and threw her work clothes into it, shutting the door behind them. She saw her zip necked walking jumper on one of the coat hooks and slipped it over her nightshirt. Only then did she put the security hook on the door and unlock it, peering through the gap to see who could be calling on her at this time of night.

"Bloody hell Excy! What on earth are you doing here at this time?" Cath exclaimed, when she saw the caller who was illuminated by the exterior wall light at the side of the door.

"Can I come in Cath I need to talk to you?" Dave asked.

"I suppose so but if you're thinking about giving me lovelorn earache about Helen for the next few hours I'm going to bed and telling you to come back in the morning,,"

She undid the security chain and let Dave into the house.

An Accidental Death

Dave walked in and sat in his usual place on the settee. Cath followed him into the lounge and leant back on the kitchen worktop. They were in their usual positions when Dave called to see her although Cath could tell it wasn't just one of their usual 'chats.' She couldn't put her finger on why she felt so awkward, maybe it was because she was feeling self-conscious about her semi nakedness or the way that Dave was sat stiffly on the settee. Whatever it was she knew that things between them were different.

Dave looked at her and she saw him glance at her naked legs. She was glad she had put some knickers on, she thought, and pulled down her nightshirt instinctively. Dave saw the instinctive gesture and embarrassed looked away.

"What the hell are you actually doing here Excy? Its half past ten at night and I'm half naked. I have known you a number of years and if something is up, spill it out or go home and if it's Helen go home anyway. I'm too tired to hear about your love life going down the toilet at this time of night."

Dave looked back at her again, paused at the sight of her naked legs and looked quickly away again.

"For goodness sake Excy, you're making me embarrassed it's only my legs get over it!"

Cath jumped onto the kitchen top and sat across it stretching her nightshirt over her knees almost down to her feet.

"Is that better?"

Dave looked back at her now fully covered body and nodded.

"I'm sorry Cath. Things somehow feel different between us now I've left. It used to be easy to talk to you, but it now just feels more difficult."

"I know Excy, I feel it too. I'm still your friend though, so come on let's hear it, you have come to ask me something, what is it?"

Dave took a breath.

"Cath I'm trying to get in with Dicks. I know I've only been working with him a couple of days, but he's been really good with me so far, but I know I'm on sort of probation. To get off it I need to show him I'm useful to him if he is going to let me hang on to his coat tails. On top of that we have got the Met crawling all over us and they are going to be taking over the enquiry by Thursday morning. If I can get some sort of breakthrough on the Traynors tomorrow, Dicks will be really happy with me, and I will be made with him for years but if I don't I might as well come back and work with you. So, I thought that seeing as you have been close to the Traynors recently, especially Karen, whether you could get anything out of her. If you could then pass it to me, then I could show I was useful to Dicks."

Cath thought quickly, she had done a favour for Karen and Ron, but it would not be seen that way by senior police officers if it ever came out. However, if she could help Dave and at the same time help herself… she played for time.

"I don't think there's anything I can do on the Traynor front Excy and I'm being honest with you about that. You have had them both locked up for a day, and I presume they have remained silent so far."

Dave nodded.

"If the Murder Incident Team can't get anything out of either of them I don't think I will. Is there anything else that could put you in Dicks's good books?"

"I couldn't think of anything Cath that's why I'm here tonight. It was a long shot I know, but I had to make it. Thanks Cath, I'll get off."

Dave went to get up.

"Hang on Excy, I'm just working through something."

Cath lapsed into thoughtful silence. She could tell him about the MacBook, get him to replace it in the exhibits store and then he could 'find' it again. That would certainly help him she thought. There was only one flaw to the plan and that was telling him what she had done and then getting him to actually do it. It was too risky, she didn't trust Excy enough; firstly to tell him, and secondly she knew there was no way he would put the MacBook back.

Dave watched as she gave thought to something, but after around a minute's silence she declared.

"I'm sorry I can't think of anything Excy."

Dave stood up to leave and turned to her.

"Thanks Cath, I'll let you get off to bed now."

Cath slid off the kitchen counter and followed him to the door.

At the door Dave turned to her and said apologetically

"Sorry to have bothered you Cath."

Cath looked at him in the doorway. He had put his personal ambition above their friendship.

"Come here Dave."

Cath put her arms around his neck, pulled him towards her and kissed his forehead. She then let go and gently pushed him out of the doorway.

"Goodbye Dave" she said softly.

Dave walked away down her path to his car. As she closed the door behind him she knew that the 'goodbye' was in more ways than one.

Cath went back into the kitchen lounge, picked up the MacBook from the far side of the settee and put it into one of the kitchen cupboards, turned off the light and went to bed.

Cath yawned. Tomorrow was another day. Tonight, she told herself, she was going to sleep soundly in Ella's imaginary arms.

Chapter 43 – Pragmatic Decisions

Wednesday 22nd January

Dave had hardly slept. He kept thinking through his plan to get on the right side of Superintendent Dicks. He also knew that Cath had known something that would have helped him, but she had chosen not to. She might have been a good friend once but the uncomfortable atmosphere between them last night had shown him that the close friendship they once had was now gone. He was moving on and she was staying where she was. If he wanted to move on in his police career he had to learn to be ruthless, and if Cath was going to be a casualty of that ruthlessness so be it.

Dicks rang him on his mobile just after 6.30 a.m. Dave had been showered and dressed for over an hour.

"Glad you're awake Excy," he greeted him as Dave answered the call.

"Meet me at White Lodge Car Park in about an hour we need to have a chat before we start work this morning. It's on the way to the incident room for both of us and seems appropriate for what I want to discuss with you."

Dave felt a sense of foreboding in the request.

"Is it something I need to be worried about boss," he asked and heard Dicks chuckle at his concern.

"No, not in the least Excy. If anything, it's good news for both of us, or could be. I'll tell you more when we meet up. See you there in an hour."

Dave looked at his watch, he would just make it if he got a move on.

Dave arrived at White Lodge five minutes early. As he pulled onto the car park he realised that it was seven days since he had pulled onto the same car park to the body of Alice Bulman. Seven days, so much had happened in such a brief period of time, not only at work but also with his relationship with Helen, Cath, Holly and Dicks. He pulled around the curve onto the car park and he almost expected to see Bill standing there, cigarette in hand, waiting for him again. The weather was similar he thought, still cold but without the covering of snow. There was no Bill Fry but there was John Dicks. Excy parked up at the side of him.

"Morning sir!"

"I like a bit of cloak and dagger stuff Excy, keeps me on my toes."

Dave was beginning to realise that a lot of what he had taken as bitterness was actually Dicks' attempts at humour. Dicks then said to him seriously

"This isn't going to take long Excy, I've got a meeting with Alan Daley and Foxley-Jones this morning that I cannot miss. Let's have a walk up to the pond and I will explain everything on the way."

Dave nodded and said conversationally.

"Lovely morning for a walk. I hope it's a less dramatic one than the last time I walked up there."

"I can't guarantee that Excy," Dicks said offhandedly and set off towards the track to the pond.

Dave took a deep breath of the fresh country air and then set off after him up the rocky bridleway. After a short distance Dicks started to explain why he had asked Dave to join him there that morning.

"I have a meeting with Alan Daley this morning and have been tipped off what it is about. There is an opportunity for you to benefit from what may happen as well as me."

Very cryptic thought Dave.

"I haven't known you long Excy, but you appear to be a very principled young man. I need to know whether you will be prepared to put some of those principles to one side to further your career or not."

Dave wasn't sure what Dicks was asking of him and so didn't say anything but kept walking at his side. Dicks carried on.

"I don't mean anything illegal but if later this morning I offered you an opportunity that could mean compromising colleagues and victims, would you put aside your principles and take it?"

Dave walked on in silence, deep in thought. He knew the answer, he had already decided to be ruthless to get on, but didn't want to say it out loud. Dicks just kept on walking, silently waiting for Dave's answer all the way up to the pond. At the pond they stood still together, and Dave turned to face Dicks.

"Yes, I would sir."

"Good lad! Let me explain what this is about. I have a feeling that the body of Dylan Oxley is going to be discovered near to where we found the body of Alice Bulman, probably in the pond here."

Dicks gestured with his arm the open expanse of water in front of them.

"Unfortunately, I have put all my eggs in the Oxley killed Alice Bulman basket."

Dicks stared over the pond and scratched the scar on his forehead.

"Depending on what happens this morning it might be best if that body never comes to light. Come on Excy we have got a busy morning."

Both men walked briskly back down the track to the car park in silence. Dave wondering what he had agreed to, and why Dicks thought Oxley was in the pond. Dicks planning his strategy for what he was going to be told and asked to do, in the meetings that morning.

At the side of his car Dicks broke the silence.

"I think this morning I will make you a cup of coffee Excy. See you in ten minutes at the office and not a word to anyone about this conversation, understand?"

"Yes sir" Dave agreed.

Twenty minutes later Dave entered Dicks' office at Buxton. Dicks was already behind his desk and the DCC Alan Daley was sat across from him. Both men stopped speaking and looked at him as he entered the room.

"Give us ten minutes Excy." Dicks said to him.

Dave raised his hand in apology, turned back through the door and closed it behind him. He looked at his watch it was 8.45 a.m. he would come back in fifteen minutes.

At exactly 9 a.m. Dave knocked on the door and Dicks shouted,

"Come in Excy!"

As he entered he saw that the DCC had obviously just stood up to go as he had his brown leather gloves and his peaked hat in his hand. He looked at Dave as he entered the office and then back towards Dicks.

"Well, I will leave everything with you then John, let me know how you get on at lunchtime. I should be in back my office by then."

"I will do," confirmed Dicks.

The DCC turned back to Dave.

"Hope you are settling in alright Excy. Superintendent Dicks was just singing your praises, keep it up and I'm sure you will go far."

Dave mumbled "Thankyou sir" and the DCC walked past him and out the door.

"Shut the door Excy,"

Dave closed the door and sat down at his desk.

"I was just discussing the cost and reputational issues of the Alice Bulman and Chatsworth Murders with the DCC."

"Are we going to search the pond for Oxley?" asked Dave.

Dicks shook his head.

"Are you still wanting to hang on to my coat tails Dave, because after the conversation I have just had with Alan Daley, our conversation this morning has now become quite relevant."

"I told you my decision this morning boss and provided it's nothing illegal nothing has changed," Dave replied confidently.

"Good. Let me put you in the picture then. I've been on major crime for two years so it's time for me to move on. Alan has just told me that Chief Superintendent Clive Morgan in the Professional Standards Department has put his date in for retirement. He will leave in twelve weeks, so I am transferring there in a fortnight with a view to taking over from him when he retires. Alan has also agreed with me that it would be helpful to your career for a spell in Professional Standards and that you can be transferred onto the department with me. You have only just been made Temporary Sergeant, so I would think when you get transferred you will be made up to substantive Sergeant and, if you get your exams in this year, Inspector in another twelve months. Well, that is the way I would see your career going. How does that sound to you?"

"It sounds very good sir; in fact, it sounds absolutely brilliant!" Dave beamed at Dicks.

"And now decisions have to be made that may clash with your high principles. We need to sort things out on all the current enquiries before we move. So, this is what we are going to do."

Dicks looked at Dave who was listening intently.

"Firstly we never had a conversation at or went up to the pond at White Lodge this morning. Our pocket books will just show that we came on duty here as normal. In relation to the Alice Bulman Murder, John Casey has already taken over the investigation and he is going to do all the media stuff on it from now on, so that means he will own the investigation and any issues that arise. Before we leave to Professional Standards however, me and you are going to do a full review of the evidence and come across the discrepancies in the statement from Matthew Hardwick, the guy with learning difficulties. A further statement will then be taken from Hardwick, identifying a man with a brown suit at the top of Bath Street around the time Alice disappeared. Annie Patel who took the statement is going to receive management advice from me about the taking of statements."

"I'm trying to keep up boss, but I don't quite get yet why we are doing this?"

"I'll try and explain it better. You see Excy, that body of Oxley is going to come up to the surface of the pond at White Lodge one day. On that day it is going to be obvious that Oxley was not the person who murdered Alice Bulman. It will be in our interests that Casey will take the blame for only looking at him and no other suspect. Any subsequent enquiry into the investigation will also show that we took a review of the case before we left it. It will show we identified evidence that had contributed to Oxley being wrongly identified as a suspect and remedied it, as well as taking action against any officers involved. There will be nothing to come back to either me or you for the mistake. You have to think about these things long term Excy, are you following me now?"

"Yes sir I think so."

"Your job is to do a review of the case and report back to me alone. I want to know in the next fourteen days anything that may have been suppressed to support the view that Oxley was the killer. I will then deal with those issues accordingly. John Casey is not to know about the review and its outcomes will be between me and you as far as possible. Are you up for that?"

"Yes sir, you can rely on me. I will go through the case with a fine tooth comb."

"That just leaves the six murders at Chatsworth a couple of days ago to sort out, …and one other thing."

Dicks looked at his watch.

"Any minute now Commander Foxley-Jones is going to walk through that door and expect a row over who is running the case. I am going to surprise him, so stay there and enjoy the fun when he comes in. The end result of all this that I am looking for is that we can both put the Alice Bulman murder and the Chatsworth Massacre on our CV's with no black marks against us, and move on to Professional Standards in a fortnight, with a promotion thrown in."

Dave thought about what Dicks was asking of him for a few seconds.

"I'm alright with everything boss."

At that moment the door opened, Commander Foxley-Jones strode into the room and looked around, he saw only Dicks and Dave in the room.

"Superintendent," he nodded towards Dicks.

"I was expecting your Deputy Chief or Chief Constable."

"It's just me," Dicks pronounced with a gesture of his arm around the room.

"Apart from Sergeant Baker of course. Take a seat. I'm just going to make a brew,"

Dicks gestured towards the seat in front of his desk.

"Do you want one?"

Foxley-Jones appeared angry and taken aback,

"No Superintendent I do not!"

Dicks checked his watch, gave Foxley-Jones his false smile and looked towards Dave.

"Coffee one sugar isn't it Sergeant Baker ?"

Dicks then walked out of the room, leaving Dave sat in uncomfortable silence with the Metropolitan Police Commander.

The next five minutes of awkward silence seemed an eternity to Dave as he pretended to read some random typed paperwork he had taken out of the first drawer on his desk. He was aware that the Commander was seething and did not want to give him an excuse to take it out on him, so had decided studious silence and avoiding eye contact was his best line of defence.

Eventually Dicks came back into the office and put down a mug of coffee in front of Dave and winked at him.

"One sugar with milk sergeant, just as I promised earlier."

Dicks circled the Commander and sat behind his desk facing him.

"Now what can we do for you this morning Commander?"

"Thank you for keeping me waiting Superintendent." Foxley-Jones, red faced and trying to keep his anger under control, sarcastically began the meeting.

"I need to know what the Derbyshire Constabulary wants to do with the Martin Gordon Enquiry as we call it. We are putting a lot of resources into this enquiry, and we need to come to some understanding on the way that it is going to be run. The hierarchy of supervision to start with. That is why I was hoping at least your DCC would be here."

"Of course Commander. Alan Daley was here earlier and wanted me to tell you that you that the Derbyshire Constabulary just like the Metropolitan Police would like to sort the administrative issues in relation to this enquiry out as soon as possible. It can sometimes be difficult for two forces to run the same investigation alongside each other. It is because of this that our Chief Constable has decided that it would be in the best interest of the victims and the investigation as a whole that the Metropolitan Police can have complete jurisdiction on the enquiry. Any offences leading to the shootings are very likely to have occurred on your force area, and the Metropolitan Police also have two further unsolved murders that you have linked to the six here I believe. Is that correct?"

Foxley-Jones nodded, and Dicks continued.

"I believe the Chief Constable is conducting a press conference at the moment, explaining this decision to the media as we speak."

Commander Foxley-Jones gave a wry smile. His own press conference that lunchtime would have to be re-written, however he was going to get what he wanted.

"That's very good of him Superintendent we may as well not be having this meeting if it's already been decided. Going back to the investigation. I had better bring you up to date. In relation to the murders in Chatsworth, we strongly suspect that the Traynors were hired by a Columbian OCG to take out Gordon and his associates. This is based on evidence that Jill Gordon and a taxi driver were shot a few hours after the shootings here, by someone we have identified through Interpol. DNA on the gun left at the scene, has come back to a fifteen year old boy wanted in Columbia and Mexico for several other drug related murders. You are right that most enquiries will probably take place in London or abroad. In the absence of watching the press conference what is the Metropolitan Police getting from Derbyshire, Superintendent?"

"You get all our forensics to date, all our exhibits, the Traynor women who are currently locked up, and a promise that anything you want doing up here will be done as soon as possible. We will expect any enquiries that you believe need doing in Derbyshire to be forwarded to us for action and prior notice of any teams being sent up to do enquiries on the area. Will that be fine with the Metropolitan Police? If you want anything else, all you have to do is ask."

"That will be fine Superintendent. I will have a Memorandum of Understanding drawn up along those lines. It's exactly what The Metropolitan Police would have asked for. Can you pass my thanks on to Alan Daley as I will need to get back to London straight away? I will get my incident room inspector to contact yours to start the transfer this afternoon if that is alright with you Superintendent?"

"Yes that's in order Commander, anything else? A cup of tea perhaps?"

This time Foxley-Jones smiled at Dicks.

"Good of you to ask but no thank you. I must get off. My driver is waiting for me at the front of the building. See you around Superintendent."

Foxley-Jones stood up and strode out of the office without looking back. He had ignored Dave's presence throughout the conversation. Dicks got up from his desk and shut the door.

"How did that go Excy?"

"Did the DCC authorise you to say all that?" asked Dave.

"Yes, the Chief was really pissed off when Foxley-Jones dropped his press conference on us on Tuesday morning intimating that we couldn't cope without their help. They were going to get the enquiry anyway, but he wanted to give them some grief back. So, he's had Foxley-Jones waiting around for a couple of days and then given him what he wanted apart from having Met detectives wandering around Derbyshire upsetting everyone. Talking about backs, let's go back to covering ours. There was one other thing that I was concerned about. I saw Cath Mulvey through the window yesterday in the back yard and wondered why she was up here?"

"I don't know why she was up here, but I called on her last night and she seemed to be hiding something but wouldn't tell me what it was. I have no idea whether it was in relation to the Bulman or Chatsworth murders though."

Dicks stroked the scar on his forehead and then picked up his desk phone and made a call.

"Jack…did Cath Mulvey come in to see you yesterday?.....What did she want?......That was very good of her, and was it a missing exhibit?....was there anything else she was interested in or seemed a bit odd?.....was there anything missing from it after she left….so there was nothing in it anyway….no there's nothing to worry about Jack I just saw her in the yard and wondered what she was doing here. Thanks Jack."

Dicks replaced the handset.

"Well, according to Jack Bainbridge she visited him at the exhibits room with a possible lost exhibit that turned out to be not one of ours. Is she looking for something that she thinks may have turned up on the Bulman enquiry?"

Dave racked his thoughts as to what Cath could have been looking for.

"There is only one thing I can think of that Cath might be looking for. The solicitor that went missing and was found burnt to death in his car, Neil Burton, had lost a MacBook with some compromising pictures on of him that he didn't want turning up. There was some suggestion from his wife that it was a reason he might have killed himself."

Dicks stroked his scar again deep in thought.

"He died the same night as Alice didn't he?"

"Yes, probably but it's not certain. He was found burnt to death about six miles away in an old disused quarry."

"Is there any link between Burton or this MacBook and Alice Bulman?"

"Not that I know of" shrugged Dave.

"It would certainly put him in the frame for her murder if there was. There wasn't any MacBook found at either her work or flat when I was on exhibits, but I don't know if one came in after I passed everything over to Jack Bainbridge."

Dicks picked up his phone and rang Jack Bainbridge again.

" Jack… has a MacBook or any type of laptop come in on the murder?......You're sure ….Thanks Jack, … No, I don't need anything else."

Dicks turned to Dave.

"No, there's no MacBook come in to Jack on the enquiry. Give her a call and let's see whether she is rocking any boats."

Dicks pulled up a chair to Dave's desk and sat back to listen.

Cath looked at the caller ID on her phone and smiled; she had been expecting the call. She took a deep breath and answered it, putting it on record and speaker. She wanted to listen back to it later to make sure that she had not disclosed anything that might cause her any trouble.

"Hi Sergeant Baker, how are things going this morning?"

"Just great Cath, how are things with you?"

"Just getting through paperwork Excy, a Sergeants job is never done, you should know that by now." Cath faked a laugh.

"Are you on your own?"

"Yes, there's just me in the office, I'm on my own at the moment," replied Dave.

"Liar," thought Cath.

"I hope that because I didn't know anything last night that was any use, that it hasn't scuppered your chances with Dicks,

Excy. He is an excellent boss and detective, and you could learn so much from him"

Cath smiled to herself; she was pretty sure that Dicks was listening.

"No, everything is fine Cath, but thanks at least for offering to help me last night, I really appreciate it. When you said you needed to think about something last night I thought there was something you knew that might help me."

"No there's nothing Excy. If there was I would have told you last night or fed it into the incident room."

"Well, If you need any help with anything, for example the Neil Burton suicide you only have to ask," Dave offered.

"Thanks Excy but it's all wrapped up. I'm playing it as a straight suicide and his wife is happy with that in view of his mental state over the last few weeks. I'm not going to create work for myself trying to turn it into something that it isn't. There's only me working from Matlock at the moment with you gone and Holly in hospital."

Cath took a deep breath. She wondered where Dave and Dicks were going with the call.

"I just wondered whether that MacBook of Burton's had turned up? You know, that one with the incriminating pictures on."

Dave looked at John Dicks who nodded towards him.

"I wish it had. It would make the Coroner's job a bit easier."

Dicks leaned back in his chair and smiled at Dave.

"Well, the offer is still there Cath if you need it. Just give me a call. Look I've got to go now the boss has just come in."

"No problem Excy and good look for the future!" she lied and closed the call.

Dave put his phone in his pocket and looked at Dicks.

"Is Cath a problem?" he asked.

Dicks face broke into a wide smile, and he stood up to go back to his own desk.

"Well done Excy, clever girl that Cath Mulvey, a very clever girl. Even if she has found it, I think we are alright to start preparing to go to Professional Standards. Let's start with getting this job packed up and moved to the Met."

Back at Matlock, Cath listened to the phone conversation again. There could be only one reason for the call she decided. Dicks had found out about her trip to Jack Bainbridge the day before and was suspicious of why she was there. Excy must also have told him about Burton's MacBook. So long as he did not suspect there was a link between the MacBook and Alice's murder she would be alright. The call had hopefully reassured Dicks that neither she nor the MacBook were a problem.

Chapter 44 – Files and Folders

Saturday 25th January

Ella had arrived at Cath's just after midnight. The Friday night traffic had made her four hour journey into a seven hour one. Cath had hugged her at the door, seen the tiredness in her eyes and after kissing her on the cheek showed her round her small home. She ran Ella a bath, and then shared a cocoa before cuddling up against her in her own bed.

Cath waited for Ella to fall asleep before kissing her neck and burying her body against her so close that she could almost feel their hearts beating as one, and then fell into a deep untroubled sleep. Ella woke Cath sometime in the night to make love and cemented their relationship after the week apart.

It was past 10 a.m. the next morning when Ella woke her with a kiss to her forehead as she put the two cups of coffee on the bedside table and then disappeared downstairs again. Cath sat up in bed and stretched, then picked up her coffee and waited for Ella to reappear. When she did re-appear she was carrying the

MacBook and snuggled back into bed placing it on the duvet in front of them both.

"So, this is the legendary MacBook!" she giggled opening it and switching it on.

"Yes, the deadly MacBook," Cath replied and took a drink of her coffee.

"You told me you couldn't get into it because of the need for a biometric password"

Ella turned the MacBook on.

"I see what you mean. Do you want me to unlock it and see what all those people died for?"

"Can you do that?" Cath asked.

"Of course! It's part of what I do. The manager's at work have these MacBook's and get locked out regularly. I spend half my working week getting them unlocked."

"Will it take long?"

"At work it usually takes as long as it takes to drink a cup of coffee, so drink that one slowly."

Cath watched as Ella went through various menus at breakneck speed for about twenty minutes before a password screen popped up and she turned to Cath.

"Give me a password you won't forget. It's got to have at least eight letters with higher and lower case, a number and a symbol."

Cath looked back at Ella vacantly and then started laughing.

"I have only one password so it will have to be that one. I can't think of anything else I would remember!"

"It will have to do. What is it?"

"One, the number, then Vodka capital V, symbol for 'and' then orange."

"That wouldn't have taken much guessing!" laughed Ella.

Ella tapped in the password and then repeated it on the prompt. The MacBook screen unlocked.

"You're in!"

Ella put the MacBook onto the duvet in front of Cath. Cath picked it up and put it back in front of Ella.

"I think you're doing a wonderful job so far and don't want to interrupt you when you're on a roll. Apart from which I have no idea how to use Apple software, we have Windows at work, and I struggle with that."

Ella opened several windows and a large number of named files came up on the screen. Ella opened them as Cath watched. After a few minutes Ella looked at Cath.

458 | P a g e

"It looks like they are company documents and accounts. Those I have opened are registered in Antigua and there are around a dozen more. You are going to need someone who knows something about companies and accounts Cath because I have no idea what any of this means."

"Are there any photographs on it?" Cath asked.

Ella opened another screen and then some files on it.

"No. There were some photographs, but they were all deleted in November and the contents of trash have also been deleted, so they can't be recovered. How far do you want to go with this Cath, you told me that no-one knows you have got it and that it's useless as evidence."

"You're right Ella. I suppose I was just curious as to what was on it. I think I know someone who might be able to help decipher what all these company documents mean, but first let's have some breakfast, I can do pancakes."

Chapter 45 – An Awful Lot Of Money

Sunday 26th January

Beryl Smith was standing outside the semi-detached council house at Moorhall in Bakewell, watching the taxi driver load her last suitcase of clothing into the back of the taxi, when her phone rang. She checked the caller and saw that it was the detective that had visited her earlier that week and took the call.

By three o clock that afternoon Beryl had moved into the vacant furnished flat above the Greengrocers on Buxton Road in Bakewell. Her clothes were the only thing she had taken with her from her marriage, and she doubted whether she would keep many of those. She had decided that they would not reflect the 'new' Beryl or the lifestyle path she had set herself on. She looked outside the bay fronted window into the dank cold afternoon and the still busy January streets of tourists below her and longed for a time when she would be able to travel to those parts of the world, where she would also be seen as a tourist by those looking out of their own windows.

Beryl plugged the MacBook into the mains and opened it. Someone had written and then sellotaped the password to the keyboard surround and Beryl smiled to herself when she saw it. Beryl typed in the password and muttered to herself.

"Right let's see what all this is about."

The following morning Beryl returned the MacBook to Cath at her home in Chesterfield. Ella made three mugs of coffee and once Beryl was settled on the settee, and the two girls on the floor looking up at her. Cath asked,

"What did you find out Beryl?"

"Well you certainly gave me an interesting task! It wasn't difficult despite there being quite a number of companies, twelve to be exact. I am not a forensic accountant, but it is quite obvious that what you have is two separate money laundering enterprises. One appears to be for the benefit of Neil Burton and Paul Trueman. This is basically a straight forward movement of money between four company accounts to confuse any authorities who might be interested in taking a look at them. There appears to be…."

Beryl looked at a piece of paper in her hand.

"Four million two hundred and thirty thousand, five hundred and ninety six pounds in the four company bank accounts towards the end of last year."

"That's an awful lot of money," commented Ella.

"…And explains why Burton wanted it back so badly," observed Cath.

Beryl nodded.

"It explains why the bastard killed Alice, but that isn't all I found. I discovered there were only a few transactions, and it was fairly easy to follow the money trail once you saw how it worked. The second separate enterprise consists of eight companies. It appears that cash was deposited on a regular basis into an account of Skona Bank, which is a small Swiss bank on the Isle of Man. It's then transferred to a company account in Antigua and then laundered through any one of five other companies who use it to purchase aircraft, yachts, and properties in London. What appears to be rental income from the properties then comes back to one of three other Antiguan companies where it is paid in dividends to the shareholders of those companies. I am not sure whether the yachts and planes actually exist as there is no audit trail on them. The odd thing is that there appears to be only two shareholders as the dividends go to an account held by a Jill and Martin Gordon. Twenty percent goes to Burton and Trueman as consulting fees. They put those fees into the four companies I previously mentioned. Burton and Trueman are the only identifiable officers of all the companies."

"Is it straight forward money laundering then?" Cath asked.

"Looks like it" confirmed Beryl.

"Other than money going in a circle around the various accounts, every few months around two million goes from one of the second set of companies to an escrow account in Mexico."

"Could it be drugs?" asked Cath.

"I don't know, but there is an instruction from Trueman for two million pounds to be transferred to the escrow account in Mexico waiting to be sent."

"It would make sense if it was drugs in view of what Helen's told me about her dad's activities in Ibiza," observed Ella.

"Anything else?" Cath asked Beryl.

"Nothing really other than it's been running nearly thirty years and that the companies were originally set up by a Margaret Burton of Worldwide Formations Limited in Sheffield."

"That makes sense,"

Cath recalled her earlier conversation with Maggie Burton.

"How much cash is in the other accounts?"

"About a couple of million pounds at the moment plus the two million that has been prepared for transfer. The companies own property worth over a hundred million pounds though."

Beryl took a drink from her mug.

"That's a lot of money! How much do I owe you for this Beryl?" asked Cath.

"Nothing. Money won't

bring Alice back and you have been honest enough with me about how you came by the MacBook. The people who killed her for this money are all dead and so justice, as far as I am concerned, has been done. Letting me be the one to find out the reason for Alice being killed was payment enough and it should be me paying you for that privilege. So, you owe me nothing. I will take what I know to my grave and never tell anyone Cath, I just want to say thank you for involving me. I feel that I can move on now I know why Alice was killed and that means more to me than you will ever know."

Beryl shut down the MacBook and handed it to Cath.

"Well at least we all know what's happened, it's just a shame that no-one else will ever know."

Cath gave Beryl a hug and then put the MacBook back into the kitchen cupboard.

Chapter 46 – The New Team

Monday 27th January

The following morning Superintendent Dicks pulled into the car park of Matlock Police Station at just after 9 a.m. and parked alongside the Red Mini belonging to Cath Mulvey. At least he would not have to chase around half of Derbyshire trying to find her that morning he thought. Buoyed by the thought of resolving the issue that he needed to speak to her about, Dicks jauntily climbed the stairs to the CID office two stairs at a time and walked confidently into the Detective Sergeants office without knocking and closed the door firmly behind him.

"Good morning Sergeant Mulvey." Dicks greeted her and sat down in the chair on the other side of her desk.

Cath looked up, surprised at the unexpected appearance of Dicks but quickly regained her composure.

"Good morning sir. What can I do for you this morning?"

Dicks looked directly towards her.

"Cath, I am a straight talker, so I won't beat about the bush. I think you have found Burton's MacBook with the photographs on. I also think it was found by you on Tuesday when you visited Jack Bainbridge at the exhibits store for the Bulman murder."

Cath stared unblinking at Dicks.

"You do not have to confirm or deny this. At the moment I am just saying my thoughts aloud as I do not really care whether you did, or you didn't find it."

Dicks stared at Cath emphasising his last statement to her.

"I would expect by now if you are half the detective I think you to be, that you know it has little evidential value because you are unable to say where you recovered it from and if you did, it would be difficult, to say the least, to prove it was actually there in the first place. Would this be a correct scenario, Cath?"

Cath didn't say anything, she could feel her heart beating fast, and she tried to control the fight or flight urge that was welling up inside her. She knew it was always the fight option that her mind would choose, but she didn't know where the conversation was going. She told herself to keep her anger under control before doing or saying something that she would regret later.

Cath looked back at Dicks with angry eyes and instinctively pushed herself back from her desk.

Dicks saw her reaction and carried on calmly.

"What I need to know is that you have no intention of returning the MacBook to where you found it. If that were to happen then there could be some very awkward questions asked, about how Oxley came to be the main suspect for the Bulman murder at some time in the future. So do I have your word that should you be in possession, or come into possession, of this particular MacBook that it will not find its way back into one of Alice Bulman's bags in the property store?"

Cath took a deep breath as the 'fight' in her subsided. Dicks was covering his own back as well as hers. The realisation that it was in both their interests that the MacBook never saw the light of day washed over her and broke her angry stare. She took another breath and leant forward on her desk.

"I understand. I won't beat about the bush either. You have my word if the MacBook ever comes into my possession I will not return it to a bag belonging to Alice Bulman in the exhibits store."

"That's all I wanted to know Sergeant Mulvey. Can I call you Cath?"

Cath nodded.

"Your word is good enough for me Cath. Just one more thing, can you get rid of the photographs on it?" Dicks laughed.

Cath leant back in her chair and smiled.

"There were no photographs. Burton and Trueman were money launderers for Martin and Jill Gordon. The MacBook was their filing cabinet, that's why Burton wanted it back so badly. They had been laundering the Gordon's money for nearly thirty years after Neil's wife set the offshore companies up when she worked for her father."

It was Dicks turn to sit back in his chair this time as he took in the information.

"Makes more sense I suppose considering what he was prepared to do to get it back," said Dicks thoughtfully.

"Is the wife involved?"

"No. I'm certain that she knows absolutely nothing about what Burton and Trueman were up to with the Gordons. She wasn't a fan of Trueman either, especially when she found out that her husband was in a relationship with him," Cath confirmed.

"There's no one else involved alive then by the looks of it," and then he laughed loudly.

"The Met are going to be going round in ever decreasing circles without the MacBook link to Trueman and Burton because it must be the only information leading to the Gordon's money, otherwise none of this would have happened. I'm pretty sure there's a copy of Burton's missing person report in the unused material so they can never allege we didn't tell them about him!"

Dicks still laughing shook his head and rubbed the scar on his head as he leant back in his chair.

"I'm sorry if I worried you there for a minute."

"It's alright, I wasn't sure where you were going that's all. Do I have your word that this conversation never took place, you have mine," said Cath looking Dicks straight in the eye.

"Of course. Look, I'm not an absolute bastard…contrary to popular belief. But I do like to protect myself against foreseeable problems. I also pay back favours when they are owed. I'm not sure at this time if I owe you one, but if I do, I will repay it Cath. Me and Excy are going on Professional Standards in a few weeks and it's always helpful to have someone on your side in that department, especially as I will be head of it."

"Thank you sir and noted."

Cath stood up and offered him her hand and Dicks stood up took it in his and they shook on their agreement.

Dicks turned to Cath as he walked to the door .

"Don't forget if you need anything give me a ring."

Dicks athletically raced down the back stairs of the police station and into the car park where he paused and looked up to the grey winter sky.

"Sorted!"

He could leave the murder incident team in the knowledge that there would be no comeback to him in the future. Excy was sorting the witness and reviewing the rest of the evidence and he had been right to eliminate any problem from Cath Mulvey and the MacBook. It had been a long shot guessing that she had found it and that it may have been linked to Alice Bulman's death, but he was glad he had taken it.

Dicks got in his car, put the key in the ignition and then stopped. It was something Cath Mulvey had just told him….but he couldn't figure out what it was…and then it came to him. Dicks thought about and then dismissed his concern as highly improbable… but he needed to be sure. Dicks got back out of his car and set off back to see Detective Sergeant Mulvey.

Chapter 47 – Dinner Decisions

Monday 27th January

It was just after five that evening when Cath arrived at Maggie's house and was let in through the pack of excited dogs at the front door.

"I'm glad that you made it because I know how things always come up for you police people at the last minute. I've done a meat and potato pie if that's alright with you?" Maggie announced as she ushered Cath into the warm kitchen.

"Now who is this mysterious guest you have told me is coming?"

"It's one of my bosses. I'll put the kettle on Maggie if that's alright with you?"

"Of course, it is," said Maggie sitting down at the table.

Outside John Dicks sat in his car and looked down over Matlock Bath. It was a grey muggy evening and even though the night was closing in, the Parades along the river were still packed with day trippers moving like ants…. with trays of fish and chips he thought to himself. Dicks scratched the scar on his head and took a deep breath, he couldn't put it off any longer. It was time to go in.

At the knock on the door, the dogs as one, shot from their baskets barking into the hallway.

"That will be your boss" Maggie said to Cath as she got up and went into the hallway shushing the dogs as she went.

A couple of minutes later the dogs filed back into the kitchen followed by Maggie and the towering figure of a shoeless Superintendent Dicks.

"It's meat and potato pie for dinner Superintendent if that's alright?"

"Yes… that's fine….thank you," Dicks confirmed.

Cath sat down putting three mugs of coffee on the table. Dicks looked towards Cath.

"Have you asked her yet?"

"Asked me what?" Maggie looked towards Cath.

"Talk about bull in a China shop!" Cath scowled at Dicks and then looked back to Maggie.

"Maggie, did you set up some companies for Neil about 30 years ago?"

Maggie Burton looked quizzically at Cath.

"Just after I married Neil all those years ago he told me he had a number of clients that needed some offshore companies setting up. I was still working for my dad at the time, and I set them up for him with nominee directors. Neil paid for them and as far as I knew they were then sold on by Neil to his clients."

Cath looked straight at Maggie Burton.

"Who were the nominee Directors when you set them up and have you had anything to do with those companies since Maggie?"

"The initial nominees were me and Neil, but Neil would have changed them when he sold them on, and I haven't had anything to do with them since I set them up."

Maggie looked worried.

"Is there a problem?"

Dicks took over from Cath.

"It looks like Neil and Trueman were using those companies to launder drug money. The directors of all the companies were Neil and Trueman but any search of them would show you as a previous director and the wife of Neil. I have been told by the Metropolitan Police that Jill Gordon was killed by an assassin linked to a drug cartel and although I do not know for sure, I think that it may have been a warning of some sort. We need to know whether you have received any threatening messages in the last few days?"

Maggie put her cup down on the table.

"I don't understand. What do you mean by money laundering? I know what it is… but what has Neil got to do with it? He was a solicitor. He's always been a solicitor."

Cath got up and took Maggie's hand off the mug and held it tightly crouching at the side of her.

"Maggie this is going to come as a shock but it's very important that you know what has happened as we think your life may be in danger. Neil and Paul have been laundering millions of pounds for some drug dealers in London and have been doing it for many years. We do not know for sure but think the girl that was murdered at Bakewell and those at Chatsworth might be connected."

Cath paused to see if Maggie was listening to what she was saying. Maggie was looking earnestly at her and so she continued.

"A woman and a taxi driver were murdered a few days ago in London and the police think it was connected to drug suppliers from South America. The woman was one of the people that Neil was laundering money for."

Maggie looked at Cath bewilderedly.

"But what has this got to do with me?"

Dicks leaned forward across the table to Maggie.

"Maggie, you set the companies up and your husband was responsible for paying the drug suppliers. It is highly likely that he and you are viewed as the head of the organisation that purchases drugs from them and that the killing of Jill Gordon was a warning. We need to know if you have also had any threats from the drug suppliers."

Maggie looked towards Dicks.

"I don't think so."

Maggie reached across to her handbag on the table and took out her phone.

"How would they get my number?"

Dicks leant back into his chair. "I'm sorry Maggie but it was probably me. Neil's Missing Person report was forwarded to the Met with all the other exhibits and documents. It has all of your personal details on it. It's highly likely that the drug cartel has informants in the Metropolitan Police."

"Oh my god! They have my address as well!"

Dicks nodded.

"What about Marcus and Laura, they are coming back from Australia next week for the funeral….are they in danger as well…I must tell them!"

Cath took Maggie's hand again.

"Maggie, we can deal with that when we know if there is actually any threat. Have you had any contact from anyone new in the last day or so?"

Maggie looked down at Cath.

"I don't know. I get lots of messages on my phone but don't read them unless I know who it is. Can you have a look.. I don't know what I would be looking for."

Cath took Maggie's phone from her and checked her messages for the previous three days. There were messages from Marcus and Laura, from Cath herself, an opticians and an unopened one from an unidentified overseas mobile number the previous evening. Cath opened the message and read the message. "Payment is still due as usual or else." followed by a bag of gold and a gun emoticon.

Cath showed the message to Dicks, who read it and nodded to Cath.

Maggie slumped into her chair.

"Do I get police protection; will I have to go into hiding….oh my god this is a nightmare!"

Cath crouched down at the side of Maggie and took both of her hands in hers.

"Maggie, we have been discussing what to do all day if you had been threatened and I have made a decision. I came into possession of the information illegally and am prepared to lose my job if you want to have police protection. In that case it is likely that you would have to be given a new identity and go into hiding somewhere as this is the normal way these things would work."

Cath looked into Maggie's eyes.

"I think that this is the best course of action for you. Superintendent Dicks has a different view and that is why he is here tonight."

Maggie looked across the table to Dicks who took a deep intake of breath.

"Maggie, if I were in your position I would think carefully about trusting the police to give you protection over a long period of time, which is what would be required. It would also mean cutting yourself off from your family and friends and starting again. This is a very difficult thing to do. What I am going to suggest is illegal and risky but would leave you free to live your life as you do now. The money that needs paying to the drug supplier according to Cath is ready to be transferred. Unfortunately, due to Neil and Paul's death's there is no company director to authorise the transfer. I think with Cath's and some other people's help you could make yourself a company director, make the transfer and get the drug supplier's off your back forever. If it goes wrong and you can't make the transfer, I will not lie to you, your life is very likely to be in danger. The choice is yours Maggie and we will go with whichever you choose. We need to know now though which path you want to travel?"

Maggie stared ahead in silent thought for a long time before she looked to Cath at her side.

"I'm sorry Cath but I want to go with the Superintendent. I know what he is asking me to do, and the risks, but he is right, I wouldn't want to live the rest of my life in hiding."

Maggie took a deep breath

"What else did that lying bastard of a husband of mine do that I don't know about? I want to know everything if I'm going to risk my life sorting this mess he has left me in."

Cath looked seriously at Maggie.

"If we are going to clear the air, lying murdering bastard might be more applicable. It's likely he killed Alice Bulman."

"Do you really think he murdered that girl?"

"Yes we think so Maggie. He may have been involved in other killings as well."

Dicks interjected.

"We can't prove any of this Maggie and only five people know about Neil's activities. They are the three of us, Cath's partner Ella and a woman called Beryl Smith. No-one outside this group must ever know either. All are willing to help you, are you alright with that?"

"Yes," confirmed Maggie after a few seconds pause.

"You live here on your own at the moment don't you?"

Maggie nodded.

"I live on my own as well so will not be missed if I stay here at night as sort of protection for you for a few days. Are you alright with me staying here?"

Maggie nodded again.

"Right, that's settled then. Let's also see if we can buy you a few extra days,"

Dicks took the phone off Cath, typed in a reply and sent it.

"Can't do any harm, they can only say "No" if we ask for an extra week."

Dicks handed the phone back to Maggie.

Maggie took it from him.

"If you are staying here I can't keep calling you Superintendent Dicks, what's your first name?"

"John," Dicks replied.

Chapter 48 – John Dicks

Friday 31st January

John Dicks sat in the armchair of his living room and looked around the sparse furnishings. He had always had little time for possessions and his living room was testament to that view. There was a bookcase with a few paperback thrillers that he had bought but never got around to reading. A television that was permanently tuned to the Sky News channel and an assortment of Private Eye magazines which littered the coffee table in front of him.

On the walls were three pictures. The first was a picture of Captain John Dicks in desert fatigues, the second was a staged photograph of his Company, titled Charlie Company 40 Commando Basra April 2003, and the final photograph was of his passing out at Sandhurst dated November 1998.

Dicks scratched instinctively at the bullet scar on his head,. That bullet had ended his army career the day after the picture of him in desert fatigues had been taken.

"

Dicks pushed his six feet four inches frame out of the chair, and walked over to a large chest by the wall, knelt at the side and opened its lid.

Dicks removed his folded and cellophane wrapped dress uniform from the chest and placed it on the floor. He then removed the box containing his Military Medal and placed it at the side of his uniform. He opened the presentation box, looked at the medal and instinctively scratched his scar again, as though digging for a memory.

No matter how far he dug, he knew that the memory of what had happened that day been lost. He had been told afterwards, whilst recovering in the hospital, that whilst leading his company against an enemy compound just outside Basra that he and his men had taken incoming mortar fire. Dicks had gone out into the killing zone and recovered two injured men and then lead an assault on the mortar battery, during which he had taken a bullet to the frontal lobe of his brain. When the bullet had been removed so had his memory of that day, together with most of his ability to empathise with people.

Dicks looked at the medal and wondered whether, before his injury, he had actually been able to consider others or whether the gallantry to win such an honour had been an aberration. He had enough self-awareness to know that his injury meant that in the present day he would have considered the risk to himself first and he would have let his colleagues die. It was the same consideration that had led him to visit Maggie Burton earlier that night. In particular what a murder enquiry would turn up if she were killed, and how such an investigation would unravel all the other deaths that Burton had been involved in. His perceived altruism towards Maggie Burton had been, he knew, selfishness for his own well-being and career.

Despite his initial reservations and lie about the scar on his head, he had quickly realised that his injury made him the perfect police officer. A man with little empathy and unbridled ambition. A police officer able to walk into any incident and see it as only an opportunity for his own progression.

Dicks took out a shoebox, removed the lid and took out the oily rag wrapped pistol and held it in his hand. One of his company sergeants had killed the Iraqi soldier and recovered the gun that he had been shot with. He had been presented with the gun when he was medically discharged six months later and two months before he had joined the police.

Dicks checked that the Tariq pistol ammunition clip was full and tucked it in the back of his trousers. He looked at the $30,000 of rolled up bundles of fifty dollar notes that lay at the bottom of the box, another relic of an unknown memory from Iraq. They may be useful to Maggie he thought as they had served no purpose for him since he had been discharged.

He had no recollection of how they had come into his possession, but he suspected that it would not have been legitimately, and once he had joined the police he had decided that they should stay in the box with the other remnants of his past life. He put the bundles in his pocket and then replaced his medal and uniform into the chest and closed the lid. It was time to go to Maggie Burton's and fulfil his side of the bargain.

John Dicks knew it was in his own interest that he had persuaded Maggie and Cath, to pursue a course of action that was not only dangerous but also undoubtedly illegal. It was also in his own interest that he had offered to spend the following four nights on the couch in the kitchen with the hope of keeping Maggie Burton and the others alive until they left on Friday. If anything happened to them overseas it would be extremely doubtful that it would be linked back to anything that had happened in the UK. Just tourists killed for being in the wrong place at the wrong time.

At Matlock Bath Cath closed her call with Ella and turned to Maggie.

"Ella's coming up Thursday night and Beryl's meeting us at the airport on Friday. That's all I can do tonight Maggie."

Maggie who had been listening to the phone conversations sat back in her chair.

"I can't thank you enough Cath, are you sure you want to get involved? According to John it could be dangerous."

Cath looked at her.

"Maggie, if it hadn't been for me I can't be sure you would be in this position. I feel responsible and wouldn't have it any other way. Beryl has her own reasons, and I will let her tell you what they are when she is ready. As for Ella, I had to tell her what was happening, we promised to have no secrets between us. Once I had told her it was no surprise to me that she would want to help. The bottom line Maggie is whether you want to go through with it or not. If you want to pull out you will get nothing but support from all of us but it's your decision."

"I've made my decision, and I'm not going to change it Cath," Maggie replied forcefully.

"There's no way I can go into hiding for the rest of my life. I will ring Marcus and Laura in the morning and cancel the funeral for a couple of weeks. On the bright side if anything happens to me I won't have to then go to it!" Maggie laughed

"You had better get off Cath, I've got to walk the dogs and make a bed up for John. Thanks for everything."

Maggie walked Cath to the door followed by the dogs and watched as she drove away.

"If he weren't already dead she would have killed Neil herself," she thought.

"He was…had been an absolute shit!"

On the Friday morning, the day that the payment was to have gone through to the Columbians, Dicks put Maggie, Cath, and Ella into a taxi to go to the airport and promised Maggie that he would look after the dogs whilst she was away. He had then walked the dogs around the garden before setting off to work.

At the bottom of the road to Maggie's house he noticed a black BMW SUV with black tinted windows parked up with two men sat in it. It looked odd and so he memorised the number and did an owner check when he got to work. The check showed that the vehicle owner was a 'blocked' number and for the person checking to contact the Metropolitan Police for further details.

It might be something or nothing he had told himself and decided to give Foxley-Jones a call. Foxley-Jones was not immediately available but called him back later that day and informed him that there were no detectives in Derbyshire conducting enquiries and if there were Foxley-Jones would have informed Derbyshire police, in accordance with the Memorandum of Understanding that had been drawn up. Dicks' suspicions about the car and its occupants were confirmed.

There was no sign of the BMW later when he returned from work and there was no sign of it when he took the dogs down to North Parade in Matlock Bath to pick up his tea from one of the café's that lined the road.

As he returned to the house and Maggie's warm kitchen, with the dogs trailing behind him, he made a plan in relation to what he expected to happen later that night.

A short time later he drove his Mercedes to the nearby New Bath Hotel parked up and walked back to the house. He then moved Maggie's car to a different position on the driveway. His intention was to make it look as though Maggie was in residence on her own that evening. He then drew the curtains and turned on the lights in the lounge and kitchen.

It was only then that he sat down to eat his paper wrapped tea, hot out the oven where it had been warming since he had walked the dogs earlier that evening. As he ate, he thought again as to why he was sat where he was.

In the previous four days the equilibrium of his life had been changed. His offer to protect Maggie had meant that the last four evenings he had been at the house with Maggie and the dogs. Maggie, he had quickly realised, was an incessant chatterer who hated any silence. So he had spent most evenings silently listening to her telling him about the stables and her life as a wife and mother. He had been unable to empathise with her concerns about her children or the hurt caused by her now deceased husband but had found that he enjoyed having company in an evening after work. He particularly liked the company of the dogs who seemed to also like his silent company and as a result, he had willingly volunteered to look after the dogs whilst Maggie was away.

He was sat where he was that evening, even though Maggie was no longer there, he told himself, to ensure that no harm came to the dogs. He knew in reality that it was the anticipation of danger that was motivating him. He had always loved danger and action and if he had asked them, he would have been told that it had been no surprise to his men, that he had led the rescue mission for his injured comrades and subsequent assault on the enemy that afternoon near Basra ,all those years ago.

He strongly suspected nothing would happen until much later when the lights went out in the house. Dicks closed his eyes, and his thoughts went to the previous night when he had sat at the same table. There had been the four of them, as Cath and Ella had slept over in order to get a taxi to the airport with Maggie the following morning.

Specks of yellow custard blew from Cath's nose as she collapsed into laughter, tears running down her cheeks and then silence as she tried to catch her breath, and then another louder burst of laughter as she collapsed giggling onto the table in front of her. Maggie was standing at the table, serving spoon in her hand, looking bemused.

"What did I say?"

She looked at Ella and then at him.

"What's so funny about spotted dick?"

Cath collapsed again in laughter at the table trying to point helplessly at him.

"I think it's the similarity with my name Maggie… and a penis" he had declared straight-faced, but watching Cath he also broke into a broad grin.

"Oh!...I'm sorry John …does anyone want any more …sponge with raisins in?"

Ella collapsed into the contagious laughter of Cath at the table.

"For goodness sake you two it's like having Marcus and Laura back for dinner!"

Maggie sat down, looked at the two still giggling women and broke into a smile herself.

He had finished off his pudding despite the intermittent uncontrolled bursts of laughter of Cath and Ella, and leant back in his chair.

"That was excellent Mrs Burton…I'm sorry…Maggie."

"Good of you to say so John. I enjoy cooking but haven't done much since the children left. Do you have any children John?"

He had shifted uncomfortably in his seat.

"No Maggie, no children."

He saw Cath nudge Ella under the table.

"That's a shame," consoled Maggie,

"So there hasn't ever been a Mrs Dicks?"

He saw Ella nudge Cath back.

"Err no Maggie, I have not been married…although I hope to be one day…I suppose I have been married to my career and not had time for affairs of the heart."

He had shifted even more uncomfortably in his seat.

"You're not gay are you?" asked Maggie

"Only my husband Neil ….."

"Oh no, I'm not gay," he had insisted as he fiddled nervously with his spoon and dropped it on the floor.

They had simultaneously gone to pick it up and banged their heads together. Both had re-emerged above the table to find Ella and Cath hilariously laughing silently in each other's arms.

"You two get worse!" Maggie exclaimed.

It was then he had noticed that Maggie Burton was wearing make-up for the first time and that her top was showing a lot of cleavage.

Around midnight he had been woken from his sleep on the settee by Maggie who had led him up to her bedroom where they had made love quietly, afraid to wake Cath and Ella. Afterwards, much to his own astonishment, he had found himself telling her about his life at Sandhurst, his Military Medal and finally he disclosed to her the adverse effects of his injury on his personality. Maggie had listened silently in the darkness of the bedroom, her head on his shoulder and arm across his chest. When he had finished she had kissed his scar and told him that she would keep his secrets.

Dicks then broke into a wide grin as he remembered Maggie, giggling like a teenager, had sat across him, bent down, and nibbled his ear and as his body had responded to her sexual touches told him it made him 'ideal for one night stands.'

He realised that it was not just the dogs he had started to feel some sort of affection for. Dicks smiled to himself, maybe there was hope, the injury would not rob him forever of feelings for others. He picked up a tennis ball from the table and whistled the dogs to him. 'Ideal for one night stands.' Dicks smiled to himself. It was something. He could work with that on a dating site he thought to himself, and his smile broke out into a wide grin.

"Come on boys!" he said to the five pairs of eyes looking expectantly up at him.

All five followed him to the rear door and Dicks and the dogs walked into the cold evening sunshine of the large walled garden.

At 10 p.m. he had gone up to Maggie's bedroom, turned on the light and drawn the curtains. After five minutes he had turned off the light and crept back to the kitchen in darkness. Once there he had placed the Tariq on the table and sat waiting for the visitor or visitors to arrive.

Just after midnight he heard the back door lock unpick and then as it opened felt the faintest drop in the room temperature that caused the hairs on his arms to rise.

Dicks felt his body ready itself with a rush of adrenalin in anticipation of danger. He was wide awake, his senses tuned to his surroundings. He took a couple of deep silent breaths to keep the 'fight' urge under control and listened intently.

There was a light shuffle of soft feet outside. Sock footed he moved silently as the door began to open towards him. Dicks silently cursed himself for leaving the Tariq on the table. The first thing he saw as the figure came through the moonlit doorway was the shadow of a raised silenced gun held in the intruders hand and then the real gun and arm came into sight.

Dicks reacted instinctively grabbing the wrist with his right hand and forcing the wrist back on itself. The gun clattered to the floor and Dicks pulled the figure towards him enveloping the neck in his left arm. He was surprisingly light thought Dicks as he raised the intruder off the floor and squeezed his neck tightly in the crook of his muscular arm. The figure squirmed, hands clawing at his arm, legs kicking wildly in the air trying to force himself out of Dick's vice like grip, and away from the dogs that were now barking and snapping at his flying feet.

The struggles were of little use against Dicks' strength and eventually the figure ceased struggling and slumped limply forward. Dicks lowered the figure to the floor and turned on the light. It was a teenager, South American by his colour and appearance, thought Dicks. Probably the same one that had murdered Jill Gordon. The silenced .45 lay at his side and Dicks kicked it away across the floor and sent the dogs back to their baskets. He had no doubts at all that the boy had been sent to kill Maggie.

Dicks felt an anger rising inside himself that he had not felt for over fourteen years, and he knelt down and punched the shallowly breathing boy hard in the head. The boy grunted with

491 | P a g e

the force of the punch and a purple bruise started to swell above his eye. Dicks took several deep breaths and regained his composure. What was he going to do with the unconscious boy on the floor? His initial plan had ended with either shooting or incapacitating any intruder. He certainly did not want any connection becoming known between the murder of Jill Gordon and either Neil or Maggie Burton.

There would be others nearby he realised, the teenager would not have been acting alone. Wherever they were, the women would be in danger once it became known that the attack had failed that night. He needed to buy them some time, he also needed to send a message that the drug supplier would understand. Finally, he had to make sure the boy on the floor ceased to be a connection between the murders in Dagenham and the murders at Chatsworth.

He decided that Cath and the others would be better off not knowing anything that had or was about to happen, it would only make them concerned for their own safety and where they were he could do nothing to help them. His decisions had been made. It was not a faultless plan, but it had a fair degree of being successful not only for himself but the others as well. There was a bonus to him personally as it would also cause confusion at some time in the future for whoever was still investigating the murder of Jill Gordon… and he really did hope it was Foxley-Jones.

Dicks knelt at the side of the boy and placed his right shin across the boys throat and rocked his weight forward, constricting the boys airway until he stopped breathing. Dicks satisfied himself that the boy was dead and then set off to find the people who had driven the boy to the address.

Dicks crept out the back door and climbed over the garden wall into the street below. Fifty yards away under a street light was the black BMW he had seen that morning. Dicks crept up to the driver's window and knocked on the tinted glass which slowly wound down and the occupant flashed a black leather wallet in his direction with the silver and red badge of the Metropolitan Police clearly displayed.

"Police!" the occupant emphasised.

"Really?" Dicks mocked

"And what are the Metropolitan Police doing up here at this time of night, a bit off your patch isn't it?"

"I'm sorry I can't tell you that, it's confidential,"

Dicks bent down and leant into the window, taking a good look at the two detectives sat in the front of it.

"Let me tell you something that's also going to be confidential. Let your paymaster know that Jill Gordon's killing has now been avenged and we will honour the payment that is owed. They will be paid by next Wednesday. Since we are now unable to trust each other, after they receive payment it will also be the last piece of business we do together. If anyone else dies there will be repercussions particularly for you two, I know who you are. Dicks put the barrel of the Tariq against the man's temple and pulled the trigger. The gun clicked loudly as the hammer hit the empty chamber and Dicks saw an ever larger dark stain appear in the drivers groin as his bladder emptied in fear. Dicks took the barrel of the gun away from the police officer's temple.

"Next time there will be a bullet in the chamber, have you two corrupt fuckers got that?"

The man in the driving seat blushed bright red, nodded, started the vehicle, and sped off in a squeal of tyres, leaving Dicks stood under the street light in the middle of the road.

Thirty minutes later Dicks drove off of the car park at White Lodge, with a broad grin across his face. When Oxley and the boy surfaced there was going to be some serious scratching of heads as to the link between them.

<u>Chapter 49 – Antigua</u>

Tuesday 4th February

Cath lay in her bikini at the bottom of the enormous bed leaning across Ella's long legs and painting Ella's toe nails a pale pink. She looked out of the open French doors to the clear blue water of the Caribbean Sea and the even clearer blue sky. Having made the last stroke of pink varnish onto Ella's little toe, she put the brush into the bottle, and screwed it tight, glancing as she did so, at, and then away from, the large wine cooler with a magnum of Champagne on ice, in the corner of the room; It was too early for that.

Cath looked back at the bikini clad Ella sitting against the headboard and for the thousandth time in the last three weeks she felt her heart skip a beat. She instinctively kissed her leg and began kissing further and further up her leg until Ella squealed and pushed her off.

"We haven't got time!" she giggled.

"I know giggled Cath. I was just getting you warmed up for later."

Ella swung her legs off the bed and checked her watch. Cath checked hers as well. Both girls looked worryingly at each other.

"It will be fine, there's nothing to worry about," Cath smiled reassuringly.

"It's just the waiting that gets you nervous ….you know not knowing what's happening," Ella leant over and put her arms around Cath.

"Tell me about it! When Helen rang and told you she had found a MacBook at Paul's house. I nearly had a nervous breakdown,"

Ella sighed and squeezed Cath tighter.

"It's a good job that she asked me if I knew how to unlock it. Rather than someone else. I've told you that I agreed to unlock it and buy it off her when we get back next week, haven't I?"

"Yes, but …" said Cath.

"There's no buts. She's put it in my room at home. The only thing she is concerned about is the £500 I am giving her for it."

A knock on the door startled Ella, causing her to jump to her feet off the bed. Both girls looked at each other and Ella walked hesitantly to the door, and opened it. Beryl and Maggie Burton walked into the room.

"How did it go?" asked Cath.

"I think it's gone alright so far," reported Maggie.

She sat down on the bed and Beryl sat at the side of her.

"The death certificates for Paul Trueman and Neil have been accepted, as has the paperwork in appointing myself and Beryl as the new directors of the companies. Mr Rousseau the solicitor had a cousin who was a police inspector, and he has apostilled the death certificates for Paul and Neil, and provided identity documents in the form of Antiguan driving licences for me and Beryl. That has allowed us to qualify as the new company directors. Another of Mr Rousseau's cousins works in the Antiguan Ministry of Commerce and he has rushed through the Appointment of Director paperwork in a few hours and then forwarded it to another of Mr Rousseau's cousins who works in the bank. That cousin has released on mine and Maggie's authority the £2,000,000 from the escrow account. In total that has cost us $20,000 to Mr Rousseau's cousins, and Mr Rousseau wants another $10,000 for arranging it all. That is all the money I brought with us. I presume that we now just wait around to see if the Columbians confirm they have received it."

"It's a good job that Mr Rousseau has so many cousins" Beryl quipped humorously.

The four women walked out on to the balcony overlooking the sea. The beach was empty, and the crystal blue sea stretched to a haze in the sun's heat. The only sign of life was a large yacht that bobbed lazily at anchor half a mile out to sea. Beryl turned towards Ella and Cath.

"I know that you two have told us that you don't want anything but me and Maggie have decided that we cannot allow that. Me and Maggie now control all the companies belonging to Neil and Paul as well as the Gordons. There are assets of over £100 million. It's more than we can spend in a lifetime and would not have been possible without the two of you. We have decided that once we are in the clear with the payment, we are going to set up a new offshore holding company that will take over all the other companies and their assets. Beryl says if we leverage the purchase against the assets of the existing companies and then wind the old ones up, we will only need to run one company which will look legitimate to any authorities that could be minded to have a look. Each of us will be twenty five percent shareholders in the new company with shares worth about £25 million. Don't say no because it's what we want to do."

"What about John Dicks, he was as involved as any of us?" Cath asked Beryl.

"Maggie says she has spoken to John. They have agreed some private arrangement, as apparently he has little interest in money. All Maggie has told me she is that she will ensure that he is always looked after financially should he require anything in the future."

Half a mile away, on the yacht, the dark haired man in the swimming trunks lay flat against the deck. The telescopic cross sights of the sniper rifle firmly fixed on the back of Maggie

Burton's head. He felt the phone lying on the deck at his side vibrate and glanced down towards its screen.

A few seconds later Maggie Burton's phone gave a loud ping and she held it up in front of her. She opened the new message from the unknown caller and read it to the other women who had fallen silent around her. "Payment received. Relationship concluded."

The man on the yacht took one last look at the back of Maggie Burton's head through the telescopic sight and laid the gun down onto the deck.

The women stood silent and transfixed for one…two… three seconds and then there was a shouting, laughing, melee of hugging and yelping together from the balcony to the bedroom where they landed in a heap on the enormous bed. Ella disentangled herself from the scrum and went over to the wine cooler, shook the magnum, popped the cork, and sprayed them with champagne and then jumped back into the orgy of happy souls on it.

Ten minutes later they were all sitting at the table on the balcony of the hotel suite, hair, bodies, and clothes, wet and sticky from the champagne but this time each of them was holding a full glass of the cold bubbling liquid. Maggie Burton raised her glass

"To our new shareholders Cath and Ella, for making this possible!"

Cath stood up and made her own toast.

"To Beryl for working out how it all could be sorted! And to Maggie for being brave enough to do it!"

The four women clinked their glasses together and emptied their champagne glasses in one.

Chapter 50 – Endings

Bright winter sunlight shone through the venetian blinds making ribbons, of light and shadow, across the bed and Cath knew it was going to be a beautiful day. She swung her bare legs out of the bed and onto the oak whitewashed floor. She stretched and then leant over and swept the long brown hair from Ella's shoulder, kissed it gently and went for a shower.

When she came back into the room Ella was awake and had made two cups of coffee. Ella was drinking hers, the duvet tucked up to her chin and Cath's sat on the marble topped bedside table. Cath went to the walk in wardrobe and threw a pair of odd socks and a pair of black tights onto the bed followed by a blue sweater, a skirt, and a jacket.

"Do you want some breakfast?" asked Ella.

Cath opened a drawer in the wardrobe and took out her bra and pants and put them on.

"No, I'm going round to Maggie's for breakfast at ten if there's nothing come in overnight. Are you coming?"

Ella yawned. "Yes I think I will."

Ella picked up her phone and looked through her social media.

"Beryl's in Vietnam, she's just posted some photos of her on an elephant."

"Let me have a look!"

Cath jumped on the bed and grabbed the phone playfully from her partner.

The phone screen showed a smiling Beryl sitting on the back of a large elephant and then as she flicked through the post, another photograph of Beryl throwing a bucket of water on its back in a muddy river, and then one of her on a hotel balcony with a cocktail on the table in front of her. Cath felt a warm glow of pride in her friends exploits.

At that moment, her own phone rang on the table at the side of her coffee. She passed Ella's phone back to her and answered it. Ella listened looking increasingly troubled as Cath talked to the person on the other end. After a couple of minutes Cath put the phone down.

Ella looked at her. "Problems?" she asked hesitantly.

"Not for me," Cath replied casually.

"A body has surfaced at the pond at White Lodge. So it looks like Dylan Oxley has finally resurfaced. They wanted me to go as the Divisional Detective Sergeant, but I've told them to contact Detective Inspector John Casey, as he will end up dealing with it and we might as well take the middle woman out of it at the start."

Cath looked at Ella's worried face, climbed onto the bed and gave her a hug.

"There's nothing to worry about Ella, there isn't anything to link things back to Trueman, Burton or more importantly us, I am absolutely sure of that."

Ella's face brightened.

"I know that really, but just needed you to tell me. See you at ten then."

"Yes. Bring some treats for the dogs will you?"

Cath gave Ella a kiss on the lips, picked up her shoes and went down the stairs. She didn't drive straight to her office at Matlock from their house on Eaton Hill at Baslow. She pulled off the road half way through Chatsworth Park towards Chatsworth House and parked up at the side of the gatehouse in the car park. Cath entered the gatehouse as the security man was filling the kettle with water.

"Time for a cuppa Cath?" he asked.

"Always got time for a cuppa with you Holly, you know that. How are you this morning?"

"I'm feeling alright this morning. I take one day at a time and today is a good day. I'm seeing Georgia later and that always cheers me up. Carpe Diem and all that." Holly smiled at Cath.

"Everything else alright Holly?" Cath asked.

"If you mean with Donna, yes it's fine. Divorce comes through next month now the house has been sold and I've given her half of my pension… Best money I have ever spent!" Holly laughed.

"And I mean that. I should have done it years ago. I couldn't have gone through everything without you and Ella, Cath. You two kept me going when I wanted to end it all and couldn't see any light at the end of the tunnel. You getting me this job and my sick pension means I'm not short of money. If you yourself ever need anything you only have to ask you know. It's a big house you have got in the village and must be expensive to run."

Cath went over to Holly and gave him a hug.

"You are such a softy! We are fine, Ella's job in IT for that company in Antigua pays her loads of money, so we are never short Holly. Look put some milk in that coffee, and I'll tell you the latest gossip from the force."

Holly poured some milk into Cath's mug.

"That enough Cath?"

"Yes that's fine Holly. Now going back to the gossip, the good news is that Excy is still with Dicks on Professional Standards and has got his promotion to Inspector. The unwelcome news for him, is that neither he nor Dicks look like they will be moving at any time in the near future. Word on the street or should I say at Headquarters, is that the Chief Constable is retiring, and the short money on his replacement is a Commander from the Met called Foxley-Jones, who apparently has some sort of grudge against them both."

"Dicks won't be happy if someone puts the brakes on his meteoric rise through the ranks Cath so there may be trouble ahead there, what do you think?"

" I would not be surprised if Dicks hasn't already got a plan to deal with Foxley-Jones, I think he's the sort of bloke who enjoys a bit of conflict."

Cath put her mug down on the table at the side of her chair, and smiled to herself. Knowing John Dicks as she did the arrival of Foxley-Jones would be just the sort of challenge that he would enjoy dealing with.